The Lady's Secret

The Unconventionals Book Two

Michelle Morrison

Printed in the United States of America
First Printing: November 2017
Amazon KDP
ISBN-9781973358398

Contents

Chapter 1

"Now Lady Eleanor, why would you worry your pretty little head about such matters?"

There was no way her expression could be deemed a smile, but Eleanor Chalcroft managed to deliver a pleasant curve of her lips despite the aggravated clench of her teeth.

"I assure you, Lord Elphinstone," she replied in a close approximation of a gentle tone of voice. "I am not the least bit worried. I simply wondered why the Turks wanted Greece in the first place."

Lord Elphinstone chuckled as if she had made the wittiest comment and turned back to the small group surrounding her and her father. The men were discussing the recent capture of the Acropolis by the Turks. Truly, she thought as she allowed her gaze to drift over the swirling masses of ball gowns at the de Wynter ball, she had absolutely no interest in acropolises or Greek islands. She'd merely asked a question. If she'd made a comment on the cut of his coat, she was sure Lord Elphinstone would have been all ears. Glancing at said coat, she frowned. What was the point of a well-cut coat when the man's posture was so terrible? No doubt the young lordling thought his pose struck a devil-may-care attitude, but really, his slouch and slightly protruding belly were anything but rakish.

"We need an independent Greek state to act as a buffer between Europe and the Ottoman Empire," her father was telling the nodding group of men around them. Eleanor promptly stopped listening and returned her attention to the two hundred guests who, like her, were not immediately concerned about the spread of the Ottoman Empire. It was the same group of people she had been socializing with since her debut three years past. Many were friends—Eleanor had been deemed a "diamond of the first water" immediately following her come out, a fact that she accepted without any real thought. While it was certainly gratifying to be considered one of the most desirable young ladies on the marriage market, she really had nothing to do with her appeal. Her mother was the source of Eleanor's golden hair and china-blue eyes. According to Lady Chalcroft, all the ladies of her mother's family shared their similar rose-and-cream complexion. Her father had certainly contributed to Eleanor's appeal; from him came the blueness of her blood and her ample dowry.

For her part, Eleanor played her role in society to perfection thanks to her mother's training since she was a child. Her manners were impeccable. She was ever smiling gently and she knew how to draw people into conversation. Moreover, her laugh had become practically famous in the London ballroom scene. It had been likened to the delicate chime of the finest Waterford crystal (a statement which had taken every ounce of Eleanor's control not to snort at—she'd always considered her laugh a bit of an embarrassment). All in all, it was mostly sheer good luck that she was deemed so desirable.

Nonetheless, there was nothing new to distinguish this Season from her previous two, except the knowledge that this year she was going to have to choose a husband. Her parents had been remarkably indulgent the past two years, but no self-respecting young woman returned for a fourth Season. However, the thought of securing herself for life to one of the men who had professed everything from poetic devotion to undying love...well it left Eleanor feeling a bit panicked if she must be truthful. Not one of these men had sparked her interest for more than a few weeks—and a tepid interest it had been, too.

Eleanor sighed. Perhaps she was being ridiculously picky. Many of the men who had courted her—who were still courting her—were perfectly nice. They just—

Her attention was diverted when she was pushed roughly from behind. Struggling not to step on her skirts and tumble headfirst into the dance floor, she gasped in surprise when her arms were roughly grasped and she was hauled up against a solid wall of man. Her heart beat rapidly from her brush with catastrophe but when she turned to find who had caught her, it began to race.

Standing before her was a man, perhaps a bit taller than average. She glanced up and noticed mahogany brown (though ill-groomed) hair. His eyes were the color of coffee, a drink she detested. His shoulders were perhaps a bit broader in an otherwise ordinary jacket of black superfine. His features—thick brows, longish nose, slightly lopsided smile—while attractive, were not exceptionally handsome. Eleanor could not reconcile why she suddenly found herself speechless, utterly transfixed.

"Are you alright? I didn't grab you too hard, did I?" the man asked. His voice was certainly distinctive—deep and a little raspy, as if he had been in the gaming salon, surrounded by pipe and cigar smoke. His accent was a little different as well—certainly well educated, but with a different cadence than she was accustomed to hearing.

She shook her head, struggling to maintain her equilibrium. Perhaps it was his scent—spicy and citrusy all at the same time—that had her feeling so befuddled. Shaking her head again, this time trying to clear it of its fascination with the tall stranger, she turned to her father who was still lecturing the group of men around him.

"Fitzhugh!" one of the younger men exclaimed. "Never thought I'd see the day you attended a London ball! How are you? And Taggart? My stars it's been a long while!" The young man, Lord Pemberly, grabbed the newcomers' hands and shook them enthusiastically.

"Well enough, I suppose," the stranger—Fitzhugh—answered. "And you? Still panting after opera dancers?"

Several of the men laughed uncomfortably, casting nervous glances at Eleanor. His companion—Taggart—elbowed him in the ribs and frowned. She raised her eyebrows at the comment. While well aware of the existence of such *demi-monde* figures as opera dancers, Eleanor had never heard a man mention one in her presence. Either this Fitzhugh was ignorant of the etiquette of ballroom conversation (in which case, what on earth was he doing at Lady de Wynter's ball?) or he thought himself above such etiquette (in which case, what on earth was he doing at Lady de Wynter's ball? She was quite the stickler for propriety at her events.)

Fitzhugh caught her speculative gaze and lifted his own eyebrow in return. Eleanor didn't know whether to be amused at his disregard for decorum, or offended. She decided to ignore him altogether and was about to turn and look for her overdue dance partner when Lord Pemberly called her name.

"Lady Eleanor, please allow me to introduce you to two old friends, Lord Reginald Taggart and Mr. Alexander Fitzhugh. Gentlemen, Lady Eleanor Chalcroft, daughter to the Marquess of Charville, who is right here." Turning, Pemberly saw Lord Chalcroft still lecturing his dwindling group of fellows and turned back to his friends. "Ah, well, I shall introduce you later.

Fitzhugh turned to Eleanor and gave her a dazzling smile, oozing charm as he reached for her hand. Eleanor waited a moment longer than was polite to give it to him. It was mild enough retribution for his slip, but she thought it best if he realized she could not be treated cavalierly in one moment and then charmed into overlooking it in the next.

"Mr. Fitzhugh," she said coolly.

"Lady Eleanor," he replied. "Again I hope I did you no harm when I sought to catch you a moment ago."

"Indeed not," she said dismissively with a slight wave of her free hand. He had not released the hand he had bent over. Finally she pulled it from his grasp with a tad more force than she would have cared to use at a ball. He grinned again and Eleanor resisted the strong urge to slap him.

Now where had that impulse come from, she wondered,

casting her gaze around the ballroom for her errant partner. She had never had the desire to slap anyone in her life, and she'd grown up with an older brother. She frowned as she failed to remember to whom she had promised this dance. The waltz was just beginning and the song was a particular favorite of hers.

"Looking for someone?" the man murmured in her ear.

She looked at him sharply. Surely the man must know one did not murmur in a lady's ear. Her initial fascination with him soured at his boldness. Ignoring him altogether, she opened the silver card case at her wrist.

"That is quite an impressive dance card. I've never seen one with all of the spaces filled. You must be ravenous by the time the midnight supper is called."

Eleanor frowned at him again, finding it harder to hold her tongue and maintain her aloof demeanor. The man was insufferable! She glanced around for her dance partner once more.

"And where is Sir Everton to claim his dance? He should not keep a lady such as yourself waiting."

Sir Everton! She thought with a mental slap of her forehead. She hadn't seen him since granting the dance at the beginning of the evening. Now that she remembered who she was looking for, she stood up on tiptoes, craning her neck to see all the entrances to the ballroom.

"Bother," she said under her breath. She wondered if he had taken ill or been called away from the ball. On the dance floor, the couples were gliding through the opening strains of the waltz and Eleanor indulged in a moment of petulance. It was ridiculous, really, as she rarely had an opening in her dance card, and it wasn't as if she wouldn't be able to dance this exact waltz in a few days at the next ball. Still, besides enjoying the song, she had the strong desire to remove herself from Mr. Fitzhugh's presence, for despite his arrogant manner, she could not quash the thrum of excitement that seemed to run through her veins. She felt the strangest pull—as if she were one of those magnets her brother had played with as a child.

"I should be happy to fill in for the errant Everton," Fitzhugh said rather too loudly.

"I'm sure he will be here any moment," she began.

"What's this, Eleanor?" Her father must have concluded his impromptu political lecture to the other young men. "Don't say you're not dancing a waltz?" He nodded at the other men, many of whom Eleanor knew had listened to the marquess's monologue only to impress her. "My gel has had men fight over the honor of dancing a waltz with her."

Eleanor glanced down to see Fitzhugh's gloved hand extended, awaiting her hand. She saw the entire group staring at her expectantly and felt compelled to accept the arrogant man's offer. She placed her hand as lightly as possible in his and refused to meet his gaze as he swept her into his arms and smoothly moved them into the flow of dancers.

Eleanor tried to lose herself in the beautiful music. Lady de Wynter prided herself on hiring the best musicians for her events. But even the accomplished orchestra couldn't distract her from her dance partner. She was acutely aware of the hand at the center of her back. She could feel its heat even through his gloves, her gown, and corset. The shoulder beneath her hand was solid. She detected none of the padding many men's tailors employed to enhance their physique. Then there was that scent again—filling her nostrils, making her long to step closer to him, to nestle her face in the crook of his neck just to get a better whiff.

They had danced nearly two full minutes before Eleanor finally glanced up. She found to her discomfort that Mr. Fitzhugh was studying her intently. She moistened suddenly dry lips and delicately cleared her throat.

"From whence do you hail, Mr. Fitzhugh?"

"I grew up in Cornwall."

"Oh? I don't know that I've met anyone who lived there."

"I don't believe its inhabitants are all that concerned with making an appearance at London events. They tend to be a bit more salt-of-the-earth and less worried with what their neighbors think of them," he said, glancing about at the glittering crowd.

Eleanor frowned at his implied criticism. "Then what brought you here?"

"Business," he replied shortly.

"Oh? Are you in the trades, then?"

She hadn't meant to sound anything other than polite but he laughed. The sound was like warm honey.

"You needn't say that in the same tone as you might ask if I roasted children on a spit on All Hallow's Eve."

Eleanor gasped and reared back slightly. "I did no such thing! And what a perfectly horrible thought!"

He laughed again and pulled her closer. "First opera dancers and now roasted children. I have made an abominable impression on you, haven't I, Lady Eleanor? Come now, you can tell me the truth."

Gazing up into eyes that were the warmest shade of brown she'd ever seen, Eleanor almost forgot to answer. She'd earlier thought them flat like coffee but the color was much richer, with flecks that reminded her of cinnamon. His eyelashes were russet—that was the only description for them and they widened in silent question as she realized she'd been staring.

With a little shake of her head, she returned her gaze to the crisp folds of his cravat. "You are certainly an original, Mr. Fitzhugh."

He laughed again at that and Eleanor couldn't help but smile in return. It was the oddest thing, really, that she should feel as if she'd accomplished something great simply by making him laugh. Normally the gentlemen were trying very hard to say something amusing to her. She'd never felt the urge to return the favor.

"Very diplomatic of you. Tell me, Lady Eleanor, do you always say and do just the right thing? It sounds terribly boring."

She felt quite certain he did not hold adherence to convention in high esteem. She heard criticism in his words and was disconcerted to discover that his disapproval stung.

"Now now," he cajoled. "Don't take offense. I can tell just by looking at you that boring is one adjective that will never be applied to you."

She glanced up to see him gazing down at her with a grin on his lips and a devilish sparkle in his eye. She felt her pulse race, felt her cheeks warm. She was acting like a first year debutante, nervous one moment, a-flutter the next. It was not a comfortable feeling.

She had the absurd desire to make him feel as off-balance as she herself had been feeling since meeting him.

"Mr. Fitzhugh, you are clearly new to London and so perhaps can be forgiven for not knowing *anything*," her emphasis was subtle but the spark in his eye told her he'd heard it. "Therefore I will seek to enlighten you." She tilted her head forward as if to impart a great secret and waited until he lowered his head closer to her own. Then she paused further still, judging the time left in the music.

"I am the most popular girl in London. This is my third year as the—oh what do they call me?—the *Golden Queen* of the *ton*. I can assure you that whatever I say or do, it instantly becomes the right thing."

And with that the music drew to a close. She broke a small bit of etiquette by not allowing him to escort her off the dance floor, but it was ever so much more gratifying to leave him there, chuckling alone as she swept off to find her next dance partner.

Chapter 2

Alexander Fitzhugh wasn't sure what he would say to the Earl of Southampton when he finally ran into him, but he hoped he was as quick on his feet as Lady Eleanor Chalcroft had been at the end of their waltz. He grinned at her departing back as she swished away from him, her blond ringlets bobbing. He had no doubt the Golden Queen was always right. He followed her off the floor and watched as she was immediately claimed for the next dance. He wasn't even aware that he continued to watch her until his friend Lord Taggart spoke beside him.

"Good luck there, Fitzhugh. Lady Eleanor has led the men a merry chase three Seasons now. When she settles, you can be assured it won't be for a mere mister."

Alex glanced at his friend with a raised brow. "I was simply admiring the lady's grace from afar, having experienced it firsthand."

"Of course you were, old boy. Come, let's find the card room. I've had my fill of marriage-minded debutantes for the evening."

Alex laughed shortly and turned to follow his friend when his eye was caught by a glimpse of a tall, gray-haired man across the room. Heart pounding, he moved his head from side to side, trying to see around the couples hopping about on the dance floor. "Move, damn you," he muttered under his breath. Finally a space cleared and he was able to see the opposite side of the ballroom but there was no sign of the man.

Unwilling to admit, even to himself, just how rattled he was, he pushed his way through the crowd and followed Reginald Taggart through a maze of hallways to a crowded noisy room at the back of the house. Smoke clung thickly to the ceiling and the deep rumble of masculine voices mingled with the gentle rustle of shuffling cards and the clink of crystal glasses. Taggart pushed his way over to the room's one open window, conveniently situated near a table well stocked with spirits. He poured two glasses of amber liquid and handed one to Alex.

"Good God, man, you look like you've seen a ghost."

Alex took a large swallow, tasting nothing but the burn of the alcohol followed by the easing warmth. Another swallow and then, "No ghost. Just thought I saw Southampton."

"Your father?" Taggart asked, surprised. "I didn't think he got out much anymore."

Alex shrugged. "Probably wasn't him then."

"What are you going to do?"

Refusing to meet his friend's gaze, Alex asked, "What do you mean?"

Taggart sloshed more brandy into both their glasses. "What are you going to do when you do finally run into your father? What is your plan?"

"I have no plan," Alex admitted.

Taggart choked discreetly on his drink. "What? You came up with a different plan to confront him every day we were at school. Surely you can't have forgotten *all* of them."

"Those were the silly schemes of a boy, Reg. A boy who wanted revenge."

"And the man doesn't?"

Alex shrugged and took another swallow. "What would it gain me?"

"Well eventually, the bloody earldom!"

"Honestly, that's not terribly enticing."

Taggart laughed. "Yes, but as the Earl of Southampton, you could have any woman you wanted—even the likes of Lady Eleanor."

"You don't think I could have her now if I chose?"

His friend leveled a skeptical look at him. "Lady Eleanor is a diamond of the first water."

"What does that even mean?" Alex said with a laugh.

"It means she is considered the best of the best. La crème de la crème. The epitome of English womanhood. She can have her choice of the best men England and probably most that Europe has to offer."

Of course Alex knew what it meant, he was simply trying to distract his friend from further questions about his father.

He stared into the amber depths of his glass. His father. He'd never called the man that to his face, not that he'd ever seen his face to be able to call him anything. A dusty portrait, a small miniature, and the assurance of his mother that he himself was the spitting image of the man were all he had to go on.

The Earl of Southampton had been nearly fifty when he'd married a fresh-faced debutante from Cornwall. Supposedly it had been a love match, in spite of, or perhaps in addition to, it being clear Southampton needed an heir and the bride's family was eager to claim connection to a more lofty title than any of them possessed. But Alice Waterston had always insisted the thirty-year age difference hadn't been an impediment to their love. She had doted on the earl and he had treated her as his cherished queen. Until, that is, she became pregnant. One would have thought the earl would have been thrilled. It was why he'd married, many said. Others thought perhaps his obsession with his wife made him resent anything that would share her affections. Very few knew the truth. It had taken Alex years to discover it himself and that had only been when he'd stumbled upon some old correspondence of his mother's. Alice Waterston had not been Southampton's first wife. His previous wife had succumbed to illness, but it wasn't childbirth fever that had claimed her but the morbid sore throat. She had not born a child, nor even suffered a tragic miscarriage for she'd never been pregnant. None of his mistresses had ever conceived either. The earl, it turned out, was incapable of siring a child. At least, that's what he believed.

Alex forced himself to unclench his teeth and swallowed

the last of his drink. Taggart, thank God, was engaged in small talk with another man and did not notice his friend's grim countenance.

Turning to fill his glass again, Alex willed his angry heartbeat to slow. He sipped his drink more slowly this time and affected a slightly bored expression as he surveyed the tables of card players wagering vast sums of money.

The Earl of Southampton had assumed his pretty young wife had indulged in an affair. Her protestations of love aside, he was convinced she had been unfaithful. Another man, facing a dearth of heirs able to carry on the family line and title, might have accepted the child, regardless of its parentage. In truth, the law held that a child born in wedlock was a man's offspring, regardless of who actually sired it. But the Earl of Southampton was a prideful man and it needled him to no end to think that his wife had found another man more attractive than him, that she had allowed another man to touch her and that another man had been able to achieve what he himself had never managed.

And so without even waiting to see the child born, he had packed a sobbing Alice into a coach and sent her away. He then sought to obtain a divorce, though this proved to be a very public and embarrassing ordeal for such a prideful man. The earl's only recourse, it appeared, was to put out that his wife and her expectant baby had died and then hope that it actually happened.

So it was that Alex grew up in Cornwall. His mother, once her tears had dried, had extracted a substantial living portion from her estranged husband and purchased a small estate not far from (but not too close to) her family's seat. She never spoke of his father beyond the most general terms and it had taken some eavesdropping on servants and reading the old letters for Alex to piece together what had happened and why he'd never met his father.

A slap on the back made him catch his balance. He and Reginald Taggart had been friends since their school days at

Shrewsbury School. It had become tradition that they never just slapped each other on the back in a camaraderie fashion. No, they sought to lay the other out, or at the very least, cause him to stumble to remain upright.

"Weak, old boy, weak," Alex said with a sad shake of his head. The stinging blow had broken the downward spiral of his thoughts, for which he was grateful.

"Let's go play some real cards," Taggart urged.

Alex raised his brow. "These aren't real cards?"

"Well of course they're real cards, but do you really wish to play crammed cheek-by-jowl in a smoky, brightly lit room?"

"I see your point. So instead we should find a gaming hell where we can play crammed cheek-by-jowl in a smoky, ill lit room I take it?"

"Precisely!" was Taggart's ringing approval. "Only three days in London and you already have the way of it. You always were a quick study."

"Good thing for you, else you'd not have had anyone to cheat off of in school," Alex remarked drolly.

"My father always said 'It's not what you know, it's who you know,' and I knew you would get me past my exams."

Their good-natured insults continued as they made their way back through the main halls of the house. They were awaiting the return of Taggart's carriage—a tedious proposition at a crowded ball—when his attention was snagged by a woman's laugh. It was melodious and joyful and he couldn't help but turn his head to see its owner.

Aha, he thought, the Golden Queen herself. He was frankly a little surprised that such a genuine sound could come from a "diamond of the first water." Or perhaps he was just surprised that she laughed, given how acerbic their encounter on the dance floor had been. Regardless, she was still smiling at something her companion—a dark haired girl of her own age —was saying. Lady Eleanor's father was waiting impatiently with a woman who could only be the girl's mother for their carriage but smiled indulgently as his daughter approached.

MICHELLE MORRISON

Alex watched her gesture and chat animatedly. The very lamp-light seemed drawn to her, shimmering in the golden threads of her hair, warming the ivory velvet of her complexion. She seemed to sparkle in the evening air, a thought that made Alex wonder just how many drinks he had downed whilst ruminating in the card room. Still, he could not take his gaze from her. It was easy to see why she'd been crowned society's queen of the *haute ton*; there was an ineffable quality about her that drew people to her. A quality above and beyond her stunning beauty and blue-blooded pedigree.

The dark-haired girl dropped her shawl and bent to pick it up. Lady Eleanor glanced out over the sea of carriages and then froze as if hearing her name shouted. Turning her head sharply, she caught him staring at her. There was nothing for it but to grin remorselessly and tilt his head in silent salute to her.

She studied him for a moment before regally returning his nod. With perfect timing, her coach arrived and she turned from him to climb gracefully up into it. He watched it roll smoothly away and fancied her hair cast a glow through the windows, though in truth it was probably only the carriage lights.

"Finally!" Taggart exclaimed, drawing his attention from thoughts of the Lady Eleanor. "I thought to die of old age before the coach arrived."

Alex snorted a laugh. "No, you'll just die of old age before you repay the money you borrowed the last time we went to play cards."

"Now that's not fair, that was in my irresponsible youth. You can't hold me to account for something that happened at university."

"Oh can't I?" Alex asked, and so their evening progressed with good natured insults and ribbing.

Chapter 3

"Come now, Juliette," Eleanor wheedled. "You know I love a good story."

"I do know. That's why you should read it yourself." Juliette Aston and Eleanor had been close friends since their debut nearly three years past. Despite Eleanor's advantage of beauty, wealth, and connections, she'd been terrified of making a fool of herself and embarrassing her parents when she entered her first season. Juliette had discovered her in the ladies' retiring room that first night, pale, sweating, and trying desperately not to lose the contents of her stomach. Juliette's confident humor—which only seemed to appear with Eleanor—had helped her gain control of herself and the two girls had felt an instant rapport with one another that had developed into a devoted friendship.

"Yes but you always do ...," Eleanor flapped her hands, trying to think of the right words. "Voices."

Juliette looked askance at her over a bite of lemon biscuit. "Voices?"

"Oh you know what I mean," Eleanor replied, exasperated. "You make your tone go up and down. You put...feeling into the words."

"If you're saying I employ inflection effectively, then I thank you. So just imagine my voice in your head as you read."

Eleanor threw an embroidered cushion at her friend who batted it away effortlessly. It was a terribly childish and unladylike thing to do, but Juliette was the one person in her life who didn't expect Eleanor to be perfect all the time. With Juliette, Eleanor could slouch, complain, or snort when she laughed and her friend would think none the less of her. Of course, excellent posture had been drilled into her since she was old enough to walk so that even in the privacy of her room, she never reclined against the back of a chair or slumped about. Then, too, her mother had been very strict about things a lady did and did not talk about and complaints of any kind were not tolerated. Eleanor's own awareness that she was a very lucky young woman had further curbed her tongue, especially around dear Juliette who had just not seemed to take to London society.

But as far as tossing pillows and snorting laughter, these were the few indulgences she participated in freely when alone with her best friend. It was ironic, really, that her public laugh had become rather famous in and of itself. While genuine, her public laugh was carefully modulated to ensure it trilled delicately out of her lips. Whereas when she was truly tickled, her laughed resembled nothing so much as a hearty guffaw with the frequent appearance of a snort to show her delight. Juliette had hugged her the first time she heard it and pronounced, "Thank God you are not entirely perfect! We shall be best of friends now!"

"Fine," Eleanor said and stuck her tongue out at her friend. She placed the novel she had wanted Juliette to read on the low table in front of them and picked up a fashion plate magazine.

"You're not going to read the book?" Juliette asked.

"I find I'm not in the mood just now," Eleanor replied loftily, and flipped through the pages of her periodical.

"Oh very well, give it here you silly goose."

Eleanor nudged the volume out of her friend's reach with the toe of her slipper. "No, truly, I need to decide on the trim for my new gown. The Andover ball is only a few days away, you know."

"Another gown?" Juliette laughed. "Eleanor, indulge me. Have you ever worn a gown more than once?"

Eleanor affected a moue of displeasure, though she knew her friend was only teasing. Then too, she'd lobbed her only missile at Juliette moments earlier and was currently unarmed. "Of course I have, you ninny. But the Duchess of Andover's ball promises to be this season's biggest, as well as one of the last. Goodness knows how many engagements will be announced at it!"

She saw her friend's animated face shutter and immediately knew why. Juliette expected Lord Worthing, Jacob Wilding, to offer for Eleanor and no doubt expected Eleanor to accept. Goodness knew her father would be happy with such an arrangement, though her mother had plans for her daughter to marry no less than a duke (a lofty goal indeed, considering the dearth of single dukes presently in England). Eleanor had done everything she could to avoid leading Lord Worthing to that event, and not just because she didn't fancy him that way. He was a decent enough fellow, and certainly handsome, not to mention heir to the Earldom of Beverly. However, all but a fool could see that he and Juliette were perfect for each other. Eleanor had realized it the moment they'd spotted him at a ball earlier in the season.

Eleanor had met him several times as a child and so was not completely unfamiliar with his character. Mostly, however, she had an unerring intuition about people. She had always been good at reading someone's character within moments of meeting them and determining best how to interact with them. Such a skill was no doubt a contributing factor to her popularity amongst society. She could sense if someone wanted to boast about an accomplishment, if another was worried about their appearance, if a third was simply a malicious person best avoided. She could just…see in a person's demeanor exactly what made them tick. So when she saw Jacob Wilding across the room, she had known in an instant that he and Juliette would be perfect for one another.

The devil was in the details, however, and Lord Worthing had been pursuing her for the last few months, even though he could not keep his eyes off Juliette whenever she was around. Eleanor suspected her and Lord Worthing's fathers were in collusion. She also knew Juliette well enough to know that her friend would do anything necessary to make Eleanor happy, even if that meant forgoing the man who was clearly meant for her.

"What will you wear?" Eleanor prodded her friend.

"It doesn't really matter. I suspect I shall be betrothed to Mr. Pickering by then. I may as well wear sackcloth." Juliette suppressed a shudder that Eleanor knew had more to do with Juliette's erstwhile suitor than the prospect of unattractive clothing.

"Nonsense," she assured her friend. "The season is not yet over. I have every confidence you will make a splendid match!"

Juliette smiled, clearly disbelieving, and tossed her a biscuit, which Eleanor deftly caught and popped in her mouth, relishing the opportunity to stuff her mouth with impunity.

"Did you happen to meet Mr. Fitzhugh last night?" This was said with an undignified spray of crumbs that sent Juliette into peals of laughter and forced Eleanor to repeat herself once said biscuit was duly swallowed.

"Mr. Fitzhugh?" Juliette shook her head. "No. When did you meet him?"

"Toward the end of the evening. He's an acquaintance of Lord Pemberly, as I understand it."

Juliette glanced at her sideways while pouring more tea. "And what is so remarkable about Mr. Fitzhugh?"

Eleanor shook her head to Juliette's silent inquiry for more tea, then paused. "Well, nothing, really. He's rather tall, I suppose. His eyes are a most unusual color—rather cinnamony if you ask me."

"Cinnamony?"

"Yes. It's a word."

"If you say so..."

"I do. His eyes are cinnamony and his lashes are russetty. But otherwise, there is nothing remarkable about him."

"Then why mention him?" Juliette asked with an all-too-knowing glance.

Eleanor shook her head and glanced unseeing at the fashion plates in front of her. The truth was, she'd been hoping Juliette had met the dratted man so her friend could tell her why she was unable to stop thinking about him. Or why he was the first person she'd met about whom she could not form an immediate impression.

They'd shared one dance, during which conversation was anything but genteel or romantic. There had been that moment on the front stairs of the de Wynter house when she had experienced a sensation not unlike a feather being drawn down her back. She had turned to find Mr. Fitzhugh staring at her. He grinned audaciously at her before bowing. There was nothing in the evening's encounter that should have caused her to wonder who he was and what he was about. And yet she found herself completely preoccupied with thoughts of the man.

Later, after Juliette departed, Eleanor wandered downstairs. Not given much to wandering, she was somewhat surprised to find herself at the open door of her father's study. She could see him seated at his desk, scrutinizing a paper in his hands. Suddenly unsure of herself—and she couldn't remember the last time that had happened—she chewed her lower lip. She had just decided to back away when Lord Chalcroft looked up.

"Ellie, my dear girl! To what do I owe this honor?"

Eleanor entered the richly appointed room, realizing she'd not stepped into it all season. It had been a bit of a whirlwind year, but she and her father had always been rather close and she suddenly felt bad for how little she'd seen him since they arrived in London.

"Don't tell me you've run out of pin money and have come to ask for more?"

"No!" she rushed to assure him. "It's not that at all," she continued, but he just laughed.

"I'm teasing you, gel. Can't a father tease his only daughter now and again?" He came around the massive oak desk and bussed her cheek, tickling her with his long whiskers.

"I came because I feel we've scarce seen each other since the Season began. It's as if we don't even live beneath the same roof."

"Silly chit. Didn't I escort you just last night to the de Wynter ball?" he chided, but she could see he was pleased that she sought him out.

Eleanor rang the bell pull to summon a maid for tea. "Yes, well it is rather difficult to hear one's own thoughts at a crush such as last night, much less converse with one's dear papa."

The maid arrived and was quickly dispatched on her errand. Eleanor joined her father in the large leather chairs in front of the cold fireplace. Once refreshments arrived, she took great pains to prepare her father's tea just how he liked it and selected several finger sandwiches for him.

"Heavens but now that you mention it, it has been a while since you poured for me. Enjoying your season, are you Ellie?"

"Yes, I suppose I am."

"You suppose? It seems you've attended every event of note in London and out. And judging by the accounts, you've enjoyed many a new gown for most of them."

Eleanor raised her brows at him in mock reproof. "You wouldn't have me appearing in last year's frocks would you? Think what people would say!"

"That you'd suddenly gained a modicum of frugality?" he inquired with equally raised brows.

"Nonsense. They'd think you were in dire financial straits. Or worse, that I'd lost my flair for fashion."

"That would definitely be the worst assumption," he replied with a nearly straight face.

She giggled and then took a breath. "Did you enjoy the de Wynter ball last night papa?"

"Oh you know I don't go much for the ballroom scene," he prevaricated. "I take it you had a good time, though. Danced nearly every dance, eh?"

She placed another sandwich on his plate and didn't answer. As was the case at most balls, she had danced every set. But it was beginning to grow a little tedious; forever appearing enthralled with whatever her dance partner chose to discuss, laughing at silly jokes as if she understood them, prettily thanking her partner for the dance, even if he'd trod all over her toes. Eleanor stared unseeing into the empty fireplace. What had come over her? Until recently, she had loved attending parties and balls, loved the laughter, the music. She had loved coaxing people into talking about themselves and flirting. Yes, flirting was divine. She loved selecting just the right gown, just the right accoutrements to her ensemble to perfectly suit each event. Well, truth be told, she still loved that part. As Juliette was fond of pointing out, Eleanor had absolutely no talent with a sketchpad or watercolors. She had absolutely no patience for practicing any musical instrument. But when it came to choosing colors and fabrics for a gown, things suddenly made sense to her. She could see details down to the trim on the hem or the embroidery around a cuff and she took great satisfaction in those details.

"Goodness but that's a serious face, Ellie."

Eleanor smiled as she came out of her reverie.

"What were you thinking about?" her father asked.

She busied herself with arranging the biscuits on her plate so they formed a perfect fan.

"Out with it. Come now, I won't tell your mother."

She laughed at that. As a child he would sneak her sweets and she would confess her childish foibles with the mutual understanding that they wouldn't tell Lady Chalcroft, who often had little patience for such indulgences.

"If you haven't overspent your allowance, you must be suffering a heartbreak. Or worse," he said ominously, though the twinkle in his eye assured her he was teasing. "You've fallen in love with a ruffian of whom I would never approve."

"No, nothing that dire," she assured him, though unbidden the image of Mr. Fitzhugh rose up again in her mind. What would her father think of a man like him?

"I just seem to be...well, tired of the whirlwind," she said with a wave at her hand to encompass everything.

Her father sat back and took a sip of his tea. He made a face and standing, fetched a small flask from his desk. He splashed the contents into his teacup. "Better," he murmured after tasting it. He resumed his seat and said, "Perhaps it's time to settle down, Ellie. You're nearing the end of your third Season. I've never rushed you—heavens knows I loathe losing your company—but that is rather the point of attending these events, you know; to find a husband and begin the next part of your life."

"I know," she said with a sigh. "And I want to. I do! It's just that none of the men I've met...really interest me. Not for very long, at least."

Her father laughed. "That's quite an indictment on the men of England. What of Jacob Wilding? He seems interesting enough."

Eleanor kept her expression neutral. She knew her father was fond of Lord Worthing and had met privately with the man, no doubt to give his blessing to a courtship. She also suspected her father and Lord Worthing's had been in collusion for some time. She needed to tread carefully.

"He is very nice gentleman."

Lord Chalcroft let out a bark of laughter. "Talk about damning with faint praise!"

Eleanor scrambled to explain. "I believe Lord Worthing has developed a *tendre* for Miss Aston.

"What's that?" he asked, looking distinctly befuddled. "That doesn't make sense."

"Yes, well at any rate," she rushed on. "I don't think he and I would suit."

Her father set his cup down and folded his hands across

his belly. "It seems you've decided no man will suit you. Am I going to have to ship you off to France just to find a husband for you? I assure you, those frogs don't treat their women like an Englishman does. I think you'd better give the men here a second look."

Eleanor nodded, studying the stray tea leaves swirling in the bottom of her cup.

"I will, papa. I promise." Frantically trying to think of a way to ask about Mr. Fitzhugh without appear interested in him, her father saved her inadvertently.

"You met Lord Taggart last night, I believe. He's a new fellow to you. Been abroad since your debut, I believe."

She had little impression of Lord Taggart beyond the fact that he was Mr. Fitzhugh's companion.

"Yes he was new. He and his friend, Mr. Fitz...Simmons?"

Lord Chalcroft shook his head. "Not Fitzsimmons. Let me think. Fitzhugh; that's it. I remember wondering last night if he was any relation to Lord Fitzhugh, the Earl of Southampton."

"I didn't realize the earl had a son."

"I don't know for sure that he does. There was some gossip years ago. What was it?" Her father frowned in concentration. "I don't remember exactly, but surely the man we met would have flaunted such a connection, even if he's only a distant relation."

"Did you converse with him at all?" she asked, wondering what her father thought of Fitzhugh.

"Not beyond a cursory introduction. Actually don't think I could pick him out in a crowd if you paraded him in front of me! Don't tell me he's caught your fancy?" he asked with raised brows.

"Hardly," she prevaricated, though her heart was beating a quick tempo. "He's just...new. And exceedingly tall."

Her father chuckled at that. "Well what about Taggart? He's 'new' as you call it and at least we know his family."

"I will certainly allow him to seek me out at the next ball

and take his measure," she replied pertly.

Her father laughed. "That's my gel! Settle for nothing but the best...but settle down soon, Ellie. You'll be happier than you are now, stuck in this limbo of the marriage mart. And don't rule out Jacob Wilding. You and he are cut of the same cloth and would rub on well together."

Eleanor presented a noncommittal smile to her father and slipped out of his study. Jacob Wilding, indeed. She had marriage plans for Jacob Wilding but they did not include her. If only Juliette were not so stubborn.

As Eleanor made her way back to her room to begin preparing for the evening's dinner guests, she wondered again why she could not get thoughts of Mr. Fitzhugh out of her mind. Perhaps it was simply because he'd been so irreverent when talking to her. Most men sought to impress her with tales of their wealth, knowledge, or exploits. They acted on their best behavior and told amusing stories trying to elicit her famous laugh. Mr. Fitzhugh, on the other hand, had spoken with complete disregard for her "delicate" sensibilities. She should have considered him rude and vowed to have no further interaction with him, except that their exchange had invigorated her. Unaccustomed as she was to men speaking to her as if...well, as if she were a man, she likened his conversation, while vexing, to that of the crisp bite of winter's air after hours in a close, stuffy, overly-warm ballroom.

She smiled at her extravagant imagery. Juliette's influence, no doubt, as her friend was forever reading poems and novels, and trying to convince Eleanor to read them as well.

As she reached the door of her chamber, a maid rushed up and handed her a folded note. "It's from your mother, my lady. She asked me to give it to you."

"She couldn't simply have you convey the message?" Eleanor said with a laugh.

"She said as how she didn't want me to forget nothing," the maid replied, shoving the note closer. Eleanor took the creamy paper and entered her room. She closed her eyes and slowly opened the missive. Focusing intently on the words, she read, "Your caizin hes asq qheq we znd clot am fooq zal to ammiz hr hr womh. Gaddd som llems you smm fit I wll hev one qhe footman pelivz it."

Eleanor felt the familiar pain begin just behind her eyes. She took the letter over to the window where the light was brighter. It didn't always help, in fact it rarely helped, but it was all she could think to do. She squinted at her mother's writing, then slit her eyes and peered from beneath her lashes but the words would not make sense today. Crumpling the note, she stuffed it in the pocket of her skirt and went in search of her mother.

Not surprisingly, she found her in her dressing room, dictating a letter while a maid curled her hair.

"Eleanor, you're not dressed for dinner yet!"

"I shan't be but a minute to dress."

"Did you receive my note?"

"I did as I was on my way to see you and thought you could just tell me what you wanted."

"Honestly, Eleanor. Why did I spend the time dictating my instructions if you had no intention of reading them?"

Why indeed, Eleanor thought, when we live in the same house and her mother knew the written word was not Eleanor's favorite method of communication. But she knew better than to voice such a question. Lady Chalcroft was a devoted mother, but she maintained a strong sense of propriety and did not tolerate responses that might be construed as disrespectful.

Lady Chalcroft stopped her maid and rearranged a curl herself. "You see how I wish it to go, Mason?" When the maid nodded, she said, "Very good. Carry on."

"What is it you would like me to do, Mother?" Eleanor asked.

"Our distant cousin, Sarah Draper has sent her yearly letter to the family asking for donations to her cause."

"Is it that time again already?" Eleanor mused. Sarah

Draper was a not-so-distant relation of her mother's, but Lady Chalcroft preferred to separate herself from her common background. Nonetheless, she also maintained a strong sense of obligation to those less fortunate than herself and so she donated money, food, and clothing to Miss Draper's cause, which was to help London's most impoverished citizens.

Eleanor wasn't sure what good a satin ball gown would do for someone who lived in a hovel if they had a roof at all. But she supposed the gown or at least the fabric from it could be sold for coin. As a result, she dutifully emptied her closet every year of those gowns and cloaks she knew she'd not wear again. She was only slightly embarrassed at the staggering number of gowns she managed to accumulate in a year, but philosophized that if she didn't have so many gowns, she wouldn't have so many to give to charity.

"I shall attend to my closets first thing in the morning," she assured her mother.

"Good. Also, please pay special attention to Lord Dunsbury. I've finally managed to get him to accept one of our invitations."

Lord Dunsbury was the only chance Lady Chalcroft had of marrying Eleanor off to a duke—in this case, the heir to a duke. He'd recently returned to England after several years abroad.

"Of course, Mother."

"You might consider that pale yellow satin gown. It sets your coloring off nicely."

Eleanor kissed the air next to her mother's cheek, being careful not to disturb her elegant coiffure, but just as carefully avoiding agreeing with her mother on what to wear. Words might make a dreadful muddle to Eleanor's mind, but colors and fabrics, designs and decorations made perfect sense. It might be a paltry talent, she mused as she returned to her room, but it was her strongest one and she was not about to dismiss it.

As she rang for her maid and chose a rose pink silk from her dressing room, she wondered if she would run into Alexander Fitzhugh again.

Chapter 4

Despite his assertion to Taggart that he hadn't an idea about confronting his father, Alex did, in fact have a plan. Several, in fact. Riding through Hyde Park, while convenient, was not particularly challenging to either him or his mount and he found his mind wandering over each plan. Plan Number One involved avoiding his father completely, focusing on building his business and fortune schemes. This was perhaps the wisest choice as his father clearly had no desire to meet or acknowledge him and any manner of unpleasantness could be avoided by simply steering clear of the man.

Plan Number Two was comprised of seeking his father out, forcing him to acknowledge who he was, and extracting some sort of penance for years of neglect; money, perhaps, but an apology at the least. While potentially gratifying (for what child would not wish retribution on a father who had denied his very existence?) it also had the greatest potential for backfiring. A man who could ignore the very heir he'd spent a lifetime trying to conceive could just as easily use his power and influence to destroy the budding business of said child. And who knew, perhaps his sire was plain evil? In which case, he might go to even greater extremes to avoid having to acknowledge him; he wouldn't put it past the man. Alex's horse responded to his unconscious tightening of the reigns by shaking its head and sidestepping. He immediately released the tension and smoothed his hand down his mount's neck.

"Easy boy. Sorry about that old chap. Didn't mean to work myself up." His horse, being a forgiving sort, resumed its easy pace along Rotten Row and Alex sank back into his reverie.

Plan Number Three, while the most nebulous, was the plan Alex was currently enacting, if only because it didn't require any immediate decisions. He would neither seek out nor avoid the Earl of Southampton. He would focus his efforts on building his shipping business and enjoy those events Taggart's coat tails could drag him to. Should he find a wealthy young lady who didn't mind a husband with a dubious lineage (an unlikely scenario, he realized), he would certainly entertain the notion of marriage, as a dowry of any size would certainly be helpful. And should he run into his father—at a ball, a horserace, a gentleman's club, he would have to think on his feet and make his next move based on how his sire reacted.

For all the ambiguity of such a plan, Alex believed in being prepared. So while he did not seek his father out, he knew exactly which gentlemen's clubs he frequented. He knew that he maintained the family townhouse in Mayfair, but kept a mistress in Bloomsbury. He had a man of business asking careful questions about the earl's finances. Though Southampton did not appear to be lacking for money, neither were half the men who would be in debtor's gaol were they not possessed of a title. It had been easier to discover that his father had a good eye for horseflesh and had bred several rather famous racehorses. And apparently, his sire had a decided weakness for toffee. This made Alex feel rather strange, as it was the one sweet he absolutely could not get enough of. His mother had always smiled so poignantly when he'd wheedled the candy out of her, and now he knew why. When he'd learned that bit of trivia about the earl, he'd very nearly sworn off the sweet. But such a move would not have had any effect on his father while it would deprive Alex of one of his favorite indulgences.

In fact, just thinking about toffee made Alex nearly cut his ride short and head into town to visit a sweet shop.

"Fitzhugh!"

He paused his mount and looked about to see Taggart nudging his horse into a gentle canter to cross the span of lawn between them. As his friend reigned in, Alex couldn't help smiling. Taggart looked like the boy he'd first met at school when they were just ten years old. Hat askew, cheeks reddened from exertion and with a devilish gleam of delight in his eyes, Taggart could have still passed for a schoolboy—or at least one in university.

"Taggart, have you escaped your nanny again?" Alex called out.

"Indeed, I left her worn out and sound asleep in my bed," was the ribald response.

Alex laughed as their horses fell into step along the graveled path.

"Fancy joining me on Friday at the Andover ball? It's sure to be a crush."

"Why not," Alex agreed. "Will there be better food than the last event?"

Taggart laughed. "Assuredly. The question is, will we get there in time to sample it. I daresay being fashionably late has its disadvantages." Taggart stood up in his stirrups and squinted across the park.

"I say, there's Miss Rosalie Spenser out for a walk. Let's join her, shall we?" Without waiting for a response, Taggart spurred his horse on, leaving Alex to follow in his dust.

Miss Spenser, as it turned out, was part of a large group of young ladies and their attendant gentlemen. For all his earlier exuberance, Taggart slowed his horse as he approached the group and swung off his mount easily, greeting the men on the edges of the group and pretending to be completely oblivious to the ginger-haired young lady. Alex suppressed a smile at his friend's machinations and slowly dismounted himself, allowing Taggart to introduce him and pretending not to notice the raised brows at the mention of his name. Surely gossip had already begun concerning his identity.

Content to let Taggart drag him along, Alex bowed over ladies' hands, nodded to the men he was introduced to, and generally tried not to say too much.

"Oh, Fitzhugh, I believe you already know Lady Eleanor, don't you?"

Grateful to step aside from a question regarding who his family was, Alex turned and found himself facing the blond beauty who had so delightfully tried to insult him the other night at the de Wynter ball.

Bowing over her hand with a ridiculous flourish, Alex looked up at her and flashed his most wicked grin. Despite the crest of pink on her cheeks, Lady Eleanor smiled polite disinterest back at him before returning her attention to the gentleman beside her. Alex mentally tipped his hat at her for maintaining her façade. She truly was a master. He found himself watching her as she conversed with the enraptured men around her. She managed to bestow a special smile or pretty comment to each man without appearing to single any out. The other young ladies in the group appeared resigned to Lady Eleanor's popularity and she in turn skillfully drew them into the conversation. Alex narrowed his eyes as he watched her adroitly manage one young gentleman to speak with a girl at her elbow. Not two minutes later, she paired another two people together. Fancied herself a matchmaker, eh? he mused, and because he could not help himself, he maneuvered himself into her circle, trying hard not to smile as he imagined her trying to pawn him off on one of her friends.

"A lovely day today, isn't it Mr. Fitzhugh?" At his murmured response, she carried on blithely. "That is a fine mount you have. I imagine he does not care for gentle walks in the park, but rather wishes to stretch his legs in the country."

"I manage to wear him out on a regular basis. Tell me, do you enjoy horseback riding?" He knew most young ladies were trained to sit a horse prettily and a few actually enjoyed it.

"If I must be honest—"

"You must," he interrupted.

She pretended not to have heard him. "If I must be honest, I much prefer riding in a carriage, although I do enjoy buying several new riding habits each season."

"And truly, isn't that the real motivation behind riding? To purchase the garments?" he teased.

She narrowed her eyes briefly but smiled benignly. "I couldn't put it better."

As they chatted, the ebb and flow of the group arranged matters such that Lady Eleanor and he were on the edge of the gathering. Taking advantage of their relative privacy, Alex said, "I couldn't help but notice your matchmaking attempts."

Lady Eleanor lifted her eyebrows delicately. "Attempts? You should know, Mr. Fitzhugh, that when I pair two people together, they end up married more often than not."

"Bit of a busybody, are you?"

She gasped but quickly recovered. "Indeed not. Otherwise, I should meddle until *all* of the people I pair together end up wedded. I simply..." she trailed off and looked out across the park as if searching for the right words. "I simply have a sense about people, you see. I don't know why, but once I get to know someone, I know just what type of person they would be happiest with. And since I know practically everyone in London—"

"Ah, so then you are familiar with my valet," he said quickly.

She narrowed her eyes at him again but did not hesitate a second. "I know practically everyone in the *ton*. Therefore I am usually able to match people who might not otherwise meet."

"And your judgment is infallible?"

"Of course not. But it is generally very good."

"And for yourself? This is not your first Season. Does your skill not work in finding yourself a husband?"

Now Lady Eleanor's eyes widened in surprise. He knew it had been an incredibly rude thing to ask. One never implied a lady might be destined to sit on the shelf, but for some reason, he couldn't help needling her. Besides, her eyes were so expressive, it was rather fun to watch them narrow and widen at his comments.

"I shall overlook your deplorable lack of manners as clearly they have a different standard of what constitutes polite conversation in Cornwall."

"That is very kind of you," he said with a grin.

Lady Eleanor glanced over her shoulder and noticed they were very nearly standing alone as some people had continued their walk and others had joined the impromptu gathering. He expected her to make some comment about joining the others but when she turned back toward him, her eyes were wide with terror and her face pale.

Thinking she'd seen someone terrifying, he quickly glanced around but saw nothing other than the well-dressed people of her circle. Looking more closely, he noticed she was breathing quite rapidly and her gloved hands were clasped tightly together as if to still their trembling.

He stepped closer to her. "Lady Eleanor?"

She appeared not to hear him, but when he reached out to touch her arm, she jumped and her gaze jerked to his.

"I...I should like to go home."

"Of course. Did you come with someone? Or is your maid about?"

Again she didn't seem to hear him. "I need to go home." Her breathing was rapid and shallow.

He was growing concerned for her. A fine sheen of perspiration gathered on her pale skin. He wondered if she was going to be ill right here and some part of him wanted to shield her from doing so in front of her friends.

"Perhaps if we sat on that bench over there," he suggested.

"No," she whispered, glancing around as if looking for an escape. In a flash of insight, Alex realized that she was not ill but panicked.

Alex was still a green lad when he'd stumbled upon the group of smugglers who operated out of the hidden coves near his home in Cornwall. It was wartime and smuggling was vastly more lucrative than fishing, farming, or any of the other trades that employed those not fighting Napoleon's army on the Continent. In retrospect, Alex realized the men could very well have killed him—the Crown had been cracking down on smugglers, even transporting or hanging some who were caught. But these men were a local gang. They'd known Alex since he was a babe and for some reason, perhaps because they considered him one of their own, or because he was so excited by their activities, they'd allowed him to hang around, even utilizing him to serve as lookout from time to time. Alex had viewed all the men as surrogate uncles and grew to know each one. One man, Sam Shepherd, had been on board the lugger the men had converted from a fishing ship as it was their fastest vessel. An otherwise smooth run had abruptly gone afoul when they'd been attacked by French pirates, intent on stealing the load of English wool the men had been smuggling into Le Havre. The fighting had been close, the French pirate ship swooping out of the fog to blast the smaller English ship with cannon and musket fire. Sam had stood between two men as their torsos had been demolished by cannonball. There was no reason he should have survived the encounter, and in fact, Alex sometimes wondered if Sam wouldn't have been happier had he died that day. Ever since, the smuggler had been struck by such attacks of nerves that he could scarce leave his house. Shaking, sweating, rapid and panicked breathing were common occurrences and most of the man's friends scarcely noticed them anymore. Alex has always sought to calm his friend, however, and had learned a few techniques that sometimes helped.

Alex had never seen another person suffer such an attack until today. Lady Eleanor's symptoms were identical to Sam Shepherd's, though he doubted the gently reared lady had ever witnessed anything as horrific as the smuggler had. Still, she was clearly distraught and seemed incapable of any sort of action.

Moving so that he blocked her from view of the others who were still chatting animatedly, he bent his head to murmur in her ear. "Take my arm."

She shook her head but Alex was certain it was the notion of moving at all that elicited such a response. "Take it," he urged, his voice low and reassuring. "Hold onto it with all your might. I won't let anything happen to you." He saw her reach for the crook of his proffered arm and then pull back. "Go on," he urged. "I'm here. No one will see. That's it. There you go." He casually stepped closer to her until he felt her pressed against his side. She clung to his forearm with a strength that surprised him.

He lowered his head again. "Easy now. I've got you." Inhaling, his senses were inundated with her scent, sweet and warm. It was intoxicating and he could not get enough. He dropped his head closer, breathing her in, gently nuzzling the soft hair at her temple before coming to his senses. Alex certainly had no concern for social niceties, living on the fringe as it were, but he was aware that Lady Eleanor lived in the midst of the London *ton* and the same protective streak that made him want to ease her attack reminded him that gentlemen did not nuzzle ladies in the park. Glancing around, he made sure no one had spotted his indiscretion before turning back to her.

"What has frightened you? Can you tell me? Perhaps I can help you."

She shook her head again and pressed her gloved hand against her lips, her eyes wide, pupils dilated, even in the bright sunlight.

"Are you going to be ill? Perhaps we should wander closer to those bushes over there," he suggested.

Another shake of the head, this one smaller and she closed her eyes as she inhaled shakily. Opening them, she lowered her hand from her mouth. "I'm not going to be ill. I...if I might have another moment."

"Of course."

"Will you...will you talk? It sometimes helps."

With his free hand, he gently stroked her gloved hand, murmuring nonsensical comments about the flowers in bloom, the shape of the clouds. He sensed some of the tension leave her body and he began telling her completely inappropriate jokes. When he heard her choke back a laugh, he knew she was on her way to recovery. He glanced over his shoulder and saw that the impromptu gathering was beginning to dissipate.

"Take a deep breath," he instructed. "Good. Now another." He squeezed her hand before smoothly stepping away from her. "Who did you come to the park with?"

She licked her dry lips and Alex felt a jolt through his entire body at the brief glimpse of her tongue. Taking another breath, she said, "Audrey. Lady Audrey. Blackburn."

He looked at the gaggle of young ladies, bedecked in nearly identical pastel gowns. "Which one is she?"

One young lady emitted a high-pitched giggle that did not seem to stop.

"Her. The giggler."

Alex turned back to her, a smile on his face. Her face was still pale, but her pupils had returned to normal size.

"Will you be alright?" he asked.

She nodded tightly. "I think so. I'll tell her I need to go home right away. We came in her carriage. It's not far away," she said, waving her hand off to the right."

"I shall fetch it. Will you be alright with Lady Audrey for a few moments?"

"Yes. I will," she said, though he suspected she was urging herself to be fine rather than reassuring him.

Alex swung up on his horse and took off at a gallop, quickly cresting the hill Lady Eleanor had gestured at and seeing three empty carriages on the other side, clearly awaiting their perambulating riders. Another couple of minutes to determine which carriage was Lady Audrey's and then an agonizing five minutes as the carriage followed Alex around the hill on the graveled path.

By the time they returned to the now greatly diminished group, he was nearly as panicked as Lady Eleanor had been. He didn't pause to wonder why he should be so concerned about a young woman he scarcely knew, but he raced ahead of the carriage to make sure she was not still suffering her attack.

She held her hands clasped tightly in front of her and

there was a brittleness to her smile, but she seemed to be holding herself together. He leapt from his mount and announced that the carriage was nearly there.

The giggling lady looked at him as if he'd lost his mind. "Who are you, sir? I don't recall bringing a footman with me to the park." She giggled at her own silly joke and the remaining ladies and gentlemen smiled—some at her, some at Alex's expense.

He opened his mouth to tell them all what he thought of them when Lady Eleanor spoke.

"Mr. Fitzhugh fetched your carriage for us so I wouldn't have to walk, Audrey. I am feeling rather faint. Would you mind terribly if we returned home?"

To her credit, Lady Audrey immediately stopped giggling and was a solicitous friend, urging Lady Eleanor to the carriage. "Let me just remind Sir Fletcher about my father's dinner invitation," she said climbing back out of the carriage.

Alex took advantage of her absence to check one last time on Lady Eleanor.

"Thank you so much for your kindness, Mr. Fitzhugh."

"Call me Alex. May I call on you tomorrow? Just to assure myself that you have recovered." He knew it wasn't a proper request, just as it wasn't at all the thing for her to call him by his first name, but suddenly he was loathe to see her go.

"That would not be...wise."

He was about to press her when she glanced past him and saw Lady Audrey returning to the carriage.

"I will be at the third bench in from Aldford Gate tomorrow at eleven o'clock," she said.

"But won't you—"

"Good day, Mr. Fitzhugh," she said firmly and Alex realized Lady Audrey was waiting for him to move so she could enter her carriage. He handed her up and glanced one last time at Lady Eleanor before the coachman started them off sharply.

Turning around, he discovered the group had dispersed. Only Taggart remained waiting for him.

"Don't know that I've ever seen you play nursemaid, Fitzhugh."

Alex threw a sour glance at his friend as he mounted his horse. "Lady Eleanor was struck ill. I seemed to be the only one not self-absorbed enough to notice. I merely offered some assistance."

Taggart neglected to look chastened, but he did forgo further teasing.

They rode briskly to the edge of Hyde Park. As they paused to say farewell, Alex couldn't resist asking after Lady Eleanor.

"How is it that one such as Lady Eleanor is still on the marriage mart? I would have assumed that with her looks and pedigree she'd have been snatched up within weeks of her debut."

Taggart laughed. "I'm sure she could have, old boy. But Lady Eleanor is not an ingénue. This is the end of her third season, if I'm not mistaken."

"Really?" asked Alex, even though she'd told him herself. "Is something...er, wrong with her?"

His friend laughed again. "Only if you consider being spoiled and coddled by her father as 'something wrong.' My mother said Lord Chalcroft thinks his daughter hung the moon and he won't push her to marry until she is good and ready. And if you ask my mother, which I pray you won't for she'll hound you to death for your interest, Lady Eleanor's mother has her heart set on a ducal coronet for her only daughter."

"Has she shown a preference for no man, then?"

"Lady Eleanor or her mother?"

Alex narrowed his eyes at his friend, who seemed to be enjoying drawing out the information. "Lady Eleanor, as one would hope that Lady Chalcroft prefers Lord Chalcroft above all others."

"One never knows, does one," Taggart mused thoughtfully. He shook his head as if to clear it from unwanted visions. "Lady Eleanor is perfectly lovely to everyone she meets. She has received dozens of offers but she has shown no man—or type of man, if you will—particular favor."

Alex's horse nipped at his friend's mount and it took a moment for the men to calm the beasts. Taggart was not put off the subject, however. "Fancy her, do you?"

"What? Of course not," Alex insisted.

Now it was his friend's turn to narrow his eyes. "You asked about her the other night at the de Wynter ball as well. You *do* fancy her, don't you?" Oblivious to Alex's assertions that he was merely curious, Taggart continued. "I dare say you'd better work on gaining your father's acknowledgement then. Lady Chalcroft might consider settling for a mere earl for her daughter, but in your current status of Mr. Fitzhugh, you haven't a chance of a dinner invitation, much less permission to court Lady Eleanor."

"I've no intention of courting anyone, Reginald," Alex said, emphasizing his friend's first name. Taggart hated his given name and Alex was wise enough only to use it when he desperately needed to distract his friend. "I told you, I'm working on building my shipping empire."

"Yes, well don't go mentioning that around Lady Eleanor's parents either. A man in trade will never win their approval, title or no."

Suddenly weary of the conversation, Alex bade his friend farewell and headed back to his rented bachelor quarters in Knightsbridge.

Despite his best efforts to think of something else, Alex found his mind returning to Lady Eleanor. He could see her pale face and fear-filled eyes in his mind and he hoped she'd made it home without further anguish. He wondered if she'd always had such attacks, or if something had occurred to her to initiate them, as was the case for the smuggler in Cornwall.

He also wondered at her parting remarks about meeting him inside Aldford Gate tomorrow. What was *that* about? he wondered. She'd refused his request to call on her at home, which should have set him straight, and yet, she'd arranged to meet him—alone as far as he could tell—tomorrow morning. He hoped she wasn't one of those ladies whose pristine exterior disguised a craven soul who thrilled at hidden associations with otherwise "undesirable" men. He'd met a couple such ladies while at university and had not found the experience to his liking.

Lady Eleanor did not seem to fit the mold of the depraved socialite, however, and he prided himself on being a rather good judge of character. Well, only tomorrow would tell, he decided philosophically as he turned his horse into the rented mews two blocks from his bachelor rooms.

Chapter 5

Eleanor woke unusually early the next morning. What's more, she woke feeling well rested and—dare she say it?—excited to get out of bed. During the London season, she generally did not go to bed before three or four in the morning and as a result, slept very late the next day. Even when she maintained country hours at her family's home, it was difficult for her to bounce out of bed bright and chipper. She generally required a pot of strong chocolate and a good thirty minutes to blearily come awake.

But today, she felt positively energetic. She climbed out of bed and padded across the room to part the heavy drapes. The day was sparklingly sunny, the sky a shade of blue that made Eleanor think of a silk gown she'd worn during her first season.

She turned at the gentle rustling of her maid behind her. The young woman gasped to find Eleanor awake and about.

"Is aught wrong, miss?

"Not at all, Mary. I simply woke up feeling wonderful this morning. I feel a bit like a child on Twelfth Night awaiting a gift."

Mary carefully set Eleanor's breakfast tray down by the window and fetched a wrapper to drape across her mistress's shoulders. "Is something exciting happening today, then?"

"Not that I—" Eleanor stopped mid-sentence. She suddenly remembered her spontaneous and possibly ill-conceived suggestion that Alexander Fitzhugh seek her out at the park this morning.

That couldn't be the reason she was looking forward to

the day, could it? She poured herself a cup of chocolate and stirred several lumps of sugar into it. As she sipped it, she considered her anticipation of the meeting. It was wholly without reason, but she was fascinated by Mr. Fitzhugh like she'd been drawn to none of the hundreds of men she'd met since her debut. He was handsome enough, she would grant him, but he was certainly not the most handsome she'd met. His nebulous parentage was certainly not in his favor, and he seemed rather indifferent to the conventions of good manners. But something in the way he'd held her when they danced, the way he'd spoken so bluntly, as if she were more than capable of verbally sparring with him, the way he'd stared at her on the de Wynter's entry stairs, the way he'd soothed her yesterday in the park...they all contributed to her not being able to think of anything or anyone else.

"We shall be going for a walk this morning, Mary," she announced.

"This morning, my lady? Before luncheon?"

Eleanor smiled. She couldn't remember the last time she had left the house before noon and she was sure Mary had grown accustomed to the later hours as well.

"Indeed. I feel as if I shall turn over a new leaf and begin waking early every day."

Though the maid hid it well, Eleanor was amused to see the girl swallow as if digesting this edict.

"What will you wear to the park, my lady? It's like to be a bit chilly. I think the clouds will move in this morning as well," Mary reported. Eleanor smiled at the girl's transparent attempts to dissuade her mistress from being about at the unfashionable hour of—Eleanor glanced at the small clock on the mantel—nine o'clock.

"Good heavens," she exclaimed. "Is that truly the time?" She would be hard pressed indeed to dress and walk all the way to the Aldford gate in two hours.

Mary looked at her with wide eyes and a startled expression. It was no doubt the first time Eleanor had ever expressed any concern over the time. While not a perpetually late person, Eleanor recognized that she'd taken advantage of her popularity to the extent that she seldom worried when she arrived at an event for she was always welcomed and her presence was always sought. Today, however, she wanted to be prompt. If she was going to go against all convention by initiating the meeting between herself and Mr. Fitzhugh, she would further defy her convention of arriving whenever it suited her even if that made her prompt.

Striding to her dressing room, she quickly chose a creamy yellow gown and, in case Mary was right about it being chilly, a matching wool pelisse that, while a bit snug in the cut under her bust, had the advantage of making her smallish breasts appear more...well, more.

She hastily washed, pausing to dab a few drops of her favorite perfume behind her ears. Mary seemed quite discombobulated by her mistress's efficiency.

As it happened, Eleanor was not quite as efficient as she imagined, for she still needed her maid to tighten her stays and fasten the tiny row of buttons up the back of her gown. She also discovered that she had no idea where her stockings were kept as she was accustomed to having Mary simply hand them to her. At any rate, she was dressed and her hair arranged by ten o'clock and Eleanor made her way downstairs where she was met by Mary who'd dashed off to fetch her coat.

"Here miss," the girl said, handing her a muslin umbrella. "In case it rains."

"Very clever, Mary. What would I do without you?" Though she and her maid had a good relationship of several years standing, Eleanor deemed it wise to put Mary in a good mood for what was sure to be a trying morning for her.

As the two left, Eleanor carefully deposited the umbrella just inside the door and whisked Mary off down the walk.

"Are you in a hurry, my lady?" Mary asked breathlessly several minutes later. Eleanor had strode with the purpose of Wellington himself and her maid, accustomed as she was to

Eleanor's usual sedate, ladylike pace, was struggling to keep up.

"Oh...no," Eleanor prevaricated. "I simply wish to indulge in a vigorous walk. Besides, if you are right—and you always are, Mary—then I wish to have my walk over and done before it begins to rain.

The two young ladies turned into the Aldford gate and Eleanor glanced left and right but saw no sign of Mr. Fitzhugh, for which she was momentarily relieved.

"Oh dear!" she exclaimed. "I've gone and left my umbrella at the house. By the door."

Mary looked about in disbelief. "But I handed it to you right there."

"I must have set it down when I arranged my bonnet. Just before we left. I'm afraid there's no help for it. You'll have to go back for it. Those clouds are dark and sure to rain, wouldn't you agree?"

The maid nodded, clearly perplexed, for the clouds were mere wisps at the moment, and said, "They are. That is, I do. I really think we should return home, my lady."

"Nonsense, I just got here. I shall take my walk and meet you back here at the gate."

"Oh my lady, no!" Mary protested. "The countess would strangle me if I left you alone in this big park. Suppose you were set upon by footpads?"

"Nonsense. I shall be perfectly fine. Go," she said, pushing her protesting maid back onto the sidewalk. "No one shall be the wiser."

Mary looked forlornly over her shoulder every few steps until she rounded a corner into Mayfair. As soon as the maid was out of sight, Eleanor turned and walked—slowly and casually—to the third bench that was a few hundred feet into the park. In the distance she could see a groom exercising a horse and on the horizon, the outline of a nurse pushing a perambulator toward the banks of the Serpentine. An involuntary shudder ran down her spine. She'd never been about London alone. Even if she didn't suffer her debilitating attacks of fear from being outside, she thought the experience would be a bit intimidating. As the whirlwind of her bravado began to fade, she wondered what on earth she would do if such an attack struck her this morning. She might go days or even weeks with no problem and then be struck with terror outside, regardless of the crowd surrounding her. Though she felt none of the tell-tale signs that an attack was forthcoming—quick breathing, tightness through her shoulders, her stomach knotted pain-fully—she was still a bit nervous as she approached the empty bench.

Suppose Mr. Fitzhugh didn't come? She'd never had a man not do her bidding, but Mr. Fitzhugh was not like other men, which had been part of his attraction. Eleanor halted in front of the bench and stared unseeing at the wrought iron curlicues that ornamented it as a worse thought occurred to her. Suppose he did come and took her bold invitation and lack of an escort as a sign that she was interested in a dalliance of some kind? Now she had no idea why she'd made such a rash sugges-tion. At the time, she'd been so grateful to him for bringing her back from her attack and so intrigued by him that she could think of nothing besides getting to know him better without the constraints of other people about.

"Has it offended you in some way, my lady?" A deep voice behind her interrupted her thoughts and made her jump. She turned to see Mr. Fitzhugh.

"I beg your pardon?"

"The bench. Has it offended you? Shall I call it out? I've never dueled before, but I can't imagine a bench would have very good aim. I should be able to avenge your honor quite handily."

She smiled at his nonsense and her earlier fearful thoughts melted away.

"Yes, but if you put a bullet in it, where would I sit?" she said with a genuine smile and realized that the only other time she genuinely smiled was when she was with Juliette. She refused to consider what that implied.

"Point taken," he conceded with a formal bow of his head. "We shall simply have to be magnanimous and allow the bench to remain unmolested. Why were you glaring at it?"

"Was I?" Eleanor asked innocently. There was no way she was going to tell him she'd been wondering if he were going to meet her and if he did, what he might think of her.

"Hmm," he said with a smirk and a speculative gleam in his eye. "Well then, Lady Eleanor, shall we sit or will we be walking during this unconventional meeting?"

"Walk, I believe," she said, and took his proffered arm. They followed the path in comfortable silence for a few minutes before Mr. Fitzhugh cleared his throat.

"Did you...that is, are you quite recovered from your... from yesterday?"

Watching the toes of her walking boots peep out from beneath her skirts at every step, Eleanor smiled.

"I am." She waited a moment and then continued. "I really can't thank you enough for your assistance. The...attacks are terrifying enough but to suffer them in public is simply mortifying."

"I quite understand," he said softly.

"Do you think," she paused, unable to look him in the eye and so still staring at the toes of her boots. "Do you think anyone else noticed?"

"Not a soul," Mr. Fitzhugh said succinctly. "I am not a small man and you are rather a petite woman."

At this, she did look at him, brows raised in question.

"You were quite hidden behind me. By the time I left to fetch your friend's carriage, you were composed, if pale. I simply told those who asked that you felt a trifle peaked."

She smiled at him again. Not a grin this time, but something nonetheless genuine.

"Do you get them often?" he asked, guiding her off onto a side path.

Eleanor felt her heart lurch uncomfortably. It was not

easy to talk about her attacks. "Not terribly often. Perhaps once a month. More if I'm tired, less if it's a busy Season."

"A busy Season? Does it keep your mind off of whatever bothers you?"

"Oh no. It's simply that a busy Season means lots of indoor activities. Balls, luncheons, musicales. I only have those... bouts when I'm outside."

"Truly?" he asked. She looked at him sharply to ascertain if he was belittling her but the look on his face was thoughtful.

"How long have you suffered them?"

She licked her lips nervously. "Since the summer of my eighth year."

"That's rather specific. How can you be certain?"

She walked for a while in silence, grateful that he did not repeat his question or in any way press her to answer. She'd never told anyone about her attacks—only Juliette was aware of them and even she didn't know the reason for them. Eleanor had no idea when she made the decision to tell Mr. Fitzhugh, or why, for that matter, but it seemed right. She took a deep breath. Finally, she was ready.

"When I was eight, several of my aunts, uncles, and cousins came to visit us at Chalkwood Manor. It was a lovely visit. All the cousins played together—we acted out little plays, rode our ponies until we were sunburnt, played hide-and-seek in the house when it was rainy. I was the youngest and would often get shuffled from group to group." She glanced at Mr. Fitzhugh and saw him scowling which had the most ridiculously warming effect on her.

She smiled and assured him, "I didn't mind in the least. I was just as happy playing dolls with the older girls as I was climbing trees with the boys. I was free of my nurse, and my mother was enjoying herself too much to scold me for acting like a hoyden.

"One day, near the end of the visit, my parents planned a huge picnic. We rode out to a remote spot on the estate. It was lovely, really. A large flowered meadow, perfectly round, in the midst of tall yew and Scots pine. The servants laid out rugs and low tables. The children were given their own rug away from the adults. No doubt it was so we wouldn't bother our parents, but of course to children, it was a treat to escape the confines of chairs and tables and manners."

Mr. Fitzhugh stopped at a bench under a large tree with a view of the swans floating on the Serpentine. At his gesture, she nodded and took a seat. He sat entirely too close to her for propriety and she wondered if he intended to kiss her, but instead he urged, "Go on."

Not sure if she was disappointed he wasn't going to kiss her or pleased that he was interested in her childhood story, she smiled ruefully.

"We played after luncheon. I suspect the adults drank quite a bit of wine. Even the servants who were with us seemed to relax, having their own picnic off to the side. The day grew later, the sun creating that perfect soft hazy light of late summer." She paused, remembering the soft, magical quality of the very air. "We were playing a game of dead man's bluff and as the youngest, of course I was it. I stumbled around trying to find one of my cousins or my brothers but I must have gotten turned around for I ended up deeper in the woods than everyone else." Here she paused, feeling a nervous clenching in her stomach as she remembered taking her blindfold off only to discover she was all alone in a vastly darker forest. Beside her, Mr. Fitzhugh took her hand. She glanced at him, saw his reassuring smile, and was amazed to feel her tension dissipate.

She took a deep breath to tell the last of her story. "As turned around as I was from wearing the blindfold, I must have headed deeper into the forest rather than making my way back to the picnic clearing.

"Apparently, my family was combing the woods looking for me, calling my name even, but I never heard them. It grew darker and darker. Thankfully it was a warm evening, but every crackle or rustle I heard sent cold shivers down my spine."

Eleanor stopped, amazed again that she'd told him her deepest secret. It also occurred to her that this was the most she'd ever monopolized a conversation with a gentleman. She'd been trained from early on to encourage men to talk about themselves, been schooled not to prattle on about herself. Suddenly unsure of herself, she looked again at Mr. Fitzhugh.

He appeared completely absorbed in her conversation. "Did they find you?" he asked.

She swallowed and licked her lips. "Yes, but not until the next morning." She cleared her throat and sat up straighter. "At any rate, from that point on, I have been afraid of being outside." Not even to the sympathetic ear of Mr. Fitzhugh would Eleanor relive the terror she'd felt as a small girl alone overnight in the dense woods. Scraped, bruised, hungry, and sure that she was going to be eaten by the myriad of creatures that filled the night with undefined noises.

"And yet you're quite alright out here today."

She gave a small shrug and smiled crookedly. "There's no accounting for when such an attack will occur. I've tried to determine what starts them, but…" she trailed off. With a shake of her head, she said, "The only reason I've survived the outdoor activities of the last three Seasons is my dear friend, Miss Juliette Aston. Were it not for her, I should either have had an attack in front of everyone and been promptly labeled fit only for Bedlam, or I should have been stuck inside like an invalid."

"What does she do to assist you?"

"Well she's mostly just *there*. I can't quite explain it except that I trust her above all others and usually just knowing she's right beside me helps stop an attack from coming on. But if it does escalate, she's ever so clever about diverting attention from me by pretending to spill her punch or tripping over her hem. She also seems to know the fastest routes back inside. She is my very dearest friend. I would do anything for her," Eleanor finished with a happy smile.

Mr. Fitzhugh was silent for so long, Eleanor was sure she'd

driven him mad with her non-stop chatter. Her mother had always warned her that men preferred to do the talking and despite the apparent unfairness of such an edict, Eleanor had obediently followed her instruction.

"I've gone and chatted your ear off, haven't I?" she said nervously. That was another novel experience. After three Seasons as the most sought after debutante, Eleanor was long past being nervous around men.

Mr. Fitzhugh smiled and squeezed her hand. "I enjoy hearing about your life. Why wouldn't I?"

She frowned even as a smile curved her lips. "Young ladies are supposed to encourage gentlemen to talk, not the other way around."

"Ah," he said. "There you have it. I'm not a gentleman. If only the men talked in Cornwall, it would be a sorry state of conversation indeed."

Eleanor cast an arch look at him. "If you're not a gentleman, I'm not entirely certain I should not be sitting alone on this bench with you."

"Afraid I might ravish you?"

She gasped. Gentlemen did not speak in such a vulgar manner to ladies. Quickly recovering, she tossed her head. "Of course not."

When he was silent, she glanced back at him only to discover him staring intently at her mouth. She licked her lips nervously and his pupils widened. He looked up at her and suddenly she could not have moved if the bench was on fire. With a slow inevitability, he leaned in and kissed her lightly once, twice. He pulled back slightly and she stifled a groan of disappointment right before he cupped the back of her head in his hand and kissed her deeply.

Her popularity had ensured that several men had attempted such a liberty before and a few of them had intrigued her enough that she had allowed a stolen kiss. Those experiences had prepared her not at all for the sensual onslaught of Mr. Fitzhugh's lips on hers. His mouth was firm and warm as he tasted her own, nibbling gently on her lower lip. Her head fell back, its weight fully supported by his large hand. He nuzzled the softness of her cheek, the line of her jaw, before returning to her mouth, this time with more intention, coaxing her lips apart, delicately flicking the inside of her mouth with his tongue.

She heard a low moan and could not tell if it had come from him or her. Sliding her hand up the fine wool of his jacket, she tentatively cupped his cheek, feeling the freshly-shaven smoothness. Emboldened, she combed her fingers through his dark brown hair, dislodging his hat. Her own bonnet was sadly askew; it's ribbons threatening to strangle her. He must have realized her discomfort for he broke the kiss to untangle the satin ribbon from beneath her chin. A breeze cooled her flaming cheeks and returned a small amount of Eleanor's sanity, for when he would have removed her bonnet, she stilled his hands. He glanced inquiringly at her, she shook her head slightly, her ingrained sense of propriety warring with her overwhelming desire to keep kissing him.

A rueful smiled tugged up the corner of Mr. Fitzhugh's mouth and he gently retied her bonnet strings before bending down to fetch his own hat. They sat staring at the gentle ripples of the Serpentine in silence until he finally suggested they continue their walk.

As they followed the path of the river in companionable silence, Eleanor was overwhelmed by her response to Mr. Fitzhugh's...well, everything, she supposed. His kiss, certainly, had affected her like no others, but his very presence seemed different. Even just sitting with him, she felt completely at ease even as her body thrummed with awareness of him. The attentive way he had listened to her, the reassuring squeezes of her hand when she grew anxious. Was this what falling in love felt like? she wondered.

They rounded a corner and Eleanor saw a familiar figure. "Juliette!" she called out, then turning back to Mr. Fitzhugh, she explained. "The friend I was telling you about." She tugged him along as she made her way to the young woman.

"Juliette, do let me introduce you to Mr. Alexander Fitzhugh. Mr. Fitzhugh, my dear friend, Miss Juliette Aston.

"Mr. Fitzhugh is a recent addition to the London social scene and I've just been showing him some of the lovelier walking paths here at the park." To her own ears, her voice sounded rushed and breathless. She strove to regain control over her ebullient emotions.

As Juliette murmured something about the weather, Lords Elphinstone and Cambers rode by on horseback. Eleanor willed them to keep riding, but upon seeing her, they quickly reined in and dismounted.

"Lady Eleanor!" Elphinstone remarked. "What a happy surprise this is. I'd not expect to find you at the park at such an early hour."

"Oh?" Eleanor said through gritted teeth. Elphinstone had made the remark much in the same tone he had the other night when he told her not to worry her pretty head about the Turks.

She introduced Mr. Fitzhugh to the new arrivals and as soon as it turned out they had a mutual acquaintance, Lord Taggart, they began talking in earnest.

Eleanor used their diversion to draw Juliette aside. Her friend was in the dire predicament of having to find a husband before the end of the Season or returning to her father's country home to keep his house. Eleanor distractedly wondered what more she could do to push her shy friend into the arms of Lord Worthing.

"I've not seen you since the de Wynter ball. Did you not receive my notes to come call?"

"I'm sorry," Juliette said. "I...was ill."

"Oh goodness. Nothing serious, I hope."

"No, no, of course not."

Sensing her friend had something on her mind and did not wish to talk in front of the three men, Eleanor changed the subject. She leaned closer and whispered, "What do you think of Mr. Fitzhugh?"

"I've only just met him. I'm sure I can't possibly think anything of him."

Eleanor surreptitiously poked her friend in the ribs, eliciting a small yelp from Juliette. The three men paused mid-conversation to cast inquiring glances at the women but Eleanor just smiled and waved them off.

"I know your father is in town," Eleanor said.

Juliette gasped. "You do? How?"

"The footman said so when he returned from delivering my last note."

"Oh. Of course."

"So I have a plan," Eleanor continued.

Her friend frowned in confusion "A plan? Whatever for?"

"To give you a little more time. In London. You said he was threatening to take you back to Hertfordshire if you were not betrothed soon."

"Yes, well...about that." Juliette hesitated but Eleanor didn't have time to push her. The men were clearly running out of conversational gambits.

Cutting right to the chase, Eleanor said, "The Duke and Duchess of Andover are retiring to the country early this year because of her condition. They are having their traditional end of Season ball in four days as a result."

"Yes? And?"

"Her Grace and I are second cousins. We played together as girls. I shall ensure you receive an invitation. You must wear your best gown—perhaps that crimson one that caused such a stir last week. When your father sees how popular and sought-after you are, he will surely realize that to take you from London early would be detrimental in the least."

"But—"

"I'm sure Mrs. Smithsonly will start to work on him as well. Your aunt really has turned into a gem." Despite her preoccupation with Mr. Fitzhugh, Eleanor's matchmaking mind was whirring with ideas.

"Yes but—"

"Has Mr. Pocock called recently?"

"What? Yes, but I really must tell you—"

Eleanor held up a hand, stopping her mid-sentence. "Mr. Fitzhugh looks like he wishes to leave. Isn't he divinely handsome?" she whispered.

Diverted, Juliette looked to her friend's escort. "Well, yes but what about Lord Wo—"

"Ah, we are off, it would appear," Eleanor said, giving her friend a quick hug.

"Now my lords, you are imposing on my morning stroll. I really must reclaim Mr. Fitzhugh for he has promised to show me a nest full of robin's eggs he recently discovered."

Feeling her friend's stare, Eleanor met Juliette's gaze. "Really?" Juliette mouthed.

Eleanor gave a little shake of her head and saw Juliette try not to laugh. With a final wave to Juliette and Lords Camber and Elphinstone, they slowly made their way back toward the Aldford gate.

They were silent again for several moments. Casting a sideways glance at him, Eleanor saw Fitzhugh deep in thought, his eyes fixed on some distant spot. She admired the strong lines of his profile for a moment before breaking the silence.

"And what of you, Mr. Fitzhugh. What was your childhood like?"

He turned to her with a crooked grin. "Mr. Fitzhugh? Surely after our earlier bit of impropriety," he said mockingly. "We can be on a first name basis."

She lifted her brows archly. "After such an impropriety, surely we should pay especial attention to the rules of etiquette."

"Very well, Lady Eleanor. What is it you wished to know?"

"Your childhood. Where in Cornwall did you grow up? What was your family like? Why have you never been to London before?"

"Who said I haven't been to London before?"

Eleanor frowned. "But...I mean how is it that we were not

introduced before last week?"

He smiled wryly at her before carefully guiding her around a steaming pile in the path. "London is much greater than the *ton*, my lady."

"Well of course...oh," she finished lamely, feeling her cheeks flush as she took his meaning. The world in which she traveled was really very small compared to...well, the world that was London. Or England for that matter.

She wondered about her father's speculation that Mr. Fitzhugh was actually the son of the Earl of Southampton. There was really no polite way to ask him, she mused. If he was Southampton's son, and wasn't using his honorific, then perhaps he and the earl had had a falling out. And yet, for him to have never entered Society until now meant that it must have been a falling out years ago. And if he wasn't the earl's heir, then who was he? Her father had thought Mr. Fitzhugh resembled Southampton so perhaps he was an impoverished relative? Or even an illegitimate son! In spite of herself, Eleanor felt a shiver of trepidation run down her spine. Associating with such a man went against everything her mother had drilled into her head growing up. From well before her debut, Eleanor had been trained to be the perfect hostess, the most graceful dance partner, the most beautiful debutante. She was expected to marry and marry well—an earl at the least, a duke, preferably. His financial straits were not as crucial. An impoverished duke would be welcome into the family and well-funded with Eleanor's generous dowry. But the wealthiest man in the world would not be welcome as a suitor in her mother's drawing room if he had been born on the wrong side of the sheets.

Striving to be circumspect, she said, "Tell me more about yourself. Your family is from Cornwall."

"My mother's family is, yes."

"Ah. And your father?"

As if she had asked a completely different question, he replied, "My mother's family consider themselves primarily landowners—farmers, really, though the bulk of their revenue in truth comes from the tin and copper mines."

"Oh…?" Eleanor said, uncertain of how to proceed. Mr. Fitzhugh plowed on as if she had asked a pertinent question.

"I didn't actually grow up with my mother's family. We lived in a small manor house near their estate. My mother was possessed of a bit of a rebellious streak."

"Something tells me you resemble her greatly," she said lightly.

He laughed and murmured under his breath, "You have no idea, my lady."

"I have no idea of what?"

"You weren't supposed to hear that," he said.

Eleanor made a great show of looking astounded. "I assure you, I am not hard of hearing. I believe those children could have heard you," she said, indicating the young brother and sister throwing bread to the geese a dozen yards away.

"At any rate," he continued as if she hadn't spoken, "My only reason for coming to London was for the sake of my business. I only happened to run into Reg Taggart a few weeks ago and he's been dragging me with him to one event after another."

"And what business is that?"

He paused a moment before answering shortly, "Shipping."

She sensed he did not wish to go into details about what exactly that entailed. Trying to decide how best to get him to tell her more, she was interrupted by a shrieked, "My lady!"

Startled, she glanced around to see her maid dashing across the lawn toward them. Realizing she was practically clinging to Mr. Fitzhugh's arm, she stepped away to put some space between them.

"My lady!" Mary gasped, her hand on her chest, her cheeks flushed from running. "I've been searching everywhere for ye! I was that close to returning to Chalcroft House and raising the alarm. I thought for sure you'd been stolen away by footpads."

Eleanor bit her lip. She hadn't thought through what

would happen to Mary when she returned from fetching the umbrella to find an empty bench.

"I do apologize, Mary," she said sincerely. "I didn't mean to give you a scare." Thinking quickly, she said, "I thought it was going to rain and I didn't want my new bonnet to be ruined so I sought refuge under the trees." She saw Mary's eyes widen and remembered Mr. Fitzhugh.

"I, uh…I happened to run into Mr. Fitzhugh here," she stammered.

"I, like her ladyship, am in possession of a new hat and, like her, sought to protect my fashionable investment beneath this sheltering tree," he improvised.

Eleanor looked quickly from Mr. Fitzhugh—surely he belonged on Drury Lane with such acting ability—to Mary, who stood open mouthed and wide-eyed. Glancing back to Mr. Fitzhugh, Eleanor bit her lip to keep from laughing. He was all but batting his eyes at the maid. Clearly the man had extensive experience befuddling women. Mary did not even seem to realize that the sun had burned through the earlier clouds. Eleanor suspected that if Fitzhugh suggested it, Mary would believe it was about to snow.

"Yes, well, I think I've had enough fresh air this morning, Mary. Let's return home, shall we?"

"Of course, my lady. Will ye be wanting your umbrella for the walk?"

Eleanor thought she heard Mr. Fitzhugh smother a laugh behind her but pointedly ignored him. Sending Mary a quelling glance, she said, "I don't believe I shall need it now. Good day to you, sir," she said with a formal little nod to Fitzhugh, as if they hadn't shared the most passionate kiss of her life less than an hour ago.

To his credit, Fitzhugh bowed correctly and only bade her farewell.

Eleanor walked as briskly as she could, hoping Mary would not speak of the incident further…especially to Lady Chalcroft. The maid rushed to catch up to her and Eleanor braced herself.

"If ye wanted a spot of time alone, my lady, ye didn't need to send me haring back for your umbrella. I could have just as easily got lost here in the park."

Eleanor looked sharply at her maid and saw not a tattle-tale, but a fellow conspirator.

"I don't expect I shall need time alone with anyone, Mary...but I thank you."

Mary grinned and the two young women made their way back to Chalcroft House, whose occupants were only just beginning to stir.

Chapter 6

Alex returned home from Hyde Park for the second time in as many days, and as he had the day before, his thoughts centered on the lovely Lady Eleanor.

After seeing her off with her maid, he'd strolled back through the park and exited through Coalbrookdale Gate, into the busy streets of Knightsbridge.

It was ridiculous, really, just how far she'd crawled under his skin in such a short period of time. His previous *affaires de coeur*, while enjoyable, had left him quite able to leave the lady in question and go about his business without another thought for her until next they met. But since that dance at the de Wynter ball, Eleanor Chalcroft had been on his mind constantly. At first he'd thought it was simply her stunning beauty, but were that the case, one dance would have been sufficient to quell his interest.

Yesterday's interaction at the park, when she'd suffered her nervous attack, had brought forth a deeply protective streak he hadn't felt since before his mother died. He'd wanted to scoop Lady Eleanor up in his arms and carry her to safety, perhaps pausing only to slay a dragon. Alex laughed at his whimsical musings, causing a dour-faced matron to swish aside her skirts and frown threateningly at him.

Smiling as much at her over-reaction as he was at the notion of himself as a dragon-slayer, he turned off the main street and made his way to the small brick building housing the set of rooms he rented. The house was nicely kept and his own quarters, while not large, were well lit and comfortably appointed.

He'd been completely satisfied with them as a bachelor's lodging. Quite unconsciously, the vision of Lady Eleanor appeared in his mind and he looked about the rooms with a new gaze.

Truly, there was scarcely space in the small living area for him to entertain anyone. It's furnishings consisted of a narrow divan, two straight-backed chairs and matching round table. A wooden chest served as his pantry and a rather ratty, but incredibly comfortable oversized armchair completed the room. The polished wood floors were softened by a colorful rag-braid rug and crisp white curtains hung over the generous windows. The thought of Lady Eleanor glancing around this meager room brought a frown to his brow—not that an unmarried lady such as herself would ever have cause to visit a bachelor' home, but...

Well, why not entertain the idea, he thought? Suppose he and Lady Eleanor were to make a match of it? he asked himself. More ridiculous things had happened in the course of his life. They certainly had a powerful attraction between them. In the highly unlikely event that he and Eleanor were to (he took a deep breath) marry, he could never bring her to such a home. She was accustomed to the very finest things in life. His entire set of rooms, small bedchamber and lavatory included, could probably fit within her wardrobe!

Alex set his hat down on the table and poured himself a mug of ale from the pot on the buffet. Taggart's warning that Lady Chalcroft was after a ducal coronet for Eleanor rang in his head like a gong.

In all his plans concerning his father, seeking to gain his acknowledgement had never been influenced by his desire to win over a lady's affections—or at least the approval of her parents.

He stood at the window watching the foot traffic on Gore Street. When he thought of it, the hand of a lady seemed the only reason to have any interaction with his father. Void of anger or desire for retribution, approaching the Earl simply for the chance to win Eleanor's hand seemed quite as noble as slay-ing a dragon on her behalf.

He must have well and truly lost his head. Noble causes, indeed. He'd seen enough of the world to be rather cynical about such things, but the image of Lady Eleanor's face would not leave his mind nor would the sweet taste of her leave his lips. He knew suddenly, as surely as he knew his name, that he must pursue her, do all he could to win her.

With that thought in mind, Alex realized he needed to refine his research on his father.

Catching up his recently discarded hat, he left his flat and made his way to Kensington Road where it would be easiest to hail a hack. En route to his solicitor's office, and then while waiting for the man to return from luncheon, Alex went over his mental list of things he wished the man to discover.

"You want to know his favorite color?" the man asked when he'd finally returned and invited Alex into his small office. His pencil was poised over the small notebook he kept in his breast pocket.

"If possible. But that's just an example. I need to know more of what kind of man he is."

"I told you he likes toffee," Mr. Hodges said, a bit desperately, Alex thought.

"Yes, and that was excellent work. Perhaps you could discover what his friends think of him. Find out how he treats his servants?"

"His servants?"

Alex nodded distractedly, his gaze lost outside the narrow window. "Indeed. You can tell a great deal about a man by how he treats those beneath him."

"Sir...it occurs to me that you would be in a better position to discover what his friends think of him than I would. I believe you mentioned Lord Taggart has been taking you along to various social events."

Bringing his attention back to the solicitor, Alex said, "Quite right. Excellent thought. I'll employ Taggart—it will give him something productive to do beyond spend his father's money in the gaming hells."

"Er, yes." Mr. Hodges replied. "As for the other details, I am afraid such investigation is quite out of my area of expertise."

"But you've done an excellent job thus far."

Mr. Hodges smiled thinly. "I thank you, sir. A bent for research is key to a solicitor's job. However for more...personal details, may I suggest a private investigator?"

Alex nodded. "Have you someone you recommend?"

"Oh indeed, a Mr. Carlson," the solicitor said, scribbling a name and address on a scrap of paper.

As he took the note and stashed it in his pocket, Alex asked casually, "Are the charge for such services comparable to your own?"

"I should expect so," the man said, not meeting his client's gaze.

Alex tried not to appear concerned about the cost, but the solicitor's fees were already more than he had planned for. Despite his father's neglect, Alex and his mother had never wanted. Alice Waterston's family, though not nearly as wealthy or prestigious as the Earl of Southampton's, had seen to that. They were a taciturn, plain-spoken bunch, but they drew ranks around one of their own when necessary and had provided for he and Alice, and even managed to cover Alex's school tuition. However, their wealth was not such that they had been able to give him any but the smallest investment for his business, and he was thankful for every penny of it.

He lived frugally to allow every penny he'd made to go into his shipping business. His plan was to coax the aging owner of one of the ships—one Captain Billingsly—into selling him the *Isabella*, and then stay on to captain a few runs while Alex built his contacts and suppliers. This would then set him on the path to becoming a shipping magnate.

He'd budgeted every penny of his savings and he was loath to part with more money but the memory of Eleanor's lips on his decided him that this was just as much of an investment as his ship stocks.

He stopped into Mr. Carlson's office on the off-chance the man was available. Fate, he decided, was smiling upon him that day for the man was in, in need of a commission, and eager to gather whatever information he could on the Earl of Southampton. Alex debated the wisdom of telling yet another person that the earl was his father, but decided that if he was going down this path, soon everyone would know. Mr. Carlson seemed neither impressed nor interested in his relationship to Southampton. Clearly, money spoke to the investigator and Alex looked forward to whatever information the man could find to tell him what sort of man had sired him.

The next week proved something of an odd time. He and Eleanor, interrupted by her maid as they were, had made no plans to meet again. His forays into London's upper society events were dependent on Taggart dragging him along and the man must be out of town for Alex didn't see him in any of their usual haunts and a knock at Taggart's slightly more fashionable bachelor's townhouse went unanswered.

He spent his days meeting with Captain Billingsly and wandering the London Docks. Two days after meeting Eleanor in the park, he had the uncanny luck of being introduced to Arthur Anderson, a former sailor and current partner in the Peninsular Steam Navigation Company. Alex had happened to sit at the same pub table as Anderson for luncheon and the two had fallen into conversation. At first, Alex had no idea that Anderson was anyone of import—the man was rough-featured, his face reddened from his years of impressment in the Royal Navy. As it turned out, Anderson was one of the most influential men in England's shipping empire.

"I've only just been a partner the two years. Started as clerk for Mr. Wilcox, I did," he said in his soft Irish accent.

"And you've the running of how many ships?" Alex asked.

Anderson glanced at him sideways. "I think I'll be keeping that to meself if you don't mind."

There was no ire to the man's tone and Alex laughed. "Of course you must. I'm only just hoping to follow in your footsteps. Not at your company, I mean," he said at Anderson's raised brows. "I mean to start my own company. Bring in luxuries from abroad. Take English goods out."

Anderson took a sip from his pint, wiping the foam off his upper lip with a swipe of his lower. "Luxuries."

"Wines, fabrics. The sort of thing that fetches high dollar even with a tariff."

Anderson nodded thoughtfully. "Aye, luxuries are good, but if you want my advice, bring them in for the common man. Don't focus all your product on the nobility. They're too fickle by half. But times are a-changin', ye see. Yer average bloke—or his misses—wants to enjoy a bar of scented soap, same as his lordship. Perhaps try a food from some far off land. There are a sight more regular folk than there are nobility, after all. You bring in things for them, price them so they can afford it and your volume will more than make up for the lower prices."

Alex pondered that for a moment and saw the worth in the idea. Still…

"Why not take your own advice?" he asked.

Anderson shrugged and glanced around but the pub was busy with sailors and dockhands eating and drinking noisily. "Me firm's been awarded a government contract, ye see. We'll be transporting supplies and troops for the crown. That's where the most money is to be made, government contracts, I mean. Good, regular money. But ye only win those if you know people, o' course."

"And you know people?"

Anderson tilted his mug to drain it. Clunking it down on the rough table, he said, "Nary a soul." He burst out laughing at the look on Alex's face and continued, "But me partner, Mr. Wilcox, knows enough people for the both of us. He's set us up with more work than we'll be able to handle."

Alex nodded and stared into the dregs of his mug as Anderson stood and flagged down a serving maid to pay for both his and Alex's meal.

"There's no need—" Alex began but Anderson waved him

aside.

"Take my advice. Start small, appeal to the masses. Then when next we meet, you buy me a meal."

Alex shook the man's hand and thanked him.

That night at home, spurred on by Andersons advice, he dug out an ancient notebook, tore out the pages of Latin notes and began furiously writing ideas for his shipping business. Even if his father acknowledged him, he would take none of the man's money. He would succeed on his own.

Lady Eleanor was as good as his.

Lord Taggart finally returned, mysterious as ever about where he'd been and what he'd been doing. Alex had learned long ago not to question his friend on his occasional disappearance so when Taggart clapped him on the back and joined him at the card table in one of the seedier gentlemen's clubs they frequented, Alex only nodded in greeting and gestured for the dealer to include his friend in the next hand.

They chatted desultorily for several minutes as they played. Alex was distracted with all of the new plans for his company and thoughts of the lovely Eleanor and her sweet lips. When he lost a third hand, he decided to call it a night. Taggart threw in his hand shortly after and the two men walked out into a rainy night. "Shall I give you a lift?" Taggart asked as his father's coach was brought round.

"Absolutely you shall. You're too spoiled by half." Taggart laughed and they climbed into the lushly appointed interior. Alex remembered his solicitor's suggestion to ask Taggart to learn more about his father.

"Does your father have much to do with the earl?" he asked casually. In all the years of their friendship, Alex realized he'd never asked this question. Theirs had been a friendship of support and camaraderie, but they each had secrets they didn't wish to share and they respected those boundaries.

"Which earl—oh you mean *your* earl?" Taggart said, equally surprised.

"He's not—yes. Southampton. Does he interact with him at all?"

"Well he knows, him, of course. Can't say as they meet for drinks at the club or anything. Why?"

Alex shifted uncomfortably and fixed his gaze on the rivulets of water streaming down the window. "I'm...curious. I just wonder what kind of man he is."

If Taggart thought this was an odd time to begin wondering such things, he did not say so. "Well a bloody wicked one, I would judge, to abandon his family because of his own insecurities."

Alex lifted one shoulder in a half shrug. "Aside from that, then. I wonder if he is well thought of, if other people would consider him a decent sort."

"Well he's an earl. People are going to call him a decent sort even if he's the worst human ever."

Alex sighed and finally looked at his friend. "Look, are you going to help me or not?"

"Help you? Help you do what? I wasn't aware you'd asked for my assistance."

Alex resisted the urge to punch his annoying friend in the mouth. "Taggart, be a sport and help me find out what sort of man my sire is."

"Are you going to approach him then?"

"I haven't decided," Alex hedged. "I thought it best to find out if he's likely to call the constable on me or if age has softened his iron heart."

"What's changed?" Taggart asked, eyeing his friend shrewdly.

If possible, Alex grew more uncomfortable, but in for a penny, in for a pound, he decided. "Lady Eleanor," he finally ground out.

Taggart whistled between his teeth. "Caught at last," he murmured.

"What is that supposed to mean?" Alex snapped.

Long inured to Alex's foul moods, Taggart simply grinned

at his friend. "Only that you were practically famous at university for never falling in love. You chased skirts aplenty but I can't think of a time you ever moped about with a broken heart."

"Just because I took my studies seriously and—"

Taggart burst out laughing. "Oh indeed. That was you. The dedicated bookworm forgoing all social distractions in pursuit of his studies. Come now, I only meant to say I'm glad to see you're human enough to fall in love—"

"I didn't say I was in love," Alex protested.

"Of course you didn't," Taggart responded patronizingly. "But good lord, Fitzhugh. Did you have to fall for *the* most sought-after young lady in London?"

Alex shrugged and returned his attention to the window.

"I know, I know," Taggart said. "There's no telling the heart what to do or who to love. Very well," he said, his tone turning business-like. "So as I see it, your quest is two-fold."

"Oh it's a quest now, is it?"

"Don't mock. You've set a monumental task and we only have a few weeks left of the Season. It is a quest. And please refrain from interrupting.

"The first part of your quest is to get your father to recognize you as his heir. I can only assume you want to know more about him to determine if he might be approachable to the idea or if you're going to have to take the legal route."

"Legal route? That sounds—"

"I said don't interrupt. That is actually the easier half of the quest. Convincing Lord and Lady Chalcroft that you're good enough for their daughter, even supposing you were to be the next Earl of Southampton, will be a positively monumental task." Taggart paused as clearly a worrisome thought just occurred to him. "Please tell me the lady returns your feelings?"

"I—well," Alex paused but remembered their time in the park and just, well, just the feeling that he had about her. "Yes. She does."

"Good, good. I'd hate to waste the tremendous amount of

effort this quest will entail for a lady who is indifferent to you."

"She's not indifferent," Alex said, quelling the niggling worry that Lady Eleanor merely considered him a flirtation or that he had misread her.

"Very well. I will approach father tomorrow and see what he knows. He'll probably assume I'm after Lady Eleanor, but it will spur him on to help us. He's been after me all Season to settle and produce an heir. Egads," he said with a shiver.

Alex laughed. "And for Lady Eleanor—"

"Oh I've just remembered," Taggart interrupted. "We've received an invitation to the Duke and Duchess of Andover's ball. You'd better come with me. You can further your courtship with Lady Eleanor, and get her parents used to seeing you."

"How do you know she'll be there?"

"It's one of the most sought after invitations of the Season. She'll be there. Besides, I might just pay her a social call and drop a hint that you will be attending as well. Then I can judge whether or not she is as lovesick for you as you are for her."

"I'm not—"

Taggart waved aside his protestations. "Just promise me you'll be on your best behavior, Fitzhugh—"

"I'm always on my—"

"And dress to the nines." Taggart inspected his friend's evening kit. "Hmmm. Perhaps you'd better come round the house tomorrow."

"Why?" Alex asked, smoothing his jacket. "What's wrong with my kit?"

Taggart lifted one eyebrow and said nothing. "Just come round. But not too early. Do you still wake at the crack of dawn?"

"It's when most people get up, you know. In order to make a living."

Taggart shuddered again. "Yes, well don't let Lord Chalcroft know you need to 'make a living.' Here you are," he said, nodding to Alex's building.

"Thanks for the lift," Alex said as he climbed down from the coach. He paused before closing the door. "And Taggart, thank you for...everything."

"Yes, yes. Don't get too effusive. You know one day I'll be calling in a huge favor in return."

Alex laughed and shut the door.

Chapter 7

Eleanor was as excited for this, which must be her fiftieth ball, as she had been for her first. It was her new gown, of course. Or at least, that's what she told her father when he commented on her excitement. It was rather spectacular, if she did say so herself. Emerald green gros de Naples with puffed sleeves and a positively flirtatious deep flounce at the hem that kicked out and drew the eye even when she took small steps. It had a lower waistline and more closely fitted bodice than the style that had been popular since her coming out and she found it altogether more flattering than the tired trend of Grecian-inspired gowns.

Her father was not convinced, however. "You look very pretty. But having paid for and viewed more gowns than I ever thought one young lady could wear, you'll forgive me if I think there's something a bit more to this rosy glow on your cheeks and sparkle in your eye."

"I'm sure I don't know what you are talking about, father," she replied, focusing on the tiny row of buttons on her long satin gloves to avoid looking at him.

"Who is he?"

At that she looked up sharply.

"Come now, what young chap has finally caught your fancy? Surely you'll not deny that's what is up and about."

Too delighted to deny it, Eleanor only allowed a coy, "Perhaps."

Lord Chalcroft laughed and turned for the butler to assist him into his overcoat and top hat. "Do I know him or will he be nipping at my heels all evening waiting for an acknowledgement."

The thought of the tall, slightly rough-cut Alexander Fitzhugh nipping at her father's heels made her smile but she refused to say anything more. She was still unsure of what exactly was developing between her and Mr. Fitzhugh, but she knew she did not want her father to pass judgment on him before she decided exactly how she felt about him. He was, after all, not the kind of man she had anticipated marrying.

In truth, she'd had no idea he was going to be at the Andover ball until yesterday when she'd been surprised to find Lord Taggart amongst her afternoon callers. Though she'd met him several times, they'd certainly never struck up any sort of friendship beyond passing pleasantries. Two other gentlemen and three young ladies were gathered with them in the drawing room. Lord Taggart was quite personable with all of them and Eleanor wondered what could have possibly brought him.

As they were both refilling glasses of lemonade at the side table, he asked her if she was planning on attending the Andover ball.

"I suppose so. It is quite the crush, but as the Season is almost exhausted, one must give a last hurrah."

"Indeed one must. I was telling my friend Mr. Fitzhugh just that the other day. Have you met him?"

Eleanor glanced at him sideways through the screen of her lashes but Lord Taggart presented only a bland smile so she answered, "I believe I have. Tall fellow?"

Taggart's smile widened slightly and he nodded. "That's the chap. At any rate, he's late to the Season so I told him in no uncertain terms that he simply *had* to attend the Andover ball. And now that I know you'll be there, I can assure him of at least one more friendly face—and quite possible a dance partner?"

Eleanor looked him fully in the face now, despite the burning flush working its way up her cheeks. Lord Taggart was clearly curious, but his curiosity did not seem to stem from any malice. Nodding regally, Eleanor said, "I should be happy to share a dance with Mr. Fitzhugh—"

"Splendid!"

"If he manages to ask me before my dance card is full. I simply can't hold spaces for men I barely know. I'm sure you understand," she finished sweetly.

Far from having the wind taken out of his sails, Lord Taggart's smile widened still further. "Quite, Lady Eleanor. I shall instruct him to rush to your side as soon as you arrive."

"Er, well I'm sure he needn't rush," she began.

"Nonsense. He'll not want to miss such an opportunity."

At that point they were joined at the refreshments by one of the young ladies who latched herself onto Lord Taggart's arm. He glanced at Eleanor and widened his eyes in mock terror, which made her cover her mouth to contain an outright laugh.

Now, en route to the Andover's enormous London house, Eleanor felt her heart fluttering in her chest, almost as if she were nervous. She glanced out the window to see how many carriages were in line before they would reach the doors.

"You sure you're not in love?" her father asked abruptly. Eleanor's mother had stayed at home with a headache and Eleanor and her father had been enjoying a relaxed conversation.

Caught unawares as she was, Eleanor started and turned to find him staring keenly at her. "I beg your pardon?"

"Are you quite sure no young man has stolen your heart?"

"No!" she answered, a little too quickly for her own ears.

"Then how about an old man?" He laughed at his own joke.

"There's no one serious, father. I fear I shall be an old maid before I find someone to live up to the example you have set for a husband."

Such teasing almost always distracted her father from his line of thought but tonight, though he smiled at her outrageous flattery, there was a shrewdness about his eyes that made her suspect he was seeing things inside her she herself wasn't yet ready to examine.

When he spoke, it was in a low, earnest voice, one she'd never heard him use before. "I know your mother is intent on you marrying high," he began.

Feeling oddly panicked, Eleanor tried another jest. "I shall bring a ladder to the wedding to please her."

He continued as if she had not spoken and Eleanor's tight smile quickly faded.

"The truth is, this family does not need you to marry to save us from ruin, gain us prestige, or even bring me allies in Parliament, though I'll admit to having talks with the Earl of Beverly, Worthing's father, about the benefits of such a union. Your mother wants the best for you but she may not realize that her idea of the best and your idea might be vastly different."

Eleanor had always been the apple of her father's eye. The two had rarely disagreed and enjoyed a relaxed, jovial relationship most uncommon in the aristocracy. But Eleanor was quite taken aback and deeply touched at her father's words. They demonstrated a depth of emotion she was certain no English father had expressed in decades.

Nibbling her lower lip nervously, Eleanor decided to throw caution to the wind and return his candor. "There is someone," she said and then qualified that with, "Possibly."

Her father smiled gently. "I don't suppose it's Lord Worthing, is it? I know you said you and he didn't suit, but—"

She looked down at her gloves. "No, it's not Lord Worthing."

"Too bad. He seems a decent chap."

"He's the very best," she avowed. "Just, not for me. I told you, papa, he and Juliette shall make a match of it. I'm quite sure of it."

Lord Chalcroft narrowed his eyes at his daughter. "Do they know it yet?"

"Perhaps not, but they soon shall," she answered pertly.

He laughed heartily and Eleanor smiled, quite pleased

with the world. Before either could say another word, the Andover footmen were opening the carriage door and handing her out. Eleanor's mother had heard just the day before that Juliette intended to settle for her dullard of a suitor, Mr. Pickering whenever he got the nerve up to formally request her hand, but Eleanor was confident she would be able to derail such an unfortunate pairing as her friend and the self-important Pickering.

Once inside, Eleanor could sense the thrum of excitement that certain events generated. It wasn't always present at the very large balls like this one, but whether it was the setting or the hosts, or simply the night air, this evening promised to be magical.

She scanned the crowd looking for Juliette, but in the crush of hundreds of people, it was impossible to pick out her friend. It was not, however, difficult to pick out especially tall men with mahogany hair that gleamed with amber highlights in the candlelight, not when one seemed to have a preternatural awareness of said man. Alex Fitzhugh was across the room, on the edge of the dance floor.

Though she may have lost her head, Eleanor had not lost her wits and she knew it was better to let Mr. Fitzhugh approach her rather than to eagerly chase him down. She could not, however, stop herself from glancing in his direction every few minutes and so far he had caught her staring twice. The first time he turned to look at her—almost as if she'd called his name—she had been dancing with the first man on her card. Fortunately the figure of the dance quickly swung her out of his line of sight, allowing her to regain her composure. The second instance, not twenty minutes later, no one stepped in front of her, or called her name, or asked her to dance. Instead, she found her gaze locked to his across half the length of the ballroom. The warm spread of a flush crept up her cheeks and still she gazed at him. Her lips tingled as she remembered that impetuous kiss they'd shared in the park. Her pulse quickened at the memory and her breath grew shallow. She felt a warm flush along the length of her body, almost as if she had a fever and yet this was delightful and felt almost decadent. Finally she could bear it no longer and glanced down at her gloved hands, clasped demurely in front of her. When she looked back up, his attention had been distracted by a crowd of young matrons who had descended upon him and Lord Taggart.

Eleanor glanced at her dance card but all the different hand written scrawls made even less sense to her than the most cleanly printed book font. It was a habit anyway. Her difficulty reading had not hindered her memory—if anything, it had sharpened it. She could recite every man on her dance card flawlessly. But ladies were constantly checking their cards, often comparing them with their friends and so Eleanor had developed the habit of glancing at it throughout the evening of a ball.

She danced two more sets and then knew she had a blank space on her card. She had deliberately saved it, "in case she needed to rest," but in actuality, she wanted to make sure she could dance with Mr. Fitzhugh if he asked her, and given Lord Taggart's comments, she rather thought he would. Still, Eleanor could not remember an event when she'd been unsure of a man asking her to dance. It gave her a rather nervous feeling that was not entirely pleasant, but for its novelty. Was she falling in love with a man she barely knew? A man whose family was unknown to her and perhaps unknown to anyone? For surely if there was a connection with the Earl of Southampton, Mr. Fitzhugh would have mentioned it to someone. That was simply how Society was. You listed your lineage as proof of your worth. It had never occurred to Eleanor to question if that was what made a man worthy in her eyes. As she stood on the edge of the dance floor, blessedly alone for the moment, she asked herself what she did want in a husband. Titled, wealthy, and handsome were the usual requisites in that order, and she hadn't questioned that order in the three years she'd been out. She didn't think her mother had actually come out and said it in so many words but Eleanor—and most other young ladies in the Season—knew what was expected of them and the suitors they encouraged. But if that was the case, Eleanor should have been happy with a dozen men over the course of the last three Seasons. Instead they all blurred together into one homogenous man. Clearly some part of her—her heart, no doubt—had been holding out for this fluttery, uncertain, exhilarating feeling.

But what else? She'd not realized until Mr. Fitzhugh came along that she actually *liked* to be included in a conversation, not just talked at. She certainly must have someone who made her feel safe outside and was understanding of her attacks. And though her father was not in business like Mr. Fitzhugh, he was constantly working to improve his holdings and expand the family's coffers. She now realized that she could not love a man who was content to simply live off the wealth acquired by his ancestors. He must have some sort of drive to improve his world.

She glanced to the side and her breath caught. Mr. Fitzhugh was walking—striding really—purposefully toward her. Their gazes caught again and she simply could not look away. She felt a bit of a ninny, but when he asked if she was free for the waltz striking up, she could only nod her head and give him her hand.

They were silent for several long moments. Truly, it had been years since Eleanor felt this nervous—perhaps since her first event three years before. She was about to force herself to make a light comment about the evening when Fitzhugh spoke.

"That color is most becoming on you."

Eleanor smiled, as much from the compliment as how it had dissipated her nerves. It was a standard opening line for a gentleman to a young lady and its familiarity allowed her to relax.

"I find it terribly unfair that men aren't afforded the same variety of colors in their own wardrobe. I suspect emerald green would suit you quite well," she said with a barely contained smile.

His gaze on her quirking lips told her he knew she was teasing and he gamely played along. "I should fancy coral, myself. Or chartreuse."

"Chartreuse, you say?" Eleanor could not contain her grin. He led her through the waltz with ease. She was acutely conscious of the muscles of his shoulder beneath her own gloved hand and equally aware of his scent—soap and shaving lotion and him. Their bodies were attuned to both the music and each other. There was no awkwardness, no thought to steps necessary as they navigated the crowded floor. There was simply a natural awareness that made it feel as if they were floating in the room alone.

He lowered his head closer to hers and she raised her eyebrows at his earnest expression. "Is chartreuse a color?"

She laughed softly, brought back to their conversation. "Indeed it is."

"What color is it?"

"A rather bright yellowish green."

"Sounds rather horrid," he said with a frown.

Eleanor tilted her head in consideration. "It is a bold choice. It's named so for the French liqueur, you know. Are you sure you wish a coat of that hue?"

He swung her gracefully in a tight circle, avoiding a collision with another couple on the floor. The move brought her flush against his body for a moment and all thoughts of teasing or fashion fled her mind. All she could recall was the feel of his lips on hers, his arm locked around her waist while the other hand cradled her head and she craved another kiss.

"Is that man wearing a chartreuse waistcoat?" he asked and Eleanor nearly had to shake her head to drag her attention from the memory.

"I beg your pardon?"

"Over there," he indicated with a nod of his head. "The man by the punch bowl."

Eleanor craned her neck to see as they whirled around

again. "Ah, yes. Sir Graham-Wright. Always bold with his fashion choices. You should do well to emulate him." In truth, the poor gentleman could not have chosen a less flattering shade for his complexion and Eleanor felt a trifle guilty mocking the poor man, who was in fact, terribly nice.

"I shall ask him who his tailor is directly after our dance and inform him of your sage advice."

Suddenly worried that Mr. Fitzhugh wasn't teasing, she gasped, "Don't you dare!"

It was Mr. Fitzhugh's turn to laugh and Eleanor felt her cheeks warm with embarrassment. Seeking to change the subject, she asked, "How is your shipping business coming along? Has your visit to London proven fruitful?"

"I've made some good contacts, developed a few ideas that I think will prove profitable."

The dance concluded and Eleanor curtseyed before allowing him to escort her off the dance floor. Loath to give up his company, she asked, "And will you remain in England or will you have to travel?"

"*Have* to travel, my lady? I should like to travel. I do not hold with the common misconception that England is the only civilized place to live. There is a whole world of adventure out there, just waiting to be taken."

His words stung a bit and her tone was more bitter than she intended when she replied. "A world of adventure for a man, perhaps. Those who espouse England as the only civilized place to live may be making a virtue out of a necessity."

Mr. Fitzhugh considered her thoughtfully and Eleanor pretended to study the couples leaving the dance floor to disguise her disquiet. She had no idea where that idea, much less the bitterness behind it had come from but now that she'd voiced it, she realized it was true. She'd spent the last three years listening to gentlemen talk about their Grand Tours, but no young lady would even consider such travel. Oh, perhaps a husband might take his wife to France or Italy for a safe honeymoon, but—

"India," Mr. Fitzhugh said abruptly.

Eleanor turned her head sharply. "I beg your pardon?"

"The East India Company."

Frowning, she said, "Yes, what of it?"

"Many ladies travel to India thanks to the East India Company."

"Mr. Fitzhugh, are you suggesting I travel to India to work for a trading company?"

Though she'd known him but a short time, she'd never seen Mr. Fitzhugh look anything but supremely confident. Now, however, he seemed as nervous as she had earlier felt.

"The Company uses charter ships to bring goods into England. Many ladies travel with family members to India. I would imagine they have all manner of adventure."

"But no one in my family is likely to ever go to India."

"Perhaps you need a new family."

"What do you—" Eleanor froze as an inkling of what he was implying struck her. *Was* he implying that he might be her new family? She stared wide-eyed at him, desperate to understand what he meant. They'd met but a handful of times, and yet, perhaps he felt the same undeniable pull she did.

A hectic color rode high on his cheekbones and his eyes glittered as he stared at her. Her mouth went dry and she felt her pulse begin to race.

He glanced past her and his eyes narrowed.

"Where does that door lead?"

Confused, she glanced over her shoulder to see a servant entering a narrow side door. "I'm not sure. I suspect it is a servant's hall so it probably connects to the kitchens and other parts of the house."

He gripped her upper arm. "Do you trust me?"

"I'm quite certain I should not."

A half laugh escaped him. "Will you meet me in that hallway anyway?"

She licked her lips nervously and whispered, "Yes."

"Five minutes. Go through that door," he said with a nod

in its direction.

She was about to acquiesce, but instead said, "Wait. Go through the door *in* five minutes or go through the door *for* five minutes?"

He smiled a lopsided, silly smile. "In five minutes, go through that door. For how long, well I shall leave that to your discretion."

"Well certainly not more than a quarter hour. I shall be missed. I shall be missed for five minutes but—"

"Lady Eleanor, I believe this dance is mine," she heard at her elbow. Glancing to her right, she saw the expectant young man waiting to escort her onto the floor.

She glanced at Mr. Fitzhugh and murmured "Eight minutes," before taking her partner's arm and joining the other couples on the dance floor.

She scarcely heard a word the young man said during their dance. It was a quadrille, thankfully, one which required elaborate steps not conducive to dialogue. It was also a dance Eleanor had done hundreds of times so it required very little thought on her part and her mind was free to race ahead the eight—no six now—minutes until she would be free to go through that non-descript door and encounter who knew what?

Her other kisses had been "stolen" in various gardens during perfectly acceptable walks outside a ballroom to ostensibly cool off. Sneaking into a quiet part of their host's house bespoke a level of intent that quite surprised Eleanor. She had no idea what possessed her to not only agree to such a scheme, but to look forward to it with pounding heart and impatient mind. Four minutes. She bobbed and swayed in time with the music. Was her color high? She felt as if her entire body were flushed, as if anyone with a discerning eye could see that she was up to no good, or would be shortly.

She smiled absently at her partner and glanced at the door in question, through which a servant carrying a platter had just passed. Good heavens, would this dance never end? Surely the orchestra was playing a longer version than—ah, there was the closing refrain. She curtsied to her partner and when he offered to escort her to the refreshment table, mumbled something about needing to excuse herself.

Eleanor felt ridiculously conspicuous as she made her way through the crush of people to the servant's door. What would people think of her going through it instead of the large ballroom doors? she wondered, but no one paid her any heed. The ball was in full swing. You could barely hear the music over the roar of conversation, laughter, and clinking glassware. Eleanor took one last furtive glance around, and plowed through the door into the dimly lit hall on the other side. Pulling the door quickly behind her, she was amazed at how quiet it suddenly was. The noise of hundreds of people enjoying themselves was muted and Eleanor took a deep breath not only to calm her nerves, but to simply enjoy being out of the press of people. She was waiting for her eyes to adjust when a hand came out of the dimness and touched her arm just above her gloves. She gasped and whirled around to see a tall shadowy figure. His hand slid down her arm to grasp hers and he silently led her around a corner and into yet another hallway. Another few steps and yet another corner. Eleanor was sure she would be completely turned around an unable to find her way back to the ballroom.

"Where are we going," she whispered.

"Almost there," he whispered back.

"Almost where?"

He stopped abruptly and she nearly ran into him. Opening a door, he gestured her in. Glancing around, she saw that they had come through a hidden door into a small library or study. The door had been cleverly covered with false book spines to blend in with the shelves on either side of it. A lamp burned low on a table by the main door and moonlight poured through the window. Mr. Fitzhugh crossed to the main door and turned the key in the lock.

"What about this door?" she whispered, feeling thoroughly wicked.

"The servants have no need to come in here while the ball is in full swing," he said, his voice low and rumbly.

She licked her lips nervously and for want of a place to look besides him, glanced at the books on the shelf to her left. A slender volume, bound in red Moroccan leather caught her attention and she slid it off the shelf. Though the letters tended to jump around on the page, she loved the feel of soft leather encasing the crisply stiff paper of a book.

She didn't hear Mr. Fitzhugh cross the room and started when he spoke directly behind her.

"Ah, that's a particular favorite of mine," he said, taking the book from her hands and flipping it open, thumbing carefully through the pages.

"Will you read this poem to me?" he asked, handing the book back to her.

"I—" she stammered. "It's too dark. I can't see the words," she prevaricated.

He took her free hand and drew her further into the room, pausing to turn up the lamp. He kissed her gloved fingers and waited expectantly.

Eleanor glanced at the page and willed the letters to stay still. "We...see...seek not the hem—heather." Her voice cracked and she swallowed. Her heart was racing and she felt a cold sweat break out beneath her stays.

She snapped the book shut and handed it back to Mr. Fitzhugh. "I fear I've developed a bit of a headache. Perhaps I shall go home." She turned to leave, thoroughly mortified but he caught her arm.

"Forgive me," he said.

"For what?" she asked breezily, avoiding his gaze.

"I did not mean to put you on the spot. I had no idea."

"No idea of what?" she asked more sharply than she would have liked.

He said nothing and she finally forced herself to look at his face. She saw neither scorn nor distaste there, but lifted her chin in defiance anyway.

"It's not that I can't read, per se," she insisted. "It's just that sometimes—most times—the letters will not stay still."

"What do you mean?" he asked softly, drawing her stiff body closer to the heat of his.

She was shocked to find herself confessing to him what she had not shared before, even with Juliette. "The letters... sometimes I can make them out and sometimes the p's turn into m's or they bounce about as if they're not attached to the paper, which is ridiculous, I know but—"

"I had a friend at university like that," he said, interrupting her rushed explanation.

"You did?" she asked incredulously. She never thought there might be another like her. "What happened to him?"

"He struggled, of course. Any written exam he failed utterly, but a few of the professors would allow him to take oral exams, which he passed with flying colors. He had an incredible memory. In fact, he was the one who introduced me to this poem because he'd memorized it after hearing it just once. It's called 'The Rush Bearing,' you see and it says—" but Eleanor interrupted him.

We seek not the hedges where violets blow,
There alone in the twilight of ev'ning we go;
They are love-tokens offered, when heavy with dew,
To a lip yet more fragrant—an eye yet more blue.
But leave them alone to their summer-soft dream—
We seek the green rushes that grow by the stream.

"You know it then," he said, clearly delighted.

"I have a rather good memory as well. One must, if one is unable to read or write things down."

"Well your reading difficulties don't seem to have hindered your prospects. You are quite the most popular young lady in London."

Eleanor shrugged. Though she enjoyed her position, she often wondered if anyone saw worth in her beyond her looks and her perfectly polished manners.

"I can remember everyone I've ever met and I have a decided knack for knowing exactly what clothes to wear at any event. Beyond that, I have no discernable skills," she said, surprised again at the bitterness in her tone. She never allowed her true thoughts to influence her tone of voice, but something about Alex drew honesty from her.

"You're artistic."

Eleanor frowned at him.

"You are. Your eye for color and lines shows an artistic aptitude. My friend was the same way. Anything regarding design, be it the cut of his coat or the architecture of a bridge came quite naturally to him."

Though she'd always considered her talents paltry against those arts like playing an instrument or painting a watercolor, she'd never considered that she was artistic. It was only now that she considered her aptitude as a real talent.

"Color and lines and symmetry are the same, regardless of the medium," he continued.

She looked up at Mr. Fitzhugh in amazement. "I never really thought of it that way."

He grinned down at her and she felt his smile the entire length of her body. Her gaze focused on the curve of his lips and she found she could not look away, not even to look into his eyes.

His smile faded and Eleanor found the new shape just as appealing. She finally raised her gaze and found him staring hotly at her. He lifted one hand to cup the back of her head and slowly, inexorably lowered his mouth to hers. She felt the pull between them as his lips descended, felt the force of their attraction as if it were physically palpable. As it had at the park, his kiss stole her breath and at the same time fed some deep longing in her. His lips slanted across hers, nipping and coaxing. His tongue explored lightly at first, then more deeply. She clung to his hard shoulders, begging support while drawing him even closer. All she could think of was how right it felt to kiss him.

Their kisses grew more heated, lips and tongues and breath mingling, tangling. He turned and backed her against the bookcase, cushioning her spine with his arm while pressing his own body tighter to hers. Her hands ended up tangled in his hair, holding his mouth to hers. She felt a rising tide of a feeling, an emotion she had never encountered. It was all consuming and invigorating. She wanted every bit of him; she didn't care who his family was or what his prospects were. For the first time in her life, she wasn't evaluating a man based on his suitability as a potential husband. She simply wanted him, needed him with a desperation she'd never experienced.

His hands were on her hips now, pulling her against the muscled hardness of his body. Breathless, she dropped her head back, allowing him unfettered access to her neck, the top of her shoulders, the expanse of her upper chest. She felt his fingers tracing delicately over the swell of her breasts, dragged her head up enough to watch him lower his own to plant hot, open-mouthed kisses on her flushed skin. It seemed incredibly trite, but her knees felt unwilling to support her and she felt her body droop against his. He immediately bent and swooped her up into his arms, carrying her the few feet to the divan where he laid her gently down, his body seamlessly following her, pressing her into the velvet-cushions. Some part of her deeply engrained training rang a warning bell in her head. Ladies did *not* engage in such licentious behavior. But a deeper part of her thrilled to his actions. Everything about him, about what they were doing felt right.

One kiss melted into the next. She slipped her hands into the warm folds of his coat, pushing his body up enough to quickly unbutton his waistcoat until just the warm crumpled linen of his shirt stood between her questing hands and his muscled chest. His own hands traversed a path down the side of her waist to cup her hip before sliding back up to caress the curve of her breast. She knew it was madness, but wanted to give herself to this man, right here, right now. She heard a low moan but could not determine if it came from him or her own throat. She felt her legs part beneath her skirts and his weight settled between them, further fueling her excitement. His fingers fumbled at the row of buttons down her back and she lifted her shoulder to give him easier access. One, two, three buttons opened in rapid succession and he returned his attention to the front of her dress, tugging the low neckline down until one breast popped out.

Eleanor gasped at the sensation of first his hand on her bare skin and then the wet heat of his mouth. She panted, trying to catch her breath while he laved the sensitive tip of her breast.

"God, you're so sweet, so incredibly perfect," he murmured against her skin. Rising up, he looked her in the eyes. "I want you, Eleanor. Like I've never wanted anything in my life."

She whispered his name, amazed at the raw longing in his face.

On the mantle, a clock chimed the quarter hour. As if in a daze, Eleanor glanced at it and realized they'd been out of the ballroom for nearly half an hour. Panic proved an effective counter to the heady rush of passion as she realized people might start looking for her.

She pushed against his chest until he sat up. Scrambling to adjust her dress, she said, "I must get back. I didn't intend to be gone so long. Someone may grow suspicious." She must have missed four or five sets—surely her dance partners were wondering where she'd gone. All she needed was for one to mention her absence to her father.

She reached behind her back to button her gown but her corset was too tight to allow much movement. She felt Alex's— she couldn't very well think of him as Mr. Fitzhugh any longer —fingers brush her own aside and he deftly buttoned her up before helping her stand. He smoothed her skirts, tugged her bodice up a bit higher, and tucked a stray curl back into her coiffure.

Then he paused for one more searing kiss that nearly undid her resolve. In fact she moaned in protest when he gently set her back.

"Come, let's get you back to the ball."

He unlocked the main door, checked outside the hidden door to ensure no one was around, and quickly led her through the connecting halls to the servant's door to the ballroom.

They were nearly there when Alex pressed her back into a doorway. "There's a woman in the hall. She's not a servant."

Eleanor peeked around the door jam and bit back a curse. "It's my friend, Juliette."

"She looks to be headed this way," he said.

"I'll go meet her and pull her back into the ballroom. You stay here for a bit."

He nodded and she stepped out of the doorway, walking rapidly toward Juliette.

"Eleanor?" she asked. "Where have you been?"

"It was so warm in the ballroom—I've not seen a crush like this in years. It went straight to my head. I simply found a quiet room in which to rest. I'm feeling much better now. Shall we return?" she asked, pulling Juliette back through the servant's door into the ballroom. The light and noise of a ball in full swing was nearly overwhelming after the quiet darkness of the library. She blinked rapidly, getting her bearings. She wondered what song the orchestra was on and whom she should be looking for to dance with.

Beside her, Juliette gasped. "Eleanor! What have you done to your hair?"

"What?" she asked, quickly lifting her hands to her head to determine what was out of place.

"Well, nothing terrible. It just looks a bit mussed."

Eleanor felt her cheeks warm. "Oh, well, I laid down. On a sofa. I told you I wasn't feeling well."

At that moment, the door behind them opened and Mr. Fitzhugh stepped into the ballroom. Eleanor felt her heart pound just looking at him. His hair was mussed from where she'd run her gloved fingers through it. She longed to extend her hand to him, draw him close, link her arm in his and announce to the entire room that he was quite the most accomplished kisser in all of England. He bowed correctly, but glanced from beneath dark brows at Eleanor with quite the most devilish gleam in his eye. His gaze never left hers and if clothes could be shed with just a glance, she knew she would be standing before him now in her unmentionables. He strode off and Eleanor watched him go until her view was blocked by the mass of people packed into the ballroom. Only then did she turn back to Juliette and the look on her friend's face made her clench her jaw defensively.

"Eleanor, how could you? Lord Worthing—" Juliette stopped abruptly, taking Eleanor completely by surprise. Juliette had always been her biggest champion and the accusation in her tone and expression was rather unsettling. She was about to ask Juliette why she was so angry when she suddenly she remembered her mother hearing that Juliette intended to settle for Mr. Pickering after all the work Juliette had done trying to bring her and Worthing together and she grew angry.

"How could I? How could you?"

"What are you—"

"How *could* you agree to marry that Pickering oaf? My mother ran into your Aunt Constance yesterday while shopping and heard the news directly from her. After everything we did to give you an opportunity to find someone—"

"Someone who would what?" Juliette asked bitterly. "Fall in love with me? Yes, Eleanor, I had several men finally show an interest in me. But just in this," she gestured to her crimson dress and elegant hairstyle. "This beautiful façade. None of them cared a fig about me. If I married one of them, I'd end up in the same position I am now. But at least this way, it is my choice and I know what I'm getting into. At least Mr. Pickering showed an interest in me before I was fashionable."

"But you hadn't given them a chance to fall in love with the real you," Eleanor protested, frustrated that London's men did not see the jewel in Juliette that she always had.

"My father gave me a deadline," Juliette said flatly. "There was no way—" she stopped suddenly and Eleanor wanted to embrace her friend but Juliette turned to leave. She stopped and said over her shoulder. "Lord Worthing doesn't deserve such treatment. He is—" Juliette broke off and tried to push her way through the crowd of people.

Frustrated and angry, Eleanor said, "Lord Worthing and I have no agreement, Juliette. Good God! I've been trying to push *you* into his arms for weeks!"

Juliette turned to stare at her, clearly shocked. "But he is quite set on you! Why wouldn't you—you said your father would push you to accept Lord Worthing when he offered."

Eleanor didn't remember making such a statement, but if she had, it must have been before she realized how perfect Juliette and Worthing were for one another.

Juliette turned once again and this time forced her way through the throngs of people, ignoring Eleanor when she called after her to stop.

"What a bloody fix this is," Eleanor muttered to herself. How was she ever to get her friend and Lord Worthing to see that they were in love with each other when the former was convinced she wasn't worthy of him and the latter was a slave to his father's influence?

Eleanor was approached by one of the men on her dance card and she blindly allowed him to escort her to the dance floor where she pasted a smile on her face. Her mind alternated between looking for Juliette and wondering how to patch things up with her, and searching for a glimpse of Mr. Fitzhugh —Alex.

Three dances later, Eleanor had no recollection of any of the gentlemen she had danced with. She had a hazy notion that she had agreed to a drive in the park with one of them and that perhaps another had an ailing mother, but otherwise, her mind was filled with thoughts of Alex Fitzhugh. She was plotting how she could spend more time with him without causing talk and trying to decide if what she felt for him was a mere infatuation or if it was, as she suspected, something more. Something life-altering.

Eleanor glanced around the room. There was still no sign of Juliette, so, thinking to settle matters once and for all with Lord Worthing, Eleanor searched the sea of people but found no sign of him either. Who she did see was Mr. Fitzhugh, standing to the side of the ballroom, watching her intently. She felt her cheeks warm, and when he began striding purposefully toward her, she couldn't have cared who was next on her dance card. She knew she was going to dance another waltz with him.

"Lady Eleanor," he said with a proper bow but a completely improper grin.

"Mr. Fitzhugh," she said with a nod of her head. She gave him her hand and he wordlessly led her onto the dance floor. They moved seamlessly into the flow of dancers, though how they didn't bump into anyone, Eleanor wasn't quite sure, as his eyes never left hers. Once again she was keenly attuned to the feel of his hand at her back, his warm and spicy scent, his shoulder, solid beneath her gloved hand. She noticed the faint hint of stubble on his jaw as if he had shaved that morning instead of right before the ball and remembered the rasp of it against the sensitive skin of her neck. She smiled to see that his hair was still slightly rumpled from her fingers. The still-fresh memory of their heated kisses caused Eleanor's entire body to flush with the desire to pull him back into that isolated library.

"I've been given to believe," he cleared his throat and began again. "I've been given to believe that your parents would be more welcoming of a titled gentleman coming to call rather than a nameless commoner."

She blinked, trying to pull her thoughts from their sensuous bent and focus on what he was saying. "Why, I suppose so. Although we frequently have untitled guests. My parents aren't *that* high in the instep."

He shook his head slightly. "I mean to call on you."

Eleanor finally took his meaning and the resulting thrill was quite potent. "Well, yes, they want what's best for me, as any parent does for his or her daughter. But—"

"My father is the Earl of Southampton," he said flatly.

"Oh. I see," She replied, unsure of how to respond, given the lack of enthusiasm or pride in his voice.

He laughed at that. "I'm sure you don't see, but perhaps if I explain it to you." They whirled several more times around the floor while he appeared to be trying to decide how to start.

"My parents had a, well, a falling out. My father—well, there's no polite way to put this. My father was convinced that my mother had had an affair and that she was pregnant with another man's child."

Eleanor gasped. "That's…that's…" she had no idea what to say.

"It's not true. My mother would not have done such a thing."

"Of course not," she assured him.

"Besides, I'm told I resemble him."

"Have you seen him?" she asked, casting a glance around the ballroom.

"He's not here," he said. When she turned her gaze back to him, he explained. "I already looked. But no, I haven't seen him face-to-face since I've been in London. I hadn't really decided to approach him until…"

"Until?" she prodded.

"Until I ran into you on the edge of that dance floor. Until two visits to the park with you. Until my recent visit to the Duke of Andover's private library."

Eleanor didn't know how to respond. He was all but telling her that she was the reason he would reconcile with his father. She'd never been so consumed by feelings. Over the course of three years out in Society, she'd met hundreds of men from England, France, even Russia and the United States. Some had been handsome, others rather clever. A few made her laugh. But none had filled her every sense like Alex Fitzhugh had—and in a matter of days, a handful of meetings. As a result, the notion that he wished to call on her caused a novel emotion; that of knowing with absolute certainty what she wanted in life.

"How will you approach him?"

He laughed again. "I have no idea. I've had a solicitor asking questions about him, trying to find out what sort of man he is. I've no idea if I should simply call on him, or try to meet him in a public setting."

"How do you think he will respond?"

"I have even less idea about that! But don't worry. I shall persevere. I've no need of his money. I will make that on my own. I just need his acknowledgement."

"What if—" Eleanor could not bring herself to finish the sentence.

"What if he refuses to acknowledge me?"

The dance was drawing to a close. Mr. Fitzhugh bowed low to her curtsey and escorted her to the far side of the dance floor so that they would have to walk all the way around to where her father was standing. Eleanor said nothing, waiting for his plan.

They'd rounded the first corner before he said, "Well, I suppose that depends on you. Will you ask your parents to accept my suit even though I may never be an Earl or even good *ton*?"

Eleanor studied her toes as they took turns peeking out from beneath the hem of her gown. Their satin beaded slippers twinkled merrily in the candlelight. While she hadn't found much in the last three years to inspire love, or even this all-consuming passion she'd experienced with Mr. Fitzhugh, the thought that she might marry outside the aristocracy had never crossed her mind. It was simply a matter of how she'd been raised, really, and faced with the possibility of marrying someone who was not a member of that hallowed group was both terrifying and invigorating.

"I—" her throat was suddenly quite dry and she swallowed before repeating herself. "I suppose we shall find out."

He gave a short laugh. "Not exactly words to inspire confidence."

She glanced at him. "You misunderstand me. I—this is all happening so quickly. No man—that is, I've never been the least bit tempted to do mad things like meet a gentleman at a park without an escort or sneak off to a darkened library before. Without trying to flatter you, I've never felt quite so… consumed before."

A snarl of couples exiting and entering the dance area brought them to a halt. The noise and bustle of a ball in full swing gave them a bubble of privacy despite being surrounded by people. Eleanor looked up at Alex and found him staring intently at her.

"I understand. I feel quite beleaguered as well," he said.

"Beleaguered?" she said with raised eyebrows. "Not exactly a word to inspire ardor."

He laughed again, more easily this time. "You, Lady Eleanor, were not in my plans. Or rather, these inconveniently strong feelings for you were not."

"Inconveniently strong? My, you do know how to flatter a lady," she replied acerbically.

"It is inconvenient when I have huge plans to build my business and make a name for myself and yet in a matter of days, feel the desire to chuck it all and spend my days mooning about outside your window, hoping for a glimpse of you. Not to mention that I had half-intended to be so successful that my father would feel like a fool for not recognizing me and now I find that I must woo him as well!"

"Oh," she said, smiling. "Well, when you put it that way"

They reached the small knot of men surrounding her father. Eleanor thought it might be best for Alex to withdraw before her father noticed them, but Lord Chalcroft turned directly to them, as if he had been awaiting their arrival.

"Ah Eleanor, having a good time I trust?" he asked her jovially, though his gaze pinned Mr. Fitzhugh in place.

"It is quite a crush," Eleanor said and when her father continued to stare at Alex expectantly, she sighed and made the necessary introductions.

"Fitzhugh?" her father asked. "Any relation to the Earl of Southampton?"

Eleanor groaned mentally, but Alex seemed oblivious to any awkwardness, instead replying, "So my mother assures me, my lord."

Lord Chalcroft's bushy eyebrows rose and his eyes took on a speculative glimmer. "Indeed? And how is your mother?"

Eleanor frowned. How on earth would her father know who Mr. Fitzhugh's mother was?

"I am sad to report that she has passed, my lord. Just two years ago of a lung ailment brought on, no doubt by the damp climate of Cornwall."

Lord Chalcroft frowned. "I am very sorry to hear that. Alice Waterston was quite the belle of London when she came out years ago."

Wide-eyed, Eleanor glanced at Alex. She was amazed her father was taking Alex's assertion at face value. Clearly Alex was also surprised Lord Chalcroft seemed to tentatively accept he was Southampton's son, as if there was nothing unusual about a man denying the existence of his progeny.

"Thank you for your condolences, Lord Chalcroft. She was indeed a fine woman."

Lord Chalcroft's attention was called by the arrival of several matrons but he gave Eleanor and Mr. Fitzhugh a significant look before turning away.

"What on earth did that mean?' Alex murmured.

"I have no idea," Eleanor whispered back. She cast him one last glance as her next dance partner came to claim her and he tilted his head and gave her a crooked smile.

Even as she danced with the next half dozen gentlemen, she was unable to avoid searching the crowds for Alex Fitzhugh. She saw him dance with a couple of other ladies, but mostly he hung about his friend, Lord Taggart, talking and being introduced to Lord Taggart's friends and acquaintances. She could not tell if he was enjoying himself as she only let her gaze sweep across him as the dances allowed. It would not do to have people speculating on her interest in Mr. Fitzhugh, especially after granting him two waltzes. It was absurd, really, how much stock people put in the silliest things like how many times a lady danced with a gentleman. As if you were to be faulted for trying to learn about someone you might spend the rest of your life with! Eleanor smiled at herself; she had never before questioned Society's rules. How funny that a few hours in Mr. Fitzhugh's company made her chafe at the strictures she had embraced for years!

"Ah, I see you quite agree with me!" said her dance partner approvingly.

Eleanor had no idea what Lord Dunsbury had been discussing moments before, but her unintended agreement made him happy so she continued nodding her head encouragingly. Her bland façade only slipped when he delivered her back to her father's side.

"Your mother shall be thrilled to hear we are in agreement on so many important issues," Lord Dunsbury said.

"Er, my mother?"

"Indeed. She was most insistent I seek you out for a dance this evening."

Eleanor felt mildly guilty for not paying the least attention to what Lord Dunsbury had been saying, but tried to make up for it by saying, "Well I shall be sure to tell her you followed her directive."

Lord Dunsbury bowed over her hand and took himself off. She was glad he had not lingered, offering to bring her refreshments or simply staying to chat. The ball must surely be drawing to a close. Normally she took great pride in dancing the last dance at a ball and arriving home just as the sun came up. Tonight, however, since she'd already danced with Mr. Fitzhugh the maximum number of times allowed, she saw no reason to linger at the ball. It wasn't likely that they could sneak off to the library twice in one night without being caught, after all.

Eleanor felt her face flush as her mind wandered to question whether in fact they *could* manage it. She glanced over to where she had last seen Mr. Fitzhugh and found him looking at her intently. She had the distinct feeling his thoughts had taken the exact path hers had. Biting her lip to keep from smiling, she turned back to her father, deciding this was the best ball she had ever attended.

At long last, the party began to break up and Lord Chalcroft finally asked Eleanor if she was ready to leave.

Once they were in the coach, with only the dimmest light from the carriage lanterns filling the interior, Eleanor allowed herself to drift off into memories of her visit to the Duke of Andover's private library. With her strange inability to make sense of most words, she rarely spent time in libraries, but she decided that with Mr. Fitzhugh in residence, a library might quickly become her favorite room of the house. She wasn't aware that she was smiling until her father commented on it.

"Was I?" she prevaricated.

"I take it you had a nice time tonight?"

"It was the best ball I've ever attended," she said solemnly.

"I noticed you danced twice with that fellow."

"I danced twice with several gentlemen."

Her father raised a bristly eyebrow at her. "Not tonight you didn't. Tonight you danced twice with only that Fitzhugh man. And both waltzes, no less."

Eleanor blinked in surprise. "How could you possibly notice something like that?"

Lord Chalcroft gave her a small smile. "I don't act as your escort to many of these events. I suppose I can do my duty when I do. Now tell me about this man. Who is he?"

"Why, I introduced you. You said you knew his mother," Eleanor reminded him.

"Who did he tell you he is?"

"He is Alexander Fitzhugh. He is the Earl of Southampton's son, though apparently he and his father are estranged."

"Did he tell you why they were estranged?"

Eleanor nibbled on her lower lip. "He did. Do...do you

know what happened?"

"I heard stories when Southampton and his wife separated, of course." Lord Chalcroft was silent for several moments. When Eleanor could no longer bear it, she asked, "What are you thinking?"

"Well, it's very easy to claim you are someone's heir to impress a beautiful woman."

"Father! What a ridiculous thing to say. If my head hasn't been turned these past three years by any number of ridiculous claims, I don't suspect it will be now. Besides, it could be so easily disproven."

"What of that?" Lord Chalcroft asked. "As you say, one word from Southampton and this man's game could be up. Has he approached the earl?"

"No. And he wasn't going to either. He is in London to broaden his shipping business."

"A tradesman?" Lord Chalcroft said in much the same tone he might exclaim. "A murderer?"

"Yes father. I believe you yourself said a smart man relies on more than an inheritance to make his way in this changing world."

"Hmmph," was Lord Chalcroft's response. "You said he *wasn't* going to approach Southampton. Why has he changed his mind?"

Eleanor looked down at her hands.

"The man has not approached me. I only know him through your introduction of him to me. He is not to blame for the estrangement with whoever his father is, but until I know who he is—"

"Good heaven's father. You act as if Mr. Fitzhugh is proposing marriage."

"He hasn't?"

Eleanor paused a split second before answering, "No." That much was true. Their conversations had seemed to contain a deeper subtext, but they had voiced no intentions. He had said he intended to approach his father so that her parents might look more favorably on his suit, but lots of men approached her parents to court her, and despite rumors to the contrary, Eleanor was not always the one who sent a man packing. Several men who'd courted her had decided they didn't suit and politely pulled back.

"But he implied he has more than a passing interest in you."

Eleanor thought of the way Alex had tugged down the bodice of her gown before saying, "I want you Eleanor. Like I've never wanted anything in my life." She felt a wash of heat over her entire body and struggled to make her voice sound as normal as possible.

"I would say that is true."

Lord Chalcroft narrowed his eyes and studied her from across the carriage and Eleanor was thankful for the dimness of the carriage lanterns. She affected a yawn and covered her mouth to further hide her flushed face.

Her father glanced outside then said, "We're home. Do not let the man approach you until he has spoken with me, Eleanor. Experienced in the marriage mart you may be, but I will determine if this man is suitable for you before his interest —or yours—grows serious."

Eleanor allowed him to help her out of the carriage without a word, but in her head, she thought, "It's too late for that."

Chapter 8

The next day Alex visited the investigator he'd hired to see if they had any information on his father. He spent a couple of hours walking the streets, planning different ways to approach his father, then casting them aside as pathetic, simpering, hackneyed, or just plain idiotic. For the hundredth time, he wondered what kind of man would spurn the woman he purportedly loved when she became pregnant? Alex's mother had never so much as flirted with the men of St. Ives, though they'd been entranced by her glistening cinnamon-colored hair, hazel eyes and gently acerbic tongue. One gentleman had even been so bold as to propose a liaison in spite of her dubious marital status. Alex only knew this because the man had called upon Alice while they were in the gardens. He himself had been up a tree investigating a bird nest or squirrel hollow or some such. The gentleman in question hadn't seen him and had proceeded to tell his mother that he loved her above all others and would sweep her off and care for her with or without the church's blessing.

Being only eleven or twelve, Alex had been rather irate that this strange man apparently wanted to kidnap his mother, but before he could scramble down to defend her, his mother had gently turned the man down. Normally she reacted to flirtatious comments from the gentlemen in town with a clever retort and a laugh, but today she only offered a sad smile and the explanation that she would not betray her wedding vows.

"Southampton is a bloody fool," the man had said.

"He is indeed," his mother replied.

"He doesn't deserve your loyalty."

"Probably not. Nonetheless, he has it."

When Alex had climbed down after the man left, his mother seemed to have forgotten he was there for she started and gasped, "Oh!"

"Why did that man want to steal you?"

She smiled and plucked twigs out of his hair. "Not really steal. He wanted...well he wanted to take care of us, I suppose."

"We don't need anyone to take care of us!" he'd exclaimed.

His mother had smiled and taking his hand, led him back toward the house. "No, I don't suppose we do."

They walked for several steps before Alex had asked, "Why is Southampton a bloody fool?"

His mother had laughed at that, but it was a choking sort of laugh and when Alex had glanced up at her, he saw tears in her eyes.

"I don't know, darling. I suppose because he is full of self-doubt and the only way he knows how to deal with that is to push people away."

"I don't understand."

His mother had smiled down at him through wet eyes. She dropped a kiss on his cheek, which he resolutely did not scrub off immediately. "I know you don't. Let's see if Cook has any of those jam-filled biscuits left, shall we?"

Duly distracted, Alex hadn't thought again of that scene until now. What self-doubt did the earl suffer from? Surely just because it had taken him years to sire a child didn't mean it could never happen. You'd think the man would be pleased that his loins had finally borne fruit. He tried to put himself in his father's shoes, but the thought of Eleanor pregnant with his child was a little too arousing for him to be considering while in public.

He wondered when he'd see her next. They'd foolishly made no plans at the Andover ball. Each time they were together they were too caught up in each other to think beyond the moment. There were only a few more weeks of the

Season left and he'd planned to be in London until he either succeeded in launching his shipping business (he paused to smirk at his unintended pun) or failed completely and found himself forced to return to Cornwall to work the small estate left to him by his mother. He knew that Eleanor would probably retire to her family's no doubt considerably larger and grander country estate and he wondered not for the first time if she could possibly be happy with his modest means. Even if his business thrived immediately, it would be years before he would see actual wealth.

He was tempted to call upon her father and convince the man that he was worthy of courting the man's daughter, but if he'd learned anything from Reggie Taggart, it was the stock the nobility put in bloodlines and breeding. While he wasn't exactly sure what constituted good breeding, he knew that until Southampton recognized him as his son, Alex was just a bloke dreaming about fortunes. Lord Chalcroft would assume he was interested in Lady Eleanor not for herself but for her dowry and connections. Alex would think the same thing were he not the one head over heels. Well, not head over heels in love, per se. He wasn't quite ready to go that far. Good God, they'd met but a handful of times. And yet...

Alex glanced up and saw a flower shop, great tubs of colorful blooms enticing customers in. Inspiration struck and he strode in to place an order.

A quarter of an hour later, he left the shop and headed for Reggie Taggart's house. He thought to warn his friend that he sent flowers in his name to Lady Eleanor (with a hopefully discernible secret message that couldn't be detected by whoever helped her read it) so that when she sent a thank you note with a hopefully responding message, the man wouldn't scratch his head in bewilderment.

"You've done what?" Reggie asked thirty minutes later. Alex repeated himself and then explained that he didn't wish to present himself to Lord Chalcroft until he had at least attempted to reconcile with his father.

"And why are you doing this?" Reg asked, yawning loudly.

Alex frowned. Hadn't he just said why he was doing it? He peered more closely at his friend and recognized the tell-tale bloodshot eyes, greasy hair, and shadow of stubble. He glanced at the clock perched on the nearby table and saw that is was nearly three in the afternoon.

"Where did you go last night after you dropped me at my flat?"

Reggie scratched his rumpled hair and settled deeper in the wide armchair of his sitting room. "Don't know what you mean. Just feeling a bit under the weather."

Alex laughed shortly. "Seriously, Reg. If our professors at school didn't buy that excuse, what makes you think I will? I know exactly what you're under, and it's not the weather." He tugged on the bell pull and when a footman answered the summons, Alex asked for a pot of strong coffee.

"Ugh," Reggie said, cupping his palm over his mouth. "Weak tea at the most." He argued.

"Coffee. Strong and dark," Alex replied implacably. He stood over his friend and urged him to down a full cup once it arrived. Reggie complained bitterly but was at least more awake-looking than he had been.

"I've half a mind to steal this girl out from under your nose just to spite you for your ill treatment of me."

Alex rolled his eyes. "Do you understand what I told you?"

"Yes, yes. I understood before you forced me to drink that bitter concoction. I just like to see the steam come out of your ears a bit. I'll forward along whatever missive your lovely Lady Eleanor Chalcroft sends me. Now be a chap and draw the blinds on your way out," he finished, slouching back into his chair and flinging a forearm across his eyes.

Two hours later Eleanor's note arrived via Taggart's manservant. It wasn't until he was breaking the seal that he wondered how her reading difficulties translated to writing words.

Her note, which instructed him to meet her at the park again the day after tomorrow, was written as a continuous sentence. Words were crammed into one densely packed paragraph and there was not a capital letter or punctuation mark to be seen. Her handwriting, however, was fluid and precise, without swoops or flourishes. Her name, signed simply "eleanor" at the bottom of the page struck him. It was so simple, without a capital or even her title. It was almost as if she were allowing him to see the real her while everyone else was treated to the façade of "Lady Eleanor." He refolded the note and tucked it in his breast pocket.

He spent the next day and a half meeting with merchants interested in importing goods. Taking Mr. Anderson's advice to heart, he proposed the idea of bringing in luxuries for the common man. He largely received responses such as, "The common man? What use has a grubby coalman got for scented soap?" When Alex replied that such a man might have a greater need than a London dandy, his audience was not amused. Several of the merchants, however, latched on to the idea right away and Alex convinced them to sign letters of agreement with him. That he didn't yet have a ship or supplier for said luxuries was a point he did not focus on. He was counting on having those letters sway Captain Billingsly into signing the final papers.

The morning he was due to meet Eleanor, he arrived at the park fifteen minutes early. He wanted to see her walk up the path. Wanted to watch the sun glint on her golden curls, appreciate the sway of her hips, the turn of her ankle. He wondered how she would convince her maid to give them privacy, but decided she was a clever woman, more than capable of coming up with a plan on her own.

He sat on the bench beneath the tree where they had first kissed. As it had been that day, the park was only populated with a few nannies and their wards. It was silly, really, that the fashionable hour was so much later in the day when the heat would make stiff collars and flounced gowns so uncomfortable. The coolness of morning still clung to the acres of grass, the breeze soft off the Serpentine. It was enough cooler that a lady might wish for the warming embrace of her suitor.

He smiled at his silly thoughts. Really, he scarcely recognized himself lately. As acutely aware as he'd been about his father's absence in his life—and the reason why—he'd always been rather cynical about love. But Eleanor made him feel hopeful. It was ridiculous, really. There were more obstacles in his path to win her than he faced in his bid to become a shipping magnate. Even still, one look at her, one conversation, even just the thought of her—and he could see one thing only: spending his life with her.

He scrubbed his hand through his hair. Christ, he thought. He'd been refusing to even think the word "love," but here he was envisioning spending his life with her. Perhaps it was better just to give over to the feeling. Unbidden, the image of his mother's face when he'd asked why he didn't have a father like the other boys rose in his mind. There had been times when he'd been glad to have his mother's attention all to himself, but there were times when he'd grown angry with her for remaining in love with a man who had so easily scorned her love.

He stood abruptly and wandered down to the edge of the lake. Was it any wonder he sought to avoid the very notion of love?

Some peripheral sense made him turn and he saw Eleanor walking quickly toward the tree. She looked neither right nor left in worry that she might be seen. She walked confidently —and alone—down the groomed path. He stepped forward to greet her as she ducked beneath the low-hanging branches of the sweet chestnut tree and walked seamlessly into his arms, raising her face for the kiss he simply had to give her.

Some moments later he raised his head and stared down into her stunning blue eyes, half-hidden beneath lids gone heavy with his kiss and pupils dilated with desire. He could not stop himself from grinning in delight that he could affect her so. It seemed only fair considering how thoughts of her filled every moment of his day.

"How did you escape your maid today?" he asked,

straightening the bonnet he'd knocked askew during their embrace.

She reached up to untie the ribbons and remove the beribboned ornament from her head. "We came to an agreement, Mary and I. She will conveniently disappear when I have the need to walk alone in the park, and I will have great need of her to try out a new hairstyle on those occasions she wishes to avoid her other duties and steal a few minutes with the new footman."

Alex chuckled. "And walking here alone brought on no unease?"

She frowned and then said, "Oh, you mean my attacks? None at all today. I suppose..." she trailed off.

"Go on," he urged.

"I suppose I was too anxious to get here to be anxious about being outside."

He smiled and touched the silky point of her chin.

"Besides, being under it is sort of like being inside."

Alex glanced at the low-hanging branches, which formed a dim cave of sorts. "I suppose so."

"It's a technique Juliette devised for me, pretending that outdoor spaces—especially those with trees—are cozy indoor spots where I never feel nervous."

"Juliette—"

"Miss Aston. She is my very best friend in the world. I introduced you to her the last time," she bit back a smile. "The last time we were here at the park."

Alex remembered well the last time they were at the park, and under this very tree for much of that time. He had no recollection of anyone other than Eleanor that day however.

"At any rate," Eleanor continued. "She is usually able to keep me from succumbing when I'm outdoors with her, but when I'm not with her, she advised me to imagine that trees are simply like little open-aired rooms. It's a surprisingly effective technique."

He couldn't help it. He kissed her again. Kissed her quite

senseless, it would seem, given that when he asked her what techniques she'd adopted to deal with her reading difficulties, she wrinkled her brow as if he were speaking Dutch.

"Never mind," he murmured and returned his lips to hers.

"You must think me a complete imbecile," she said against his kiss.

"What?" He nibbled at her lower lip. "Of course not," he said before delicately licking the corner of her mouth. "Why would you say such a thing?" he asked before claiming her lips in a deep kiss.

Long moments later, she lifted her head and stared at him through passion-dazed eyes. "Because I grow fearful of the outdoors and I can scarcely read my name much less write it. I suppose I could only be more worthless if children and small animals ran from me when they saw me."

Her self-deprecating humor was laced with bitterness and Alex forced himself to stop kissing her. "I beg to differ, my lady. In the first place as I told you, you are not the first person I've known with your particular difficulty reading. But you are also not the only one I've known who suffers such episodes."

"What?" she asked, clearly amazed.

"I suspect your condition is not terribly uncommon, but most people probably hide their condition, as you do."

"But who—"

"I shall tell you later," he said, giving into temptation and kissing her again. "I suspect there are many others like you who simply hide their affliction."

Lady Eleanor's perfect symmetrical beauty was marred by a cynically arched eyebrow and the compression of her lips into a disbelieving smirk. And yet the expression was so shrewd and humorous, he found himself even more attracted to her.

"I mean it. But you said you can scarcely write your name. Did you not pen the note to me?"

Eleanor toyed with the folds of his cravat. "I wrote it. It takes me forever and often gives me a wicked headache, but I can force my hand to make the correct words. Is my handwriting as terrible as my governess insisted?"

"Not at all. It's quite legible, though not the handwriting I would expect of you, actually."

"What do you mean by that?" she asked with a frown. "What kind of handwriting would you expect of me?"

He paused, then chuckled at himself. "I suppose something very curly and, er, swoopy. Perhaps with little flowers in the margins. Instead your handwriting is...bold. Strong, I suppose you might say."

Eleanor considered his words. "Is that a good thing do you think?"

He smiled and tilted her chin up until she looked at him. "I think it's a very good thing. I know we scarcely know each other, but I think you are far stronger and more able than most people give you credit for, Lady Eleanor."

A horse drew to a stop just beyond the sheltering limbs of their tree and it's rider dismounted. Eleanor stepped quickly back from him and into a stray shaft of sunlight which struck gold off her pale curls.

"Lady Eleanor?" the horse's rider called.

Alex moved to stop her, but Eleanor squared her shoulders and stepped out from beneath the tree. Alex followed close on her heels, realizing his presence might make matters worse, but unwilling to let her face a potential ugly situation alone.

"Lord Worthing," she said coolly, and Alex was impressed at her bravado.

"How fortuitous I should find you here," Lord Worthing said.

"We had no arrangement, my lord," Eleanor said quickly.

"No, no. Of course not. Actually, I wished to see you because...well, because." Worthing paused, clearly uncomfortable. "I need to reach Miss Aston."

Eleanor inhaled sharply but Alex couldn't tell if it was surprise, hurt, or exasperation.

"She has left London," he continued. "I know she lives in Hertfordshire but I do not have her address. I thought you might be able to give it to me," Worthing finished, his hand turned up in supplication.

"Why?" Eleanor asked, her tone sharp.

"I beg your pardon?" he said.

"Why do you want to reach her?"

"That's not something I'm prepared to discuss with you," he answered awkwardly.

"Well you will discuss it with me if you want my help," she said sharply. Alex stepped forward and touched her elbow. He had the sick feeling in the pit of his stomach that Eleanor might be hurt that this man was asking after her friend. She glanced over her shoulder and nodded reassurance to him and he saw that she was not upset, but angry. Turning back to Worthing, she said, "Juliette is engaged to be married."

"What? To whom?"

"Mr. Pickering, if you must know. He approached her father the morning after the Andover ball. It was quickly arranged and they packed up and left before luncheon." Her voice had rose in volume.

"But..." the confused man began.

"You're too late, Worthing. You were a fool not to win her sooner. Now you've lost her," she finished fiercely.

Alex felt ridiculously relieved that Eleanor was upset on her friend's behalf and not because she was hurt over the man's clear fixation on her friend.

"Are they married?" Worthing hissed.

"I beg your pardon?"

"I said are they married yet or simply betrothed?"

"Of course they're not married yet. The banns have yet to be called. You don't think Pickering would go to the expense or trouble to obtain a dispensation, do you?"

"If they're not yet married, then I am not too late," Worthing replied tightly.

Watching Eleanor's expression, Alex could see she considered the man to be the worst sort of fool. "And do you really think Juliette will appreciate your sweeping in at the last moment and 'rescuing' her?"

Worthing frowned. "What do you mean?"

"You've had weeks to appreciate her, to fall in love with her, to beg her to marry you! Do you know why she agreed to marry him? Do you?"

Worthing shook his head, at a loss.

"She accepted him because he was the only man to woo her *before* she became popular. Her aunt Constance and I assured her that if she were more outgoing and talkative in public, the men would flock to her. But she didn't want someone who only saw her as a pretty prize. Even though Pickering hasn't the first idea who she really is, at least he didn't choose her based on her ability to act like a social butterfly. You, however, had scads of time to get to know the real her. You had plenty of time to see that you were perfect for each other. Yet for some asinine reason, you kept trying to court *me*, even when I all but pushed you away!"

"My father is dying."

Eleanor stopped short and Alex wondered if the man was lying simply to gain her assistance. "What do you mean?" she asked warily.

"I mean my father's heart is failing. He's had several attacks over the last...well apparently over the last year, but several serious ones more recently. Since he found out he may not have long to live, he's been pressing me to marry. Once I agreed I would actively seek a wife, he decided that you were the best choice because, well, for a variety of valid reasons. I'm not sure if you know, but he and your father have even discussed a union between us."

Alex couldn't fault Worthing's sire. The more time he spent in Eleanor's company, the more reasons he discovered to marry her.

Eleanor nodded distractedly, then frowned and brought her fingertips to her lips. "I am so very sorry," she murmured behind them, then lowering her hand, said, "So why are you here trying to track down Juliette instead of challenging Mr. Fitzhugh," at this she gestured to Alex and he lowered his brows at Worthing accordingly, "to a duel or some such nonsense?"

At that, the other man finally smiled. "Duels are not at all the thing anymore." Sobering, he continued, "I could not bear the thought of *not* spending the rest of my life with Juliette. I finally told my father as much. I'm sure I should be chagrined to admit that my mother assisted in my cause, but I'm just glad my father came around and agreed that I should marry who I choose. Er...I mean no offense to you, Lady Eleanor."

She waved her hand dismissively. Alex had the notion that she had really gone to quite a lot of work to push the errant lovers together. "Really, we would not suit at all. I could have told you that weeks ago." She took a deep breath and gazed out across the Serpentine. Clearly coming to a decision, she turned back to Worthing.

"Berkhamsted. It's a ways past St. Alban's. I don't know further direction than that. John Coachman always takes me right there."

"I will find it."

"You'll not have an easy job of it," Eleanor warned.

"What do you mean? Finding Berkhamsted?"

Eleanor shook her head slightly. "Convincing Juliette to accept you."

"Why? Does she not—" the man paused and Alex felt a touch of sympathy for the bloke. "Does she not care for me, do you think?"

"Oh I'm sure she loves you. But she will have some idiotic notion that she's not good enough for you or that she's being disloyal to me, or that she shouldn't go back on her word to Pickering, or some such nonsense. Our girl can be stubborn at the most inopportune times."

Worthing looked like a man on a mission. Alex fancied he himself wore the same expression when he thought of Eleanor.

"I'll convince her," he assured her.

Eleanor sniffed. "Yes, well, make sure you do."

The man grinned suddenly, grabbed Eleanor by the shoulders, and kissed her forehead. Alex instinctively stepped forward with a growl, but Worthing waved him off with an apologetic grin as he sprinted to his horse and spurred the beast on.

"Good heavens, perhaps my plans will come to fruition after all," Eleanor said, tapping her gloved fingers against her lips—lips that were still swollen from his kisses.

"Matchmaking again, were you?" Alex asked, smiling at the devious gleam in her gaze.

"Have you ever noticed that people often can't see what's best for them, even when it's staring them in the face? I just helped Juliette and Worthing figure that out." She glanced back to where Lord Worthing's horse was disappearing from sight. "I believe I shall insist they name their first daughter after me."

"And how have you taken it when someone has told you what's best for you?"

She gave him an arch look. "Well if it's my modiste, I take her word for it, though I daresay, she hasn't had to steer me away from a fashion faux pas in years."

"I'm certain she hasn't," he murmured, admiring the snug fitting pelisse of palest yellow.

"My father did try to convince me to marry a gentleman my first season out."

"Oh really?"

"It didn't take me five minutes to explain to him all the reasons the man was completely wrong for me."

"That long, hmm? And what of your mother?"

"Mothers always know best. I never contradict her."

"Never?" Alex said, wondering just what her mother would say about his suit.

"Well," she prevaricated. "Never that she need know about." She put her bonnet back on, then took his arm and gestured to the still empty path that followed the course of the manmade river. "And what of you? Did your mother always know what was best for you?"

"I'm sure she did. I was just too stupid to listen to her," he said ruefully.

"I wonder if your father will try to guide you once you two make up."

Alex huffed a short laugh. "I'm fairly certain we won't be 'making up.' The best I think I can hope for is that he will grudgingly admit my identity."

"Yes but to admit your identity will be to accept you as his heir and I can assure you, men think they know what's best for their heirs."

"So long as he approves of you, I shall take all of his other life directions," he said dramatically, knowing he would do no such thing.

He saw Eleanor glance at him from beneath the brim of her bonnet. They had danced around his intentions since their encounter in the Andover library, but he had yet to formally ask for her hand. He was waiting until things were settled, until his father acknowledged him, until her parents met him, until he was able to formally court her. An insidious voice—one he normally only heard in the dark hours of the night—suggested that he was unsure of Eleanor's feelings. The voice proposed that perhaps she was only toying with him, that in the end, she would want a man without the taint of accused bastardy, a man who had spent his life learning how to act, what to say, and how to dress. He normally tried to ignore the voice and was surprised, in fact, that it dared whisper it's doubts in broad daylight, when the lady in question was on his arm and the taste of her still on his lips.

"Perhaps he shall want to invest in your shipping business," she mused.

"No," Alex said sharply.

Eleanor glanced quickly at him, then away. He cursed himself for his outburst and willed himself to explain.

"I should like to...that is. Well, this is something I must do on my own. It's my own version of sink or swim."

"Sink or what?"

"Sink or swim. You know, you throw someone in the water. Either they swim, which means they succeed and live, or they sink to the bottom, disappearing from view and sparing everyone the hassle of cleaning up after them."

"That sounds horrible!"

"Worry not. I'm a very good swimmer." They walked round the bend of the river and he finally noticed the dark looming storm clouds. The breeze had picked up and he wondered if he should send her home.

"If you had more capital, though, wouldn't it make expanding your business easier?"

"Well of course, which is why I'm trying to talk a few captains into going into business—"

"My dowry is quite large," she said abruptly.

"I beg your pardon?" he stammered.

"My dowry. It's ridiculously large. You'd think my parents were trying to get rid of me, but my father insists he just thinks I'm worth it."

"Er, I'm sure you are," he said, at a loss for how else to respond.

A low rumble of thunder distracted him. The scent of rain was heavy on the increasing wind and his sailor's blood told him the storm would be a strong one. Finally, the implication of her statement sank in.

They walked in silence for a bit and his head swam with her words. First, she clearly considered him marriage material, which went far to allay his doubts of a moment ago.

Being the acknowledged son of the Earl of Southampton would help his business prospects, but having a huge lump of cash a dowry would provide would help even more. Still, the thought of using a wife's money to fund his dream went against the need he had to prove himself, succeed by his own wits and acumen.

"Your dowry should be spent buying pretty dresses and objects d'art. Not financing ratty old ships."

He was surprised to see a look of displeasure cross her face. Her jaw clenched and he was about to speak (though what he would say, he didn't know) when she snapped, "I am more than a pretty mannequin spending money on countless gowns. I am actually capable of interest in more than *pretty dresses and objects d'arte*."

"I didn't—that is," he began when the threatening clouds suddenly burst open. He didn't want to part from her with bad feelings between them. He glanced around and noticed that they were near the Knightsbridge entrance. He guided her as they ran out of the park and down the two blocks to his flat. She paused at the building's entrance. "I live here. You'll be safe and out of the rain while I find you a hansom cab."

She agreed, but when he made to leave her in the vestibule, she grabbed his arm. He looked at her in question. Her cheeks were flushed from the cold and their run and her eyelashes were spiky with raindrops and he simply couldn't help it. He bent his head and captured her cold lips in a kiss that quickly warmed them both. She clutched the lapels of his jacket and he drew her closer to him, his hands recognizing the thinness of her dress, the inadequacy of her fitted Spenser jacket to keep her warm.

"Would you—" he began. "Shall I take you to my rooms so you can get warm?"

She gazed at him steadily for a long moment and then nodded.

He took her gloved hand in his and led her up the stairs. The clomping sound of his booted feet and the softer patter of hers filled the narrow passage and yet could not drown out the pounding of his heartbeat.

They reached the first landing and he was relieved to find it empty. It seemed one or another of his neighbors was always coming or going and he would not have wanted Eleanor to feel embarrassed to be seen going into a gentleman's flat.

He fumbled with the key a moment, feeling like a nervous lad with his first woman, then realized that it was a bit of a momentous occasion; Eleanor was the first woman he'd ever wanted to spend the rest of his life with. The thought was daunting to say the least. He pushed the door open, glanced in to make sure he'd not left any random bits of underclothes lying about on the floor, and gestured for her to precede him.

She entered the small set of rooms and glanced around with obvious interest. Alex followed her gaze and knew she must be appalled to see how meagerly he lived. He'd not seen her house, but he doubted the Marquess of Charville would have resided in anything less grand than the Mayfair homes Alex had seen. Suddenly the comfortably broken-in armchair and faded braid rug seemed a bit shabby and the small rooms less inviting and more pathetic.

"I, ah, haven't yet taken a larger townhouse. I've been putting all of my capital into my shipping business," he explained, hating that he felt the need to.

She turned to face him, nodding slowly. "I've often heard my father say a man should put all of his focus on his main investment and not be distracted by less important ventures." Her smile did as much to reassure him as her words, especially when she said, "It's quite cozy."

He smiled at that and his unease of his humble lodgings dissolved. He lit a few candles to combat the dimness from the overcast skies. With the sound of the rain pattering against the windows and Eleanor here, he decided it *was* cozy.

"Would you like, ah," he began, rummaging through his small cupboard and finding only a few crumbled tealeaves in the canister. He opened another door to see a wine bottle with only a dregs-filled swallow left. With a sigh of relief, he reached into the back of the cupboard and pulled out a nearly full bottle of whiskey. He turned to offer it to Eleanor, only realizing as he held it triumphantly aloft that well-bred ladies did not indulge in strong spirits.

A smile curled the corners of her mouth up and she shook her head, but as he turned to replace the bottle, cursing himself for being an awkward host, she said, "Wait!"

He glanced over his shoulder and saw her crossing the short distance between them.

"I—I've never tried that before. Is it brandy?"

"Whiskey," he corrected.

"I've never tried that either. May I?"

"Of course," he said quickly, and scrambled to find a glass. He poured a small splash and handed it to her.

"Don't men usually drink more than that?" she asked, eyeing the small bit of golden liquid skeptically.

"Well, yes," he admitted. "But it's very strong, especially if you're not accustomed to spirits."

"A good point," she conceded.

"You can always have more if you like it."

She smiled at that and sniffed the glass gingerly.

"It smells...smoky?"

He nodded, absorbed in the way the candlelight glinted off the antique gold of her hair. He smiled at the little wrinkle of concentration between her brows and at the surprising intimacy of her now-ungloved hands. Even during their torrid encounter in the Andover library, Eleanor had worn long satin gloves. Now she'd removed both gloves and hat, no doubt while he'd been rummaging through the cupboard and the effect was nearly as erotic as if she'd removed her gown.

Eleanor's sudden cough pulled his focus from her bare hands with their dimpled backs and elegant fingers. Her eyes were watering and her lips were scrunched in a moue of distaste. He inspected the glass.

"Did you drink it all at once?" he asked.

"Of course. Isn't that what men do it?" she rasped.

A huff of laughter escaped him. "Some do. Others prefer to sip it slowly to savor it."

"Oh," she said. "May I have some more then to savor it?

"Certainly," he said, adding another small splash to her glass. "Do you like it then?" he asked as he recapped the bottle.

"Not terribly much, no," she admitted and he laughed, giving into the impulse to touch the velvety softness of her cheek.

She tilted her head into his palm and he stepped closer, cradling her face in both hands, gazing into her eyes before slowly lowering his lips to hers.

While her cheeks were still chilled from the rain, her lips were warm and damp and welcoming. He kissed and nibbled at their softness, relishing every caress.

Her lips parted and her tongue darted out to graze the corner of his mouth. He obligingly opened to her seeking tongue, delighting in the taste of whiskey added to her own sweet essence.

They kissed for long minutes, learning each other's secrets, sampling the tastes of mouths and necks and earlobes. Alex's body was rock hard with desire and though Eleanor was pressed willingly against the length of him, he thought he'd better cool things off. He didn't want to alarm her with his response.

He opened his eyes and stepped back, grinning when her lips followed him, her neck stretching to keep contact. Her cheeks were now flushed with warmth and when her lashes fluttered open, her eyes were glazed with the same desire he felt raging through his body. It was all he could do not to gather her against him and respond to that desire.

She gazed at him steadily for several long moments and then peeled her tightly fitted jacket from her arms.

"It's warm in here," she murmured.

"It is," he choked out. She struggled a bit to free her wrists from the damp sleeves and the movement caused her breasts to thrust out in a way that made the breath freeze in his lungs.

She tossed the garment onto a chair and took a half step closer to him. "It's *very* warm in here," she said, sliding her hands inside his own coat and pushing it off his shoulders.

He pulled the jacket ruthlessly from his arms, his gaze never leaving hers.

"Hmm," she said, eyeing his waistcoat before her nimble fingers quickly unbuttoned it. He pressed her hands flat against his chest.

His breath caught as only the linen of his shirt separated his skin from hers.

She ran her hands over the contours of his ribs and he couldn't help but tighten the muscles of his abdomen and expand his chest. Some small part of his brain chided him for acting like a vain peacock, but he dismissed it. He wanted her to like what she was exploring.

Eleanor stepped even closer and began delicately nibbling his neck while she untie his cravat. He ran his hands up and down her back, feeling the rigid confines of her short corset and below that the deliciously soft curves of her bottom. She turned in his arms and he thought she'd changed her mind, but she simply said, "Unbutton me?"

Her words sent a jolt through his body but he forced himself to ask, "Are you sure?"

Eleanor glanced over her shoulder, her heart pounding with nerves and excitement. "I'm sure," she said. When she'd agreed to come up to his rooms, she hadn't intended more than a repeat of the delicious interlude they'd shared in the Andover library. But somewhere in the midst of their passionate kissing, their roaming hands, and their labored breaths, she knew she wanted more. She knew the feelings she had for Alex were stronger than anything she'd ever experienced. She could hear Juliette's voice in her head saying, "You goose, you're in love!" But she was afraid to think the words, much less say them. And yet she knew it was true, suspected it had been so since that day at the park when he'd saved her from her nervous attack. She wanted to give herself to him fully, wanted to learn what the physical side of love entailed, wanted him to show her his feelings as well.

She glanced up at him from beneath her lashes and the intensity in his gaze as he slowly raised his hands to loose her buttons made her insides tingle in a way that made her suddenly want to tear her clothes from her body.

The delicate touch of his finger against her back, even

through her chemise, caused goose bumps to rise on her arms. When he freed the last button, she took a breath and shrugged her shoulders, allowing her gown to slip to the floor.

"Shall I unlace you as well?" he asked, his voice a husky murmur at her ear. The timbre of his voice, low and deep, caused a visceral reaction between her legs and she found herself unable to respond beyond a jerky nod of her head.

It seemed to take an inordinately long time for him to loosen the constricting laces enough that she could unhook the busk of her corset and she wondered if he was nervous as well. The notion excited her and made her feel less hesitant.

Finally she was free of her corset and it joined her gown on the floor. Alex offered her his hand and she stepped delicately out of the puddle of fabric at her feet. Turning to look at him, she glanced pointedly at his clothes and raised her eyebrows at him. He stripped himself of waistcoat, shirt, and breeches so quickly she almost laughed. Then when his boots went sailing across the room to thunk against the wall, she gave in and giggled. His laugh joined hers and suddenly her nerves slipped away and she was as comfortable with him as she'd been since the very beginning. She laughed again.

"What's funny?" he asked.

"I was just thinking that I've always felt comfortable with you until I remembered the night we met."

He frowned. "You weren't comfortable with me then?"

She stepped closer to him and tentatively laid her hands on his lightly furred chest.

"I was distinctly uncomfortable, as well you know, for you went out of your way to unnerve me!"

"I don't know what you're talking about. I was intimidated by trying not to step on the toes of the most beautiful woman in the room," he protested.

She raised her eyebrows again. "You mentioned opera dancers and roasting children within minutes of meeting me. I think you sought to put me in my place," she said archly.

He grinned sheepishly. "I think it was just that you

seemed so far above me. I wanted to know if you were real at all."

"And what do you think now?" she asked.

"Oh you're real," he said, sliding his hands around her waist and drawing her flush against his body. "You're very real."

Only her chemise and his smallclothes separated them and Eleanor could feel every hard, muscled ridge of his body. He was very real also.

He lowered his head and nuzzled the sensitive skin below her ear. As his hot mouth and tongue laved her skin she felt shivers of pleasure ripple through her body, awakening sensations she'd only wondered about. His hand slid down to cup her bottom and he pulled her up against him, his hardness fitting naturally against the tender apex of her legs. Whatever remaining sense of propriety Eleanor had clung to dissolved and she let instinct take over, allowing her hands to roam over his arms, shoulders, and back. She grabbed his head and directed his mouth back to hers for a breath-stealing kiss that heated her blood and infused her with a frantic desire. She tore at her chemise, then tugged at his smallclothes.

Though he was panting as heavily as she, he soothed her with a "Shh. Easy love," as he slipped the straps of her chemise off her shoulders and pushed it down her body. His smallclothes disappeared in a push and Alex swept her up into his arms to carry her into the tiny bedroom. He laid her down on his bed gently, his lips never leaving hers as he stretched out next to her. One hand tangled in her hair and his muscled leg slid along hers. Her thighs parted instinctively, cradling the weight of his leg.

His other hand, which had been exploring her ribcage, slid around to cup her breast, the rough pad of his thumb as it rasped over her nipple sending answering quivers to the juncture of her thighs. As if knowing just what he had caused, Alex slid his hand over her stomach to toy with her private curls, parting them to explore deeper.

Eleanor's hips lifted of their own accord when he found the most sensitive spot and when he gasped, she knew he'd discovered her wetness. She tugged on his shoulders, urging him atop her, craving the weight of him, and she curled her legs around his as she felt him poised at her entrance.

He lifted his head, his dilated pupils making his eyes appear black in the dim light. "Are you sure?" he asked again.

She tilted her hips, causing his hardness to slide along her wetness and eliciting a low groan from him. "I'm sure," she said with all the love she felt in her heart.

He gently slid forward as his lips sought hers and though they'd not said the words aloud, Eleanor felt his love for her in the tender way he brought her pleasure. Though she was initially shy when he asked if she liked when he nibbled the underside of her breast or thrust at a certain angle, within a few minutes, as the pleasure built, she found herself crying, "Yes!" and "There. Right there!"

His low chuckle of delight turned into a groan of his own pleasure as she allowed herself to explore the curves and hollows of his own body. Soon, however, her entire being was focused on the intimate meeting of their bodies as the tension within her built. She clung to his back, dimly aware of the roar of the rain against the windows as it matched the storm raging through her veins. She tossed her head as she reached for whatever destination Alex was guiding her toward. He reached between them and touched the sensitive crest of her womanhood, circling it delicately and making her eyes fly open in surprise.

His eyes were dark coals, blazing with intensity as he held her gaze, his body thrusting rhythmically.

Eleanor found herself unable to breathe as her body tightened, contracting around a tiny core of pleasure that remained frozen in time before it exploded in a flood of heat and sensation that tore a low scream from her throat. She clung to Alex's back, her nails biting into his skin as if that would keep her from shattering into a million pieces, but when Alex himself cried out in pleasure, she embraced one last ripple of delight and let herself float into blissful oblivion

Alex slowly opened his eyes, noting that while it was still raining, the downpour had lightened to a gentle patter. He wondered how long he had dozed and carefully climbed out of bed so as not to awaken Eleanor who lay on her stomach, her golden hair covering her face.

He pulled his battered watch from his waistcoat pocket, relieved to see it was not yet one. He sat back on the bed and ran a hand down Eleanor's silken back. The sheets were bunched over the gentle curve of her backside and he forced himself not to push them lower. He didn't know how long she'd planned her alibi, but as neither of them had anticipated ending up in his flat, he imagined she would not have much more time.

"Mmm," she moaned as he ran his hand back up her spine and smoothed her hair from her face.

"The rain has lightened. We should get you home."

"I don't want to leave," she mumbled, reaching to pull him down next to her. He obliged, stretching out beside her and kissing her brow.

She turned so he could reach her lips and within seconds they were panting with desire. Employing his one last shred of reason, he tore his lips from hers and said, "I'm perfectly happy to spend the day in bed with you, but it is past noon. I wasn't sure how long you could be away without rousing suspicion."

She sighed and pushed herself upright. "You're right. I suppose I should return. My maid is hiding out in my room so my mother thinks I'm chaperoned, but I imagine she's run out of sweets and fashion magazines by now."

Alex helped her dress, pausing for a well-placed kiss at the base of her spine, the back of her knee, the crease of her elbow. The words "I love you" filled his mouth but he could not force them past his lips. He stared into the crystal blue depths of her eyes, trying to read her own emotions, but some part of him simply wouldn't believe that the warm light in her gaze was proof that he was as important to her as she had become to him.

Finally she spoke, tearing his attention from his tormenting doubts.

"The Season is drawing to a close," she said. "My father likes to remain in London until the very end, but then we will retire to the country." He instantly took her meaning.

"I intend to call upon your father tomorrow."

She smiled and smoothed the rumpled linen of his shirt. "My family always attends the Henley and the reception held after by Lord and Lady Blakely."

"The Henley..."

"A regatta. Boat racing. I only mention it because last year I saw both Lord Taggart and the Earl of Southampton at the race and later at the Gresham's."

She looked at him directly and Alex knew he had a deadline. He would gain his father's acknowledgement at the very least and approach her family at the Henley Regatta.

He left her to hail a cab and then escorted her downstairs, his scowl sending one of the building's young imps scampering back into his own flat.

They stepped outside and he handed her up into the hansom cab, noting its shabby interior and hating that he was not able to send her home in more style. "I don't like sending you off like this, with no escort."

She smiled and touched his cheek briefly. "I'll be fine. It isn't but a few minutes' drive to Mayfair." He stepped back and closed the door of the cab, wishing they could have had one more kiss. As the coach drove off, he smiled at his love struck thoughts. But right then he had the feeling that he would never get enough of Eleanor.

As he climbed the stairs to his flat, Alex mulled over Eleanor's oblique offer of her dowry for his business. He didn't need it, not really. He had planned well, knew his abilities. He was only waiting on Captain Billingsly to sign on with him to put everything in motion. Still, with a huge infusion of cash, he could start his business at a level it would take years to achieve otherwise.

He abruptly changed course and headed back downstairs to flag a hackney to take him to the London Docks. He had intended to meet with Captain Billingsly tomorrow for the man's decision. He would simply find him today and perhaps drop the suggestion that he might be coming into large capital. Then if the old seaman still hesitated, Alex would know it was time to start searching for another business partner.

Several hours later, Alex turned onto Gore Street, a spring in his step despite his tiredness. He'd had to chase all over both the east and west London Dock—an area of some thirty acres—until he finally found Captain Billingsly, but his quest had proven fruitful. Even before he mentioned the possibility of more capital, the captain had been enthusiastic about Alex's ideas. Well, Alex reflected with a grin, as enthusiastic as any salty old man who'd survived two wars with Napoleon could be.

Lost in his thoughts of Captain Billingsly's saltiness and Lady Eleanor's sweetness, he did not hear the two men come at him from behind, only realized he was not alone on the street when they each grabbed an arm and hustled him into a narrow passageway between two brick buildings. Alex bided his time, waiting until one of them released an arm. As soon as he did, Alex swung with all his might, clocking one of the men— a bushily bearded Goliath—on the side of the head. The man staggered back, but as Alex had punched with his off hand, it was not as effective as it could have been. At any rate, the second man, short but wiry and clearly not so hampered by such a thing as an off hand, delivered a blow to Alex's midriff that sent his breath whooshing out. Goliath, recovered by now, delivered a sharp upper cut that clacked Alex's teeth together and knocked his head back against the brick wall. His vision blurred and he shook his head trying to clear it. He tasted blood in his mouth but before he could spit it out, Goliath grabbed him by the throat and lifted, forcing Alex to his tiptoes to avoid choking to death. The man was built like a stone wall and though Alex was strong from years of wrestling sails and battling storms at sea, he could not budge the larger man so much as an inch and the behemoth's accomplice had no compunction about beating a man who couldn't fight back. The wiry attacker delivered one more blow to Alex's ribs before hissing his warning. "Ye've been nosy, me glocky friend. A boy should be more respectful of a man's privacy."

"Wha—" Alex rasped. Goliath didn't loosen his grip any so Alex rasped louder. "What man?"

"Don't play coy wi' me. Yer having people ask questions about a...mutual acquaintance and 'e don't take kindly to bein' investigated, wassat?"

Blood and spittle dribbled from Alex's mouth onto the Goliath's hand. The man made a disgusted noise and released Alex's neck to wipe his hands fastidiously on Alex's jacket. The respite allowed Alex to take a full breath and say, "You mean Southampton?"

"Oi, Zeb," the wiry man said to his partner. "You 'ear that? Soufhampton he says, bold as brass." A knife appeared in the man's hand and he held it in front of Alex's face. "It would behoof you to speak respectfully of yer betters. But yes, I mean the earl. Not keen on people poking into his private affairs, is he Zeb?"

The Goliath, Zeb, remained silent, his enormous bulk blocking any hope of escape.

The wiry man cast a scornful glance at Zeb and shook his head before turning back to Alex.

"Go back to whatever bodging hole ye climbed outta and pretend ye never 'eard of the Earl of Soufhampton. It'll ensure ye a nice long life that way."

Staring as he was at the glimmering knife blade, Alex didn't see Zeb deliver a final one-two gut punch before the two men melted into the shadows of the encroaching night. Alex crumpled slowly to the ground, retching. A few minutes later, he pulled himself up the wall and staggered out of the alley-way. Thankfully his rooms were just down the street. By the time he made his way up the two flights of stairs to his door, he was sweating profusely and it hurt to stand upright. He flung himself onto his narrow bed that still smelled of Eleanor and waited for the nausea to pass. Once the room stopped spinning, he stared at the ceiling wondering what the hell that incident had meant. Why on earth would Southampton react so to his trying to learn more about him? Surely the questions the investigator and man of business had asked were neither too prying nor out of line for a son to know.

With a groan, Alex rolled out of bed and stripped off his clothes. He was achy in places he hadn't realized he'd been hit. Pouring the last of the water into the chipped ewer beside his bed, he splashed water on his face and gingerly swished a mouthful, probing with a finger to determine the blood had come from the inside of his lip. After a quick scrub down, he dropped back onto the bed and stared at the ceiling in the dark grey twilight.

There were only two reasons he could think of for the earl to send such a brutal message: one, he thought Alex was going to approach him for money (an understandable suspicion), or two, the man had something to hide and thought Alex was intent on exposing it, perhaps out of malice for being neglected. Given the fact that Southampton had never laid eyes on him, much less knew Alex, this was also understandable. Still, sending two thugs to deliver his message was a rather coarse way to deal with his son. Having so little experience with the nobility, Alex was a bit surprised to find one of them—and his own father, to boot—could act like a common dock thug.

By the time Alex woke the next morning—sore and stiff, but otherwise no worse for wear, he'd had another thought. Perhaps he needed to approach his father directly and explain that he only hoped to gain his acknowledgement, bluntly assure him he wanted neither money nor to do him ill.

Shaving revealed a dark bruise where his wiry assailant

had clocked him in the jaw and his lower lip was a bit swollen, but the majority of his other injuries were easily hidden—no doubt that was professional courtesy on his assailants' part. Breathing shallowly so as not to jar his bruised ribs any more than necessary, he made his way to a pub where breakfast and a pint did much to restore him. He had a busy day ahead of him. His first stop was at his investigator's offices where he intended to lay blame for his physical state. Surely an investigator worth his salt should be able to make discreet inquiries without letting the subject of the inquiry know.

Said investigator was disturbingly unmoved at Alex's beating, implying that such an occurrence was to be expected, which reminded Alex of one of his mother's favorite sayings: You get what you pay for. No doubt a better and more expensive investigator would have been more discreet.

His luck finally turned when he appeared at Reggie Taggart's townhouse. His friend was not only in, but awake and sober. Furthermore, he knew when the Henley regatta was and planned to attend it himself.

"Mind if I tag along then?" Alex asked.

"Course not. More the merrier. Never knew you were into rowing. Thought you were more of a big water type of sportsman."

"Do you think Southampton will be there?"

"I should think so. Have you not approached him then?"

"Well I was about to," Alex began, and then relayed his previous evening's adventure.

"Egad! Are you sure you want to be related to this man? He sounds a right lurker."

"Where do you pick up this cant? I'm at the docks every day and I don't even hear these words."

"I am always seeking to improve my vocabulary," Taggart said, his nose in the air.

"Right. Well at any rate, lurker or not, I have to get Southampton to at least acknowledge me in order to approach Lord Chalcroft."

"Chalcroft—ah. The plot thickens. Tell me…how have you managed to progress things thus far with Lady Eleanor? By my accounts, you've only seen her at two balls and a chance encounter at the park, where I believe she went home ill."

"Yes, well, you never were terribly good at accounting, were you? I believe *vocabulary* is more your strength."

"No need to hit below the belt, old man."

"Sorry," Alex said unapologetically. "What does one wear to a boat race? And where do people watch it from? Do you think it will be difficult to find Southampton there?"

Taggart shook his head and held up a hand to stop Alex's questions. "I need a stiff drink and good food before I can possibly solve your life problems yet again, Fitzhugh. Call my carriage round and let's go to my club. We can put on the nose-bag. A man can't think properly on an empty stomach."

"Put on the nose-bag?" Alex asked with an incredulous shake of his head, but dutifully went to call for his friend's carriage.

Chapter 9

Eleanor's mother sailed into her daughter's room the next morning while Eleanor was just waking.

"Goodness, you're up early," Eleanor said.

"There is much to do, daughter. I'd advise you to ring for your maid," Lady Chalcroft said briskly, though not unkindly.

Eleanor dutifully crawled out of bed and pulled the bell cord. "What is there to do?"

"Your father has decided to retire to Burton early this year." Lady Chalcroft's tone was even but Eleanor knew her mother well and knew that this abrupt change of plans was irksome to her mother's love of precise routine. A second thought caused her stomach to clench.

"Will we not attend the Henley races?" That was where she planned for Mr. Fitzhugh to seek her father's permission to marry her. She'd never before been interested in rowing before but suddenly the event had become momentous as the symbol of the beginning of her new life.

"Oh no!" was her mother's high-pitched reply. Eleanor reflected that she'd never heard her mother's voice in anything other than a carefully modulated tone. "We are attending the regatta and then proceeding directly to Burton." Normally, Lord Chalcroft brought the family back to London where he wrapped up last minute parliamentary business while Lady Chalcroft and Eleanor oversaw packing and closing of their London house. Eleanor didn't see that packing before leaving was any great inconvenience. In fact, it made sense, actually, as it would eliminate at least a full day in a carriage by proceeding to their estate near Burton-Upon-Trent from Henley. Her mother, however, clearly saw the break with routine as catastrophic.

"What a crimp in our schedule. Tell me what we need do then," she said in as supportive a tone as possible. Her mother visibly relaxed and began rattling off the usual list of "settle accounts with the butcher," "decide on what clothes to pack and what to leave," and "make sure the maids thoroughly beat the carpets and cushions before covering them."

It was nothing they didn't do every year, but Eleanor knew that if she tried to point that out, her mother would only grow more agitated. In fact, the more Eleanor sympathized with Lady Chalcroft, the more her mother calmed until she was her usual, unflappable self. As Eleanor quickly dressed and instructed her maid on a simple hairdo, she wondered if that had been part of her success in society. She'd always had an ability to read what type of reaction people needed and deliver it sincerely. If only she'd been able to read books as easily, she mused, but for the first time did so without rancor. Alex's blunt acceptance of her problem and his assurance that she was not the only person with such an affliction, had done much to reassure her.

She assisted her mother in their self-assigned chores, soothing her mother whenever she started fixating on Lord Chalcroft's abrupt decision.

"I don't know why he would change our perfectly timed schedule this year," her mother complained after they met with the housekeeper (who, in truth, had the various jobs of closing accounts with the butcher and overseeing the maid's cleaning).

"Perhaps he has finished whatever work he can do this Season and longs for the coolness of Staffordshire. It has been a very warm summer," she said distractedly, thinking as she was of the afternoon spent in Alex's bed.

"I suppose," her mother grudgingly allowed. "Still, I told Fiona Witherspoon that I would attend her luncheon. It was for the ladies who had contributed to the Ladies' Compassion Society—you know, the one which sponsors Miss Draper's charity."

"Ah yes. How is cousin Sarah?"

"I'm sure I don't know," her mother said, in much the same tone she might deny knowing about a plot to blow up Parliament. "Up to her elbows in lice-infested children, I imagine."

"Why only lice-infested?" Eleanor asked. She knew only that Sarah Draper worked with London's poor and rarely attended family functions.

Lady Chalcroft sighed with exasperation. "It was a turn of phrase, Eleanor. Now do go tell your maid which clothes to pack for Henley and which to pack for Burton. Oh why couldn't we have just kept to our usual schedule?"

As Eleanor dutifully trudged upstairs, she shrugged off her mother's exasperation but a sense of unease displaced the feeling of sensuous languor she'd been enjoying. Perhaps her mother's anxiousness had finally rubbed off on her. Out of the blue, she thought of Alex's response when she had offered her dowry to help him with his business rang in her ears. It had been so like the comments she'd heard all her life and so out of character for what she thought of him. She stood in front of her window, fingering the silk fringe on the draperies, staring unseeing at the cloudy sky. She was not a woman given to doubt when it came to men, but never had she felt so vulnerable with a man.

Despite his reassurances to the contrary, what stuck in her mind was the notion that he thought she needed her dowry for more clothes and fripperies. It was true, she knew next to nothing about the shipping world; only that it brought her beautiful silks for the modiste and pearls for the jeweler. Nonetheless, she knew it took money to make money. She'd heard her father expound many times on the need to be well-supported when beginning a business venture. She knew her mother would be aghast to know her father had been speaking of money and even more distraught to learn he'd spouted such notions in front of his daughter. In truth, Eleanor had ignored half of his lectures (they'd been directed at the swarm of young men who were actually after her attention) but some salient points must have stuck in her mind.

She'd never met the Earl of Southampton before and had no idea if he had money to lend or would be so inclined to a son whom he'd never acknowledged. She was fairly confident Mr. Fitzhugh had little enough of his own. Her eye for ladies' clothing extended to all fiber arts. She knew that his clothes were well made, but clearly purchased for longevity over the changing whims of fashion. His shoes were of quality as well, but thicker of leather and heel. Clearly made to last, clearly worn for several years already.

Turning from the window, Eleanor absently opened her cabinet and began sorting through gowns. For some reason, the normally pleasurable task of picking just the right ensemble for an event was muted today.

Your dowry should be spent buying pretty dresses and objects d'art. Not financing ratty old ships.

Did he really think that was all she cared about? The phrase rang too close to the one Eleanor had heard more times than she could stand: "Don't worry your pretty little head about such a thing."

Eleanor flung the handful of gowns on her bed and paced the length of her room. If Alex thought she was just a bit of ornament, fit only for attending balls and modeling finery, she would be sorely disappointed in him. She wondered if she had made a mistake telling him of her inability to read. Surely that had shown him that she hadn't a brain in her head. She didn't doubt his feelings for her...well at least his attraction to her. In the midst of her musings, the memory of their passionate interlude made her cheeks flame. Had he told her he loved her? He couldn't have. She wouldn't forget such a declaration. Granted, he had told her he'd never experienced the feelings he had for her, but that really wasn't the same, was it? As she thought of the previous morning, how passionate and tender he'd been, she'd never felt so absolutely cherished, so vitally necessary to another. A man couldn't counterfeit that, could he?

But of course he could, a cynical part of her brain said. She'd been warned since before her debut three years before about nefarious men who would seek to steal that which was only a husband's right. But we *are* going to marry, she told herself. The cynical brain lifted her right eyebrow in a skeptical expression and said nothing.

Eleanor felt a bit lightheaded and sank onto the cushioned ottoman in front of the fireplace. Her breathing was rapid and shallow and her fingers felt a bit tingly. She was having one of her attacks, she realized. Here, in the comforting safety of her very own room! Oh she wished Juliette had not left town. She gripped her knees in her hand and forced herself to concentrate on a flower pattern in the rug as she willed herself to breathe more slowly and deeply. A few black spots appeared in her vision and she bent at the waist to hang her head between her knees. She imagined first Juliette, and then Alex speaking to her calmly, assuring her she was going to be fine, but that made her feel worse. She discovered she was bouncing her heel up and down in a seemingly random pattern and started counting the bounces. "One-two-three…one-two…one-two-three-four-five." She wondered if she could control the pattern, which of course she could, so she bounced out the rhythm of a waltz for a minute, then began making up patterns. She had no idea how long she sat there, bent over, bouncing her heel to an imaginary rhythm, but suddenly she realized she no longer felt alarmed. She sat up suddenly which made her head swim for a moment, but after it settled, she sat and waited for the feeling to return. It didn't and she smiled broadly to herself.

"I did it," she said aloud to the empty room. "I got over it on my own!" She'd had the attacks when she was alone before, but generally she'd resorted to curling up in a ball and waiting for them to pass—occasionally after a few minutes, sometimes after hours. Juliette had a remarkable ability to talk her out of the attacks, but this was the first time Eleanor had been able to do it on her own.

She waited another moment and then cautiously stood. Unlike the times she'd merely waited it out, she was not exhausted. Instead, she felt rather invigorated, so pleased with herself was she.

She returned to her task of sorting gowns and let her thoughts return to Alex. In her more charitable frame of mind, she considered that he might not have intended to make her feel like a featherbrain. It was conceivable that he had his own demons and the notion of his business succeeding only because he married well might not sit well with him. She laughed softly. Clearly he had not been in the *ton* long, for marrying a dowry was the accepted and encouraged reason behind the proposal of many a man in need of a fortune.

He might also think she placed great importance on marrying a man with a title, and until a fortnight ago, he would have been right. She had been raised to expect to marry a man of rank and she'd never questioned that expectation until she met Alex. Of course, she had urged him to gain his father's acceptance, but that was simply so that her parents would more readily accept his suit. Her parent's approval had always been important to her and she hated the thought of disappointing them. But he wouldn't know that—they'd had so little time to learn about each other, after all—and perhaps he thought she was very concerned with appearances.

She marveled again at how quickly such thoughts had dissolved once she met Alex. She'd always acted correctly, dressed properly, and worked to make everyone around her get along smoothly. But for some reason such concerns no longer seemed to be at the forefront of her mind.

She added to the two piles of dresses on her bed and for some reason thought of her distant cousin, Sarah Draper. She only knew that there had been some furor surrounding Miss Draper a few years back, perhaps regarding a man? She'd disappeared for several months and the family had assumed she'd eloped with a nobody until she was discovered working at a Southwark soup kitchen. She'd flat out refused to return to her family and the only contact Eleanor and her mother had with her was when they made a yearly donation of old clothes, linens, and funds to Sarah's charity. Eleanor always thought Sarah must have been soft in the head, but now she wondered at the details behind her abrupt about-face.

It seemed that love could make one abandon all one had been brought up to believe. She suddenly wished she could talk to Miss Draper and ask her if she had changed her life because of love and if so, did she regret it? Deciding she had spent entirely too much time wondering about what was going on in other people's heads, Eleanor abandoned her clothing task and went downstairs to order tea and biscuits in the conservatory.

The day before the regatta, Eleanor and her parents climbed into their travelling coach. They weren't even out of the city proper when Lady Chalcroft made her announcement: "Lord Dunsbury will be joining us to watch the races. I've invited him to dine with us tomorrow night."

"Oh?" Lord Chalcroft replied, barely glancing up from his newspaper. Eleanor quickly shifted her gaze to the window

"You'll need to make yourself available to him this weekend."

When there was no reply, Eleanor glanced at her father who had lowered his paper. "To whom are you speaking, dear?" he asked.

"To the both of you," was the succinct reply.

Eleanor and her father glanced at each other before returning their attention to Lady Chalcroft.

"I have it on the best authority that Lord Dunsbury has a decided preference for Eleanor. You," she said, turning her gaze to her daughter. "Will be welcoming, pleasant, and attentive."

Without even the merest shift of her head, just a quick cut of her eyes, Lady Chalcroft stared meaningfully at her husband. "You will not make him feel foolish, young, or in any way imply you are not approving of his suit."

"Good heavens, woman. What are you talking about?" Eleanor bit the inside of her lip to keep from laughing at her father's affronted expression.

"You know exactly what I mean. You like to needle and test a young man until he's so intimidated, he crawls away with his tail between his legs."

"And do you want your only daughter married to a man who will crawl away with his tail between his legs? If he can't stand up to a blustering old fool like myself, how will he stand up to the real scoundrels in life? I should think any daughter of your loins—" Lady Chalcroft winced at the word—"would chew up and spit out any man who could not stand up to her father."

Eleanor tucked her hands under her skirts to keep from applauding.

Lady Chalcroft's lips twitched and Eleanor realized her mother was trying very hard not to laugh. "Oh very well. Just promise me you'll encourage the man in some small way."

"Once I take his measure and find him to be acceptable, I shall be as encouraging as—" he paused and Eleanor had the sneaking suspicion he was about to say something even more inappropriate than "loins." He caught himself and instead repeated, "I shall be encouraging."

"Thank you," her mother said graciously.

"Dunsbury, you say? Is that the Duke of Devonshire's heir?"

"He is."

"Ah, well if he's anything like his father, he'll be a good sort." He glanced at his daughter with a wink. "You could do worse than Dunsbury. Always a good idea to look to the sire."

Recalling their conversation after the Andover ball, Eleanor hoped he would prove just as encouraging to Mr. Fitzhugh when he arrived at Henley. Of course, by then he and his father should have reconciled and he would be Lord

Fitzhugh.

"I do hope I'll be allowed some say in the matter," she murmured.

"Bearing in mind that you are still unwed after your third Season—a third Season of which you were considered to be the most sought-after young lady—perhaps you would consent to some guidance by your parents," her mother said wearily.

Stung, Eleanor looked to her father but he was gazing at his wife with concern. Eleanor realized that while her mother was often serious, she was rarely unkind. Some unspoken message seemed to pass between her parents and Eleanor decided to let the matter drop.

"Well you'll be happy to know that Juliette has settled. Lord Worthing has come to his senses and asked her to marry him. Or at least, I believe that was his plan." She watched her mother carefully for a response. She'd actually been a bit surprised her mother hadn't pushed her more to encourage Lord Worthing. He was heir to an earldom and his family was without reproach. "I suspect the wedding will be in the next month or so. I should very much like to attend."

"We will consider all invitations after we see how this week end goes," her mother replied and Eleanor blinked in amazement. She'd never been given a condition before. "Do be sure and ask after Lord Dunsbury's sister. He is most fond of her and she has recently wed."

Lady Chalcroft was clearly determined. Eleanor sighed quietly and stared out the window. Lord Dunsbury was nice enough, and if she hadn't met Alex Fitzhugh, she would no doubt encourage his suit. She was well aware that three Seasons, even for a "diamond of the first water," was dangerously close to being considered on the shelf. For the first time, she wondered why men were allowed to wait until in their thirties to marry and yet young women were considered old by twenty-two. And not for the first time in the last few days, she missed Juliette. She would certainly have an opinion on the matter as she herself had been given a deadline to marry this year as well. Juliette had survived her ultimatum with a near miss at the altar with the wrong man. Perhaps she would share her friend's luck and she and Juliette would both be wed by autumn. With that happy thought, she allowed herself to indulge in her favorite new pastime, daydreaming about Mr. Fitzhugh.

Arriving some hours later at the house of Lord and Lady Blakely with whom they stayed every year, Eleanor was glad to be out of the confines of the carriage. Her parents had been taciturn for the trip, her father reading and her mother "resting her eyes," and she'd had only her musings about wedding dresses and flowers to keep her occupied and even for her, it had grown tedious.

The races were only a two-day event, but there was a whirlwind of activities planned around them. Picnics, parties, and balls, with Lord and Lady Blakely's being one of the most sought after invitations.

Dinner the next night saw a variety of noble guests at the Blakely table and true to her mother's word, Lord Dunsbury was present and seated right next to her. They enjoyed pleasant conversation; he was exceedingly solicitous of her, and never once told her not to worry her pretty head about something. He was classically handsome with carefully pomaded curls, a well-trimmed mustache, and dark blue eyes. He made her laugh at a self-deprecating story and surprised her by listening attentively when she spoke. Truly, he was the perfect husband prospect. Except that she felt no overwhelming pull toward him. Her body didn't thrum to the rumble of his voice, her cheeks didn't warm when he gazed at her, and she felt not a single butterfly beneath her corset. She was meticulously polite to him for he seemed a truly good man, and had she not met Alexander Fitzhugh three weeks ago, she would have no doubt encouraged his suit.

She pleaded a headache after dinner and retired early, even pretending to be asleep when her mother entered the room to check on her to avoid hearing further instructions on Lord Dunsbury.

The next morning she dressed with exceptional care, choosing a striped pale pink muslin gown and deep rose Spencer. She sat patiently while her maid tugged and twisted her hair until it rippled beautifully around her face and gathered it in a low knot at her nape so as not to interfere with the set of her hat, a beribboned confection with yards of lace that tied quite jauntily beneath her left ear.

As they made their way to the grassy banks of the Thames, she scanned the crowds. She knew it was ridiculous to expect to find Alex Fitzhugh so soon, but it had been days since she'd seen him and with no word of his success with his father, she was anxious to lay eyes on him and assure herself that their mad, whirlwind romance was a real thing. She didn't doubt her feelings—not for a moment. But, well, it *had* been a mad whirlwind of a romance and for all that they'd rather jumped the gun on a wedding ceremony, they'd not once mentioned love. She'd never been so consumed by thoughts of another and it was proving to be a bit disconcerting, especially as she'd become rather accustomed to men pledging undying love after a few dances, much less anything more intimate. Of course part of his appeal was that Alex was unlike any other man she'd met and so she could not predict his every move as she'd been able to do with the men of the *ton*. Despite her best efforts to the contrary, a small insidious voice whispered that perhaps Mr. Fitzhugh, now that he'd had the distinction of "ruining" Lady Eleanor Chalcroft, was now no longer interested in furthering their relationship.

Eleanor shook her head and clenched her fists. No, she told the voice fiercely. Mr. Fitzhugh had surprised her at every turn, from the first night they met to his gentleness at the park when she'd suffered one of her attacks, to the intensity of passion he'd aroused in her from their first kiss. She trusted her feelings for him and she trusted him as well as she reminded herself when the doubts began their whispering. Nonetheless, it would still be reassuring to actually see him, feel the warmth of his gaze on her face and have her heart surge to life at his nearness.

She watched the races from beneath a large canvas pavilion with only half-hearted attention. Her gaze constantly scanned the crowds on both sides of the Thames, though she could scarcely make out the faces of those on the other side of the river. She listened for his deep voice with that slight hint of an accent, a roundness of the vowels that betrayed his upbringing in Cornwall. With all the straining to see and the sun glinting off the water, she gave herself a headache by luncheon and her mother worriedly pulled off a glove to check for fever.

"Perhaps you should return to the Blakely's and rest. You won't want to miss the dance this evening."

"I'm fine, mother," Eleanor protested. "I simply go too caught up in the excitement of the races. Our team won, you see."

Lady Chalcroft looked at her daughter as if she'd never seen her before. "And who is 'our team?'"

"Why, the one I've been rooting for, of course. You should see them; they have lovely rowing costumes. Quite dapper."

Her mother looked as if she wanted to check her temperature again, but instead pulled her glove back on and turned to leave. "Lord Dunsbury will be joining us this afternoon. Do see that he has a nice time."

Eleanor only just stifled a groan. Her mother had been remarkably restrained during Eleanor's first two seasons out, but apparently that was simply because there were no ducal heirs about. Now that Lord Dunsbury had appeared on the scene, her mother was stepping up to her matchmaking duties with the tenacity of, well of a matchmaking mama, Eleanor thought with a grin. And why had Lord Dunsbury only appeared this season? Ah well, it would give her something to ask him during the long afternoon. Once that conversational gambit was exhausted, she hoped he would stay predictable and fill the time with stories of himself. She was quite good at nodding and smiling encouragingly. Eleanor frowned as she stared unseeing into the haze of the afternoon. How ridiculous that young ladies should be expected to do all the listening in conversation. She bit her lower lip, chewing it thoughtfully. How odd that she should only now question what she had accepted and even embraced her entire life. She should blame Juliette, and no doubt Alex Fitzhugh for her positively bluestocking thoughts, but somehow she could find it in her to blame anyone. If anything, she suspected she should thank them for—

"Don't gnaw on your lip, Eleanor. And for heaven's sake, why are you frowning?" Her mother's reprimand was issued in a low tone of voice but Eleanor knew better than delay in smoothing her expression into one of serene cordiality.

"Are you quite sure you're not ill?"

"Quite sure, mother. A momentary lapse, I assure you."

"Yes, well mind your lapses in public, dear. Here comes Lord Dunsbury."

Her mother greeted the man warmly, urging him to sit with Eleanor while she saw that the luncheon would be served on time.

The afternoon passed pleasantly enough. Eleanor valiantly attempted to appear interested in whatever it was Lord Dunsbury had to say while surreptitiously watching for Mr. Fitzhugh. Nonetheless, and despite having only sat in the pleasant coolness of the shade all day, she felt exhausted by the time they returned to the Blakely's house that evening. She would have pled a headache and skipped the public dance but she wanted to be available for Alex to find her, and a public ball would be easier for him to attend than the Blakely's private ball tomorrow. She gamely trudged upstairs to bathe and dress for the evening.

The Henley Dance was a crowded, boisterous affair but try though she might, Eleanor couldn't find Alex. She danced several times, twice with Lord Dunsbury to her mother's approval, thinking that she might be more visible on the dance floor in case Mr. Fitzhugh was looking for her as desperately as she was for him. She allowed herself to be escorted to the refreshment table four times, made as many trips to the ladies' retiring room, and in general used any excuse to travel throughout the large hall, all to no avail.

There was still another full day of races, she reminded herself as they took the short carriage ride to the Blakely's house. And the Blakely's ball tomorrow night. She hadn't specifically told Alex to come to the first day of the Henley. And who knew what was keeping him. Perhaps his business required his attention. Or his father wanted to meet with him, perhaps spend time catching up. Perhaps his horse threw him and he was bleeding to death in a ditch somewhere between here and London.

Eleanor and her mother departed earlier than her father the next morning as Lady Chalcroft wanted to stop by the apothecary for ingredients for one of her simples.

"Why not have your maid fetch them while we're at the races today?"

"She can't tell milk thistle from marshmallow root. Would you have me make your father's tonic from milk thistle?"

"Certainly not," Eleanor said with as much indignation as she could insincerely manage.

The footman helped them both down from the carriage but Lady Chalcroft said, "There's no need for you to come in. I shall only be a minute."

Rather than climb back in the carriage—she would be sitting again all day, after all—Eleanor elected to walk along the street, peering in shop windows.

She was perhaps three doors down when she was approached by a young woman holding a toddler. Eleanor's first thought was that the woman could have been her sister. They had the same fair complexion, dark gold hair, and blue. The differences, however, far outweighed their similarities. The young woman's cheeks were wind chapped, her hair was tied back in a tight knot, and she weighed perhaps a stone less than Eleanor. The bones of her shoulders looked as if they were about to poke through the worn fabric of her dress and there was air of resignation about her.

"Forgive me, my lady," the young woman said. "I don't mean to bother you, but I was wondering if you might spare a coin to feed my brother."

"Oh!" Eleanor said, completely at a loss for words. "I—"

"Here now!" the footman exclaimed, rushing to Eleanor's side. "Don't you be bothering my lady."

"No, no," Eleanor said, finding her voice. "It's alright. Let me see what I have."

"My lady, she's just begging so she can buy more blue ruin. I've seen it before."

"I'm not!" the woman protested, clutching the toddler closer to her. He squirmed wanting to get down and she was so slight it was all she could do to keep a grip on him. "I don't touch a drop of that," she said vehemently. "I've never so much as touched spirits."

"I believe you," Eleanor said. "Let me see what I have," she said as she opened her reticule.

"My lady," the footman interjected as she pulled out a handful of coins. "That's too much. She'll just waste it—"

"Aye, waste it on food. Perhaps buy my poor brother a new nappy." The girl looked worn down, but Eleanor admired her spirit.

"Hush, John," Eleanor said to the indignant footman. She handed the money to the young woman. "What's your name?"

Behind them, she heard the tinkle of a shop bell and knew without looking that her mother had emerged from the apothecary.

"Eleanor?" her mother called.

"Coming," Eleanor called at the same time the young woman said, "Yes?"

Startled, Eleanor looked at her. "Is that your name as well?"

The other Eleanor nodded, looking as surprised as she felt, and as the footman shepherded her away, the other woman called out, "God bless you, my lady."

"Good luck to you," Eleanor replied before allowing the

footman to hustle her into the carriage.

Sitting, she turned and saw her mother scowl at the footman before climbing in herself.

"What were you thinking, Eleanor, talking with such a woman? Suppose someone saw you?"

"I suppose they would have seen me give her a few coins to feed her brother."

"It wasn't seemly. Besides, giving money to people like that merely encourages them to beg more rather than seeking gameful employment."

Eleanor frowned and studied the tip of her glove. "I thought ladies were supposed to do charitable work. You are on the committee for the hospital."

"That is very different. We help gather supplies through various social events. We don't interact directly with the hospital staff."

"But—" Eleanor had the strangest sensation: a bit like she'd awoken from a nap in the middle of a party, or perhaps as if someone had opened the drapes after she'd been stumbling in a dimly lit room. "But how can you know what the hospital really needs if you don't talk to them? Perhaps crocheted doilies and baskets of preserves don't do them much good. What if what they really need is," here Eleanor struggled to think of what a hospital might actually need. She'd never even driven by one, much less stepped inside. "Blankets!" she exclaimed on a moment's inspiration.

"Then they can simply sell what we provide for the funds to buy blankets," her mother replied shortly.

It seemed like unnecessary work for hospital staff who were, as far as she knew, serving poor people who couldn't afford a private doctor to come to their home. Another thought occurred to her.

"That girl's name was Eleanor."

Her mother looked up from the contents of her reticule, clearly confused. "I beg your pardon?"

"The girl I gave the coins to. Her name was Eleanor as well.

What do you think she would do with her little brother if she did work."

"What little brother? Eleanor, whatever are you talking about?"

"She asked for money to feed her little brother. You told me that I was just encouraging her to beg instead of work, but I can't help wonder what she would do with her little brother if she had to work all day. Surely a child that young cannot take care of himself." Eleanor had absolutely no experience with children of any age. Her older brother and his wife had yet to have a baby and caught up in the social whirl of the Season, she'd found herself disinclined to visit those friends who had married and borne children.

"You've been talking to her, haven't you?" her mother said sharply.

"What? Who?"

"Sarah Draper. Did she approach you on the street? Send you a letter?"

"Cousin Sarah? No! I've not seen her since last year and even then we scarcely spoke. I think she considers me a ninny."

"Then what is this nuisance all about?"

Eleanor sat back. "I wasn't trying to be a nuisance. It just occurred to me—the questions, I mean."

Her mother pressed two fingers against her forehead as if it hurt and Eleanor was surprised to notice how wan her mother looked today.

"Well please try to focus on your task at hand today."

"My task?"

"Lord Dunsbury. He will be joining us again. I trust you encouraged his suit last night?"

"I...ah, well I danced with him. Twice, in fact. He escorted me to the refreshment table. He seemed to, er, enjoy himself."

"Your father has decided that we shall depart for home tomorrow. That means you only have today and tonight's ball to further his interest."

"Surely—"

"Eleanor, please," her mother said wearily, and again, Eleanor was again taken with how fragile her normally indomitable mother looked.

"Please just do as I ask for one day without arguing."

Eleanor couldn't recall a time she'd ever "argued" with her mother. Even if she had disagreed with her, Lady Chalcroft was not a force to be denied. Opposition had never even entered her daughter's mind in all her years of instruction.

"Of course, mother."

"Thank you," Lady Chalcroft said, and turned to look out the window.

The day passed with tedious slowness. By luncheon, Eleanor gave up scanning the crowds for a glimpse of Alex and was beginning to fear he may never appear. That horrible voice in her head would not stop gloating. Thankfully Lord Dunsbury did not seem to require her constant attention, visiting with the other gentlemen, and he was most sought after by the other ladies who had joined them in the pavilion. It was only when she would catch her mother's disapproving eye that she felt compelled to seek him out and engage him in some bit of nonsense or another.

By the time she and her parents made their way back to the Blakely's to prepare for their hosts' ball, Eleanor was in a foul mood. She was tired, her cheeks hurt from holding them all day in a smile she didn't feel, and despite her bonnet, parasol, and shade pavilion, her nose was sunburnt.

She swatted the offending organ with a powder pouf, blinking rapidly at the resulting cloud, and grumbling under her breath.

"Is anything the matter, my lady?" her maid asked. "You don't seem yourself these last few days."

Eleanor sighed and smiled—grimaced, really—at Mary in the mirror. "Uncertainty is not an emotion I am comfortable with, Mary. I find it makes me quite irritable."

Mary secured a diamond brooch in the curls above Eleanor's right ear. Though Eleanor had not confided the details of her association with Mr. Fitzhugh, she was fairly certain her maid knew exactly what was going on. "You must have faith, my lady. You're a good person and good things will happen to you."

"Faith," Eleanor repeated. She'd dutifully attended church every Sunday since she was old enough to sit still and was well schooled in the virtue of faith, but the comforts of her life were such that she'd never needed to put much stock into the notion of believing something would happen and waiting patiently for it. Thoughts of her comfortable life brought to mind the young woman who had approached her this morning. She wondered where she was and if she relied on faith to feed her brother.

Her contemplation was interrupted by her mother who swept into the room to inspect her daughter's appearance with her usual resolute poise. There was no hint of the fragility Eleanor had noticed earlier.

"You will make yourself available to Lord Dunsbury tonight, Eleanor. You scarcely paid him much notice today. Don't think I wasn't watching."

"Mother, do give me some credit for knowing how to attract a man's attention. Sometimes not being too available encourages the chase. Haven't I received half a dozen offers since my debut?"

"More than a dozen, I should say," her mother conceded. "Very well, point taken. But if Lord Dunsbury does not come to scratch tonight, it may be months before we see him again."

"But surely there is no rush. I mean—"

"There is not another eligible man with even the slimmest chance of a ducal coronet in all of England."

"But why must I—"

"I'm not going to discuss this further, Eleanor. I've let you have your head for three seasons. Now it is time to focus on Lord Dunsbury." With that pronouncement, her mother swept from the room, leaving only a delicate wash of French perfume in her wake.

"Have faith, my lady," Mary said as Eleanor slumped in her chair.

"That's easier said than done," she grumbled, but resolutely straightened her spine and applied another layer of powder to her red nose.

.

Chapter 10

Alex was in a fine fit as he and Taggart walked up the wide, gracious steps of Lord Blakely's home. He'd spent the last three days trying to approach his father and he had met with nothing but failure. He wasn't sure if it was fate that his father was deliberately avoiding him that was setting him more on edge.

After the brutal warning he'd received, he thought it best not to present himself at his father's townhouse so instead he'd written a short, respectful note assuring the earl he wanted nothing but to meet him. He'd purchased the best paper he could find and thought out his words carefully before writing, but the effort had been for naught. The boy he hired to deliver it and receive a reply returned with the letter unopened.

To make things worse, he'd been plagued with doubts about Eleanor as well. Despite what had occurred between them, he couldn't quell the notion that she may have come to her senses in the days they'd been apart, surrounded as she no doubt was with dozens of more eligible men who didn't have to convince their fathers of their identity.

That evening, Alex watched from down the street as his father's carriage pulled away from the house. On horseback, he followed the carriage all the way to the Theatre Royal on Drury Lane. Once inside the crowded lobby, he craned his neck to find the earl. Southampton had begun ascending a carpeted staircase when something made him pause. He turned and scanned the crowd and Alex lifted a hand to draw his attention. The earl gave no indication he even saw Alex—though did his eyes narrow slightly?—before he turned and continued his ascent. The show had been sold out so Alex had been forced to wait in the lobby despite the attempts of the theatre ushers to urge him to leave, but Southampton did not appear during intermission and Alex found no sign of him in the departing crush.

The next day he made the rounds of his father's club, his Parliament office, and even his tailor trying to run into him. He even went so far as to knock on the Southampton's front door, but the butler had informed him that the earl was not in to callers.

"If you will take him my card, I believe he will change his mind," Alex persisted, pointing at his calling card which looked very small and inconsequential on the engraved silver salver in the butler's hand.

"I'm sorry, sir. I have my instructions."

Alex tried to read any hint of his father's mood in the servant: was he disdainful or inquisitive? But the man's expression was as granite, impervious to the elements of human emotion. Turning away with a sigh, Alex reminded himself to never sit at a card table with a butler.

The next day was equally frustrating. Another note sent to his father disappeared in the depths of the manor.

"What do you mean, 'disappeared?'" he asked the messenger boy.

The boy shrugged. "I gave it to some stuffy gent what answered the door and told 'im I was to take a reply, but 'e shut the door i' my face an' never came back. Waited near an hour, I did."

Alex dropped a coin in the upturned hand and nodded absently at the thanks he received. He was at a loss. He and Taggart were to depart in just an hour for Henley. He'd hoped he could go directly to Eleanor's father and present himself with his father's acknowledgement as an eligible suitor. Instead, he had one last chance to approach his father. He would have to track him down at the Blakely's ball, hope the presence of a crowd would prevent his father from causing a scene, then further hope the man could be reasoned with. Alex tried to tamp down his anger with Southampton. He was the injured party here, not his father. He was the one who'd had to live off the charity of his mother's family, who'd had to grow up without a father. His mother had borne the heartache until the day she died, though she was fierce enough to deny it, and Alex hated his father for the grief he caused her. The earl had been a fool to doubt such a wife. At any rate, clearly the man was foul of heart. Alex just hoped he could be reasoned with. He was prepared to sign off any legal right to Southampton's wealth, lands, or properties. He just needed the connection to the earldom to win over Eleanor's parents.

Inside the stately Blakely mansion, the air was thick with the late summer heat and the press of hundreds of overdressed bodies. Alex strained to scan the crowds, looking for both Southampton and Eleanor. Beside him, Taggart was doing the same.

"Egads, we'll be lucky to find the refreshment table in this crush," Taggart grumbled as they pushed their way through the crowded entry hall into the series of connected rooms that served as ballroom.

They made a slow sweep of the perimeter of the three large rooms. It was only as they were completing the first circuit that Taggart said, "There she is!"

Alex turned sharply to catch a glimpse of Eleanor in the arms of a dark-haired man on the dance floor. The sweep of the waltz spun her around and he knew she spotted him. Her eyes widened and she craned her neck to keep him in her sight as her partner twirled her down the length of the dance floor.

"Who was Lady Eleanor dancing with?" He had to practically shout the question at Taggart, so noisy was it in the ballroom. Clearly his question had gone astray for a pair of older ladies turned at his query.

"That's Lord Dunsbury. Heir to a dukedom, he is. Which one is it, Millicent?" the first lady asked of her companion.

The second lady tapped her lips with the edge of her

closed fan. "Let me think. Oh! Devonshire. The Duke of Devonshire. She'll not make a better catch if she waited for ten seasons!"

"True, true," the first lady said.

"Is he courting her?" Alex asked sharply. Both ladies looked at him in surprise, but the first lady nodded amiably. "It's been quite the spectacle, watching Dunsbury chase after Lady Eleanor these past three days. Waiting on her hand and foot, he is. Won't even speak to another lady."

"I heard he gave Miss Stoneworth the cut direct in his haste to fetch Lady Eleanor a cup of lemonade at the races today," Millicent said to her friend.

"Well, Lady Eleanor is a beauty, I'll grant you. And such a connection to the Chalcrofts would benefit any family, ducal or not."

Alex tried to spot Eleanor again. A sick feeling was clenching his stomach, causing bile to burn the back of his throat. Even if he had his father's public blessing, wealth, and promised title, he was no competition for the heir to a dukedom. The doubts he'd been trying to quash for the last week chuckled evilly in the back of his head.

He turned to ask Taggart's opinion but the man had wandered off.

He skirted the room, trying to catch sight of Eleanor, to ascertain for himself if she was gazing at this ducal heir the same way she had looked at him. A woman on the side of the dance floor caused him to halt in his tracks. For a second, he thought she was Eleanor but he instantly realized the older woman must be her mother. They shared the same antique gold hair and heart-stopping beauty, though this woman was older and her expression more calculating. He made his way to a column that was just behind the lady.

"—each other for years, you know," she was saying. "Why the duchess and I grew up near each other and Chalcroft was at secondary school with Devonshire."

"Nonetheless, you must be very proud," said the dark-haired woman next to her. "Dukes—or should I say, future dukes—are few and far between on the marriage market. Tell me truly, Elizabeth, was Eleanor waiting all these years for Dunsbury to declare himself?"

"All these years?" Eleanor's supposed mother said. "You make it sound as if a decade has passed and Eleanor pining away through all of it. Dunsbury was out of the country until recently, you know. Besides, Eleanor has had plenty of offers during her three Seasons out."

"I marvel that you allowed her to wait so long." Alex chanced a peek at Lady Chalcroft's companion but the woman didn't seem to be speaking maliciously.

"Yes, well, that was her father's doing. He quite dotes on her, you know. Still, you might consider it...destiny, shall we say, that Dunsbury returned when he did."

"She won't refuse him, will she? I daresay any daughter of yours will have a stubborn streak," the woman said with a gentle chuckle.

"I don't know what you mean," Lady Chalcroft replied, but Alex could hear the humor in her voice. "No," she said, sobering. "Eleanor will marry Dunsbury. She knows her duty and she knows how lucky she is to have captured his interest."

Alex pushed away from the column behind which he'd been skulking, his throat constricted, his stomach in knots. He recognized Lord Chalcroft as he came to claim his wife for a dance and ducked back behind the pillar. His heart was pounding and his fingers felt numb. Staggering through the crowd, he told himself it couldn't be true. He tried to call to mind Eleanor's face as she'd kissed him in the Andover library, the intimate hours spent in his flat, or the expression in her eyes when she'd all but told him to settle his affairs and approach her father here at Henley. But he couldn't picture anything more concrete than a halo of golden hair and a dimpled smile.

Get a grip on yourself, man, he told himself. It had only been a few days since he'd seen her. Her affections would not have waned in so short a time. He was certain of her. He was.

It was just the strain of trying to confront his father, the hoops through which he was having to jump to approach *her* father, all while he should have been devoting every waking hour to getting his business afloat. He'd not been in contact with Captain Billingsley for days. Suppose the man had taken changed his mind? Or worse, that he'd taken Alex's plans as his own? The burning in his stomach intensified. This was insane, he thought. Suppose I've jeopardized my entire business plan— my life plan—for a woman who is going to throw me over for a more illustrious title? Who better than her mother would know Eleanor's intentions? The fantasy that had blossomed in the last few weeks of him and Eleanor and the possibilities for their life seemed to pop like so many soap bubbles, and the doubts were now roaring.

Alex found himself on the other side of the ballroom without any memory of walking there and looked up to discover Eleanor in his direct line of sight. She turned as if he'd called her name and smiled widely at him. Some of the tightness in his chest eased at her expression and he took a step in her direction before he noticed his father just off to her left. The tightness resumed tenfold, yet he felt remarkably calm as he adjusted his route and strode purposefully toward the earl. He suddenly had not a thought for Lady Eleanor or Taggart who called out after him to slow his pace.

He pushed methodically through the throngs of people, weaving his way around groups, nudging individuals out of his path with a distracted "Pardon me."

When he was but a dozen steps from his father, Southampton glanced up. Upon seeing Alex's determined face, he promptly quit his conversation, turning to force his own way through the crowd of people surrounding him.

Clenching his jaw, Alex redoubled his efforts, finally catching up to the man in the main hall of the Blakely's home. While there were considerably fewer people here than in the main rooms, they were not alone and Alex strove to keep his voice low as he called out, "My lord Southampton. Wait!"

With a sour look on his face, the earl paused and turned around.

Alex stopped directly in front of him, suddenly at a loss of what to say.

"Well?" Southampton snapped? "Make your pitch so I may turn you down and get on with my evening."

"My pitch?"

"Try and sell me whatever it is you're so determined to hawk and let me have done with it."

"I'm not trying to sell you anything," Alex said through gritted teeth. "I just—" He paused.

"You just what? Go on. Spit it out." The earl's voice was sharp with impatience and not for the first time, Alex wondered what his mother had seen in him.

"My mother—your wife—is dead. She passed last year." Perhaps the earl had heard this news, but somehow, Alex felt he should be the one to tell him in person.

Southampton's eyelids flickered and a muscle twitched under his left eye, but to someone who wasn't closely scrutinizing his expression, he would seem to be unfazed by the news. After a moment, he said, "I repeat, sir, what is it you want?"

Taken aback that the man had nothing to say of his wife's death, Alex ground out, "I—"

"Useless," the earl muttered and moved to push past Alex, whose anger quickly replaced shock. Alex stood his ground, forcing the older man to step back. "I want nothing from you. I require only your acknowledgement. It is the least you can do after abandoning your pregnant wife."

"How dare you," Southampton snarled. "You cur! You have no right to approach me, much less to imply—" the earl broke off, his face darkening, his brows lowered over deep set eyes.

Surely the man did not seek to deny he was Alex's father? They could have been the same person, years apart. They shared the same height, carriage, and russet brown eyes. While the earl's hair had gone to grey, it had that underlying reddish tone that hinted it had once been the very color Alex's was now.

A soft voice split the tension between the men. "Alex?"

Tearing his gaze from his sire's, Alex turned his head to see Eleanor in the hall, just a few feet away from them. For a moment, he forgot what her mother had said, saw only her sweet face filled with concern for him.

"Is there anything I can do?" she asked.

"My acknowledgement, eh?" Southampton snarled and Alex whipped his head back to see the earl staring at Eleanor, sizing her up as if she were a racehorse to be wagered upon. "I'm sure you do. Chalcroft won't be keen to turn his daughter over to a nameless cur."

Alex clenched his teeth until he felt his pulse pound in his temple. He had to stay focused. He had to convince this man— his father—to do the right thing.

"I want no money from you, no lands—"

"Of course you do. It's all tied together. Do you take me for a fool? I know what you're about. Your petty little dreams to be a shipping magnate. Your infatuation with a woman who will never settle for the likes of you. I'll see my title rot before I give it over to a bastard." "

"No!" Alex said tightly. Why was this man so loath to ac-knowledge his own son? "My mother—"

"Likely didn't know who your father was either."

Alex felt the blood drain from his face; felt, as if his skin were wax, the expression melt from his visage until he pre-sented a cold, stony front. "Don't you dare speak of my mother. You were not worthy of her when you had her. You certainly haven't the right to mention her now."

"I will speak of her or anyone else who seeks to play me false."

"Then you are a fool. Look at me, man! I look nothing like my mother." He saw the earl's gaze travel over his face, knew the man was not blind to their similarities. "Do you run into so many men who so closely resemble you, then?"

His father's lips pressed into a straight line of bitterness.

He glanced over Alex's shoulder, presumably at Eleanor again, but when he nodded shortly then jerked his head toward the front entry, Alex looked around. Two large men in livery were bearing down on him. Before he could so much as protest, they each grabbed an arm and manhandled him toward the door.

"No!" Eleanor called out.

"Trust me, my dear, you'll thank me when you are a duchess," Southampton said, carelessly brushing off the sleeve of his jacket.

Alex struggled against the grip of the two men, each of whom outweighed him by at least two stone. He managed to pull one arm free and swung around to point at his father. "You stupid old man!" he yelled. "My mother was better off without you! Why she let you touch her in the first place is beyond me!" The footman he'd escaped came at Alex from another angle, pushing him toward the door.

People began pouring into the hall, drawn by his shouts. He saw Eleanor struggle to push her way through them. Lord Blakely made his way to the front of the crowd. "What is going on here?"

Southampton flicked his fingers in Alex's direction. "I am doing you a service Blakely. I'm having your servants take out a bit of uninvited rubbish who sought to invade your party."

"No!" Eleanor said fiercely. "He's not uninvited! He's—" she was jostled again and Alex lost sight of her. By this time the footman were at the door, then at the top of the steps. Somehow Southampton was beside them, his face coldly triumphant.

"Alex!" Eleanor called and he saw her behind the earl, held back by Lord Dunsbury, who gripped her protectively. The sight of Eleanor in the man's arms caused a cold, fury, distinct and separate next to the rage he felt at his father. She looked as foreign to him as if she had traveled from the farthest reaches of Asia. A small crowd had gathered, drawn by the sound of raised voices and the hope of titillating gossip. Suddenly, irrationally, he was angry at Eleanor for putting him in this position, for making him approach his father like a beggar, for distracting him from the business that he'd been working on for four years.

He looked back at Southampton and forced his muscles to relax.

The footmen released him, clearly expecting him to depart peaceably.

Keeping his voice deliberately light and mocking he said, "Perhaps you're right about me. I certainly couldn't be the son of such a petty, impotent coward." He saw a rage that matched his own flare up in Southampton's eyes. With a roar, the older man launched himself at Alex and though his sire lacked his strength, his momentum—and Alex's surprise—enabled him to propel Alex back down the front steps to land in a bruised, ignominious heap in the dirt. Before he could leap to his feet, Eleanor was at his side, tears streaming down her face as she knelt in the dusty drive.

"This man is an imposter and a villain! You would be wise to guard your pocketbooks and your daughters from him," Southampton shouted.

"Eleanor!" a man called and Alex realized that he must have hit his head because his ears were ringing and he couldn't determine who had called her name. Regardless, she kept her attention on him, smoothing his hair back from his brow, whispering soothing sounds he could not distinguish as words. He thought his vision was doubled as well when two men appeared behind her and bent to lift her off the ground.

"No!" she screamed. "Leave me!"

"Eleanor," said one quietly while the other snapped, "Hush!"

Alex realized it was Dunsbury and Lord Chalcroft, no doubt seeking to save Eleanor from ruin. Alex looked at the three of them and they may as well have been his father: privileged, pampered, confident in their superiority.

"Eleanor, you're not helping the man," Dunsbury said gently. "Come with me and we'll sort this all out without an audience."

Eleanor glanced at the man as if he were her savior. She nodded and allowed him to help her to her feet.

"Alex," Eleanor called, reaching a hand to him but he scrambled to his feet unaided.

"Get away from me!" he snarled. "All of you!" he said more loudly to the crowd who'd gathered on the front steps, ladies tittering behind their fans, men looking down their nose at him. Rage burned like acid in his stomach. He saw not Eleanor's tears, but her advantage, heard not her cries for him, but the mocking words of the other guests. She stepped closer to him and grabbed his arm, staring up at him with tear-filled eyes but he felt nothing. He jerked his arm away and she stumbled.

"How dare you!" Dunsbury spat and strode forward, his hands clenched in fists.

Eleanor grabbed Dunsbury's arm, crying, "Robert, no!"

Robert? Alex thought. Clearly she and the man were more familiar than mere acquaintances. He wondered if Dunsbury had convinced her to visit the library or even his rooms. The thought was bitter gall in his mouth and he glared at her, heaping the blame for this entire awful scene on her shoulders, even as he knew it was unfair and petty.

"You'd better listen to him," he said through gritted teeth. "I'm sure he's the only man who will be able to afford your endless gowns and the tutors you'll likely need." He saw her face whiten at the insult and though no one could know what he meant by the last slur, he knew also that it was a cruel remark to make. Why he felt the need to lash out, to hurt her in such a petty way, he wasn't sure but he seemed unable not to.

"I think you had better leave," Lord Chalcroft said bleakly. Alex looked at Eleanor's father and saw neither scorn nor anger, but something akin to pity, an emotion that made Alex even more furious. Without another word, he spun on his heel and strode down the drive. A nervous young lad intercepted him with his horse and he swung up on the animal and rode off without a backward glance.

"Alex!" he heard Eleanor cry out but he closed his ears and his heart to the sound and raced on.

Chapter 11

Eleanor's maid woke her the next morning before dawn. Urged her to rise, to be frank, as Eleanor hadn't slept a wink since falling into bed late last night, tear-streaked physically, crushed emotionally. She had little recollection of her father and Lord Dunsbury hustling her back into the Blakely house last night after Alex had left her, the expression on his face as he'd looked at her one of disgust and hatred. She knew her mother had been summoned, had registered the deathly pallor of her face as her father spoke in low tones of the altercation, but she'd been unable to meet her mother's eyes. All she knew was that Lady Chalcroft had hoarsely instructed Eleanor's maid to put her to bed and then pack immediately. They would be on the road by sunrise.

Numbly, Eleanor allowed her maid to strip off her gown —the very same she had been sure she would become engaged in. Her tears had temporarily abated; she was holding onto her composure with the merest thread of restraint. She woodenly pulled her earrings and necklace off, and winced not once when Mary tugged at the jeweled brooch that was tangled in her hair.

"I'm sorry, my lady," Mary had gasped, but Eleanor just stared straight ahead, trusting in the frozen cloak that seemed to have settled on her shoulders to get her into the privacy of her bed where she was certain she would die.

Die, however, she did not. As Mary quietly tiptoed out of the room, Eleanor felt her control slip. Lying on her side, she felt a tremor begin low in her belly. In her mind's eye she could see the scene on the front steps as if she were a bird, high up in the air. She saw her own frantic tears, Dunsbury's attempts to restrain her, her own father's stoic expression, Southampton's self-satisfied sneer. But most of all, she saw Alex, glaring at her as if she had brought about his ruin. A fat, hot tear slid over the bridge of her nose to drip onto the pillow. Another leaked into her hairline.

Why would he have cast such hatred at her? Had someone said something? Vaguely she recalled Southampton saying something about being a duchess. Did Alex think she had thrown him over for Dunsbury? It was utterly mad, but perhaps Southampton had lied.

A hiccupping sob escaped her. Surely Alex would have given her the benefit of the doubt, asked her directly before condemning her?

By the light of the single candle burning on the mantle, she saw her ball gown lying across a chair, waiting for Mary to return and gather it to be packed. The pale gold of the heavy satin gleamed richly in the candlelight. She'd spent hours choosing it, having Mary take in a few seams so it fit her like a glove. She'd wanted everything to be perfect when Alex finally approached her.

Mary crept back into the room and as silently as a wraith gathered up Eleanor's stockings and slippers. As she reached for the gown, Eleanor said, "Get rid of that."

Mary jumped, no doubt thinking her to be asleep. "My lady?"

"The dress. Get rid of it. I don't want to see it again."

"But my lady—"

"Get rid of it!"

Mary nodded and departed as quietly as she'd come in, the gleam of the satin seeming to sap the light from the room as it billowed around the doorframe.

Again and again Eleanor poured over the whirlwind events of the night. How had the disaster come about? She replayed the ugly words she'd heard Southampton hurl at Alex.

They must have only met tonight. That would explain why Alex had been so late coming to Henley. He must have been trying to track the earl down, meet with him and present his case.

But why would the earl have been so virulent? Finally seeing them together, it was clear the men shared the same blood. Southampton had no other children, no other heir. Surely he must wish for a son to inherit.

She pressed her face into her pillow, trying to suffocate the pain within her. Why had Alex not approached her first? Perhaps if they had both gone to Southampton, they could have convinced him to see reason. A rapid succession of scenarios played out in her mind of what she could have said to convince the man until she flopped on her back in exasperation. Such thoughts were pointless. Alex hadn't asked for her help—whether because it didn't occur to him or, the more despondent thought, he didn't believe her assistance to be of value. He would not be the first to discount her contribution to anything beyond what color gown to wear.

Eleanor flung herself out of bed and began pacing the short length of her guest room. Regardless of the value Alex placed on her ability to argue and convince, nothing explained how he'd turned on her before storming off. It was almost as if he'd blamed her…for what, she wasn't sure, but the anger in his face was clear and she'd felt the full brunt of it.

She sank to the floor in front of the cold fireplace. She'd never been a pacer, having been trained from a young age that ladies sat perfectly still for hours at a time. Fidgeting, fussing, and pacing were not the hallmarks of good breeding.

She sat there until the cold of early morning drove her back under the covers of her bed where she lay with a heart as cold as her feet. There was really only one explanation: Alex had not trusted her, had not believed in her. Even taking into account how upset his father had made him, he had no right to take that anger out on her, especially when she had tried to stand with him.

Her tears were long dried by the time Mary crept back

into the room and coaxed her from bed with a pot of tea. She stoically washed her face and dressed, then braced herself to go downstairs and face her parents. They were leaving like thieves in the night, departing before any of Lord Blakely's other guests had arisen, before they were the focus of virulent gossip. Lord Blakely was at the door with her parents and as Eleanor approached, she heard his solicitous murmurs, assuring them that he would stem the tide of speculation.

Eleanor did not greet her parents, nor did they say anything to her. They climbed into the coach and drove off. The first hour was spent in numb silence. She and her mother stared out opposite windows while her father pretended to read the newspaper in the seat across from them. Eleanor watched the late summer scenery pass with none of her usual appreciation. The lush greens of the fields and riotous colors of the flowers left her unmoved. Everything had a pall to it and she felt as though her heart and head were wrapped in wool felt, muffled and removed from the world. Finally, Lady Chalcroft turned to her daughter, though her mother had to call her name twice before Eleanor realized she was being addressed.

"I should like to give you the benefit of the doubt and allow you to defend yourself before your father and I decide what to do with you." Her voice was low and even, but Eleanor could hear the underlying strain in it. Whether that strain was from grief or anger, she could not tell, so stoic was her mother's expression.

Still, Eleanor paused. What had she to defend herself against? She'd done nothing wrong. Lord Southampton was the only culprit in last night's debacle.

"Defend myself?" She heard the note of hysteria in her voice and pressed her lips together, willing herself to calm. When she spoke again, her voice was as low as her mother's. "I do not take your meaning, my lady. What have I to defend myself against?"

Lady Chalcroft's lips pressed so tightly, her mouth appeared to disappear. Ah, Eleanor thought (for she knew that expression well), it was anger her mother was bottling.

"I require an explanation as to why you behaved in such an ill-bred manner on the front steps of our host's home. In front of a crowd—a crowd, Eleanor!—of people who will be keen to spread the tale of how Lady Eleanor Chalcroft threw herself at a nobody. A nobody who scorned her, I might add."

She felt her mother's words like a physical blow to her heart. Lady Chalcroft had always been a stern parent, expecting much more of her daughter than most mothers of the *ton* did their own offspring, but she had always been Eleanor's first supporter, bending over backwards to make sure Eleanor was given freedoms most young women weren't, and helping Eleanor hide and cope with her difficulties with written words.

It was a full minute before she was able to respond to her mother. She licked her lips and took a slow, steadying breath before saying, "I do not believe I threw myself at anyone. I went to the aid of a friend who was being sorely abused by...by a man who should have been proud to call him son. Lord Southampton was an utter brute. It was his—"

"Lord Southampton is not my daughter. I care not what he said or did. You should have had the presence of mind to remove yourself from such a disgraceful situation."

"I sought to stand by—"

"Yes, yes, your 'friend.' Tell me; who is this friend and why have I never met him if he is so worthy of your support."

Eleanor felt her heart pounding, her hands grow clammy. "He is Mr. Fitzhugh. Alex Fitzhugh. His father is the earl, though they are estranged."

"Few men are close to their illegitimate offspring," her mother said coldly and Eleanor didn't know if she was more shocked at Lady Chalcroft's tone or the fact that her mother had mentioned illegitimate offspring. It was certainly one of those topics on the mental lists of "do NOT discuss."

"He is not—he is Lord Southampton's legitimate son and heir. He sought to reconcile with the earl before he presented himself to you and father."

Lady Chalcroft's expression did not soften. Eleanor cast a desperate glance at her father who had heretofore remained hidden behind his newspaper. She saw that the paper was now lowered and her father's expression was somber. Eleanor silently pleaded for his assistance.

"I believe young Fitzhugh to be telling the truth—about his parentage, anyway," he said to his wife. "I don't think you were out in society when the Southamptons had their falling out."

"Be that as it may, you do not handle such personal matters in a public arena. You especially do not subject a young lady of good family to the type of gossip that such a scene will spark." Turning to Eleanor, Lady Chalcroft's voice rose. "Do you have any idea what people will say about you?"

"What could they possibly say? I did nothing beyond try to assist him to stand when Southampton attacked him— without provocation, I might add."

"You threw yourself to the ground, sobbing, begging for him to take you with him."

"What?? I did no—"

"He had to pry you off his leg. He said in a loud voice he never cared for you, only sought your dowry, and could never want a woman who behaved in such a manner. Then he left while you fainted into a heap in the dirt."

"That is patently untrue!" Eleanor cried. "Why would you say such horrible things?" The weight she'd felt like a strike against her heart intensified. She had no idea how her own mother could speak so cruelly, so falsely. "Why would you say such terrible things?"

"I did not say them. That description came to me by way of the Duchess of Devonshire. Yes, Lord Dunsbury's mother. Because we are friends, she came to me directly last night to warn me of what had happened, that I might be prepared for the fallout."

"But that's not what happened!" Eleanor protested. She felt hot tears race down her cheeks but she didn't even bother to wipe them away. "Father, tell her please! You were there. You know that's not what occurred!"

Lord Chalcroft spent an inordinate amount of time folding his paper and setting it aside. "I know that's not what occurred and your mother does as well. But Eleanor, that's what Lord Dunsbury's *mother* reported and she is a close friend of the family. Imagine what those who aren't friends will say."

"With your popularity these past three years comes jealousy, Eleanor," her mother said more gently. "There are those who will delight in your downfall, who will embellish what they've heard to make it sound more salacious."

"But it wasn't salacious—"

"It doesn't matter, Eleanor!" her mother said sharply, and then more gently, "It doesn't matter."

Eleanor sat in stunned silence, staring at her mother whose face was a pale mask of grief and disappointment. Her father's expression was filled with sympathy.

"What—" Eleanor's voice cracked and she swallowed before speaking again. "What do I do now?"

Lady Chalcroft pressed a hand to her mouth and turned her gaze back out the window, an act that worried Eleanor more than anything else. Her mother was unflappable. She'd had an answer for every question Eleanor had ever asked. Even when she hadn't known if squirrels lived in nests like birds or holes like gophers, Lady Chalcroft had had an answer: "Rest assured, they live as cozily as you do in homes befitting their station." To which Eleanor had assumed they lived in turreted houses and slept beneath velvet coverlets, for at the age of eight, she thought squirrels were noble creatures, indeed.

Lord Chalcroft stepped into the silence. "We shall retire to Chalcroft Manor where we will regroup. Your mother will correspond with her friends and let them know that absolutely nothing untoward occurred. London is nearly empty at this time of year. With so few social events at which to gossip, people will forget about the incident and by next Season, there should be very little fallout."

Eleanor thought this was a very optimistic scenario and so, apparently, did her mother.

"The only way there will be little fallout is if we can get Lord Dunsbury to marry Eleanor before then. And I really don't see how that will happen. Clarice Dunsbury, friend though she may be, will not want to bring scandal to the family name."

"The duchy of Devonshire can weather this little tumult. We shall have them all up for hunting next month," said her father confidently.

Eleanor stared from one parent to the next. "But I don't wish to marry Lord Dunsbury."

Her mother turned to her with an expression of disbelief on her face. "I don't see how that has any bearing on the matter. If we can coax an offer from him, you will accept and be thankful that his feelings for you were greater than his concern for a fiancée who's the topic of sensational gossip."

"His feelings for me? I don't believe he has any feelings for me beyond that of an acquaintance. And what of my feelings? I love Mr.—"

Her mother made a sharp hand gesture cutting off her words. "Do not speak that man's name to me. Your feeling will evaporate as rapidly as he did once he realized Southampton wasn't buying into his plea."

"That's not fair!" Eleanor protested.

"Life is seldom fair, Eleanor," her mother said firmly.

"Father?" Eleanor asked, remembering that he had always wanted her happiness above a marriage of status.

"I'm afraid—well, while I perhaps don't share your mother's grim outlook on life's fairness, I'm afraid her plan is the best we can hope for. Even if Southampton relented and reconciled with this Fitzhugh and he was able to convince me that he was worthy of you. No," he said when Eleanor would have spoken to defend Alex. "He should have settled matters with Southampton before coming to the Blakely's ball. That was bad form and I would tell him so to his face. It shows impetuous judgment and I would scrutinize his character even more before I agreed to let him marry you."

"So I'm to have no say in who I wed, then?" Eleanor said petulantly.

"I would say your judgment has proven rather impetuous as well," her mother cut in, then pressed her lips tightly together as if regretting her outburst.

"Of course you have a say in who you wed. But as your father, I must insure the man is worthy of you and our family. Lord Dunsbury, if he is able to rise above this incident, will prove himself worthy of protecting and caring for you."

"But I don't love him!"

Lady Chalcroft started to speak but at a glance from her husband, returned her gaze to the window and remained silent. Her father continued, "I am sure that once you get to know him and see how suited he is to you, you will grow to love him. Successful marriages are rarely based on the infatuation that we take for being in love."

"That is perhaps the most disheartening statement I have ever heard," Eleanor said softly.

Her father smiled sadly. "Don't be disheartened. Trust me in this. Now," he continued briskly. "Let us turn our thoughts to where we will stop for luncheon. Last time the Lazy Gander was not up to your mother's standards. I think we should give the White Rose a try."

Eleanor made an attempt at a smile for her father's benefit. It had always bothered him to see her unhappy and since there was clearly nothing to be done today, it was the least she could do to lessen his distress.

Their journey home proceeded in uneasy silence. Eleanor vacillated between the sweet torment of remembering stolen kisses in a library, passionate embraces in his room while the rain pounded on the windows, the feeling of utterly understanding and being understood by another person, and the bewildering despair of those last minutes with Alex when he seemed so completely different from the man she thought she knew, when he'd spewed hatred and contempt at her. She wondered where he was now, if he'd had any further contact with Southampton, if he would try to contact her.

During the next day in the carriage, her parents began discussing the events they would host before the weather made travel difficult. Eleanor was trying to distract herself by practically hanging out the open window of the carriage, studying the passing landscape. When she heard Lord Dunsbury's name mentioned, however, she sat back and while still pretending to look out the window, she listened intently to her parent's conversation.

The entire Dunsbury family would be invited in September if correspondence between the duchess and Lady Chalcroft remained cordial. Eleanor's mother was full of ideas to woo Lord Dunsbury and convince him that Eleanor was an innocent victim in the unfortunate scene with Southampton.

Eleanor bit her lower lip to keep from responding. She knew her mother had no idea of the depths of her feelings for Alex Fitzhugh, knew she wanted only the best for her daughter, but the thought of marrying another man was unimaginable. In fact, given her increasingly mixed feeling about Alex, the thought of marrying *any* man was unappealing.

She felt her head start to pound, as it did when she tried too hard to make the words on a page stay still. She massaged her temples and told herself she could figure something out. Oh if only Juliette were here. Her friend's unflappable demeanor and dry sense of humor would be inordinately calming. They would hatch some mad scheme, laugh about it, and then figure out a real plan. She hoped Jacob Wilding's plans to win Juliette had gone better than hers and Alex's, and that her friend was now deliriously happy. Juliette deserved nothing less.

She spent the remainder of the trip determinedly focusing on her friend and imagining a splendid wedding gown for her. It was difficult to think of anything wedding related considering the shambles of her matrimonial plans, but it was infinitely more productive that ruminating on her own miserable predicament.

Chapter 12

For all her parent's talk about hosting social events as though nothing had happened, when they returned to Chalcroft Manor, they refused all invitations, putting out that Lady Chalcroft was ill. Eleanor's mother did keep much to her rooms and while she seemed to write volume's worth of letters, she rarely seemed to post any of them, instead asking the butler twice daily if any letters had been received.

After a week of isolation, a letter did arrive, but it was for Eleanor. She took it with some trepidation; would Alex have written her? It seemed in order; an explanation of his actions, an apology, perhaps a begging of forgiveness.

Though she'd never seen his handwriting before, one glance at the script addressed to her told her it was not from him. She battled a feeling of intense disappointment even as she was glad to see that the letter was from Juliette. She tore it open standing in the hall, scanning the beautifully written words. But as was always the case, when she tried to read something quickly, the letters hopped about even more frantically. With a sigh of frustration, Eleanor shoved the missive in her pocket and set out for the walk she'd been about to embark upon when the letter was delivered.

She walked for nearly an hour before she took a seat in the covered folly and willed her mind to relax. She slowly withdrew the letter and trying not to strain, allowed her eyes to slide over the words. While she couldn't make out all the words, she was able to decipher Juliette's message. "Thank heavens!" she exclaimed, for it appeared that Juliette and Jacob

Wilding had finally come to their senses and planned to marry —as soon as the banns were read, it appeared. She stared at some of the dancing words, sure that juicy details were contained therein, but she only succeeded in bringing on the start of a headache.

"It doesn't matter," she told herself as she carefully refolded the letter. "I will get all the details from Juliette herself. And I shall remind her that she has me to credit entirely with her happiness!"

Back inside the house, she asked after her mother's whereabouts until a maid directed her to her mother's private drawing room upstairs. Eleanor knocked lightly and took a deep breath when bid to enter.

"Good day, mother. You look well this morning." In truth, Lady Chalcroft was rather pale, as she had been since their return. But she was dressed as if to receive callers and her hair was, as always, perfectly coiffed.

"Eleanor," her mother said with a glance up from the letter she was reading. Then she looked again at her daughter. "You're looking rather sun-dappled. I hope you didn't go out without a bonnet. You know how I've warned you about the detrimental effects of the sun on your complexion."

Eleanor hadn't been outside without a bonnet since she was six years old. Besides being rather vain about her complexion, she also loved hats and wearing them had never been a point of contention for her. But rather than remind her mother of those facts, she simply said, "Of course not, mother. My rosy glow is simply excitement."

"Oh?" her mother replied, turning back to her letter. "What is there to be excited about?"

"Juliette and Lord Worthing are engaged to be married. The wedding will take place in just a fortnight."

At that, Lady Chalcroft set the letter down altogether and stared out the window. "I am happy for Juliette. She is a fine young woman. I suspect you played a strong hand in their matchmaking?"

"Well, only in so far as to help them see how well they got along." When her mother remained silently staring out the window, Eleanor found herself rambling on. "I—I know father had hoped Lord Worthing and I might hit it off, but really, anyone could see that he and Juliette were a perfect match and he and I really weren't suited to one another."

"No, you don't seem to prefer the men who would be considered acceptable husbands by your parents or society."

Eleanor recoiled as if her mother had struck her. She stood silent, unsure of how to respond. Her mother drew her gaze slowly from the window and looked at her daughter. "I suppose you wish to go to Miss Aston's wedding?"

"I do. She is my dearest friend."

"You do not think you will bring censure on yourself, spoil the wedding with ugly gossip directed at you?"

Eleanor frowned. "If people would censure me for going to the aid of a friend—"

"Clearly you considered him to be more than a friend."

Eleanor took a deep breath and held it for a moment before releasing it as quietly as possible. She had no idea what she thought of Alex anymore. Each day seemed to bring a new emotion: longing, anger, frustration, grief. She chose to ignore her mother's remark and instead said, "And as for ruining Juliette's wedding, I shall do no such thing. I believe she says it will be small affair. You know her family is not that prestigious." She pulled the letter out of her pocket and made to offer it to her mother.

"But surely Lord and Lady Wilding—" Lady Chalcroft finally noticed the letter and her daughter's pleading expression. Her lower lip trembled before she pursed it tightly against the upper lip. She took the letter from Eleanor and quickly read it over before folding it carefully and handing it back.

"You are correct. It will be a small affair."

"I...I could not tell. Is it to be the twenty-second or the twenty-fifth?" Twos and fives often flipped on her.

"The twenty-fifth. But I...I do not wish to go out just yet.

I will write your aunt Violet and see if she can be persuaded to chaperone you."

Lady Chalcroft's widowed older sister was a dour woman with a predilection for retiring early. Eleanor did not want to be stuck with her for five or six days—especially if her mother "warned" her about the "situation." Eleanor could hear Juliette commenting on her excessive use of emphasis, as if Eleanor had written her thoughts on a blackboard and Juliette was correcting them. The thought made her smile and miss her friend even more.

"It occurs to me that Juliette's great aunt and former chaperone will be travelling to the wedding as well. She is sure to pass right by us and I'm sure it would be no imposition for her to take me with her."

She saw her mother frown and rushed to convince her. "It's just that she'd be coming from London and we could hear, ah, what news there was. Besides," Eleanor had to carefully modulate her tone of voice. She needed to strike the right balance between sympathy and critique. "It upsets me how Aunt Violet is so critical of you, mother. I know we needs respect her position, but the way she seems to take every little issue and seize upon it..." She saw that her mother, rather than taking offense was considering her words and she pushed her argument a bit harder. "Well, she quite reminds me of a cat hoping a mouse will stick its neck out of a hole!"

"And I suppose I am the mouse in this scenario?" The first genuine smile in days tugged at her mother's mouth.

"Only the dainty adorable ones who we wish we could keep as pets instead of hand over to those mean cats."

At this, Lady Chalcroft laughed aloud and while it was only a quiet huff of air, it relieved Eleanor greatly to hear it. "Eleanor, I have known you only to run shrieking from the vicinity when any creature comes near you. You must realize how dubious my comparison to a rodent—regardless of how dainty and adorable—seems."

"Surely not every creature, mother. I quite like some animals, after all."

"Need I remind you of the day the squirrel perched upon the window sill of the drawing room last summer?"

"It merely surprised me, that's all. I quite liked squirrels as a child, after all."

Her mother cast her a skeptical look but spoke before Eleanor could say more. "At any rate, I confess you have the right of my sister Violet. She has ever sought to criticize me and she would never let me live this scandalous debacle down."

Eleanor clenched her teeth together to keep from contending yet again that she had done nothing scandalous.

"Very well, if you are certain Mrs. Smithsonly will not mind, I shall send her a note today."

"Mrs. Smithsonly and I grew quite close during our endeavors to see Juliette betrothed to Lord Worthing," Eleanor assured her.

Eleanor had other reasons for wanting to travel with Mrs. Smithsonly. A plan had been forming in her head—a mad idea that she would only enact if it she did not hear from Alex in the next fortnight.

Eleanor's prediction about Juliette's great aunt proved to be true and two weeks later on the arranged date, Mrs. Smithsonly drew up to Chalcroft Manor in her carriage. Once inside, she proceeded to interrogate Eleanor on the events at Henley.

"One only hears bits and pieces, especially now that everyone has scattered to their various country homes," Mrs. Smithsonly complained. "All I could get out of Gertie Bessom was that you'd quite tossed aside all social mores and practically flung yourself at that young nobody."

"He is not a nobody!" Eleanor hissed quietly, looking around to make sure her mother had not come downstairs yet. She ushered Mrs. Smithsonly into one of the smaller drawing rooms and closed the door.

"He happens to be the son of the earl of Southampton, who is an evil, heartless man."

"Southampton, you say? Oh my yes. He is, well I wouldn't say evil. Bitter, perhaps."

"Well what he did to his son was downright evil."

Mrs. Smithsonly frowned. "I don't recall Southampton having a son."

Eleanor took a deep breath, trying to think of the most succinct way to explain the situation when Mrs. Smithsonly sucked in a quick breath.

"Just a moment—I do remember something..." The older woman stared at Eleanor for a moment. "So it *was* true. Or rather, it wasn't."

Eleanor frowned in confusion and was about to ask Mrs. Smithsonly for clarification with the lady's brows drew together. "Are you certain he is Southampton's son?"

"If you saw him, you would not need to ask that question. The resemblance is striking."

"I always thought Southampton was a fool. Sending off his young wife because he thought she'd betrayed him instead of thanking God that she'd been able to coax seed out of him."

Eleanor felt her mouth drop at Mrs. Smithsonly's rather crude description. This feisty dowager was a far cry from the drowsy chaperone who had overseen Juliette's first two Seasons. She wondered what had changed the old woman, but decided they would have plenty of time to discuss that in the carriage. She had more important things to tell Mrs. Smithsonly now.

"How is your dear mother?" the dowager asked, glancing around as if surprised Lady Chalcroft had not joined them yet.

"I'm glad you asked, ma'am. She is quite distraught—"

"One needn't think too hard to discern why."

Eleanor stifled an exasperated sigh. "Yes, well, as I've explained—"

"Actually, you really haven't explained anything, dear."

For the second time in her life, Eleanor felt her jaw drop open. She paused a moment, debating how much time they had left before her mother came down to greet their guest.

Rallying her wits, she held up her hands. "I promise to tell you every last detail once we are on the road. In the meantime, I pray you will hear me out."

"Well carry on, my dear. I'm hardly stopping you."

Eleanor ignored that debatable point and spoke hurriedly. "This incident has affected my mother uncharacteristically hard. She knows society is always full of gross rumors and sensational stories and that they always blow over."

She saw the dowager's eyebrows rise and rushed to finish before the woman spoke again. "I assure you, my part in this incident was negligible. Once people know what truly happened, the only one who shall be maliciously talked about will be the earl. But in the meantime, won't you please spare my mother the agony of believing her only daughter has been shamed in front of her friends? I very much fear she will make herself ill if she dwells on this much more."

Mrs. Smithsonly sat in contemplative silence for several agonizing seconds. Just when Eleanor thought she would shriek with impatience, the dowager spoke. "You are wrong to believe that Southampton will be the one to suffer from this incident, as you call it. Even were he not a member of the peerage, he is a man and you are an unmarried young woman. You're not a first year debutante. You know as well as I that women are always held accountable for any social missteps and punished cruelly. I very much fear you may be ruined, my dear."

At this Eleanor felt the blood drain from her cheeks and her fingers went numb.

"But I like your mother very much and can sympathize with her situation. Therefore, I shall do as I believe you are asking, and lie about how big a fiasco you've created."

"I didn't—" Eleanor practically shouted.

Mrs. Smithsonly held up a hand to stay her. "As I just reminded you, it doesn't matter. You will still bear the brunt of the gossip. Now ring for refreshments and let us present a soothing façade for your dear mama. I do hope she's been notified of my arrival?"

Eleanor quickly tugged the bell pull and returned to her seat. "Of course, ma'am." She had sent her maid to inform her mother of Mrs. Smithsonly's arrival herself with specific instructions to first walk completely around Chalcroft Manor before doing so.

Lady Chalcroft arrived with the tea and sandwiches Eleanor had sent for and Mrs. Smithsonly proceeded to paint a benign picture of the gossip floating around London. Eleanor's mother seemed greatly relieved by Mrs. Smithsonly's overstated assurances and Eleanor knew it had been the kindest thing to do. Besides, she'd had a nagging certainty that if the gossip had proven too virulent, her mother might forbid her attending Juliette's wedding.

Eleanor and Mrs. Smithsonly departed the next morning and they weren't out of the drive before the older lady pounced on her temporary ward.

"Alright, I've deceived your mother for you. Now tell me everything."

Even though she'd been expecting it, Eleanor was a bit taken aback by Mrs. Smithsonly's keenness. She cleared her throat and smoothed her skirts. When she could delay no longer, she took a deep breath and told the older woman everything. From the first night she'd met Alexander Fitzhugh to their secret park meetings to—she paused as she thought yet again of the hours in Alex's rooms. No, she quickly decided. Mrs. Smithsonly didn't need to know *everything*. She proceeded to recall their understanding that Alex would offer for her once he'd approached his father. She finished with the long wait at Henley for Alex to appear and seek her father's permission, how she'd been unable to talk to him before he and his father had had their run in, and what she remembered of Southampton's cruel words.

Mrs. Smithsonly sat in thought for at least a mile. Eleanor worried her lower lip between her teeth as the old woman stared in contemplation at the velvet-covered squabs across from her. Finally, she spoke.

"And has Fitzhugh contacted you?"

Eleanor paused but knew there was no hiding from the question. "No."

"No? Not even a note?"

Eleanor shook her head, unable to make her voice work. It had been the most worrisome part of the past weeks, the lack of word from Alex. Wouldn't he want to know she was all right? Wouldn't he want to apologize for inadvertently putting her in such a terrible position? Wouldn't he want to further their courtship? Though she tried not to think of the negative possibilities behind his silence, her fears and doubts had grown each day she did not hear from him. Then, too, were the cruel things he'd said to her. At the time she brushed them off as his reaction to being made to feel like an outsider. But as each day passed with no contact from him, she couldn't help but wonder if he'd truly believed that she was only interested in a wealthy man and "endless gowns." Then there was that oblique comment about needing a tutor. She'd heard little "jokes" about her penchant for clothing since she was a young adolescent, but no one beyond her mother knew of her difficulties with the written word and as a result, she'd never heard an unkind word about it. For Alex to reference it, when he knew how self-conscious she was about it was the hardest thing for her to rationalize out of that horrible encounter.

"Hmmm," Mrs. Smithsonly tapped a gloved finger against her lips as she stared in contemplation out the window. Eleanor felt her stomach knot again.

"Well, he's either furious with you, and—assuming you've truly told me everything—unjustly so."

"I have!" Eleanor exclaimed.

"Or, he's mortified by the encounter and the fact that you were in the front row to see his disgrace."

It was Eleanor's turn to stare unseeing out the window as green fields rolled by. She had considered that Alex might feel humiliated by his father's actions, but surely he would realize that the shame was his father's and not his own.

Mrs. Smithsonly answered her unspoken question. "A man's pride can be a fragile thing. Especially a man in a difficult social position such as Mr. Fitzhugh's. For you to see him brought low, stripped of his dignity would be the worst thing. He could find himself unable to face you, even by letter."

"But I—"

"Yes, yes, you love him and don't think ill of him, but you've had a bit of a hasty courtship, haven't you? What assurances does he have that an earl's daughter would wish to be associated with a man with no name or fortune to offer her?"

Eleanor nodded and studied her gloved hands. She saw a stray thread poking out of a finger seam and tugged at it with her other hand. It was true that she and Alex had never even hinted at their feelings for one another: they'd made their oblique plans to marry without a single word about what was in their hearts. And if he had happened to hear that Lord Dunsbury had been courting her...she could see how he would feel ashamed to contact her. Another thought made her frown.

"But what if that's not the case? What if he is, as you say, furious with me? Why would he be angry? What could I have possibly done to provoke him?"

"Why nothing, of course."

"Then—" Eleanor began, but the older woman cut her off.

"Nothing except being born into a wealthy, respected family of title. Nothing except being terribly popular and able to draw men to your side with a snap of your fingers—"

"I never—"

Mrs. Smithsonly gave her A Look and Eleanor promptly pressed her lips together. "You know very well you've been able to draw every man you found even remotely appealing with barely a glance.

"Be that as it may," Mrs. Smithsonly plowed on before Eleanor could draw a breath. "If indeed he had heard that Devonshire's heir was sniffing at your heels, it would be natural to assume you would choose him over a nameless pauper.

Wouldn't you be angry if the person you were enamored of —who'd have everything in life simply given to them—were suddenly taking up with someone infinitely more suitable for them?"

Eleanor's brows drew together. She thought a moment and then said very low, "Yes, but only if I doubted their feelings. Only if I doubted every encounter we had shared. Only if —" her voice broke as she thought of the way Alex had looked at her when Dunsbury had pulled her away. She took a deep breath before continuing. "Only if I thought the very worst of that person."

Mrs. Smithsonly pressed her lips together and stared at Eleanor in sympathy. Several miles rolled by before she finally spoke and even then her voice was a bit raspy. "I do hope Juliette sent to London for her wedding gown. The seamstress in Berkhamstead knows nothing about proper fit. She has a fine hand for embroidery, but I very much fear Juliette will be wed in an elaborately embroidered sack."

Eleanor smiled in appreciation of Mrs. Smithsonly's attempts to distract her and said, "Juliette will be beautiful no matter what her dress looks like."

"Well, she is fortunate to have taken after her mother in looks. You should have seen her mother in her day. Why she ever chose to marry Sir Aston, I'm sure I can't say. Why she could have had…"

Mrs. Smithsonly proceeded to fill the remaining hours of the journey with light commentary on people long dead or at the very least, completely unknown to Eleanor. Fortunately for Eleanor, she had long since mastered the ability to appear attentive while her mind wandered.

She knew her mother nursed a secret hope that they would be able to salvage a match with Lord Dunsbury. She also knew that, even if Dunsbury were still interested, she could not marry him. Alex may have believed the worst of her, but falling in love with him had taught her a great deal about herself—things that didn't match up to the persona of the perfect debutante. She was curious to see just how different she really was from the careful façade she had spent years cultivating. To that end, an idea had taken root that was too mad to consider except in the darkest moments of her sleepless nights these past weeks. If she were brave enough—or foolish enough—to go through with it, she would need to implement it during this trip. She—her courage failed her at this point and she forced her attention back to Mrs. Smithsonly who was detailing how she was the mastermind behind the match behind Lord Worthing and Juliette.

Respect for her elders was too deeply ingrained in Eleanor's mind to allow her to contradict the matron, but she did smile to herself at Mrs. Smithsonly's outrageous claims of subterfuge and manipulation. Eleanor was confident in the role she had played in helping her friend find love and it was enough that her efforts were successful.

They arrived at Juliette's father's estate with just enough time to change for dinner. Juliette greeted her with a tight hug and a smile so heartfelt, Eleanor could only wonder at the joy she must be feeling. Her own heart ached a little with envy to see her friend's happiness, but she pushed the feeling aside. The next few days were for Juliette and Eleanor would not dampen her friend's celebration with her own woes.

"So," Juliette whispered, after pulling Eleanor aside before they went in to dinner. "What of that tall gentleman who captured your fancy?"

Eleanor started visibly. She realized that so much had happened since the two friends had last spoken, she didn't know where to begin. At her reaction, Juliette grinned. "Don't think you can hide it from me. I saw how enamored you were of him. Who is he? Tell me everything, but quickly. We'll have to go through as soon as Aunt Constance comes down."

Eleanor's vow to spare Juliette worry was sorely tested. She so longed for her friend's level-headed advice. Juliette knew just how to tell Eleanor what to do without making it seem like she was telling her what to do. But one glance at Lord Worthing, who stood across the room talking with guests but could not resist stealing glances at his betrothed, firmed her resolve.

"Oh you know me, Juliette. I can't even remember a man's name once the newness has worn off."

Her friend gave her a look, and in it Eleanor could see the family resemblance to Constance Smithsonly, so to distract her she said, "Introduce me to your fiancée."

"You already know him, you goose," Juliette said, though she was already turning toward Lord Worthing.

"Yes, but not as your future husband. Besides, he is greatly indebted to me. He'd have never found you if I hadn't given him your direction."

Juliette happily complied, clearly delighted to have any reason to be near Worthing who, for his part, was duly grateful for Eleanor's assistance.

She spent the rest of the evening trying to blend in with the wallpaper while Juliette held court. While many people had clearly not heard the gossip about her and were quite friendly, she had noticed a few censorious stares and knew it was only a matter of time before she was snubbed by everyone. She only hoped it was after the wedding, for she wanted nothing to spoil Juliette's day.

Hiding behind the rim of a teacup, she reflected that she and her friend had effectively swapped places—here Juliette was the reigning queen, laughing and dancing, sought out by all the other guests, while Eleanor sought refuge amongst the potted ferns.

"He's a fool, you know."

Eleanor started, splashing tea into her saucer. She turned to find that Lord Worthing had discovered her hiding place.

"I beg your pardon?"

"Fitzhugh."

Eleanor felt her heart clench at the man's name but kept her face smoothly impassive. "I'm sure I don't know what you're talking about."

"Of course not. I'm just making idle chit chat to avoid the wrath of Juliette's Aunt Constance who finds me a bit of a blockhead for not snatching up her niece earlier."

"Well, she has you on that count," Eleanor replied.

"Couldn't agree more. Still, Fitzhugh didn't handle his delicate situation well and I shall tell him so the next time I see him."

Eleanor forced herself to take a sip of tea before she said as casually as she could manage, "Oh? I wasn't aware you and Mr. Fitzhugh were acquainted."

"We're not. But I suppose since Juliette considers you the closest thing to a sister, that makes you and I practically related and so I feel compelled to do the brotherly thing."

"That is not necessary," she murmured, though she smiled at his caring. A thought struck her, "Does Juliette know?"

"Not that it would change how she feels about you, but no, she's not heard what I'm sure are wildly inaccurate stories."

A short, bitter laugh escaped Eleanor. "It doesn't matter if they're inaccurate. I'm the fool who fell in love with a no-account swindler and threw her good name away for a man who doesn't care enough about her to—" She clamped her lips shut and stared through the screen of palms at the partygoers.

"What of Dunsbury?"

"What of him?" she asked abruptly, her gaze still locked forward.

"I think he cares for you. I imagine if you..." His voice trailed off at the incredulous look Eleanor gave him.

"Forget I said that. I know you can't force yourself to love someone." His gaze scanned the crowd and his expression softened when he saw Juliette laughing with a group of relatives.

He turned back to Eleanor and said, "Just know that Juliette and I will stand by you no matter what."

Eleanor felt tears sting the back of her eyes and she gulped another swallow of tea to give herself a moment to push them away.

"Thank you, Lord Worthing," she said.

"And now if you will be alright, I should mingle with the other guests."

"Of course! I'm perfectly fine, I assure you." She gave him the smile she'd perfected over the years and while it was obvious Lord Worthing was not fooled by it, he squeezed her hand reassuringly and left her in her foliage hiding spot.

Juliette's wedding, though small by London standards, was beautiful and genuine. Sitting next to Aunt Constance, Eleanor shed tears of joy with most of the women in the church as a radiant Juliette became Lady Worthing.

Once they returned to Sir Aston's house for the wedding luncheon, however, Eleanor's invisibility seemed to melt away. She saw whispers behind hands and felt the resulting stares as knowledge of her "indiscretion" worked its way through the room like a rising tide. Still, Eleanor might have stuck it out, plastered to Aunt Constance's side and pretending she was unaware of the hostile glances cast her way, except that Aunt Constance had taken ill and retired. "Too much excitement," the elderly lady had declared. "And perhaps too many celebratory spirits, though I'll deny it to my deathbed if you dare repeat that."

At any rate, Eleanor was alone at the table while the rest of the guests who had finished eating were milling about. She might still have persevered—censorious glares were rarely fatal, after all—if she had simply been left alone. But some wrinkled dowager with bad breath and a sour look about her felt it necessary to cross the room to tell Eleanor how distasteful her presence was, especially at the celebration of a true lady such as Juliette.

"My mother taught me to treat the elderly with respect," Eleanor said, her voice shaking, "So I shan't tell you to your face what an ignorant old biddy you are." She stood to leave but the dowager gripped her wrist with a claw like strength.

"We all knew you'd come to no good. You were always too big for your britches, too spirited for polite society."

Eleanor was torn between the opposing desires to rage, cry, or laugh. She felt every muscle in her body tense with the strain to contain all three emotions and said coldly, "I have no idea who you are which leads me to believe you have even less understanding of who I am." She wanted to say more, wanted to cry out against the injustice of being judged for falling in love, but she could tell that the tears were winning the battle to escape her physical control so she pulled her arm from the old woman's grasp and fled the room.

Upstairs in the tiny guest room, she quickly threw her clothes into her trunk and rang for a maid. "Please have a groom fetch my trunk and instruct Mrs. Smithsonly's carriage to be readied."

She wasn't stealing Aunt Constance's carriage, she told herself, merely borrowing it. It would be back at Sir Aston's house by late evening and she was sure Aunt Constance wouldn't have need of it for several more days yet.

As she waited for the carriage to be readied, she went over the plan that had been forming in the back of her mind for the last week. It was ridiculous, really. Hare-brained, her father would say. Shocking, her mother would declare. But the more she thought about it, the more it made sense.

It was only a matter of time until the rest of society knew about her "scandalous" behavior. Once the Little Season opened and more people were in London, word of her downfall would spread like wildfire. In even less time, the story would take on a life of its own with embellishments and details that would have no basis in reality but would titillate all who heard of it. Numb at least for the moment to the insult of it, Eleanor couldn't blame anyone for reveling in her shame. It was like one of those romantic adventure penny dreadfuls Juliette was forever sneaking: lurid details and shocking actions were downright entertaining. If Eleanor had been able to make out more than a page of those books, she surely would have been as avid a reader as her friend.

It was also a given that Eleanor was ruined. Oh, her parents would surely find someone to marry her off to, though not Lord Dunsbury. It mattered not how close of friends their mothers were, Eleanor knew the Duchess of Devonshire would demand only the best for her son. And truth be told, Eleanor agreed. He was a good man and deserved better than she could give him. He deserved someone who loved him. Nonetheless, they would find someone—perhaps an elderly titled gentleman who didn't pay heed to gossip or lived in the wilds of the Lake District or Yorkshire where people were more concerned with the quality of their sheep than the reputation of a young miss they'd never heard of. The problem was, Eleanor didn't want to be married off. Her parents had allowed her the freedom to reject suitor after suitor because they were utterly confident she would make a brilliant match in the end. She'd assumed she'd have to settle on a man eventually, she'd just held out hope he'd stir her heart and fire her blood. Well, she'd found that passion, for all the good it had done her. She'd found it, lost it, and had no desire to revisit it again. But neither did she want a marriage of convenience to a man as old as her father, who would see her as nothing more than a trophy—or worse, a brood mare.

"The carriage is ready, my lady, and your trunk is loaded. Are you sure I shouldn't call for Mrs. Smithsonly?" the maid said, clearly dying of curiosity but trying to appear circumspect.

"I've already spoken with dear Aunt Constance. She is confident I shall come to no harm on this short portion of my journey. And," she improvised hastily. "My parents will have sent their coach to pick me up in Berkhamstead," she said, referring to the small town nearby.

If the maid wondered why her parent's carriage wouldn't simply come the extra distance to pick her up directly, she didn't mention it. Eleanor nodded a dismissal and descended the staircase as quickly and unobtrusively as possible. She paused twice when first a matronly woman then a young man walked through the entrance hall en route to the powder room or perhaps the card room, but fortunately neither person had glanced up. As she neared the last few steps, she took a deep breath, kept her head down, and raced across the parquet floor to the door and her waiting carriage.

Her heart beat as if she were having one of her attacks, but as she kept glancing back and saw no one in pursuit—she almost smiled at the thought of being pursued like a cutpurse —both her heart and breathing slowed. As the carriage turned out of the long drive onto the road, she sat back and continued her train of thought from earlier.

Upon reconsideration, she decided that her parents would not *force* her to marry. Of that she was fairly confident. But the thought of living year after year with her mother's quiet disappointment and her father's perplexed gaze made her stomach clench and her palms grow clammy.

But more than that, something had fundamentally changed in her that night on the steps of Lord Blakely's manor. Or perhaps it was in the days and weeks that followed when Alex remained silent and she'd had countless hours to wonder what had gone wrong. Regardless, she was no longer the same naïve, sheltered young woman she had been. Neither was she going to dwell in heartbroken banishment. Somewhere in days following the arrival of Juliette's letter, a plan had budded in her mind. A rash, perhaps foolhardy plan, but one that she believed would give her the fresh start she so desperately desired.

She would make her way to London and she would seek out Cousin Sarah. They had barely spoken a handful of times as Cousin Sarah was rarely invited to family events, and even more rarely attended. Their conversations had been stilted as was to be expected with two women so completely divergent in interest. And yet, something told Eleanor that Sarah Draper would, if not understand her need to change her life, at least support it.

As the carriage drew to a halt in front of the posting inn

where Eleanor planned to purchase a seat on a public coach—
something she'd never before done—a worrisome thought occurred to her. How on earth would she manage her large, well-
packed trunk? She might be able to pay the coachman to load
it for her but once she reached London? Thinking frantically,
she stepped from the carriage and instructed the footman to
bring her trunk inside the inn. Once there she procured a room
(to the consternation of the prune-faced inn keeper's wife) and
had her trunk delivered there.

"Please inform me when the London coach arrives," she
said tartly, hoping to brazen her way through this. Young
women did *not* take rooms in public houses.

"Mmph," was the disapproving reply, but a boy was called
for and her trunk wrestled to a small room on the second floor.
Quickly opening it, she rifled through the contents. She owned
few gowns could that could be considered plain but she had
snuck her two most somber frocks into the trunk at home.
Had her maid Mary seen them, she surely would have pulled
them out. Thank heavens she had convinced her mother that
traveling with a maid was unnecessary. She'd told Lady Chalcroft Juliette's maid would serve them both, but in truth, she'd
planned her time at Juliette's wedding to be a crash course in
dressing herself.

Pulling out the gowns—a dark blue with a fine white print
and a burgundy with a prim high collar, she bundled them as
neatly as possible and wrapped them in the one pelisse she'd
brought. The few bits of jewelry she'd brought she wrapped in
a chemise with her comb and tucked it in the middle of her
bundle. She opened her reticule, counted out her funds, and
spied her small silver card case. A thought occurred to her
and she took one of the creamy cards out and looked about
for a quill. She didn't travel with writing instruments as she
avoided writing as much as reading, so she marched downstairs and asked for a pen and ink with scarcely a quaver in her
voice.

She took a deep breath to calm her mind and willed herself to see the words before she wrote them. "I am fine. I am safe. I shall return home in time." That was all the room she had with her blocky lettering, but it would have to do. She didn't expect it would keep her father from scouring England looking for her, but perhaps it would alleviate her parents' greatest worry—that she'd been kidnapped.

"The coach to London's pulled up," the prune-faced woman announced.

"I shall be down directly," Eleanor replied with more confidence.

Rushing upstairs, she placed the calling card in the center of her trunk and shut the lid. She plucked a threadbare table covering off the rickety bedside table and draped it over the luggage. Gathering up her bundle of clothes as if it were the most natural thing for a lady to do, she returned downstairs, paid her fare, and boarded the oldest coach she'd ever seen.

The ride to London, though slightly crowded with two elderly gentlemen and a young mother with her son, was not as intimidating as she'd anticipated. They pulled into London in late afternoon and stopped at a posting inn as the sun was setting.

Eleanor climbed down, stiff from the cramped accommodations, to a dizzying array of sights and smells, few of them pleasant. Gathering her bundle in tightly, she quickly entered the common room of the inn. She pushed her way between two burly men and ran smack into the ample and nearly exposed bosom of a red-headed serving maid. The young woman held two tankards in each hand that she tilted to keep from spilling at Eleanor's collision. "I'd think ye was takin' liberties had ye a cock. Yer not hidin' one under them skirts, are ye?" she said, laughing at Eleanor's wide eyes and flushed cheeks. She moved adroitly through the full room to deliver her ale and Eleanor pushed through the throngs as quickly as possible. Behind a timeworn wooden bar, she spotted a man who appeared to be in charge. After several attempts to gain his attention, she beat her fist on the planks and said as loudly as possible, "Excuse me!" He didn't stop filling tankards from a large vat beside him, but he nodded in acknowledgement.

"I am in need of a room."

"That's too bad. We're full."

"Full?" Eleanor asked, stupefied. "How can that be?"

The innkeeper didn't even glance up. "Because I've people in the rooms."

He turned to speak to a serving maid and dazed, Eleanor looked around the bustling common room, completely at a loss. Gathering her wits, she asked if there were other inns nearby. She had to repeat her question before the busy innkeeper admitted that there were, "But they're most likely full too. Market tomorrow."

"But surely—" Eleanor began but the man had turned to draw a pitcher of ale.

Clutching her small bundle of clothes, she pushed her way to the front door of the inn. Outside the front of the inn was lit with torches. She stood in their warm glow wondering what on earth she could do. She supposed she could hire a hackney coach to take her to her family's town home, but she had no idea if there was even a caretaker present to open it. Besides, that would be the ultimate defeat: barely making it to London only to retreat to the safety of her father's house. She was trying to ignore the idea of a night spent out of doors that was making her heart beat an anxious pattern in her chest. Flickers of the night she'd spent lost outside as a child flitted through her mind.

She wasn't aware she'd been chewing her bottom lip until a country-accented voice interrupted her worried reverie.

"Are ye alright, then, miss?"

Eleanor turned to see the young mother from the carriage, her arms full of a sleeping boy.

"I—" she began, then shook her head to dispel her more frightful thoughts. "There's no room at the inn."

"Ach, this is the more popular inn," the young woman replied with a nod. "They've a reputation for their kidney pies and their buxom serving maids."

"I've no idea of the quality of the pies, but I can attest to the state of the maids," Eleanor replied, feeling the tightness in her throat ease a bit.

The young mother laughed and shifted the weight of her sleeping child. Eleanor had no idea how old the boy was, but his legs dangled nearly to his mother's knees.

"Allow me," Eleanor said as she relived the woman of the bulging canvas bag dangling from her straining arm.

"Thank ye. He's only six," she said, indicating her sleeping son with a movement of her chin. "But he takes after her father who's a tall man. Well," she said with a laugh. "He takes after him in his ability to fall asleep anywhere as well!"

Eleanor smiled but couldn't think of a thing to say.

"Have ye another place to stay then?" The woman asked. "Or family you are here to see?"

Eleanor shook her head no then paused. "Well, I've come to London to find my cousin but I don't have her direction beyond Southwark."

The woman's eyes flitted over the cut and fabric of Eleanor's gown. "Sure it's Southwark? That's a rough area."

"Yes. I've heard." She hadn't, of course, but it seemed the thing to say.

"Well ye'll not want to be wandering Southwark at night. You need a place to stay. Ye'll not want to be wandering Southwark in the day either, but that's a worry for tomorrow."

"Do you...do you know where I might find a room? The innkeeper here said every inn was full tonight."

"I've no doubt. No," she said with a shake of her head. "I'm sure there's no room to be had in this part of town. But a lady like yerself should not stay alone regardless. Come with me. I'm staying with my parents. They'll find room for ye as well."

"Are you sure?" Eleanor asked hesitantly. She didn't know what the etiquette of the situation would be, but she was truly terrified of not having a place to stay.

"Ach, aye, they'll have a place, though it'll no doubt be

cramped since my sister and her unruly lot moved in with them. Besides, if ye save me from havin' to carry that bag and this boy, I'll give ye my own bed!" she finished with a laugh.

Chapter 13

Two years later...

Alex Fitzhugh stood at the helm of his newest ship, the *Marianna*, his knees softening to take the swell of the waves beneath the hull. He had a captain and a crew full of men who could take the wheel, but he'd started a tradition of bringing each new ship into harbor and he liked the connection to the wood of the ship, the salt spray of the sea, and the kiss of the sun.

He was returning from nearly five months in India where he'd set up his second field office, trained a manager, and met with suppliers. He'd fallen in love with the heat and color of India, the food and the people, but he was looking forward to settling into his own home in London. He'd purchased a large but rundown town house from a viscount who'd outspent his income for too many years. The place had fallen into such disrepair that it was uninhabitable, so Alex had hired a team of contractors and given them three months while he was out of the country to renovate it. Since he was two months later than he'd planned, he figured the contractors should almost be finishing up with the work.

The sun was just setting over London's crowded skyline when the *Marianna* was finally secured and the crew paid. By the time Alex found a hackney cab and made his way to Mayfair to his town house, he was ready for nothing more than a hot bath and the extra-long bed he'd ordered made. Drawing up in front of his residence, it was clear that neither would be possible. Not only was the house dark, scaffolding still masked the front and piles of lumber littered the side yards. With a curse, he wondered what had become of the staff he'd hired to put the insides to right.

He called out to the driver to take him to the Charing Cross Coaching Inn where'd he'd stayed when first coming to London. With a start, he realized he had no need to stay in a humble coaching inn any longer. He rapped on the coach window again, redirecting the driver to the Cavendish Hotel.

Alex sat back in the worn leather seat with a feeling of satisfaction. This was the first time in nearly two years he'd actually recognized his successes. Of course he'd seen his bankbook balance grow, but it had always been with the idea that he had more capital to invest in merchandise or a warehouse or another ship.

He'd scarce had time six months ago to meet with the estate agent who had found his house, much less the contractors to give them their marching orders. He could scarce remember the inside of his tiny set of rooms on Knightsbridge, as he'd spent every day of the last two years in his equally tiny office in the west docks, on board his ships, or more recently, setting up his two field offices—the first in Morocco, the second in India.

He would forever be indebted to Arthur Anderson whose offhand comment at their chance meeting more than two years ago had been the basis for Alex's business plan. Bringing in more affordable luxuries for the common man had proved even more lucrative than the expensive items the *ton* purchased.

The hackney coach pulled to a stop in front of the imposing façade of the Cavendish Hotel. A footman opened the door and Alex leapt down, tossing a coin to the driver. He checked in and followed the young man carrying his luggage to his suite on the third floor.

The richly appointed rooms seemed ridiculously large after the tiny quarters on board the Marianna. In fact, his old rooms on Knightsbridge would probably fit in this suite's bathing room.

Tossing his jacket onto a chair, Alex crossed to a buffet and poured himself a drink. A maid lit a small fire and the candles before leaving and the light cast a mellow glow on the dark brocades of the furniture and rich patterns of the rug underfoot.

Suddenly alone for the first time in months, he felt the hectic rush of his new business slowly slide from his shoulders, and a feeling of deep contentment filled him. He sat in front of the fire and rested his booted feet on the grate.

There was still so much he wanted to do with his business, but he'd brought it further than he'd ever thought possible in so short a time. Still, it had been a killing pace. He would spend a few months in London seeing his house finished and enjoying it. There was certainly plenty to do in town while his hired captains sailed the seas. Perhaps he would even see about acquiring a mistress. He had no idea how one did that, but some companionship of the feminine variety would be greatly welcomed after months in the company of rough sailors. He hadn't enjoyed the more refined company of a woman since—

Alex surged to his feet, tossed back the last of his drink, and grabbed his coat. He was in need of a meal and perhaps a good deal more alcohol. Though he was appreciative of his ability to stay in a fine hotel, when it came to grabbing hearty food and a pint without a wait or the encumbrance of manners, the Cock Tavern was Alex's favorite spot. A platter of cold meats, two bowls of the tavern's famous soup, and a third pint of beer later, Alex sat back in his chair and sighed contentedly. The headaches of having to deal with his contractors while still running his growing shipping business seemed much more manageable on a full stomach.

"By Jove! It's Fitzhugh!" roared a drunken voice Alex recognized as his old school friend Taggart, whom he'd last seen at the Blakely ball two years ago on the most humiliating night of his life. He braced himself for awkward questions, but Taggart was so deep in his cups he could barely shake Alex's hand.

"How've you been, ol' boy?" Taggart asked. "No, wait. *Where've* you been? I've not seen you in—" here he paused and seemed to count random numbers on his fingers before dropping his hands and finishing, "In a bloody long time!"

"Good to see you too Taggart. I've been building my business, traveling quite a bit as a result."

"Well it's been too long by half!" his friend exclaimed enthusiastically.

"It has," Alex agreed and was surprised to find he meant it. Taggart had been a steadfast friend since their school days and he had been wrong to avoid him.

"You must join us!" Taggart declared. "We've heard of a new dance hall with girls fresh from Paris!"

"I've only returned to London this afternoon," Alex said with a shake of his head. "The only bed I'm seeking tonight is my own."

Taggart scowled as he tried to decipher what Alex had said. Finally, giving up he asked, "Does that mean no?"

Alex smiled and slapped his friend on the back. "It means not tonight."

"Oh very well," his friend said. "But you will join me tomorrow—I've scads of entertainment planned. Where are you staying?"

Alex told him, convinced Taggart's alcohol-sodden brain wouldn't remember, then made his way back to the Cavendish where he luxuriated in a bed in which he could actually stretch to his full height.

The next day, he travelled to his warehouse down by the docks where he was to meet with his man of business and address some of the issues that had arisen in his absence. As he sifted through the pile of personal correspondence on his desk, he was frankly shocked to see a heavy cream envelope bearing his father's crest. He forced his hands to calmly slit the edge of the paper with his penknife and slowly withdrew the thick sheet of paper within. It was a request for Alex to call upon Southampton as soon as he returned to London. The earl, it would seem, was desirous of civil conversation

He shoved the missive in his jacket pocket and forced his mind not to wonder at the reason for the old man's sudden change of heart. Southampton had made very clear in Henley how utterly he detested Alex's very presence. This letter was downright conciliatory. With a shake of his head, he looked up as his man of affairs entered the office, glad there was a pile of work to take his mind off the letter.

As it happened, Taggart did remember Alex's hotel, but it was nearly a week later before Alex finally felt he had the time to take the evening off and enjoy his friend's company. They started at a gaming hell but rapidly progressed through an assortment of clubs before Taggart finally dragged him to a ball.

"No, old boy. Anything but that," Alex protested—genuinely reluctant. Though it had been two years, his last brush with the nobility had left a bad taste in his mouth. And though he'd deny it with his dying breath, he was loath to run into Eleanor Chalcroft, though surely by now she had a new last name; Dunsbury if he were a betting man.

Taggart would not be denied, however. "I promised Lord Hubert I would stop by. It's his wife's first ball, by which I mean it's the first one they've hosted since marrying. He's ridiculously besotted with her and he wants to make sure her first event is a success which is why he's pulled out all the stops and cajoled all his old friends into making an appearance."

"Why don't you stop by and we'll meet up afterwards at the club?"

But Taggart would not be denied and Alex found himself walking up the lantern-lit steps to a large town house, trying to tamp down the uncomfortable memories of the last ball he'd attended. He hadn't seen Southampton since that awful night—hadn't seen anyone in "society," busy as he'd been building his business. He was fairly confident he would not run into the man tonight or any night, really, but it occurred to him again that he could very well see Eleanor. He wondered dispassionately if she were a duchess yet. He had no idea if the old duke had died and it didn't really matter, of course. He just hoped to hell she was not at the ball tonight. He cursed Taggart for forcing him to come to this blasted event. Inside it was a mad crush and the two men pushed their way through to the refreshment table where the few remaining crumbs implied the food had been better than was normally provided at events such as this.

"Drat," said Taggart. "Hubert promised me good food as a reward for showing up."

At that moment a servant appeared bearing a tray stacked with delicate finger sandwiches. Taggart loaded a plate with two handfuls of sandwiches and barely stepped out of the way before devouring them.

"Aren't you eating?" he asked around a mouthful of food.

"How is it you are considered to be a gentleman of noble birth when you eat with the manners of a hog at the trough?"

"What? I'm hungry!" Taggart protested, swiping a glass of punch off the tray of a passing footman. "Besides, I've never seen a hog before."

"You don't say," Alex remarked drily.

When Taggart was finished, he announced his intention to find and pay his respects to their host. "Then we're off," he promised.

They took up a position alongside the dance floor as it allowed them the clearest view of the room. As Alex had never met their host, he was of no assistance and found himself unconsciously scanning the dancers on the floor. While there were innumerable blondes curtsying and twirling on the floor, none had that distinctive sheen of old gold. He realized he was straining to hear a laugh like the chiming of bells, but all he could discern was the jumbled buzz of hundreds of conversations over the music. He felt the tense knot beneath his breastbone begin to dissolve when suddenly he saw Lord Dunsbury making his way off the parquet floor. His entire body tensed and he moved to his right to keep the man in his line of site.

Dunsbury's partner was a petite brunette, but surely he would return to his wife's side. A large group of young men halfway in their cups pushed past him and he lost sight of Dunsbury.

"Come on, move along," he muttered, craning his neck to see over them. After they passed, it took him several moments to locate Dunsbury again. He was faintly surprised to see an elegant woman with chestnut hair on Dunsbury's arm. Dunsbury smiled at her possessively and they chatted with an ease that belied a familiarity greater than mere acquaintances.

"Ah, I see Hubert." Taggart's exclamation broke Alex's reverie and he started.

"Come along, I'll have us in that new gaming club in no time."

"Taggart, wait." His friend paused, his eyebrows raised in question.

Alex found his throat was suddenly dry and he had to clear it to force himself to speak.

"What is it old man? Have a burning desire to dance the quadrille?"

Alex ignored the jest and jerked his chin to indicate Dunsbury.

"Dunsbury. Lord Dunsbury."

Taggart glanced across the room and nodded. "Yes, that's him. Did you wish to make your greetings?"

Alex shook his head sharply. "Did he…did he not marry Lady Eleanor Chalcroft?" He heard the quaver in his voice and was ashamed of it, but could not quell it.

Taggart's smile faded. "Don't say you don't know? Oh but you couldn't, I suppose, busy as you were sailing the seven seas and becoming a shipping—"

"Taggart!" Alex rasped.

"No, old boy. She didn't marry him. Good lord, how to tell you? Here, let's get out of this crush." Taggart led the way to a small alcove. Alex could still see Dunsbury through the scrim of a potted palm.

Taggart took a deep breath and suddenly Alex feared the

worst.

"Lady Eleanor disappeared nearly two years ago."

"What? What do you mean, *disappeared*?" Alex felt his hands curl into fists and the muscles in his neck tightened.

Taggart shrugged. "She just...disappeared. It was a few months after...well after Blakely's ball. You know—"

"Yes, I know," Alex said tightly. "Go on."

"Well not many people know the actual details, but my mother is a close friend of the Chalcrofts. Lady Eleanor went with a family friend to a wedding—Worthing and some chit—"

A memory sparked in Alex's mind and he interrupted, "Juliette. Lady Eleanor's dearest friend."

"Yes, that sounds right. Well, at any rate, Lady Eleanor left during the wedding festivities leaving a note saying she was fine, but she hasn't been seen or heard from since."

Alex felt the blood drain from his face. "And Dunsbury?"

"He married Mrs. Catherine Purcell not three months after the Blakely ball. A widow, she was. Not at all what his mother wanted for him, so I heard." He shuddered and Alex knew he was in sympathy with Dunsbury.

"Then he and Lady Eleanor were never betrothed?"

"Dunsbury and Lady Eleanor?" Taggart said, surprised. "Not that I'd ever heard."

It was the oddest thing, really, the physical reaction Alex was experiencing, as if he were slightly outside his body with scarcely any feeling in his fingers or toes. He wondered if this was what ladies felt like when they had a fainting spell.

"I say, old boy, are you quite alright?" Taggart said, clutching Alex's arm.

With a Herculean effort, Alex pulled himself together. "Yes, yes. Of course," he said, though he knew Taggart didn't believe him. Showing a bit more sensitivity than Alex would have ever given him credit for, however, his friend remained silent, just squeezing his arm briefly before dropping his hand and looking out at the crowd.

"Ah, there is Lord Hubert. I'll just go say hello and meet

you at the coach, shall I?"

Alex nodded, distracted, and didn't notice Taggart's departure. He tried to reconcile what he'd just learned with what he'd thought for two long years, what he'd heard Eleanor's own mother claim. And then, with a sick feeling in his stomach, with how he had treated Eleanor when he'd thought she'd toyed with his heart.

But it had been her mother who'd sworn her daughter would be the next Duchess of Devonshire, his brain argued. Who would know better? Eleanor hadn't said so, his heart answered. And either way, you acted like a complete ass, it added for good measure. His brain was silent, having no rejoinder for that. He had been an ass, pushing Eleanor away when she'd knelt by his side with tears in her eyes.

For two years he'd avoided thinking of Eleanor, of the emotions she'd brought to life in him and how horribly it had all ended. Every once in a while during the past two years, he'd catch sight of shiny gold curls and his heart would freeze until he saw that it wasn't her. That was nothing compared to when he heard a laugh that sounded like hers. She'd told him how ridiculous she thought it was that people had made such a to do over what she considered to be a rather braying sound, but Alex knew why her laugh had been famous. For all its melodious tones, it always sounded genuine, which made it unique in a sea of people who spoke and laughed without sincerity.

And so, anytime he heard a woman's laugh that reminded him of Eleanor, he knew that if he was to sleep that night, it would only be at the bottom of a bottle.

His traitorous dreams had replayed her sprawled beneath him in that small set of rooms he used to rent, or more fancifully, he would fantasize about her lying naked in the tall grass near his home in Cornwall. In each dream she would croon her love for him and the feeling the words evoked was as intense as the physical reaction. But when he would awake, he would punish himself by reliving that awful night when he'd learned that she'd never intended to marry him—a night compounded in hurt by the vile run-in with his father. Such musings inevitably put him in a foul mood, but they would allow him to force his thoughts and feelings for Eleanor away for weeks at a time.

To learn now that half of that awful night in Henley had not been as he'd believed it shook him to his core. His father was still a spawn of the devil, but Eleanor had never played him false. The tears she'd shed when she tried to help him up had been genuine. Dunsbury hadn't pulled her away because she was his intended, but because he was trying to shield her from censure and Southampton's unpleasantness as any gentleman would.

Bitter regret burned in his chest. If he'd not been so unsure of himself, if his father's rejection had not been so virulent or if he'd had time to get over it before seeing Eleanor and hearing the speculation about her betrothal, perhaps he would have waited, heard Eleanor out, seen the truth for himself, instead of leaping to devastating conclusions. And then to learn that Eleanor had disappeared? She must have been waiting to hear from him. Waiting for him to send a letter or show up at her father's house. What must she have thought when he did not? Alex closed his eyes, the bitter burn of regret like acid in his heart.

Suddenly the noise and gaiety was too much. He had to leave. Pushing his way through the throngs of talking and laughing people, he didn't hear his name called until he was in the much emptier hallway and headed down the stairs.

"Fitzhugh!"

It was not Taggart's voice calling him. Alex stopped and turned, shocked to see Eleanor's father rushing to catch up to him. He'd met the man but once, but his impression had been of a hale, vibrant man. While still recognizable, Lord Chalcroft was much thinner and grayer than he had been, with deep grooves along either side of his mouth.

Alex had no idea what to say to the man. Why on earth would Eleanor's father follow him: to call him out, perhaps? He certainly deserved it. He issued a brief bow and said, "Lord

Chalcroft."

Lord Chalcroft paused a moment to catch his breath or perhaps collect himself. Alex could not read from his expression what the man was feeling or thinking.

"My daughter," the older man finally said.

Wary, Alex said nothing, wondering if an accusation or threat was about to be issued, prepared to accept both as his due.

"Eleanor," Lord Chalcroft repeated, his voice holding a note of pleading. "Where is she?"

Taken aback, Alex said, "My lord?"

"She left to be with you, did she not? I told her mother once she set her heart on you we may as well give up, but her mother wanted the world for Eleanor."

"Lord Chalcroft, I—" Alex stopped, wishing for all the world that Eleanor had tracked him down, rung a peal over his head, and then married him.

"All is forgiven—tell her that, will you? We only wish to see her, know she is well."

Alex swallowed, feeling like broken glass was in his throat. "My lord...I've not seen Eleanor since Lord Blakely's ball in Henley." The words seemed not to register on the earl. He continued to stare expectantly at Alex.

"I do not know where she is."

Lord Chalcroft straightened as if pulling himself together. Without another word he turned to leave. Alex stopped him with a hand on his arm.

"I do not know where she is—I only just learned she was missing." At Lord Chalcroft's frown, Alex explained, "I've been abroad a good deal these last two years and...well, it doesn't matter.

"I will find her, Lord Chalcroft. I swear it."

At that the older man's face softened. "You think I haven't looked? You think I haven't had solicitors and investigators roaming the continent trying to find her?"

Alex paused. Of course the powerful marquess would

have had every resource at his fingertips. What more could Alex do? And yet, he felt keenly that he could not rest until he located Eleanor.

"I will find her," he insisted.

Lord Chalcroft smiled sadly. "I wish you every luck then." He turned again to go and this time, Alex let him.

Chapter 14

Eleanor straightened and pressed her hands to the small of her back to ease the ache there. A newborn's wail interrupted her and she turned to bend once again to the low pallet on which the new mother lay, exhausted but well. Eleanor tucked the swaddling more tightly around the baby and nestled it closer to its dozing mother.

"Ye'd make a fair midwife did ye set yer mind to it," said the old woman in the corner, packing her bag with the herbs and tools of her profession.

Eleanor smiled, "Ah but then who would be around to make sure Miss Sarah wasn't swindled by the butcher?"

The old midwife smiled in return. "Aye, don't know how she's managed so much in her short years, but ye've certainly helped her. Everyone says so. Still, the world always needs a midwife."

"Yes but I don't do so well with the births that don't go as smoothly as this one," she said, gesturing to the bed.

"Smoothly?" rasped a dry voice. Eleanor quickly fetched a cup of water and helped the young woman drink it. "Didn't feel so smooth from this end."

Eleanor chuckled at the jest and forbore from mentioning the half dozen births she'd attended where mother, child, or both had not survived the grueling process of delivery.

The first time, when a baby had been stillborn, she'd cried bitterly, unable to control her sobs until Nan, the old midwife, had shook her roughly by the shoulders.

"What good will your tears do, girl? Ten babies a day

die here in Southwark alone." The midwife's face softened as she'd looked at Eleanor. "Have ye naught seen a stillborn babe, then?"

Eleanor shook her head, wiping the tears from her face and forcing her emotions into check.

"Aye, well, I'm sorry to say this won't be your last. Poor food, worse water, and hard labor even before the work of birthing a babe mean death is as common an end result as life." She gently nudged Eleanor out of the room and said, "Get ye to home and have Miss Sarah give you a dose of brandy." At Eleanor's moue of distaste, she said, "No don't make that face at me. You're no gently bred miss are ye?"

"Not any longer," Eleanor had murmured and followed Nan's instructions that night and on all the successive childbed deaths she'd attended.

But tonight was a good night and so any libations would be of the celebratory kind.

Gathering her shawl and basket of supplies, Eleanor bade the new mother and Nan goodnight.

"Have one of the boys walk ye to home," Nan called after her.

Eleanor waved but didn't obey. In the two years since joining her cousin Sarah in her work here in the part of Southwark called the Mint, she'd gone from being a terrified young miss who jumped at every sound and shrank from the strangers on the streets to a woman who knew her way around the roughest streets of London. Being known as Sarah's assistant who helped people with food and medical care had given her no small amount of protection from the criminal elements of the borough.

She was not foolhardy, however, and kept her knife in hand beneath the folds of her shawl. She'd never had to actually use it, though Cousin Sarah had made sure she knew how to wield it, but she had pulled it out it as a deterrent on more than one occasion when she'd been concerned for her safety.

But now the sun was just dipping below the ragged skyline of tenements and the people in the street were more concerned with closing up shops and getting home than harassing a lone woman.

Eleanor passed by her favorite shop—an apothecary who routinely shared his vast knowledge about herbs and simples with her. She paused to glance in the small window but the angle of the sun had turned the thick panes into a reflective mirror. It took her a moment to realize that the young woman she was seeing was herself.

Cousin Sarah's tiny set of rooms had no mirror and Eleanor had long since grown accustomed to arranging her hair and smoothing her collar without one. Now, however, she saw a young woman who was both familiar and strange. Lacking a ladies' maid, curling tongs, or rose-scented pomades, her hair was pulled back into a simple knot at the nape of her neck. Her dress—one of the two she had brought with her two years ago—had been turned, but the color was faded and her cuffs were beginning to fray.

But beyond her physical appearance, the greatest change Eleanor saw was in her carriage: she held her shoulders back strongly, her head held high. She'd lost the delicate plumpness that had given her soft curves, but she knew she was physically strong. Two years of working with Cousin Sarah trying to feed, clothe, and tend the desperately poor of Southwark had honed her. She would not be considered the epitome of English womanhood in a ballroom now, but Eleanor realized she much preferred her new appearance.

"Hey bird," said a rough voice as a large hand sought the curve of her waist. "Fancy something in there do ye? How bout ye make it worth me while to buy it for ye?"

Eleanor whirled around, knocking his arm away and wielding her knife close to her body but clearly visible.

"Why don't I wing you instead and send you home to your mother?"

Far from being threatened, the rough man laughed. "Easy now, pigeon. I was only making an offer. Now put your wee pig sticker down and let's get a pint to start our friendship off right."

They were joined by a second man and Eleanor's apprehension grew. She knew she'd be recognized in any of the pubs they might go into, but she was afraid the men might change their minds about getting an ale. She wondered if the apothecary was still in his shop and if he'd hear her if she screamed.

"C'mon ye lout. We're late enow as it is," said the newcomer.

"Hold on," said Eleanor's antagonist. "I've found me a fresh one and I've a mind to take her wiv us for a bit o'sport."

The second man glanced fully at Eleanor then smacked his friend on the side of his head.

"Oi! What'd ye do that fer?"

"Leave this bird be. She helped me mam last spring when she was on her deathbed. Pulled her right back from the brink, she did." With a tug at his cap, the man gripped his friend by the neck and steered him away from Eleanor.

She felt the tension leave her shoulders and she loosened her death grip on the handle of her knife. Taking a deep breath, she willed her racing heart to slow, then looked around to make sure there were no other immediate threats before turning and hurriedly walking back to the set of rooms she shared with her cousin.

Though she still felt the pulse of urgency from the encounter, Eleanor felt no qualms or fears as she wended her way through the maze of streets. And that, she realized with a smile, was her greatest change.

From her first night in London, she should have suffered nervous attack after nervous attack, worrying about where she would stay and how she would find her cousin. But something had changed inside her. From the moment she'd made the decision to leave her old life behind and start anew, she'd felt nothing but a bullheaded determination to see it through. That first night when she'd been taken in by the young mother from the traveling coach had reinforced her determination and banished the overwhelming fear she'd experienced outside since she was a child.

Reaching her destination, she climbed the three narrow flights of stairs in the shabby but somewhat respectable building where she lived with Sarah. She unlocked the door, then stooped to pick up a sealed note that had been slipped under the door. No doubt another request for assistance. Her cousin was unable to say no to the residents and other aid societies in Southwark and such notes were a frequent occurrence.

Eleanor tossed the note on the small table at which they ate, drank tea, sewed, and answered correspondence. Her inability to read properly was of little concern in a borough where most people signed their names with an X and relied on the pictures on shop signs to determine what was sold inside.

She could have helped Sarah more had she been able to pen letters requesting money or supplies from their various patrons, but Sarah had never begrudged Eleanor her difficulties with the written word.

A clatter at the door heralded the entrance of Sarah. They greeted one another warmly and Eleanor pointed out the note that had been delivered.

"Shall we wager what aid we'll need to cobble together?" Eleanor joked as Sarah opened the missive and began reading.

Her cousin was a tall brunette with dark eyes beneath two severe slashes of brows. Her nose was straight and no-nonsense with no cute upturn or softening ball at the end. Eleanor had seen Sarah's wide mouth curved in laughter and smile with joy, but those occasions were few and far between. She'd set herself a mammoth task trying to eradicate poverty in London's poorest neighborhoods and the never-ending work usually left her mouth compressed in a determined line. Now, however, it was pinched with disgust and tears glittered in her brown eyes.

"Sarah! Whatever is wrong?"

In response, her cousin handed her the now crumpled note. Eleanor scanned the florid handwriting and noticed the elaborate seal at the top but could not calm her mind enough to focus on deciphering the rippling words.

"What does it say?"

Sarah beat her fists against her thighs, and took a deep breath, forcing her emotions under control. She took the note back and stared at it, though Eleanor suspected the words by now were just as jumbled for Sarah as they had been for her.

"They've withdrawn their support."

"What? Who?" Eleanor asked, urging her cousin to sit and putting a kettle on to boil.

"Oh no, don't waste the tea on me. Save it for something important."

Before coming to Southwark, Eleanor had never considered the cost of tea. She would order whole pots discarded if she thought the flavor off or if it cooled too quickly. Now she knew the exact cost per ounce and knew that they'd only been able to afford it these past six months because a new shipping magnate had begun bringing lower priced luxuries into England to appeal to those who had to pinch every farthing.

"Nonsense. This is clearly important and there is nothing so soothing as a cup to put things into perspective."

Sarah huffed a short laugh but tears escaped her eyes. Unnerved, Eleanor bustled about, collecting their meager tea utensils. She put a hot cup into Sarah's hands and sat across from her.

"What has happened?" she asked as calmly as she could.

Sarah took a fortifying sip and smiled. "How silly I am."

"You're not—"

"The Ladies' Compassion Society has withdrawn their financial support from our program."

"What?" Eleanor gasped. The Ladies' Compassion Society, the LCS as Eleanor and Sarah referred to the ungainly-named group, was their main source of funding. Comprised of the wealthiest ladies of the ton, the group held lavish though rather ineffective fundraisers but nonetheless wrote hefty checks to Sarah, which she used to house, feed, and provide medical care for hundreds of families.

They received funds from several other groups and individuals—a church, a wealthy merchant who remembered his humble roots—but for nearly five years, the LCS had been Sarah's financial backbone.

"Do they say why?"

Sarah picked up the letter. "They feel five years is a sufficient length of time to support one organization. They're going to focus their fundraising on a war widow's group."

"But more than half of the families we help *are* war widows!" Eleanor exclaimed.

"That's not the worst of it. They have concerns that the money is not being used wisely."

"What?" Eleanor shrieked. "Are they mad? How are food, shelter, and medicine not a wise use of their money?"

"I believe they are implying that I am using funds for my personal use."

"That is complete bollocks!"

Sarah choked on her tea and laughed. "I don't believe I've ever heard you use such…colorful language before, dear."

"Yes, well," said Eleanor, flushing. "Desperate times call for desperate measures. The point is, don't they know absolutely every penny they give goes to the poor?"

Sarah had a small annuity from an inheritance. Had she remained "in society," and not married, she would have had to take a position as a companion or governess in order to make enough to live alone respectably, but here in Southwark, she was able to pay her meager rent and buy a new gown or cloak every three or four years.

Eleanor had arrived two years ago with a small amount of cash and a handful of jewelry, which she'd sold with Sarah's help. She had thought it was enough to last her a few weeks, but with Sarah's instruction, she still had enough to support herself for at least another year.

As a result, the notion that she and Sarah were somehow living in luxury off the donations to Sarah's organization was preposterous.

"We have to show them," Eleanor decided. "Have them come visit. Show them your ledgers," she said, gesturing to the stack of cloth-covered books in which Sarah kept track of every farthing she spent.

"Those ladies would never come here, Eleanor. Would you have?"

"Yes, well, I was a ninny. I thought helping the poor meant donating my old ball gowns once a year. What did you do with those, by the way?"

"Sold them of course. Taffeta and silk are not much use here, as you've learned, so we sold them for a mere fraction of what they cost, I'm sure. The point being, even for the ladies who invest a little more into our cause than you did, the notion of coming to The Mint would be outside their realm of possibility."

"Then we will have to go to them. Write them and ask for a meeting. You can convince them, Sarah. I know you can."

Sarah smiled sadly. "I know you think highly of me, dear, but to the ladies of the Compassion Society, I am scarcely a step above the people I seek to help, having abandoned polite society so many years ago. They would not receive me and if they did, they would not be predisposed to change their minds."

"Then I will have to go," said Eleanor, surprising herself as much as Sarah. "They will surely listen to the daughter of an earl."

"Don't be silly. There's no way word of your visit would not reach your parents. They've never stopped looking for you. Why it was only last week someone was asking after a blond lady of high birth over on Clack Street."

"What? Why did you not tell me?"

"I didn't want to worry you. Besides, it was young Robbie MacGibbons who brought me word. He told the man asking that a lady of good birth would be mad to take up here, that she wouldn't last a day without—well, wouldn't last a day."

Eleanor nodded, somewhat assured. Robbie Mac was a

bright young man, one who surely would have gone far in life had he been born into even the lowest merchant or tradesman class. Doomed as he was to have been born into abject poverty, he made the most of his quick wits by knowing everything there was to know about the goings on in the borough. Eleanor suspected he knew she was much more than she appeared and that she was hiding from someone, but he had also taken a brotherly liking to her, showing her the ropes of life in the tenements and she trusted him implicitly. Still…

"If one man has come, more will follow. It is only a matter of time before I am discovered," Eleanor said pragmatically, doing a good job of suppressing the tremor in her voice. "I would rather be found out on my own terms. And if I can do some good for your organization—"

"*Our* organization," Sarah interrupted. "You've given of yourself completely. Together we've accomplished so much more than I ever could have alone."

Eleanor smiled, her eyes watering.

"Besides which," Sarah continued. "You've been the greatest friend to me. I don't need to tell you how lonely a vocation this is. We are outcast from the society into which we were born but there always seems to be some distance between us and the people we seek to serve. But since you've come, I've felt like I was not alone anymore."

The tears that had flooded Eleanor's eyes now spilled over. She swiped at them before clutching her cousin's hands across the table.

"If I have helped you, you have changed my life. Who knew I had abilities beyond choosing the right gown for an occasion or making a man feel like everything he uttered was the most fascinating thing I've ever heard?"

Sarah laughed and rummaged in her battered reticule, pulling out two threadbare but clean handkerchiefs.

"You are so much more than that," she said firmly. "Though I wouldn't discount the skill of knowing how to dress. I fear I wouldn't know a spot of lace if it choked me."

They finished their now cold tea and Eleanor carefully set down her empty cup.

"I think I shall have to first reconcile with my parents before seeking to influence the LCS. I shall no doubt need their assistance."

"Well you should reconcile with them first no matter what your intentions," Sarah said. "They love you very much and I am certain your absence has been devastating for them."

"Of course...I just mean, my influence as a marquess's daughter is only as great as the marquess's support of me."

Sarah nodded. "How do you think they'll respond? Your parents, I mean, not the LCS."

Eleanor pressed her lips together. "I...I think they'll welcome me back. I did send them those letters through Juliette, letting them know I was safe. I know they've been hurt and I'm sure my mother was bitterly disappointed I did not make the match of the century,"

"Surely she wanted more for you than to simply marry," Sarah said with a frown.

Eleanor laughed. "You've been too long away from the *ton*, Sarah. That is all a young woman of good birth can aspire to: making a good match."

"Have you ever regretted not marrying?"

"You know I haven't," Eleanor assured her.

"You might yet, of course. You're still very young."

"You're scarcely three years my senior! Besides, I can't imagine leaving my life here. I feel so much more...fulfilled. Can you imagine any of the men who courted me before allowing me to continue my work? Now, help me write my parents to warn them of my impending return. Have we any ink left?"

"There should be enough for a letter or two."

"Good. I think I shall enlist the aid of Juliette. Next to you, she's been the best friend I've ever had."

Chapter 15

A fortnight later, Alex ran his hands through his hair in frustration. He'd had investigators retracing Lady Eleanor's stops from Sir Aston's home in Hertfordshire all the way to a coach inn in London, but there she seemed to disappear into thin air. He knew her father had reached the same conclusion; he had simply hoped he might have more luck, find someone who'd seen where she went, who'd taken her in.

He absolutely would not allow himself to consider that any harm had befallen her. She was too good at charming people. He just knew if she'd encountered anyone who wished her ill, she'd have them eating out of her palm in a quarter hour. Alex recognized this was an incredibly naïve thought. He'd enough experience in the world to know there was a whole class of people who had nothing but malice in their veins, regardless of their station in life, but he would torture himself to insanity if he let his imagination go down that path.

He knotted his cravat and inspected the results in the mirror. He should probably employ the services of a valet soon. He was preparing to attend the first ball he'd been invited to on his own merits. It was not the upper tier of society, but it was a clear indication that he was making a name for himself, he thought. His wealth and business were beginning to attract attention. Unless, he thought grimly, this had something to do with his father. He'd still not answered the old man's summons, even though the latest missive had been written in what he assumed to be the old earl's own hand.

Gaining acceptance into the ton had never been one of his

goals—the few weeks he'd hoped to win Eleanor aside—but his growing wealth and business interactions with those noblemen who were seeking to augment their estate income by investing in his growing ventures had pulled him into the outer fringes of society.

He made his way downstairs and had one of the hotel footmen flag a coach for him.

Once at the ball, he and Taggart made the rounds, greeting those people who received him, meeting a few, mostly young noblemen who wished to attach their dwindling fortunes to his growing business.

He and Taggart took up a position just off the dance floor where the opening cotillion was just starting.

"Can we find the gaming room now?" Taggart asked. "I've had as much bright light as I can handle."

Alex glanced at the warm golden glow cast on the hundreds of guests. "I'd hardly call candlelight blinding."

"I prefer my candlelight diffused with a comforting layer of cigar smoke," Taggart explained, his bleary eyes glancing balefully at the sparkling chandeliers overhead.

Alex huffed a brief laugh. "You should be looking for a wife. Isn't that what men of your position do at your age?"

Taggart shuddered and took two small steps back as a swishing skirt from the dance floor swept past.

"My family's title is not so prestigious that it won't survive being passed onto a distant cousin."

Alex smiled at his friend whose aversion to all things involving young marriage-minded women had started back in school. Actually, he suspected Taggart's aversion was to all women, but Alex would never ask him about it; Taggart had always been a good friend and Alex had no desire to put him on the spot.

He slapped Taggart on the back. "You're right, old boy. I was just teasing. You'd make a terrible husband."

"I would, wouldn't I? I've always appreciated your honesty, Fitz."

Alex nodded distractedly, and glanced at the double doors where a couple was just being announced. They looked familiar, but Alex could not place them until he heard their names.

"Lord and Lady Worthing," the butler called out. Worthing was Eleanor's former suitor who had married... Eleanor's best friend.

He started and made to move to intercept them in the crush of people. Perhaps Eleanor had been in touch with her friend, Lady Worthing. He lost sight of the couple as a crowd of debutants and young men pushed between them. He craned his neck to determine which direction they were moving when the next announcement froze him in his tracks.

"The Marquess and Marchioness of Chalcroft and their daughter, Lady Eleanor Chalcroft."

A hush fell over the entire ballroom. Or perhaps—more likely, a part of Alex's brain observed—perhaps it was the roar in his ears that drowned out all other sounds. That roar abruptly receded and was replaced with the decided increase in volume of conversation as people informed their ignorant neighbors of the significance of Lady Eleanor's arrival.

He pushed his way through the throngs of people until he could see her.

She was very composed, though there were two patches of color high on her cheeks. Her coiffure was absent the shiny ringlets she used to favor. Instead, it was smoothed back off her face in a simple chignon.

Her gown, while perfectly fitted, was equally simple, a rich dark green muslin edged in matching velvet ribbon, but no flounces or lace.

The family had scarcely made it a dozen steps into the ballroom when they were stopped by many people wishing to pay their respects in theory, but no doubt wishing in truth to learn the details behind Eleanor's absence.

Alex saw Eleanor's friend Lady Worthing double back and link her arm through her friend's, offering moral support. Eleanor smiled her thanks but seemed perfectly composed as she greeted old friends. Alex wished he had a right to approach her, but knew he'd lost that right on the front steps of Lord Blakely's home in Henley. He contented himself with watching her from a partially obscured nook behind a tall column. A potted palm allowed him further camouflage as he watched the Chalcroft family make their slow way through the crowds of people.

Whatever Eleanor had been doing or wherever she had been, she seemed to have suffered no ill effects. She was more slender than she had been two years previously, and the loss of her fashionably plump cheeks made her appear older and more mature, though perhaps that was also due to the way she held herself. She'd always had a graceful carriage, but now there was a stillness to her—an economy of motion that was lacking in the young ladies of the ton who fluttered their fans and coyly tilted their heads.

Alex felt a tight knot form in his chest at the hurt he had caused her. The fact that it was her mother's own words that had influenced him bought him no relief. He should have trusted her as she'd clearly trusted him to show up and approach her father.

"There you are, old boy! What are you doing skulking in the shrubbery?" Taggart handed him a glass of spirits and pretended to be absorbed in watching the dancers while Alex took a drink and collected himself.

"I see Chalmers is about to find himself betrothed to one of the Patterson daughters, though don't ask me to tell you which one. Those chits look like they were pressed with a biscuit mold, so identical are they to one another. I dare say, I wouldn't be surprised to learn he'd kissed one in the garden but asked for another's hand from their father."

Alex had no idea who his friend was talking about, but he appreciated the time for the brandy to work its magic on him as the knot in his chest unwound enough to talk.

"Taggart," he said. His friend turned expectantly and Alex felt himself gaping like a fish out of water.

Taggart indicated he should take another sip and said, "She's been living in Southwark with a relative."

Alex choked on the mouthful of spirits, causing his eyes to water and throat to burn. "Southwark?"

Taggart pounded him none-too-gently on the back. "Yes, according to what I overheard while looking for you. Not near as exciting as if she'd been living in Paris if you ask me, but of course you won't, seeing as how you're head over heels for her."

"What? I—"

Taggart waved his hand dismissively. "You were completely smitten with her two years ago and I can only assume since she took such radical action as to leave her family that you broke her heart."

Alex's fingers tightened painfully on his glass at the words "broke her heart." Self-loathing coursed through his veins as well as bitter regret that he had lost the one person in the world who had loved him.

"How'd it happen, old man?"

Alex hesitated but realized he needed another person's opinion, and though Taggart had travelled to Henley with him, he didn't know the details behind the evening's debacle. He briefly outlined Eleanor's directive to approach her father in Henley, his failed attempts at meeting with his father here in London, overhearing Lady Chalcroft's assertion that her daughter would be marrying Dunsbury, and then the final humiliating occurrence on the front steps with his father and Eleanor.

Taggart whistled low between his teeth. "I say, you fucked that up good and proper, didn't you?"

Alex almost laughed at his friend's accurate summation. "No sense in doing a poor job of fucking it up," he mumbled.

"What are you going to do about it now?"

Alex glanced over to where Eleanor was now nodding regally to a distinguished-looking gentleman.

"What the hell can I do but try to stay out of her life?"

"If you do any such thing, I shall call you out as a base coward." Though the tone was joking, Alex heard his friend's truth and turned to stare at Eleanor again. She must have felt his gaze, for he saw her brows crease right before she glanced in his direction. He ducked back behind the column and scowled as Taggart snorted with laughter.

"You've faced the dangers of months at sea, yet the gaze of Lady Eleanor sends you scurrying for cover."

"Shut up, Taggart," Alex grumbled, a reluctant smile tugging at his mouth. "Make yourself useful why don't you, and try to find out what she's been doing in Southwark."

Taggart executed a mocking bow. "Aye aye, my captain." And with that, he wove his way through the partygoers with the grace of a panther and approached his quarry, the outer edges of the group of people surrounding Eleanor, with the focus of a hawk going after a pigeon.

He met up again with Alex, who was skulking behind yet another potted plant, nearly an hour later, but the din of conversation was at such a level that Alex could scarcely hear him.

"Let's get out of here," Alex told his friend. "I need a drink stronger than this watered down brew."

In the coach en route to their club, Taggart shared what he'd learned of Eleanor's missing years.

"Apparently she was struck with the inspiration to run off and save the world. In Southwark. The Mint."

"The Mint?" Alex said, appalled. Burly men hesitated entering that borough for fear of being robbed, attacked, or worse. The thought of Eleanor living there for two years was unfathomable. Eleanor with her anxious attacks when she was outside in unfamiliar places; how had she survived?

"What was she doing there? What do you mean by 'saving the world'?"

"Just that, old boy. She has an acquaintance, or perhaps it's a cousin? At any rate, this person runs some sort of business feeding the poor, though it doesn't seem there'd be much money to be made feeding people who can't afford food."

"A charity, you dolt," Alex said.

"No need to grow offensive," Taggart said, frowning at the interruption. "Now where was I? Ah yes, so she went off to feed the poor and teach them to read, thus saving the world from having to see more of those—"

"Teach them to read?" Alex interjected, remembering the difficulty Eleanor had making out letters.

"Their sums, perhaps? I know there was food in there. She's been a sister of mercy at any rate, though I wonder at how her reputation will fare, having lived there and mingling with the lesser sorts."

"Her parents seemed to be supportive tonight," Alex mused.

"Yes, well, Chalcroft always doted on her if I recall"

"And her friend...Juliette Worthing?"

"Ah yes, wife to the future Earl of Beverly. Yes, she's got some backing. We'll have to see what the society papers say tomorrow. They'll either applaud her as a paragon or crucify her as a who—fallen woman."

"Did you learn why she's returned now?" Alex asked, squelching the ridiculous thought that she may have heard of his successful business and rise in society.

"Something about bringing attention to the plight of the suffering women and children, which of course means her charity needs money. What I want to know is why no one cares about suffering men?"

The coach drew to a stop in front of their club and Alex thumped his friend on the back as they climbed down.

"That's because it's usually the men causing the suffering."

Chapter 16

Despite the rather late night (by her current standards—they'd left the party at one in the morning, unheard of when balls often lasted until three or four), Eleanor awoke shortly after sunrise. Two years of rising before dawn and going to bed by nine had reset her body clock. In Southwark at night there was little enough candle or firelight to warrant staying up late. Then too, she and Sarah were usually exhausted from their long days of cooking and serving food, lugging meals to those too infirm to come to their small shop-front, and the endless rounds of visiting the ill and wounded, dispensing what herbs and tinctures they'd been able to afford from the apothecary.

Add to that the daily rounds of tending the random children whose mothers had found a day's work, and trying to talk the pickpockets out of their given profession, and it was no wonder that both young women often found their heads nodding over their suppers.

She rose from her bed and went to light a small fire before washing and dressing. She sniffed the finely milled honeysuckle-scented soap, closing her eyes in pure enjoyment at the simple luxury. When she'd joined cousin Sarah, she put away all thoughts of the many comforts she had always taken for granted. Though having to haul and heat her own bathing water had been a huge adjustment—as had learning to cook and set broken bones—she'd thrown herself into the process, refusing to even think of the first twenty-one years of her life.

Now, however, she found a childlike delight in what she used to take for granted, like down pillows, desserts, and servants to haul hot water for an actual bath.

Without thinking, she made the bed and only as she set the last pillow on it did she laugh at herself, remembering the horror on her chambermaid's face when she walked in on Eleanor straightening sheets last week.

Her growling stomach reminded her she'd been too nervous the night before to eat supper. She made her way downstairs to the kitchens where the staff, still unnerved by her presence, had grown accustomed to her dashing in to help herself to tea and biscuits.

Hours later the butler announced the arrival of Lady Worthing.

"Juliette!" she said, running to hug her friend, though she'd just seen her the night before.

"What are you working on so industriously?" Juliette asked, pointing at the huge workbasket on the floor and the piles of fabric spread across the damask-covered sofas.

"I'm tearing old linen sheets into bandages. Here, help me roll," she said, handing Juliette a handful of strips.

Juliette removed her hat and gloves with a laugh. "I always knew you had hidden depths, Eleanor, but somehow I never pictured you rolling bandages."

"I'll go mad if I don't do something," Eleanor said and then used her teeth to start another tear. "Besides, you've no idea how quickly we go through bandages. They're worth their weight in gold."

"Surely not gold," Juliette said with a smile that faded at Eleanor's earnest expression.

"If you'd seen a young boy die for want of a clean dressing on his wound, Juliette but—oh!" she said, clapping a hand over her mouth. "I forgot I mustn't share such stories with you. Mother will have my head if she knows I'm telling you gutter stories in your condition."

Juliette shook her head and laughed. "I haven't even begun to show, Eleanor," she said, lightly resting her hand on her midriff. "Besides, my constitution is not so frail as that. But what are 'gutter stories'?"

Eleanor stacked the neatly rolled bandage in her work-basket. "That's what mother calls it when I start talking about my life in the Mint—that's the area of Southwark where cousin Sarah and I live and work. She doesn't mean it unkindly, I don't think. She just doesn't really know what to make of my life there."

"Well you must admit, it was a bit out of character for you to run off to work in the poorest slums in London, not to mention doing so without a word to your family." There was no judgment in Juliette's voice, but Eleanor recognized the trauma she'd forced her parents to endure.

"I did write," she said meekly.

Juliette moved to sit next to Eleanor and put her arm around her. "I know, dear. But you must credit your mother with handling your return with a great deal of grace and not hold it against her if she's unable to understand what exactly you were doing there."

"I was helping—"

"Yes, yes. That's what you do now, but that's not why you fled there in the first place."

Eleanor sat in silence, tugging at a loose thread on one of the rolls of linen. She knew Juliette wouldn't force her to talk of her disastrous and brief courtship, but she'd not discussed it with another soul in the two years she'd been in Southwark. Cousin Sarah knew something traumatic had happened, but with her own mysterious background, she'd never asked Eleanor for details.

Now, however, Eleanor found herself wanting—no, craving—Juliette's advice. Her friend had always supported her and she knew she would not judge her rather unorthodox behavior.

"Well, you remember Mr. Fitzhugh."

"The tall chap with the chestnut hair? I do."

"You probably suspected I was taken with him."

"Only from the first moment you met him," Juliette said

with a smile. "Yes, I remember, though at the time I thought you mad for not appreciating Lord Worthing."

"Yes, you ninny, because he was clearly meant for you! Well, Mr. Fitzhugh, he seemed to return my regard and things progressed rather quickly between us."

Juliette's brows rose. "Did you—"

Eleanor felt her cheeks warm at the memory the rainy afternoon in his flat.

"Say no more," Juliette said, suppressing a smile.

"We…well, we had an understanding, I was sure of it. But you know my parents. They wouldn't have allowed me to marry a man without a title. He's the Earl of Southampton's son, you know."

"I've heard rumors to that effect, yes."

"You have? But—"

"Later," Juliette admonished. "Finish your story."

Eleanor nodded. "I don't believe Mr. Fitzhugh had originally planned to approach his father—we never got round to exactly why they were estranged—but he decided to seek his recognition so that mother would at least entertain his suit."

"But he was not successful," Juliette said.

"No. He—well I'm not sure what happened here in London. He was going to speak with him here and then travel to Henley to speak to my father but I didn't see him until the final event."

"Lord Blakely's ball?"

Eleanor nodded. "He and his father were having words. I don't remember exactly what the old man said, but it was horrible. Mean and vile."

That was a lie of course Eleanor remembered every world the Earl of Southampton had said, but she could not bear to repeat the things the bitter old man had said.

"So your parents denied Mr. Fitzhugh's request to court you?"

"He never even spoke with them. I approached Southampton as they were arguing, hoping I could smooth things out. I though surely the earl would not be so rude with a lady present."

Juliette's laugh was a faint huff and Eleanor returned it with a half-smile.

"Yes, well, he *shouldn't* have spoken like that in front of me. But then he should not have spoken thus to his very own son."

"What happened next?"

Eleanor frowned. "The earl's own footmen tried to remove Mr. Fitzhugh by force. There was a bit of an altercation. I —" she stared unseeing at her clasped hands. "The next thing I knew, Mr. Fitzhugh was outside at the bottom of Blakely's stairs. I rushed to him to assist him, but—" Eleanor was surprised when her voice broke. It had been more than two years, after all. Clearing her throat she continued, "But he pushed me away. He said—he said I should go ahead and marry Dunsbury, that I wasn't worth the bother."

"Not worth the bother?" Juliette repeated, incensed.

It wasn't what he'd said, of course. He'd made a crack about Eleanor needing a tutor, but she could not bring herself to confess that. It was too painful. Besides, she'd never told Juliette of her reading difficulties.

"Well, perhaps not those exact words, but he made it clear he wanted nothing to do with me. He stormed off into the night and I never saw him again. When I realized he did not intend to contact me. Yes," she said at Juliette's raised eyebrows. "Yes, I thought it was a misunderstanding and that he would at least write to clear it up. I'll admit it, I was an utter ninny."

"You were in love," Juliette protested softly. "When you love someone, you are willing to forgive things."

Eleanor nodded her head slowly, remembering those awful weeks after the Blakely ball.

"Well, mother was keen to marry me off right away to quell the gossip and this time father did not gainsay her."

"Is that when the idea of joining your cousin came to you?"

Eleanor frowned. "I'm not really sure when the idea formed." She paused, thinking of the beggar girl who had shared her name. Perhaps that encounter had planted the seed. She shrugged. "All I know is that I had to do something different with my life. I had to learn what I was capable of."

"Clearly a great deal, if you must know!" Juliette said passionately. "Have you truly been delivering babies?"

"Only six by myself. I'm really only an assistant. I help what physicians and midwives cousin Sarah can coerce into donating their services. The babes I delivered were simply too impatient to wait until the midwife arrived."

"Was it terrifying?" Juliette asked, and Eleanor saw her fingers twitch against her midriff. She smiled reassuringly at her friend.

"Not at all. It's a good deal of work on the mother's side, but it's a straightforward, natural process. You will rise to the challenge spectacularly!"

She pushed the memories of the women and babes who had not survived the grueling process from her mind. As Lady Worthing, Juliette would be well fed, warm, and rested when her time came. The women she'd had to wrap in linens with their equally still babies had had none of those luxuries. She shook her head slightly and smiled at Juliette, who was clearly reassured.

"And now you've returned to—forgive me, I didn't quite understand your note."

"The Ladies' Compassion Society, who has provided the bulk of cousin Sarah's donations has decided to fund other charities instead. So I've come, well, back, I suppose you'd say, to convince them otherwise."

"How do you intend to do that?"

"I know how their minds work. They mean well, but I know they can't imagine that anyone would willingly live as Sarah does—"

"And you," Juliette interjected.

"And me," Eleanor amended. "Without skimming money

off the top, or embezzling it outright."

Juliette drew back. "But why on earth would they think that? That's positively horrible! To be so cynical—"

"Wealth is simply too important to them. They can't conceive of anyone, especially a wellborn lady—willingly living without it. It is no matter. I also know how to talk to people—that was my one skill from my time as a debutante—"

"Not your only skill," Juliette said quickly.

"It is a good thing we are such close friends, else I'd take exception at your constant interrupting."

Juliette stuck her tongue out at her.

"Such behavior from Lady Worthing! What would people say?"

Juliette tossed her half eaten biscuit at Eleanor who deftly caught it before resuming.

"As I was saying, I believe I can convince the ladies of the Compassion Society not only to renew their sponsorship of Sarah's charity, but to increase their funding."

"That's quite ambitions. Do let me know if I can assist you. I've no influence to speak of, but my husband's mother is no one to be trifled with amongst the leaders of the *ton*." Juliette plucked another biscuit off the tray. "What will you do if you should run into Mr. Fitzhugh about town?"

Eleanor felt goosebumps rise up along her arms. She'd not allowed herself to consider such an occurrence and the very thought made her stomach clench.

"I shall simply—" she began airily, intending to brush the idea away. Then, remembering it was only Juliette with her, dropped the pretense of nonchalance, slumped back in the cushions, and confessed, "Truly? I shall probably suffer one of my attacks, then find a very deep hole to climb into!"

Chapter 17

Eleanor spent the next few days receiving visitors and attending much smaller functions than the first night's ball. She told her mother she wanted to ease back into society gradually, with which her mother fully agreed. In truth, however, Eleanor did not feel prepared for the huge crush of people again. While making her way through the crowd the last time, she'd felt those precursors of an attack of the nerves, which she afterwards found interesting considering she should have felt right at home in a ballroom. It had been her most natural habitat, as it were, the place she'd been accepted and praised.

That first night, however, she'd found the noise grating and the press of bodies rather oppressive. She was sure the feeling would fade, but in the meantime, she felt it best to visit with people in less rigid settings. Having a few guests to call felt far more comfortable, but more importantly, Eleanor used the interactions to try and influence the individual members of the Ladies' Compassion Society before she attended their charity ball the next week.

The few ladies she'd visited with had been noncommittal when she'd mentioned the need for continued funding. They would follow the will of Lady Augustus, who ran the group with the ruthless determination of a general. Eleanor knew that she would have to win her over fully or Sarah's work would come to a standstill. It would be impossible to gain enough individual donations to replace the funds Sarah had come to rely on from the LCS. She'd devised a plan she hoped would make it impossible for Lady Augustus to withdraw her support. She prayed she could pull it off. When Eleanor's mother stopped by her room one morning five days after her return, she wondered if her mother was a mind reader.

"I'm visiting Lady Augustus today, Eleanor. Would you like to join me?"

Eleanor paused in the midst of coiling her hair. Her mouth was full of hairpins, which gave her an excuse not to answer right away. She did want to talk to Lady Augustus, but something told her that given the opportunity to turn her down in private, she would. But if Eleanor was able to put forth her plea in a more public venue—the upcoming charity ball, for example—Lady Augustus might feel uncomfortable about denying the Marquess of Chalcroft's daughter in front of the very society she sought to lead. Eleanor was not above manipulating the emotions of the ton for Sarah.

"Eleanor, you know you have a lady's maid to do your hair," her mother said, coming fully into the room and tucking a stray wisp into Eleanor's chignon.

Eleanor poked the pins into her hair and stood to kiss her mother's cheek.

"I know. It's just quicker to do it myself."

Lady Chalcroft seemed poised to say more, but clearly decided to choose her battles wisely and let it go.

"If you don't mind, I will forgo visiting Lady Augustus today. Please tell her I am very much looking forward to her event on Thursday."

Lady Chalcroft's eyes narrowed. "Eleanor, what do you have up your sleeve?"

"Not a thing, mother," she said, waving the gathered sleeves of her gown to distract her mother from detecting any guilt in her countenance. "I simply promised Juliette I would join her as she shops today for her layette."

"How far along is she? Wait! Eleanor, unmarried ladies should not—" Her mother stopped abruptly.

"You know I'm no longer an ordinary unmarried lady."

"Don't remind me," her mother sighed.

Eleanor laughed softly. She and her mother had skirted around many emotions since her return. Eleanor now felt it was time to be forthright. "I am sorry mother. I hope you know how much I regret worrying you. And not marrying as you had hoped." She saw Lady Chalcroft's eyes fill with tears and she caught up her mother's hand between her own.

"I thought I could be your perfect daughter. I truly did. I just…realized that I needed to see if there was more to me than a perfect daughter and debutante."

"And what did you discover?" her mother whispered.

"Oh mother! Did you know I can organize huge groups of people? I can convince them to work together on common projects. I can—well I'm sure you won't approve, but I can treat any number of ailments and injuries."

"Why wouldn't I approve?" her mother asked gently.

"Well, I suppose those skills mightn't seem ladylike."

Lady Chalcroft drew her daughter over to sit on the frilly sofa in front of the fireplace.

"When I thought you'd been abducted, when I worried you might be—" Eleanor's mother pressed her lips together before continuing. "When I thought the very worst, I can assure you, I wasn't worried about what was ladylike or proper or seemly. Then when I received your first letter, well, I was so relieved. Then I was furious, because really, Eleanor, could you not have warned us?"

Seeing that her mother didn't actually expect an answer, Eleanor remained silent.

Lady Chalcroft continued, "As the months turned into a year and then two, I mostly wondered what you were doing to keep yourself occupied. Your letters, in addition to being infrequent, were frustratingly lacking in details. Oh I know," she said holding up a hand. "You couldn't have told us much without giving us clues as to where you might be."

"I did miss you terribly, mother."

Lady Chalcroft took a deep breath and patted her cheeks delicately, her equilibrium returning.

"Well you are home now and it strikes me that the skills you have acquired are the same it takes to help run a large estate."

"Are you suggesting I apply for employment as an estate manager?" Eleanor said with a smile.

"I am such suggesting that a man, such as Lord Fletcher of Yorkshire would be thrilled to marry a woman who was not only refined and elegant, but duly capable of helping him manage his very large holdings."

"Oh mother, I—"

"Is that the time?" Lady Chalcroft asked, peering at the ornate gold clock on the mantle. "I must be off. Just consider my words, Eleanor. I do not know if you will be able to resume your place in London's society, but I do think there is a chance we can still settle you happily." And with that, Lady Chalcroft was off.

Eleanor slouched back against the brocade cushions—something she'd never have done two years ago—and sighed wearily. She had no plans or desire to regain her place in London's society. But now that she had returned, she very much feared she might not be able to return to living and working full time in Southwark. She didn't think her parents would stand for it, regardless of her being of age.

The charity ball for the Ladies' Compassion Society was a lavish affair far more befitting the arrival of a foreign dignitary than an aid society, but Eleanor did not begrudge the enormous guest list of nobles and society darlings who would be attending. In fact, the more prominent the guests, the more their reaction to her plan could help her win over Lady Augustus.

Eleanor entered the room behind her parents and heard the volume of conversation increase as her name was announced. Having avoided large events like this since that first ball, she'd accidentally created a mystique around herself. She would have laughed at the notion were she not feeling the tightening of her throat that warned her nerves were stretched taut.

She made her slow way down the shallow stairs into the great room, scanning the crowd for Juliette. Not finding her, she stayed close to her parents, reminding herself that she had thrived in this environment for longer than she'd flourished in Southwark. She thought of cousin Sarah and how bravely she'd carved her vision out of nothing and how she was relying on Eleanor to save their organization. The thought straightened Eleanor's spine. She lifted her chin and took a steadying breath. She could do this, she reminded herself.

She nodded at the crowds of people who converged around her, warmly greeting those who were genuinely welcoming of her and coolly turning aside those who seemed interested in salacious gossip. She heard Alex Fitzhugh's name whispered several times and forced herself not to respond, though that proved to be the biggest challenge as she sipped tepid punch and tried to pretend she didn't know his name, though every time she heard the distinctive "tz" of his name, her heart pounded.

She realized that by throwing herself into Sarah's work for the last two years, she'd largely avoided thinking of the heartbreak of her whirlwind romance with him. To hear his name was like experiencing the bitter disappointment of his betrayal afresh, as if two years had not passed.

"Why Lady Eleanor, how lovely of you to attend our ball. I daresay your appearance will make this the most talked-about event of the season."

Eleanor forced a bright smile to her lips as she curtsied to Lady Augustus while her mother stopped to speak to an acquaintance.

"Yours is the only event I wished to attend. Its importance cannot be overstated."

Lady Augustus preened a bit before lowering her voice. "And may I add how glad I am you have returned to your family. This is where you belong dear and it was too cruel of you to disappear like that, no matter the reason."

"But surely you know the call of a spiritual vocation, Lady Augustus. For you have spent so many years organizing the ladies of the *ton* and providing such invaluable assistance to England's less fortunate souls."

Lady Augustus struggled to look humble though she was clearly pleased by Eleanor's words. "Well, one must do what one can, mustn't one? Nevertheless, sometimes we need to recognize when it is time to move on—as you so wisely have done. I feel it is best you're no longer associated with Miss Draper's activities."

Eleanor clenched her teeth at Lady Augustus' supercilious tone.

"I'm not sure what you mean."

"Well she is such a forward young woman. She puts many people off, you know. It's best you're not tarred with the same brush, what with your mother being such a pillar of society and all."

"But surely you cannot deny the excellent work Miss Draper has done. Why, she's single handedly saved thousands from utter starvation!"

Eleanor's mother turned at her raised voice and Eleanor smoothed her face into a benign smile. "What I mean to say is you would know best what good works you have been single-handedly responsible for."

"It is true, we have done excellent work in that region— what do they call it?"

"It's known as The Mint."

"Yes, such a quaint name. Still I think—"

"Lady Augustus, it has occurred to me that few people realize just how much you do for our great city. With your permission, I should like to address everyone so that I may publicly thank you for your tireless work and for making me feel so welcome tonight."

Lady Augustus was clearly pleased by Eleanor's effusive praise, though she strove to seem modest.

"Well I'm sure it's not necessary to thank me. A lady does

not do good for public recognition."

"Of course not, but this is a fundraiser, is it not? Surely it wouldn't hurt to remind those who do so little that they should perhaps contribute a bit more."

"Well, the Ladies' Compassion Society is always trying to aid more people."

"Of course you are. So it's settled. Perhaps when the musicians take their break?"

"Why yes, that would have the greatest impact." Lady Augustus said, and rushed off to speak to the orchestra master.

"What are you up to, Eleanor?"

"I don't know what you mean, mother," Eleanor said innocently.

Lady Chalcroft gave her daughter a meaningful gaze but forbore from saying anything more.

"There you are!" Juliette said as she rushed to join them. "I've been looking everywhere for you."

"You're just in time," Eleanor said, turning so her mother couldn't hear. "I've Lady Augustus right where I want her."

"That sounds positively diabolical," Juliette replied.

"Not at all!" Eleanor protested. "I'm merely going to state the truth in such a way that she'll be unable to withdraw her funding."

"As I said, diabolical."

Eleanor laughed and looked behind Juliette. "Where is Worthing? Already in the gaming room?"

"No, no. He was detained at his father's office in parliament. He'll join me here."

"Excellent. In the meantime, you can lend me moral support. Come along," she said tugging Juliette after her.

It took several minutes for the raucous partygoers to quiet when Lady Augustus took the stage. Eleanor scarcely paid attention to her words as she was suddenly struck with nerves. She felt Juliette squeeze her hand reassuringly.

"You truly are the very best of friends, you know," Eleanor said.

"Oh, I do know. You are completely lucky to have me," Juliette said out of the corner of her mouth.

Eleanor laughed aloud and felt her nervousness recede. She was still smiling as she took the stage.

"Thank you, Lady Augustus," she began, speaking as loudly as she could. "And truly, that is why I am here tonight: to thank you.

"As you all know, Lady Augustus has spearheaded the Ladies' Compassion Society for many years, helping the less fortunate of London through her tireless work." Eleanor paused for the round of applause this elicited and snuck a glance at Lady Augustus to see her smiling benevolently. When the crowd quieted again, Eleanor paused to let the tension build.

"As many of you also know, I have been absent the social scene for the last two years." A rumble of murmurs greeted this announcement and Eleanor waited patiently. "Like Lady Augustus, I too felt the urge to help my fellow man. I have spent the last two years in the company of my dear cousin, Miss Sarah Draper as she has sought to feed the hungry of Southwark. She has also provided medical care to countless people and taught many women valuable vocational skills to help them provide for themselves."

More applause and another glance at Lady Augustus to see her looking a bit unsure of what Eleanor was going to say next.

"The Ladies' Compassion Society has been the main source of funding for Miss Draper's work. Under Lady Augustus' generous direction, the Society has funded food, medicine, and other vital supplies. My cousin, Miss Draper, has used every penny she's ever received from the Society to ensure she never turns a person in need away." Eleanor sensed the crowd growing restive and sought to lighten the mood.

"Can you believe *I* have not bought a new gown in two years?" She smiled at the laughter this drew. "I assure you, the hardship of wearing a turned dress has caused me the greatest strain," she said, with a delicate back of the hand to her forehead. "Why," she said, affecting a mock horrified tone. "When

I asked my cousin if I might at least buy some new gloves to spare my hands from the sun, she refused!"

More laughter greeted this and Eleanor felt the interest return to her.

"And do you know what my cousin said when I asked why not?" The crowd seemed to hold its collective breath waiting for another humorous quip.

"Why, she said that one pair of ladies' gloves cost enough to feed a dozen children for a month." This was met with silence, but Eleanor sensed that her point had hit home.

"Well, I couldn't very well argue with that, could I? But as a result, my nails will never be the same again," she finished, as vapidly as she could to more laughter.

Eleanor decided it was time to deliver her *piece de resistance*. She took a deep breath and glanced up, but froze before she could utter a word. There in the middle of the crowd was Alex Fitzhugh. His expression was unreadable as he gazed at her steadily. She felt her heartbeat pounding in her ears and she struggled to remember what she'd been about to say.

In a flash, she remembered Cousin Sarah and their work. She also remembered why she'd fled her life to join Sarah in the first place and felt her concentration sharpen.

"You can imagine Miss Draper's and my distress when we received a letter from the Ladies' Compassion Society stating they'd be unable to fund us any longer."

She paused to let the censorious grumbles build, then held up a hand to quiet them. She kept her gaze from Lady Augustus for fear of losing her courage. She'd never done anything quite so bold as this...if one didn't count running away from home.

"No, no, please. There is so much need in our country and Lady Augustus and the other ladies must do as they see fit. But I knew if I appealed to you directly," and here she gestured imploringly to the crowd, making sure she avoided looking in the direction where Fitzhugh stood. "On this, a night of generosity extraordinaire, you would see fit to help the Compassion Society not only continue to fund Miss Draper's and my work, but to even increase our budget so that we might help even more people." She batted her eyes and tried to project every wile she'd ever mastered to sway the crowd. "My dear friends, what say you?" she cried out, flinging her arms wide, and her plea was met with wild applause and cheering. She chanced a look at Lady Augustus and saw her displeasure as she made her way back onto the dais. Displeased she might be, but Lady Augustus was shrewd as well and when she spoke, she was nothing but graciousness.

"Well Lady Eleanor, you have certainly rallied the troops, as it were. Of course we shall continue to fund Miss Draper's project—" more cheers followed this announcement. "And perhaps you will deign to have a more active role in the Ladies' Compassion Society as well, seeing how passionate you are about our causes."

Eleanor smiled weakly and allowed herself to be ushered off the stage.

"Oh well done!" Juliette exclaimed as she hugged Eleanor moments before she was swarmed with well-wishers. Eleanor knew many of these people had considered her actions scandalous, but caught up as they were in the emotions of the evening, they now had only encouraging words for her. She made slow progress through the crowd on her way back to her parents as she was stopped over and over by friends, former suitors, and people she'd never before met. She was growing weary of the constant press of people when a touch at her elbow and a deep voice stopped her.

"I feel compelled to offer my congratulations as well as a substantial donation."

Without turning she knew it was Fitzhugh and as the crowd around her grew silent, she knew others were realizing who he was as well. Drat the man! He could ruin everything if he made people think of her behavior in Henley instead of her impassioned speech.

She glanced desperately at Juliette who immediately leapt into the fray. "Now is not the time, Mr. Fitzhugh," she hissed, then put a hand on her barely discernable belly and loudly proclaimed, "Eleanor dear! The baby...I fear I shall faint!" She flailed about quite believably and Eleanor hurried to take her friend's arm, imploring people to clear a path. She glanced back over her shoulder to see Mr. Fitzhugh looking pale and uncertain.

Pale and uncertain? she scoffed. He'd been quite certain when he had cast her aside two years ago. She told herself she was angry and that her shaking hands and clammy skin were a result of her ire, but she very much feared she was fooling herself. She wished she had prepared herself for the possibility of seeing him. Oh, she should have had a witty and biting remark for him so all would know how what contempt she had for him, how little he mattered to her, even if in truth she had no idea what she thought of him.

Thankfully, with Juliette's supposed ailment—and the crowd's shock at her unplanned announcement of her pregnancy—she was able to leave the ball soon after and was spared encountering the hurtful man again.

She tossed and turned all night, torn between triumphant thoughts of saving Sarah's charity and wondering why Alex had been there tonight and why on earth he'd approached her. A hundred different scenarios ran through her head and she would not admit even to herself just how many centered on him falling to his knees and begging her forgiveness. In those imaginings, half the time she scorned his pleas, leaving him a broken man, but the other half...well, those were simply too foolish to even contemplate as the sun peeked between her curtains and she finally gave up trying to sleep. She wearily climbed out of bed and made her way to her small desk where she painstakingly wrote out a note to Sarah.

When she judged it was finally late enough for breakfast to be laid, she dressed herself and headed downstairs for a restorative cup of chocolate. While she fully intended to return to Southwark in the next day or two, while she was at home, she planned to fully enjoy such luxuries as feather mattresses, baths she didn't have to heat herself, and chocolate.

She was just debating having a third cup of chocolate when her father entered the breakfast room.

"Well, daughter, I think it's safe to say no one has ever gotten the better of Lady Augustus before. I suppose you are to be congratulated."

Eleanor grinned at her father. "I'm sure I don't know what you mean, papa. I merely asked the guests at her ball to help her do the right thing."

Lord Chalcroft slathered butter on a piece of toast and abruptly changed the subject. "And what of Alex Fitzhugh?"

Eleanor dropped the sugar spoon into her chocolate, splashing dark brown droplets onto the pristine linen tablecloth. She scrambled to regain her wits. "Oh? Was he there?" she tried to feign.

"Indeed. I believe he even approached you. Right before Lady Worthing made her rather startling announcement."

Eleanor found herself unable to meet her father's gaze and busied herself with carefully spooning jam onto a muffin she had no intention of eating. "Oh, that's right. I scarcely remember speaking to him."

At her father's prolonged silence, Eleanor grew uncomfortable and finally glanced sideway at him. Lord Chalcroft was staring at her steadily, his eyebrows raised in inquiry.

"Oh very well, yes, he approached me," she burst out. "He said some nonsense about congratulating me and wishing to make a donation." She huffed a scornful laugh. "As if the man has two shillings to spare."

"I'd take him up on that offer," Lord Chalcroft said. "Alexander Fitzhugh has become quite the shipping magnate these past two years."

Eleanor squashed the brief spurt of happiness she felt that Alex's dreams had come to fruition. She certainly couldn't give a fig what had become of him and told her father so.

"If you're sure about that," was all Lord Chalcroft said, then turned his attention to his crisply pressed newspaper.

Chapter 18

Alex had never felt so nervous. On second thought, there was that time when he and his crew had been boarded by pirates off the coast of Portugal. He had felt like this, then too, as if his entire life could change in an instant. He was astride his horse and had just turned down the street for Chalcroft House, Eleanor's family home.

The night before he had acted on impulse, approaching her after her magnificent speech. She was the same young woman he'd fallen in love with two years before and yet she was so much more. She'd been society's darling by dint of her beauty and breeding and manners, but last night she'd entranced the crowd with her passion and strength. And, if he wasn't wrong in reading the subtext of her speech, she'd convinced Lady Augustus to do something she hadn't intended.

He'd been swept along with the crowd of well-wishers and without thought had said the first innocuous thing he could think of to gain her attention. Then she'd turned and her cheeks, flush with her success, had gone pale. He'd ached to say something more, but she'd cast an imploring glance at her friend who'd chastised him in a furious whisper and then given an impressive and extravagant display of preparing to faint. Alex snorted aloud. He seriously doubted Juliette Wilding had ever fainted in her life.

The laugh helped steady him and he took a deep breath as he drew closer to Eleanor's family's stately home. He pulled his horse up short at the sight of a shabby hired hack out front.

He frowned as he saw a young woman—a housemaid

by the cut of her cloak—leave the house and make her way down the walk. Surely a maid would leave by a back entrance, he thought. As the young woman climbed into the coach, he caught a glimpse of her face and realized it was Lady Eleanor. His frown deepened and he wondered what she was about.

He knew the Marquess of Chalcroft owned at least two carriages, and even if both were out, surely Lady Eleanor would call for a nicer hackney cab than this sorry conveyance. Not to mention that she'd be accompanied by at least a lady's maid if not a footman as well.

Without a second thought, he nudged his horse into motion and followed the battered cab.

They took a circuitous route through Mayfair and into the city, finally making their way to London Bridge. It was no surprise that Eleanor would not take the family coach and crest into the Mint district of Southwark. What was a surprise was how protective he suddenly felt of her. It was ridiculous, he realized, as he guided his horse around a pool of fetid water. He'd been—well, he'd been a complete ass to her two years ago. He'd attempted to banish her from his thoughts and those dreams that had slipped through in the dark of night had not been about keeping her safe. He had absolutely no right to the protection of her, and yet the feeling was strong.

The hackney cab finally drew to a stop in front of a building that was slightly less dilapidated than its neighbors. He watched Eleanor pay the driver and turn to enter the building.

"Miss Eleanor!" called a grimy young boy as he ran down the street, waving his hand. "Miss Eleanor! Come quick!" He reached her and Alex could not hear what he said to her, but he was clearly agitated. Eleanor smoothed his unruly hair and spoke to him at which point the boy seemed to calm and nodded. Eleanor quickly entered the building while the boy waited, hopping from foot to foot. Alex waited, backing his horse into an alley so as not to be seen when she returned.

Within a couple of minutes, Eleanor hurried out of the building, a large basket on her arm. She followed the boy who took off the way he had come not five minutes before.

Alex waited to make sure she wouldn't spot him before following. They wended their way deeper into the maze of the Mint, finally slipping down a narrow covered alley, at which point Alex had to dismount and coax his horse to follow.

"Yes, yes, old boy," he said, holding back a gag at the smell. "I don't want to know what that is either."

Thankfully, the alleyway was short, opening into a large yard that clearly had access from another street for there were several carts and piles of hay and horse dung. One of the carts lay on its side, its slats broken, the wheels jutting into the air. From the darkness of the alley, he quickly spotted Eleanor as she knelt on the ground next to a man who was pinned beneath the overturned cart. Eleanor quickly stood and looked around for assistance, but there was no one else about.

She tried to lift the wagon herself and Alex ran forward. He grasped the rough wood, grunting with the effort to lift the cart up. Out of the corner of his eye he saw Eleanor immediately grasp the man under the arms. She heaved with all of her slight weight and the boy rushed to help her pull the man free. The injured man howled in pain and mercifully passed out. Alex lowed the cart, the muscles in his arms trembling from the strain. He rushed to Eleanor's side and said, "What can I do?"

She glanced up from her basket and he saw her eyes widen as she recognized him. For a timeless moment, nothing else existed. It was as if no time had passed since that rainy afternoon in his flat when the world outside their embrace had disappeared. Finally pulling her focus back to the man who was moaning as he regained consciousness, she held him still as she spoke soothingly to him.

"Johnny," she called, and the young boy knelt across the man from her. "Talk to him. Keep him calm."

As the boy reassured the man—his father? Alex wondered —she ran her fingers over the man's scalp and neck. Alex crouched nearby and watched as she ran practiced hands down each arm, then began palpating his torso. The man jerked and inhaled sharply when she reached his ribs on the right. She deftly unbuttoned the man's coarse shirt and revealed an already purpling contusion easily the span of Alex's hand.

"Broken?" he whispered, and Eleanor nodded.

She turned back to the injured man and told him, "You're going to be fine Lenny. It's naught but a wee crack in your ribs, though I'm sure it must hurt like the devil."

Lenny nodded but said, "It's not so bad, missus."

Eleanor smiled and smoothed the hair back from the man's sweaty brow. Though Lenny looked old enough to be her father, he clearly took comfort from the maternal gesture and admitted, "It does hurt awfully."

"Of course it does. I've some willow bark tea I'll brew for you, but first we need something a bit more expedient." She reached in her basket and withdrew a small brown bottle. When she uncorked it, Alex caught a whiff of cheap whiskey. She carefully lifted Lenny's head and poured several swallows in his mouth.

"Ah, missus, ye are indeed an angel of mercy."

"Yes, well I doubt you'll say the same when I have to bind your ribs. Here, finish it off and we'll get started."

Lenny obliged by polishing off every last drop. The alcohol seemed to have an almost immediate effect as his head lolled back, though he still remained conscious.

"What else was in that?" Alex asked.

Eleanor shook her head as she fetched several rolls of linen from her basket.

"It's just whiskey, but his body is in shock from the injury so the alcohol affects him more potently than it normally would." She paused and stared at Lenny with a frown.

"What can I do?" he asked.

"I must bind his ribs, but rolling him from side to side will be excruciating and I don't know how severe the break is. There is a chance we could puncture his lung."

"What if we stood him up?"

"Yes, that would be best, but again, the bending and flexing required to do so could injure him further. I don't remember what Dr. Kendall told me to do in cases like this.

Alex glanced around the yard and saw a wide, loose board on the wreck of the cart that had pinned Lenny. He ran to it and wrenched it free.

"Here," he said. "If we can slide this under him, I can use it to lift him without his having to bend."

Eleanor nodded and gently rolled Lenny away from his injured side so Alex could wedge the board beneath the groaning man. Alex moved up to his head and grasped the board.

"Lenny, we're going to lift you. Be prepared to stand, alright?" Eleanor said.

Lenny nodded and Alex heaved with all the strength he had acquired rigging ships and lifting cargo the last two years.

At last Lenny was on his feet, though he wavered and clutched his ribs protectively. Alex dropped the board and gently took the man's shoulders to steady him while Eleanor efficiently bound his ribs beneath his shirt.

"Can you make it inside?"

Lenny nodded and with the guidance of Johnny, they maneuvered their way into one of the buildings and up a flight of stairs to a tiny set of rooms. There was a bed against the wall and they eased Lenny onto it.

Eleanor glanced at the flat bit of wool that served as a pillow and turned to Alex. "We need to prop him up. See if you can find blankets to put behind him."

Though tidy, the small living space was sparsely furnished. Struck with an idea, Alex ran back downstairs.

When he returned, Eleanor asked, "What is that?"

"A bolster made of straw."

"And your jacket?"

He nodded. "There are no extra blankets to be found."

Eleanor took the makeshift pillow and they got Lenny situated as comfortably as possible. She brewed willow bark tea, instructed Johnny on dosage, and arranged a small table with all the injured man might need close at hand.

When she was done she said, "Now you mustn't lift anything heavy for a month. Longer, if possible."

The numbing effects of the whiskey were clearly wearing off but Lenny looked more distraught at her instructions.

"Missus, I can't stop work for a month! I can't stop work for a day. There's naught but me and the boy. We'll starve and loose what customers I have."

"I'll have food brought round," Eleanor assured him.

"What is your business?" Alex asked, but Lenny's breathing was shallow and rapid from pain and distress.

"He uses his cart to transport things for merchants—supplies and goods," Eleanor explained.

"Is there much business in that?"

"He gets by," Eleanor said with a shrug. "It's more than many people here can do."

Alex squatted by the bed and laid a hand on the man's shoulder. "Lenny, when you are healed, see Lady Eleanor. She will put you in touch with my warehouse manager. I've always a need for hard working men if you'll come to the shipyards. In the meantime," he dug in his waistcoat pocket and withdrew what money he had. "This will help during your recovery."

Eleanor returned from the small hearth with a fresh mug of something acrid.

"You see Lenny, nothing to worry about. Now you must drink this. It will ease your discomfort."

Lenny made a face after one sip. "Think I'd rather have that other medicine you gave me, missus."

"Yes, I'm sure you would. But this is what you get now. Make sure he drinks every drop," she instructed Johnny who looked relieved to have something to do. Eleanor fussed over the man a bit longer. Alex hoped the pair would be alright until Lenny healed. He realized how easy it had been to simply hand over money, but how challenging it would be to put it to use in Southwark

Alex followed Eleanor down the stairs and back into the small courtyard. He glanced around looking for his horse and did not realize Eleanor had stopped and turned toward him until he ran into her. He instinctively clutched her to him as they staggered, trying to stay upright. As soon as they were steady, Eleanor backed several steps away, her cheeks flushed.

"Thank you," she said, fiddling with the handle of her basket. "For helping, for promising him work, for the money." She forced herself to meet his gaze. "Thank you."

The rush of caring for the injured man over, Alex found himself unsure of what to say or do. "You are welcome," he said soberly.

"What are you doing here? How did you—"

Alex looked around the courtyard, unable to return her gaze as he tried to think of a response that wouldn't sound completely mad.

"Did you—did you follow me?"

He opened his mouth to respond when his brain finally processed what his eyes had been seeing.

"Where's my horse?" He ran to the larger entrance and looked up and down the narrow road beyond. "Someone's stolen my horse!"

Without a word, Eleanor went inside and called for Johnny, who bolted downstairs. They came out and Alex heard her say, "The boys have been at it again, I'm afraid. Will you fetch Mr. Fitzhugh's horse?"

Johnny nodded and headed for the road. "If they give you any guff, mention Miss Sarah's name," she called.

The boy waved and was gone, darting quickly out of sight.

"He'll retrieve it," she assured him and suddenly the awkwardness returned.

They stared at each other for a long moment while the sounds of the city washed over them.

"I was intending to call on you this morning."

"What?"

"I—I arrived at your father's house this morning. I intended to pay a proper call. I saw you getting in the hired hack and I—well, I didn't think. I just followed you."

"Why?"

Alex shrugged and felt like a schoolboy caught making mischief. "I don't know. I suppose I wanted to learn more about you. You have changed a great deal in the last two years."

He regretted those last words as Eleanor's face hardened.

"Indeed," she began.

"I just—can we talk? Can we go somewhere and just talk? I would like to—"

"What, explain why you treated me with such contempt and disdain and then left me and my reputation in tatters?"

Alex closed his eyes in regret at the bitterness in her voice. He nodded. "Yes, I would like to explain all that."

Eleanor looked away from him and he could tell her thoughts were warring. They were distracted by the return of Johnny, sporting a black eye and leading Alex's horse.

"Found 'im just in time. They were just about to strip his saddle and sell it."

Eleanor rushed to inspect his black eye. "What happened?" She knelt and began rummaging through her basket.

"I forgot to mention Miss Sarah's name right away."

Eleanor stood and began applying a thick salve to the small cut on his cheekbone.

Johnny stood still for a moment, then wriggled away. "I'm fine, miss!" He caught Alex's eye and smiled sheepishly. Alex recognized a fellow male delighted to be fussed over, but embarrassed to like it at the same time.

"Go and check on your father," Eleanor said. "Make sure he finishes the willow bark tea."

After the boy left, Eleanor turned to Alex, though she refused to meet his eyes.

After a long moment of silence during which she seemed to be debating something, she said, "I shall meet you tomorrow at eight o'clock in St. James' Park. The northernmost corner."

"Eight o'clock in the morning?" he asked.

At this, Eleanor did look at him, her brows raised in disdain? Challenge? "Is that too early for you?"

"Of course not," he replied, stung. "I was simply verifying. St. James's Park is not the wisest location for a lady to be seen." It was in close proximity to many gentlemen's clubs and ladies of questionable virtue were often seen there.

"I won't be seen," she retorted. "Well?"

"I will meet you there," he agreed. "Shall I escort you home?"

"No. Thank you. I have business to attend to. I shall return to my cousin's."

"May I see you safely there?"

She shook her head. "I daresay I'll be safer on my own than in the company of a coatless toff."

Alex was about to respond when he realized she was suppressing a smile. Taking this as a good sign, he watched her go and forced himself not to follow to ensure her safety. He reminded himself again that had no right to that duty any longer, if he'd ever really had it. And she certainly had managed quite well without him for a long time.

Alex had no idea what the future held for himself and Eleanor, but he hoped she would at least forgive, if not understand, his actions that fateful night. And if she could forgive him, well, the possibilities for them were great indeed.

"Come along, old boy," he said, leading his horse home.

Alex arrived early the next morning and found a small bench that afforded him a view of the entrance gate. He tried to sit but found himself pacing, going over what he would say to Eleanor when she arrived. Since learning of his devastating mistake two years past, all he'd been able to think about—other than what an ass he'd been—was Eleanor and how she'd made him feel, as if he were the most interesting man in the world, as if she'd only truly come alive when they met. Even though they'd had vastly different backgrounds, even when she knew his father refused to acknowledge him, she'd never treated him as anything other than an equal. It had been his own insecurities that had caused him to doubt her in the end. Those few halcyon weeks with her had opened a world to him that he had closed off since his mother had died—one that saw the purpose of life as more than work. While his feelings for her were obviously different than those he'd held for his mother, it was still love and it filled a need in him he'd ignored for too long.

This new Eleanor appealed to him even more. Her purposeful life, the bravery she'd shown leaving everything comfortable and familiar to forge it, the aura she had of not caring a fig what people thought of her proved she'd clearly come into her own and he wanted to learn her anew, love her anew.

If there was any way she would forgive him, any way she would give him a second chance, he would seize it and prove to her he was worthy of her.

A light step on the path drew his attention. She wore a cloak and simple, face-hiding bonnet, but he knew it was her. She saw him and headed directly toward him.

"Shall we take the path through the trees?" she asked without preamble.

"Certainly."

They were each silent for a full minute and then spoke at the same time.

"Did you—"

"Were you—"

They both smiled and the tension dissipated somewhat.

"Please," Alex said, indicating she should go first.

She shook her head. "It's nothing. Small talk."

He nodded and took a deep breath. He couldn't very well jump right into explaining his asinine behavior right away, so he decided to ease into conversation.

"Have you enjoyed your time working with your cousin?"

She paused before answering. "I'm not sure if 'enjoy' is the right word. I get a great deal of satisfaction out of it. Helping people, making a difference in someone's life is very satisfying. But it is very hard to see such suffering, knowing that no matter how hard you work, there will always be more."

He nodded his head in understanding. "You seem to have become quite the healer."

She glanced at him then, as if suspicious of his sincerity or interest. Apparently deciding he was in earnest, she shrugged her shoulders and returned her gaze to the path in front of them.

"I've barely scratched the surface. I offer makeshift care at best. You could say I simply...patch up injuries and hold off sickness or death until actual medical help arrives."

"And how often does actual medical help reach the Mint?" he asked.

She smiled. "Not often."

"Then I would say there is nothing makeshift in your care. And I doubt Lenny would agree that your care of him was makeshift. No false modesty now," he said teasingly.

The eyes she turned on him were wide and imploring. "I'm not! It's just that the more I learn about caring for the sick and injured, the more I realize there is to learn."

"That makes sense," he said, and they walked a moment in silence. "Tell me, what's the thing you've missed most while living there?"

She gave him an odd half-frown, half-smile expression. "It's not as if I was living in the wilds of Africa or the steppes of Russia, you know."

"Yes, but the Mint is a far cry from Mayfair. Tell me," he said with a teasing smile. "Was it feather beds? Ices from Gunther's? Silk gowns?"

She shook her head, her expression wistful. "I missed my family. My father, my mother. Even my brother who I hadn't seen in over a year before I left. He's much older than I and as a result we were never close when we were growing up, and yet I found myself yearning to see him."

Alex nodded. He still felt his mother's absence keenly. He sensed a way to ease into his intended topic and said, "Was your mother disappointed?"

She looked fully at him then, confusion evident on her face. "Disappointed? What do you mean?"

He took a deep breath and plunged ahead. "Just that—I know she wanted you to marry well that season."

Her mouth fell open and before she could say anything, he rushed on. "That's what caused the problem. At Henley. Well," he rushed to add. "Not the only cause, just the final straw, as it were."

"What do you mean?" she whispered.

He felt his heart pounding and he glanced around, realizing they'd come to a standstill.

"That week. After your family departed for Henley...I tried to meet with my—with Southampton. Every day I would go to his house. Every afternoon I would try to track him down at his club. Every evening I looked for him at the theater or the few social events I could get into.

"He refused to see me. He even sent two rough blokes to physically convince me to leave him alone."

She caught her breath and reached out to him before catching herself and holding her hands tightly in front of her.

He took heart at the gesture, nonetheless.

"I went to Henley anyway. I didn't arrive until that night. I looked everywhere for you and finally saw you dancing with Dunsbury."

She started to say something and he held up a hand. "No, no. That wasn't—I mean—" he sighed and took his hat off to run a hand through his hair before replacing it.

"I saw you dancing and I was struck dead in my tracks. You were so incredibly beautiful. I thought to myself that I'd never be worthy of you."

She took a short gasp of breath.

"I had no idea who Dunsbury was. I only learned his name because—"

"Because why?" she whispered.

He paused. He certainly didn't want to drive a wedge between her and her mother, but there was no other way to tell his story.

"I was standing right behind your mother while you were dancing with Dunsbury. She was sitting with another lady, discussing your marriage prospects. She said—" he broke off, remembering the devastation of his dreams that night.

"What? What did she say?" There was an edge of tension in her voice.

"She said your betrothal to Dunsbury was all but done, that there were only a few formalities to be addressed, but that you would most assuredly be the next Duchess of Devonshire."

Eleanor inhaled sharply and covered her mouth with a gloved hand. After a moment she lowered it and whispered, "How can you be certain it was her?"

He smiled without humor. "I don't think your father is in the habit of kissing other ladies' hands and calling them 'dear' before whisking them away for a dance. Then, too, you resemble her greatly."

Eleanor nodded, staring unseeing into the grove of trees.

"I was devastated," he continued hoarsely, and her gaze snapped back to his face.

"Utterly gutted. I'd been so desperate to gain my father's acknowledgement, prove myself worthy to your family and then...and then marry you. To learn that all that time you'd been allowing Dunsbury to court you, encouraging him—"

"But I never did!" she cried.

"I know that now. I learned it my first week back in London. I think I knew it that night. I was just so *uncertain* of myself, of my worthiness for you."

She frowned at that, lost in thought for several moments. "You said your first week back. What did you mean by that?"

"I've spent most of the last two years outside of England, establishing my shipping firm. I couldn't—I couldn't bear to remain here where I might see you married to another, so I changed my original plan of hiring a captain to set up outposts and travelled to Africa and India myself."

Eleanor was pale and seemed a bit dazed. He didn't blame

her: it was a lot to digest.

"I only learned that you had disappeared the first event I attended after I came back just a few weeks ago. I began searching for you the next day."

"You did? Why?"

"It was my fault you'd fled. I'd ruined your reputation, your life."

Eleanor suddenly snapped out of her daze, her eyes glaring fury, her shoulders squared as if for battle. "What reputation you left me with two years ago you managed to finish off in the last two days."

"What? How could I—"

"First," she snarled, holding up a finger. "You dared approach me at the charity ball when absolutely everyone was looking at me."

"I didn't think. I was just so glad—"

"Second," another finger joined the first. "You were seen following me when I departed my parent's house yesterday."

"What? By whom?" Alex was completely floored by that accusation. She'd been nearly unrecognizable in her humble garb and he—well, he certainly hadn't disguised himself, but surely he was not so obvious as that and he was certainly a nobody as far as the *ton* was concerned.

She waved her hand dismissively. "I don't know. Perhaps Lady Biltings across the square. She positively lives for gossip, and the more it can hurt someone, the better. Perhaps someone driving by or out for a stroll. The point is, it is assumed you followed me for an assignation. Everyone also doubts whether I actually spent the last two years working with Sarah. They think I've been with you!" she said, the disgust evident in her voice.

"And third," she didn't bother with another finger, but paused.

"Third?" he asked, dreading his next crime.

"Well, one and two were sufficient to ruin everything." She wrung her hands and stared off into the thicket of trees.

"Oh how will I tell Sarah?" she whispered.

Alex tore off his hat again and scrubbed his fingers in his hair in frustration. "I can fix this. I can tell everyone the truth."

"They don't care about the truth," she said bitterly.

He couldn't help it; he took her by the arms and drew her closer to him.

"I will fix this, Eleanor. I will save your reputation. I swear it."

She s glanced up at him and laughed. "My reputation? I don't care about that. Well, not beyond the shame it will cause my parents."

"Then what?" he asked, confused.

"Lady Augustus. The Ladies' Compassion Society. They'll cut Sarah's funding for sure now. Lady Augustus wasn't happy I manipulated her into continuing our funding. Our charity will be ruined—no one will donate so much as a tuppence again."

Alex was devastated, more so when her face crumpled and she began weeping into her hands. After her fierceness thus far, it was somehow harder to see her now break down. He gingerly drew her against his chest and when she didn't object, he wrapped his arms around her and stroked her back.

Her tears finally stopped but she remained in his embrace, resting her cheek against his lapel. He closed his eyes and soaked in the feel of her in his arms.

After several long minutes, she slowly lifted her head and gazed up at him. Her eyes were red and puffy as she delicately wiped her nose with a gloved hand, but to him, she was still the most beautiful woman he'd ever seen and she'd never looked lovelier.

He slowly lowered his head. She tipped her chin up at the same time and their lips met in a fusion of warmth, tender and exploring. It lasted an eternity and then slowly grew in intensity, lips and tongues clashing.

He tightened his arms around her and felt her fingers in the hair at his nape, holding his head to hers. The small glade in which they stood was quiet, the only sound their gasps and erratic breaths as they kissed ever more deeply. Alex knew the damp ground smelled of leaves and moss, knew the scent of the pines was pungent in the air, and yet all he could smell was her skin and hair. She wore no fancy perfume or powder; she smelled of clean, warm woman. It had been two years since their lips had touched and yet it was as if they'd never parted, so perfectly did their mouths fit as they devoured one another.

Nothing existed outside their embrace and Alex pulled her tighter to him until they were pressed from lips to knees. He could feel every ragged breath she drew as if it were his own.

So attuned to her was he that he felt when she slowly began to pull away, the distance between them a mere breath, then a handbreadth, and then she stepped slowly back. The cool air between them woke him from the sensual stupor their kiss had cast and he opened his eyes to study her, looking for any signs of distress or regret.

She seemed to be caught in the same web of desire that had entangled him and he watched as her dreamy expression slowly dissolved, her resolute mien returning. She did not seem to regret their kiss, a fact for which he was grateful.

He tried to speak, cleared his throat, and tried again. "I didn't realize how much I'd missed that. Or you. I had—I had closed off that part of myself when I thought you'd..." he trailed off, not wanting to revisit that hurt again today.

"I know," she whispered. "Me too."

He reached up to brush a stray tendril of hair off her forehead and then gently traced the curve of her cheek. She tilted her head ever so slightly toward his caress.

"I *will* fix this," he vowed.

The dreaminess left her eyes and she straightened away from him, squaring her shoulders again.

"There is nothing you can do," she said flatly.

"I refuse to believe that. Look at how easily you won people to your side the other night. The people of the *ton* love you. Once I make it known that there is nothing untoward about..." his voice trailed off. He knew all too well how unforgiving society could be, especially when it came to ladies who did not abide its strict rules of behavior. Or people whose lineage was distinctly lacking.

That thought sparked an idea.

"Wait a moment," he interrupted when it looked as if she was about to speak. "Forgive me—that was rude. It's only that —well, I think I might have something. It's a mad idea, but it just might work."

Eleanor shook her head and the wounded look in her gaze was like a knife to his heart. "I do not want your assistance. I trusted you before. I placed my entire future in your hands and you cast me aside without even giving me the courtesy of an explanation, much less the chance to answer for my supposed crime."

"I know," he admitted in a raspy voice. He could barely make his throat form words. "Eleanor, if you knew how much I regret my asinine behavior."

She shook her head, her face pale and set. "I cannot trust you to save the most important thing in my life."

His idea was too new, too unformed to convince her that he could save her and her charity. Instead, he stared, completely flummoxed, as Eleanor studied his face as if memorizing his features. Her own expression softened briefly.

"I forgive you, you know."

"For which of my many failings?" he asked, half joking.

She smiled and said, "If you had not—not broken my heart, I would have never had the courage or the impetus to join my cousin in her work. Had we married, I would have lived the life I was trained for. I would never have discovered what I was truly capable of, would never have learned all the many things the last two years in Southwark have taught me. So for that, I must actually thank you." She smiled again, tears in her eyes. She took a deep breath.

"I bid you good day, Mr. Fitzhugh." And with that, she

turned on her heel and strode down the path.

He reached out a hand to stop her but forced it to drop. He watched her walk out of the grove of trees, saw the sun glint off a renegade curl that had escaped her somber bonnet. She strode to the park gates, looking neither left nor right, and within a moment, she was gone.

Alex exhaled wearily and rubbed the back of his neck, trying to release the knotted muscles there.

She was completely right in her accusations, of course. If he'd taken but a moment that night in Henley to approach her and ask her if she was engaged to another, all of this could have been avoided. But he had allowed his damnable pride to get in the way and it had cost him Eleanor.

He made his slow way back to his hotel, thinking of her last words, of her thanks. Had they married, he of course would have continued with his business, but certainly not at the level he had achieved by travelling the world himself. And while he would not have expected her to be a typical society matron (for in truth, he had no idea what that entailed), their life most probably would not have included her fulfilling a vocation.

Once at his hotel, he collected his stack of mail and climbed the stairs to his suite of rooms.

There was another missive from the Earl of Southampton. He pulled it from the stack of correspondence, then dug through the piles of papers on his makeshift desk until he located the other three letters.

All were open, but unanswered. He'd wanted nothing to do with his father, but he'd been unable to toss them in the fire or return them unopened as the old man had done to his letters two years ago. The missives asked for him to visit to discuss a matter of import. There was not apology or overture of reconciliation, but something about the shaky handwriting, clearly not that of a secretary, made Alex feel that was exactly what the earl intended.

He sat in front of the cold fireplace and stared at the most recent letter. He finally tore it open and scanned the wavering script. His father—for it seemed the old man was finally admitting his paternity—had been apprised of some new information and greatly wished to meet with Alex as soon as possible.

Alex felt conflicted. No, that wasn't true. He knew he would do anything he could to help Eleanor, and the Earl of Southampton was the only ace he had up his sleeve to sway public opinion toward her. The hesitation he felt was simply from having to ask for help from the man who'd never recognized him as his son and then seen to his utter humiliation two years ago.

Still, swallowing his pride and going to visit Southampton was a small price to pay for what he'd done to Eleanor.

Deciding he did not want to sit around ruminating on the meeting, he leapt to his feet and headed downstairs to call for a coach.

Alex's knee bounced erratically as he waited for the hackney coach to arrive at his father's house. He should have ridden, he thought, and expelled this nervous energy.

At long last, the coach drew to a stop in front of his father's palatial Mayfair home. Alex glared at the front door that had been slammed in his face repeatedly two years past. As he strode up the brick pathway, the door swung open and the butler greeted him cordially.

"Good day, my lord. May I take your hat?"

It was the same stone-faced butler who'd implacably denied any information before, but now practically oozed welcome. "*My lord*," indeed, thought Alex. Well that was telling.

"I shall inform the earl you have arrived. If you will wait in here?"

Alex found himself shown to an opulent sitting room. Though the furnishings were elegant and not a speck of dust was present, it had the air of disuse, as if no one had laughed in it for many years. He shook his head at the fanciful thoughts and forced them back to what the earl was likely to say to him, and more importantly, what Alex would say in return.

A soft knock at the door heralded the butler's return and Alex followed him across the massive entry hall and down another passage to what must be his father's study.

Alex came to a standstill just inside the doorway—not because he was unsure of himself, but because he was unsure the man standing beside the fireplace was the earl. Southampton was radically changed from the last time Alex had seen him. Gone was the muscular frame and straight carriage. The earl had lost easily two stone and his shoulders were stooped.

His hair had thinned considerably and lay limply against his head. But most changed were the earl's eyes. The haughtiness in his bold gaze of two years ago had been wiped away, replaced with a sad cloudiness that Alex had only seen in men facing their death.

He suddenly understood why his father now wished to reconcile. He must be facing death with no other prospects of an heir to succeed him. Alex had the urge to turn on his heel and leave the old curmudgeon to his doom, but Eleanor's face flashed before his eyes and he remembered the reason he was here in the first place. He tamped down his disgust of the man who had denied his existence and shunned Alex's mother and he strode across the room to stand in front of his sire.

"Thank you for coming," the earl said and Alex noted that his voice was still strong, though there was no trace of the usual haughtiness. "Won't you sit?" he asked, gesturing to one of the two leather chairs positioned in front of the fire and sinking into the other. "It is good to see you," he continued as his eyes travelled over Alex's face and frame. While they now shared very little resemblance, Alex knew he was seeing a younger version of himself in Alex.

"You're the very image of me at your age," he said with the ghost of a smile. "Except for your mouth—that is the exact shape of your mother's." He gestured to Alex's face. "I suspect you share her smile."

Alex felt his hands shaking and clenched them into fists to steady them. "You dare mention my mother?" he hissed.

The earl went on as if Alex had not spoken, though Alex realized it was merely because his distant gaze was looking into the past.

"She had the most beautiful smile, your mother did."

"I wouldn't know. She didn't smile much after you cast her aside." It wasn't true, of course, and Alex felt like a petulant five-year-old for wanting to lash out. He felt even worse when the earl wiped a shaky hand down his face.

Unable to remain seated, Alex stood and paced to the window that overlooked an immaculate back garden and mews.

"I assume from your letters that you have decided to acknowledge me." When his father did not respond, Alex turned to look at him. The older man was hunched over and his shoulders were shaking.

Alex had no idea what to do. Years of antagonism toward his father were difficult to let go, but the man was clearly distraught. Glancing around, Alex saw the liquor shelf behind his father's desk. He poured a healthy dose of brandy and took it to the earl.

"Thank you," the man rasped, and drank as if it were a life-saving elixir.

Alex resumed his seat and waited. As the soothing effects of the brandy seeped into his father's blood, the older man calmed and dashed a hand across his eyes.

"I know I must seem a foolish old man." He took a deep breath and looked Alex in the face. "I do mean to acknowledge you, if you'll allow it."

Alex was silent for several long moments. "Why? Why now?"

"I'll tell you, though I know it will make you hate me even more than you must now."

If the earl was seeking reassurance, Alex did not intend to accommodate him. After another long silence, the earl began speaking.

"I don't know what you know of your mother's and my marriage. She was a fresh-faced debutante and I was well beyond my youth when we met. Of course, the age difference was nothing for an arranged marriage—happens all the time, a young girl given to a man nearly as old as her father. But ours wasn't such an arrangement. We fell in love on a bench in Hyde Park. We met quite by accident when we rescued a young boy who'd escaped his nanny and wandered too far into the Serpentine. We each heard the boy's screams and plunged into the water to haul him out. Couldn't save him from the wrath of his nanny, unfortunately," he said with a chuckle.

"We sat on that park bench and talked for hours. Our clothes were completely dry by the time we left the park and my heart was completely smitten. We were married within two months."

"So you were happy?" Alex couldn't help but ask.

"Deliriously so. And yet," the earl admitted, closing his eyes as if to avoid Alex's judgment. "And yet, I constantly worried that she would fall out of love with me just as quickly. She was so vibrant, so personable and I...well I enjoyed nothing so much as spending an evening with a book in front of the fire. How could I possibly hold her interest?

"Did she ever indicate she was falling out of love? Or not happy?"

"Never. She was...she was the light of my life."

Alex frowned in frustration. "Then what could possibly have gone amiss?"

The earl picked up his brandy glass, noticed it was empty, and set it back down. "Your mother's maid had an...attraction to me. One time when your mother was visiting her family, this woman—she was no more than a girl, really—she thought to...well she climbed into my bed in the middle of the night. Started touching me. I was asleep and, er—"

"Responded?" Alex suggested.

"Indeed. Thought she was your mother, didn't I? When I finally awoke, I was shocked and did not comport myself well. I...I threw her from the bed. She was furious, I suppose, though at the time, she was full of tears. She told me—" his voice choked.

"What did she say?" Alex said, his voice low.

"She told me that your mother had been having an affair for months. She said Alice was not visiting her family, but was with her lover. She must have known or suspected how insecure I was, for she knew just what to say to destroy me. She told me—" a sob interrupted his confession. "She told me your mother was pregnant—with you, as it happens. But she swore it was her lover's baby. Your mother had not yet told me she was expecting. She didn't tell me until she returned which somehow seemed to confirm the maid's story. Plus…well, your mother had not conceived in the three years of our marriage. To my knowledge, none of my past mistresses had either. I suspected that the problem was with me and then after all that time, to have your mother end up pregnant. It…I," he took a ragged breath.

"I judged without question. I cut her out of my heart and out of my life. And you with her. If I'd only just talked to her —" he broke off as Alex surged to his feet and strode back to the window.

He pressed his forehead to the glass, almost wishing he could push his head through it, experience physical pain to distract himself from the pain he felt in his heart, partly for what his father said, partly because it hit too close to home.

He had judged Eleanor just as quickly, just as harshly, just as wrongly.

"I don't blame you for hating me." His father's voice was right behind him. Alex whirled around and saw the older man flinch.

"I don't hate you," he said hoarsely.

His father studied his face and nodded. Neither man was able to speak for a long minute.

"What made you realize your mistake?" Alex asked.

"You. Looking at you that night in Henley, really seeing you up close and face to face, I could no longer tell myself I'd been the righteous one, the injured party. I said…horrible things that night. I was desperate to protect the anger and betrayal I'd nursed for so many years. But after that night, I hired an investigator to track down that maid. She confessed to lying. You cannot imagine my grief and guilt."

"I can imagine it," Alex said more gently than he'd intended.

"I know it's poor recompense, but I'd like to recognize you as my son, my heir. As the next earl, you won't have to work, but if you wished, the contacts you'd gain with the title would be useful to your growing shipping business."

"I don't care about that—not right now at any rate. But if you truly wish to make amends, there is something you could assist me with."

"Name it," his father said firmly.

In a few brief sentences, Alex described his and Eleanor's aborted courtship.

His father moaned low in his chest and Alex grasped the earl's elbow, sure the man was dying. "That was my fault, wasn't it? She was that lovely young woman who tried to assist you, wasn't she?"

Alex thought of how the awful confrontation with his father was perhaps made worse by his own anger at thinking Eleanor had thrown him over for another.

"That was her, yes. But I made an error in judgment that would have doomed us regardless, I think." He continued with his story, bringing the earl up to this morning's meeting with Eleanor.

"And now, again because of me, her reputation is compromised. And, as she says, what's worse is her beloved charity will not survive. Lady Augustus will pounce on the reason not to fund them any longer."

"You're telling me this Lady Eleanor went off on her own for two years and worked in Southwark?"

Alex felt his muscles tighten—if his father disparaged Eleanor—

The earl slapped the arm of his chair and laughed aloud.

"By Jove, she's got spirit, hasn't she? Sounds a bit like your mother, I'd say."

Alex felt the tension leave his body and he couldn't help but smile at the delight his sire took in Eleanor's actions.

"And what exactly did she do there?"

Alex explained about Eleanor and her cousin's work.

"Doesn't sound terribly interesting to me, but women do have softer hearts. And of course they can only operate if they receive donations."

"That is correct. There is a lady's group that has been their main source of funding, but—"

"Lady Augustus, did you say?" his father interrupted. The old man looked ready to burst into laughter.

"Yes. Do you know her?"

At that, the earl did laugh. "Oh indeed, my boy. I know her. She and I had an arrangement a while back.

"At any rate, Lady Augustus—Iris as I know her—presents herself as a self-righteous woman, but in private, I can assure you, she is not so pure."

Alex suppressed a shudder at the notion of hearing of his father's sexual exploits, but his expression must have given away his revulsion for the earl laughed.

"Fear not, I'm not a man to kiss and tell. Fortunately for us, Iris Augustus doesn't know that."

"Are you intending to blackmail her?"

The earl frowned and made a dismissive flicking motion with his fingers. "I intend to remind her that people can still do good works even if they are not so morally impeccable as society might wish them to be."

"Nothing untoward happened between Lady Eleanor and me yesterday!" Alex protested.

"It doesn't matter, not to someone like Iris. What does matter is that I guarantee she will continue to fund your Eleanor's work. Now tell me: you do intend to marry her, don't you?"

Alex started to say the thought hadn't crossed his mind,

but he knew that the moment he'd learned Eleanor was not married to Dunsbury, the idea had been in the back of his mind, coursing through his veins with every beat of his heart.

"I—I don't know if she'll have me after everything that has transpired."

"Well, you'll have to grovel, son. You'll have to beg her forgiveness and vow you'll never be such an idiot again. And if you would grovel a little bit on my behalf, too, I would be grateful," he finished hoarsely.

Alex extended his hand and his father grasped it tightly. And while he wasn't quite ready to forgive the years of neglect, his greater understanding of his father might allow for at least a peaceable future.

Chapter 19

Eleanor snuck back into the house and made her way upstairs where she changed into one of her old morning gowns. She smiled as she considered that while the dress was from three seasons ago, she'd worn it perhaps three or four times and it certainly didn't qualify as "old."

Despite being dressed by eleven o'clock, she still had a while to wait until Juliette was due to call. A tap at her door revealed a footman who informed her she had a caller.

"This early? Who?"

Her cousin Sarah stood awkwardly in the center of the drawing room. She turned as Eleanor walked in.

"Sarah!" Eleanor exclaimed, rushing to embrace her cousin. "I missed you yesterday when I came."

"Yes, I heard you had quite the excitement with Lenny Mitchell."

"Have you heard from him? Is he well?"

"I stopped by on my way here. He's still in a bit of pain, but his son is taking care of him and I take it a benefactor has seen to it that he will not suffer for income while he recuperates."

"Oh. Yes," Eleanor prevaricated. Sarah laughed and poked her in the arm.

"I'm not judging you, goose. But I do insist you tell me what's been going on. I received your note that you'd secured on funding. Brava, cousin!"

"As to that—" Eleanor began.

"Oh dear. Well, do tell so that we may plan our next steps. But may we plan with food? I feel I've already walked miles today."

"Sarah! Forgive me. Of course, sit and let me order some refreshments."

She tugged on the bell pull and within minutes they were feasting on sandwiches, biscuits, and tea.

With their initial hunger addressed, Sarah insisted on hearing every detail of Eleanor's return to the *ton*. After Eleanor reunited with her parents, she'd insisted on returning to work in Southwark, but she understood her parent's desperate need to have her close, so she'd been spending most nights of the past fortnight at her parent's home. As a result, she and Sarah had had little chance to catch up, and after two years of living and working together, Eleanor sorely missed their chats. They were finishing the last two sandwiches when the butler announced the arrival of Juliette Wilding.

"Juliette! Oh I'm so glad you're early. I want you to meet my cousin, Miss Draper. Sarah, Lady Worthing."

Juliette and Sarah exchanged warm greetings. Eleanor ordered more food and a slightly awkward silence settled over the room.

Eleanor leapt into the quiet by saying, "Between the two of you, you know all my foibles and flaws so there are no secrets here." Turning to Juliette, she said, "I just finished telling Sarah about the Lady's Compassion Society event and Lady Augustus' promise to fund us."

"Oh, she was fiendishly clever," Juliette said. "Lady Augustus didn't stand a chance."

Sara smiled warmly. "I'm so proud of you."

"Yes, but then events transpired which have placed everything in jeopardy once again." She quickly described Alex's following her to Southwark and the resultant gossip.

"Damned man," Sarah muttered and Juliette laughed aloud. "How can you say 'events transpired,' Eleanor? Everything was fine until he pushed his way back in your life."

"Well that brings me to the most recent events—this morning's in fact."

The new tray of food and tea arrived and once the maid left, Eleanor told the other two women of her early morning meeting with Alex, leaving out the passionate embrace they'd shared. She finished with Alex's vow to fix the mess he had inadvertently created and then reached for her now cool tea.

Sarah and Juliette were silent and Eleanor chewed on her lower lip before exclaiming, "Well? What do you think?"

"Of his apology?" Juliette asked and Sarah followed with, "Of his promise?"

"Well, both, I should say."

The two other women looked at each other and an unspoken communication passed between them as if they'd been close friends for years.

Juliette turned to Eleanor and said, "The important thing is, what do *you* think about what he said."

Eleanor leapt to her feet and began pacing. She thought of how vibrant she felt in his presence. The air fairly crackled with some mysterious force that made her skin tingle. She'd never felt so—so excited to be alive and at the same time, so completely comfortable in her skin and in her place in the world. The only other time she'd felt that had been two years ago with Alex, but now this feeling seemed to have intensified —and that with only a few minutes in his presence! Realizing the other two women were staring at her, she whirled around. "I don't know what to think! That's why I'm asking you, isn't it?" She caught a glimpse of Sarah's raised eyebrows and said, "I'm sorry. I didn't mean to snap. I'm just so bloody confused."

Juliette half-gasped, half-laughed at Eleanor's curse.

"Do you love him still?" Sarah asked bluntly.

Eleanor stopped in her tracks, her mouth agape.

"She still loves him," Juliette said. "Otherwise she'd have denied it immediately instead of making that fish face."

Eleanor wrinkled her nose and stuck her tongue out at her friend before dropping back onto the sofa.

"Two years ago I was mad for him. I think—I think if he had asked father for my hand and been refused, I would have eloped with him."

"Which is what many people thought you had done until you returned home," Juliette said softly.

Eleanor grimaced. "The point being, I would have done anything for him and he hurt me dreadfully that night in Henley."

"And does his explanation change that hurt?" Sarah asked.

Eleanor gazed across the room at the window. "My mother was so determined I marry Dunsbury. To be honest, I don't think he was the slightest bit interested in me. But she was determined he should offer before we left for home. I believe she and his mother had been plotting." She turned her gaze back to her friends. "I'm sure she sounded quite credible when he overheard her talking about it."

"And it was your mother," Juliette said. "Anyone else and he would have attributed it to gossip."

"You still haven't answered the question," Sarah said impatiently. "Did his explanation and apology allay your hurt?"

Eleanor took a deep breath. "Yes. I believe it did."

"Did you tell him that?"

Eleanor smiled grimly. "Not quite. I believe I called him to task for not giving me the chance to explain. Then I berated him for destroying my reputation—twice—and ruining our chances of funding."

"How did he respond to that?" Juliette asked.

"That's when he promised to fix everything."

"Who promised to fix what?"

The three young women jumped as Lady Chalcroft swept into the room, looking as if she knew exactly what they were talking about. "Juliette, Sarah, it is good to see you both."

"Lady Chalcroft," the two women replied, sounding like schoolgirls caught in the act.

"Mother," Eleanor began.

"Your father has had a letter from the Earl of Southampton."

"What?" three voices exclaimed together.

"We shall be attending the Duke of Devonshire's event this evening."

"Dunsbury's father," Juliette whispered in explanation to Sarah who seemed unimpressed.

"Sarah, you will borrow a suitable gown from Eleanor."

At that, Sarah's impassive expression evaporated. "But—" she began.

"She's more of a size to me," Juliette interrupted. "I'll give her something."

While Sarah frowned at Juliette, Eleanor said, "What is going on mother?" I've no wish to—"

"You," Lady Chalcroft said, pointing at her daughter (Eleanor had never seen her mother point at anything and the shock made her hold her tongue). "You shall allow your maid to fix your hair. You shall wear your jewels and your finest dress."

Duly chastened, Eleanor asked, "What is this for?"

"As your father might say, we are putting all our cards in. Or is it chips? There is some gambling reference, I'm sure. In short, we are hoping a show of force tonight will squash these silly rumors once and for all." Eleanor was impressed her mother was taking this second round of gossip so well.

"But the Earl of Southampton? How did he come to be involved?" Eleanor asked, confused. Surely the bitter old man would not care one whit about her or her troubles.

"As to that, I am not sure. Your father is playing his cards close to his arm, I believe the expression is."

"Chest," Sarah corrected and Lady Chalcroft raised her eyebrows.

"A lady does not say that word."

"Will this plan save Sarah's funding?" Eleanor persisted.

"I believe that point was mentioned as well," was all they could get out of Eleanor's mother before she launched into a list of directives they all must follow regarding what to wear, who to speak with, and how to act.

Eleanor arrived with her parents at the Duke of Devonshire's grand house directly behind Lord Worthing's coach. Eleanor saw Worthing help Juliette down from the carriage and then a gorgeous young woman followed.

Eleanor gasped. "Sarah!" she called, trying to lower the window on the carriage door.

"Eleanor!" her mother chastised. "A little decorum, please. We are trying to mend your reputation, not ruin it further."

"But Sarah looks—"

"Yes, well, her mother was considered quite the beauty. It's no surprise her daughter should be as well once we got her out of those drab gowns she favors."

Eleanor waited impatiently for the footman to assist her down and hurried over to her cousin who looked distinctly uncomfortable.

"You look gorgeous," Eleanor said by way of greeting. Sarah glanced down at the lush folds of midnight blue satin said, "I feel as though I'm naked."

The off the shoulder sleeves and deep décolletage showed off creamy skin, smooth shoulders, and a generous cleavage.

"Well, you're not," Eleanor said matter-of-factly. "And if I have to throw my shoulders back and pretend to belong here, so do you."

"Ah, but you have always belonged here whereas I never have," Sarah protested as Eleanor pulled her along.

Once announced, there was a flurry of conversation around the large drawing room. Connecting doors all along the house had been opened so that people might converse in one room and dance in another.

Flanked by her parents and with Juliette and her husband leading the way, Eleanor felt she was as prepared as she could be for what the evening may bring. They stopped in the second room where they greeted Juliette's in-laws, the Earl and Countess of Beverly. When Lord Dunsbury and his wife joined them, Eleanor understood exactly what her mother had meant by a show of force.

"Is it as bad as that?" she only half joked, a slightly panicked feeling creeping through her veins when no one responded.

Footmen delivered glasses of champagne and conversation buzzed all around them. Glancing around, Eleanor noticed that everyone except Sarah seemed relaxed and confident, but Eleanor sensed they were waiting for a final player this evening.

She was chatting with Dunsbury and his wife whom she'd just met, when over the din of conversation she heard the butler announce the arrival of the Earl of Southampton and his son, Alexander Fitzhugh, Lord Reading.

Eleanor felt the blood drain from her cheeks and she gripped her father's arm, lest she loose her balance. Was this part of Alex's plan? How had he convinced his father to acknowledge him and how on earth would that possibly help her and Sarah?"

"Patience my dear," her father said, reading her expression as astutely as he ever had. "I suspect we are in for quite a show this evening."

Eleanor glanced up at her father and felt her heart contract with love. "I'm so sorry to put you in this situation, Papa."

Her father glanced down at her in surprise. "My dear girl, why are you sorry? This is quite the most excitement I've had in years. Parliament can be a bit of a bore, you know."

"Yes but people will never forget. No matter tonight's outcome, I will always be marked with scandal."

Her father laughed at that. "Anyone who knows you knows the goodness of your heart. And if they judge you without knowing you, their opinion is of little value. Besides, I suspect our contingent of supporters will sway those with small minds. He gestured with a subtle nod of his head and Eleanor glanced around to see that their friends had dispersed themselves among the immediate crowd and would no doubt guide the conversations.

"I find myself a bit overwhelmed by your show of force, as you call it." She glanced covertly across the room and saw that Alex and his father—who looked as if he'd aged a decade—had stopped to talk to—no, could it be? The Earl of Southampton was deep in conversation with Lady Augustus who was blushing like a debutante and practically giggling at whatever he was saying.

"Eleanor." Her father's somber tone immediately caught her attention and she looked up to see a deep crease between his brows. "For all my bravado about society's gossip, I fear there may be only one way to stop tongues wagging."

"What is that?" Eleanor asked, but her fingers chilled. She refused to acknowledge what she suspected she already knew.

"I fear the only way to ensure you a life without constant censure is if you marry."

"What?" Eleanor said loudly and at the startled glances her way, smoothed her face into a pleasant smile.

"Have you spoken at all to Lord Reading?"

"Lord Reading? Who is—oh," she said as she realized he had called Alex by his newly acknowledged title. "A little. He explained what led to the, ah, occurrence at Henley."

"Did he? I should like to hear that myself." The earl glanced across the room and Eleanor followed his line of sight and saw Southampton, Alex, and Lady Augustus making their slow way toward Eleanor. She quickly turned and pretended she didn't see them. She knew the crowds of people surrounding her were watching avidly, no doubt hoping for a scandal they could chew on for months during the gossip-starved off season.

"You know it to be true," her father continued. "Besides, I want you to have a family and some security for when your mother and I are gone."

'But—"

"We'll work out the details later."

"Details?" she parroted and when her father hushed her, she realized she'd spoken loudly again. The two matrons directly opposite here were whispering furiously to each other as they stared at her.

She felt a touch at her elbow and turned to see Sarah had returned to her side.

"What macabre beings we humans have become," Eleanor whispered to her cousin. "That we should take such interest and delight in other people's perceived downfalls."

"What do you mean, 'have become'? The Romans threw Christians to the lions for entertainments. We as a species have long taken great delight in the suffering of others."

"It's terrible," Eleanor said with a frown.

Sarah tilted her head in acknowledgement. "Perhaps we're simply excessively relieved that we are not the ones being fed to the lions."

"Well, I for one—"

"Shhh," Sarah whispered. "The lion has arrived."

Eleanor slowly turned, making sure her expression was composed. Unsure of what to say to Alex or his father, she settled on, "Lady Augustus, how lovely to see you."

Eleanor's father turned from his conversation and greeted Alex's father. "Southampton."

"Chalcroft, always a pleasure. It's been a while."

"Indeed. You are well, I trust?"

Eleanor fought the urge to shift her weight from foot to foot as the men exchanged the requisite banalities.

"You know Lady Augustus, of course," Lord Southampton said.

"Indeed. Ever a pleasure to see you, my lady. I ran into your husband just the other day at the club."

"Oh?" Lady Augustus said, glancing sideways at Southampton. The strange thought crossed Eleanor's mind that Lady Augustus did not want to remind the earl of the existence of her husband.

Southampton seemed not to notice her furtive glance, instead turning to Alex. "You may not have been introduced to my son, however. Allow me to present Alexander Fitzhugh,

Lord Reading and my heir."

Eleanor could hear people around them whispering and she knew all eyes in the room were focused on their small groups. She called on her years of social etiquette training to keep her face carefully neutral as she pretended that this was a normal introduction, though inside her heart was racing as was her mind, wondering how these events would play out. She could not quite believe that the only solution was to marry Alex, even as she secretly wished for that very thing.

"I am pleased to make your formal acquaintance," her father said, then turned to Eleanor. "In return, allow me to introduce you to my daughter, Lady Eleanor Chalcroft."

Eleanor smiled and curtseyed as Southampton beamed and said loudly, "Is this the plucky gel who took it upon herself to feed the masses?"

"Well, actually, my cousin—" Eleanor glanced around but there was no sign of Sarah. She frowned as she noticed that people had crowded rudely close to their small party, the better to eavesdrop, no doubt. Southampton's booming voice drew her attention back to the performance unfolding.

"Now now, don't be modest. I know your project has the full support of our lovely Lady Augustus here, and she knows a worthy cause when she sees one."

At that, Lady Augustus looked distinctly uncomfortable. She laid a tentative hand on his arm. Southampton gave her a firm glance and Eleanor wondered what on earth he meant by it. Southampton didn't give her a chance to reply as he returned his attention to Eleanor.

"Lady Eleanor, I believe you have the acquaintance of my son, though at the time he was perhaps not up to your, ah, standards, shall we say?" His voice seemed unnecessarily loud and Eleanor wondered if it was so that everyone could hear him. "When you first met him, society did not know him as my heir. Now that he's established himself as an independent man of wealth and business, he has claimed his due, the title of Lord Reading."

Eleanor could tell Southampton required a response from her, but her brain felt sluggish with Alex standing right next to her and she didn't know what her role was supposed to—

"Oh!" she said aloud, for the pieces suddenly clicked together in her mind. Southampton was making it seem that Alex had been the one to avoid public association with his father so that he might establish his company on his own, and now that he had successfully done that, he would accept his father's title.

She snapped back to attention in time to hear Southampton say, "—and I for one couldn't be happier. In fact," he looked to Eleanor's father who gave a tiny nod. "I think we should take advantage of this smashing event."

Eleanor chanced a look at Alex and while he at first seemed as confused as she, a dawning look of comprehension and horror spread across his handsome face. He glanced at her and Eleanor found herself unable to look away. Suddenly, fear, nerves, and uncertainty all dissolved as all she could remember was how right she'd felt with him, as if she needn't hide her flaws, as if she were perfect, just as she was.

"Eleanor?" Lady Chalcroft had returned to her daughter's side and Eleanor pulled her gaze from Alex's.

"Yes, I'm alright," she said. She realized Lord Southampton and her father were making their way to the center of the room and she allowed her mother to draw her along.

Southampton stopped in the middle of a large Abusson carpet and commandeered a footman's tray of champagne flutes. Eleanor absently accepted one as her father's earlier words about marriage and Southampton's words about Alex previously not being up to her standards clanged in her head.

She inhaled sharply and Alex lightly touched her elbow. She looked up at him and saw his own dawning realization of what was about to happen.

"I didn't know—that is I didn't realize he was going to—"

"Hush," Lady Chalcroft said. "Smile the both of you. There will be time to sort everything out later.

Southampton cleared his throat loudly but it was unnecessary as everyone in the room was staring at their small group. A hush quickly descended and Southampton smiled jovially at the congregation.

"It has been too long since I've been out in society and I must say, I have missed the lot of you."

This was met with chuckles and a smattering of applause.

"As you no doubt have heard, my son has returned to England after successfully building a shipping business. I assure you, dear friends, I am in no such dire straits that he needed to earn his own fortune, but you know how young men like to make a name for themselves."

Eleanor suppressed a snort of laughter. Most young men were more than content to live off their family's wealth. In fact, it was considered gauche for a nobleman to dirty his hands in trade, but as Eleanor glanced around, it seemed that no one was thinking of that long-held edict. Instead, they were nodding indulgently, caught up in Southampton's bonhomie.

"But now that he has returned and assumed his rightful place as my heir—" Eleanor chanced a look at Alex's face. His expression was carefully bland, but something in his eyes made her think Southampton's words were as much a surprise to him as they were to the rest of the world.

"Now it is time he settled down, wouldn't you agree?"

This time the applause was more energetic. Eleanor felt like she was trapped in the path of a runaway horse, able to do nothing but watch her impending doom draw closer. Except that it didn't feel like doom, quite the opposite, in fact. There was an odd flutter of excitement in her stomach. She glanced again at Alex and found him staring at her with an expression of hope? Contrition? She wasn't sure. His father held up a hand to silence the partygoers.

"I'm sure I need not introduce Lady Eleanor Chalcroft to you." The whispers resumed but Eleanor pretended not to hear them.

"She, like my son, felt she needed to make a difference in

the world. And what a difference she has made! Why, Lady Augustus was telling me how proud she was to be funding Lady Eleanor's work."

At this, Lady Augustus again looked appalled. She opened her mouth as if to speak but Southampton bent his head slightly and said something in her ear. Lady Augustus's cheeks flamed red and she visibly swallowed before pasting on a weak smile and nodding woodenly.

Eleanor realized that Lady Augustus had indeed intended to cancel the funds after the latest gossip, but whatever Southampton had said to her—and it must have been good to shut her down so quickly—had saved Sarah's charity. Eleanor was inclined to forgive Southampton's abominable behavior two years ago if he could save Sarah's funding.

Suddenly realizing the polite applause was for her, Eleanor smiled and nodded her head at the gathering.

"But now that she has returned home where she belongs, it is time she settled down as well, wouldn't you agree?"

There were some cheers, some applause, and quite a few confused looks, as if people wanted to follow along, but were unsure where he was leading.

Southampton appeared to note everything and said, "I've kept you from your entertainment long enough! Without further ado, allow me to announce the betrothal of Lady Eleanor Chalcroft to my son, Lord Alexander Fitzhugh."

Although Eleanor had suspected this was Southampton's plan to squelch gossip, she was still a bit shocked to hear the words said aloud. She heard offers of congratulations and best wishes as though through a blanket, muffled and indistinct.

Somehow she found herself next to Alex and he took her arm, squeezing her hand. He ducked his head and said, "I had no idea he intended this for tonight. I—we can make this right. After talk has died down and your charity is funded, you can call off. I can leave England or—"

"Is that what you want?" she interrupted, looking at him intently.

"No!" he replied immediately, then had to pause and shake the hand of another well-wisher. "That is—" he looked around and saw the crowds of people waiting to congratulation them.

"Meet me on the veranda in ten minutes," she whispered, feeling a ridiculous thrill at his emphatic denial.

He nodded, his eyes dark and intense.

As soon as she could, Eleanor ducked out of the room, claiming the excitement had made her lightheaded. She wove her way through the maze of rooms. Fortunately she'd been in this house several times over the years and knew which doors would gain her access to the wide verandah that wrapped around the side of the house.

Outside, the air was cool and fresh. She paused a moment to inhale and calm the fluttering in her stomach. When she turned the corner, she saw Alex standing in the shadows, staring at the few stars that peaked through the clouds above.

Though her slippers made not a sound, he turned as if alerted to her presence. She stopped in front of him and they stared at each other in apprehensive silence.

Alex finally spoke, his voice low and gruff. "I apologize for my father's actions in there. He told me he had a foolproof plan to stop the rumors about you and save your charity, but I had no idea he intended to..." he trailed off as if unable to believe what had happened.

"Betroth us?" Eleanor pressed her lips together and then said, "You seemed as surprised as I was. Did you truly not suspect?"

"I—I suppose I thought he would try to make light of the rumors, convince people what they'd heard was ridiculous. I knew he had something on Lady Augustus so I thought he was simply going to intimidate her into funding your charity."

She took a step back, putting a careful distance between them. There was a sinking feeling in the pit of her stomach and her cheeks felt a bit numb. She'd thought Alex might have felt as she did, shocked but not displeased at the turn of events... clearly she'd been mistaken.

"Well I shan't hold you to it, of course. I appreciate that your father convinced Lady Augustus to continue our funding." She took a quick breath. Why did she feel she was about to cry? "I shall return to Southwark to continue my work with my cousin. People will assume you wanted a wife who…" she trailed off, not sure how she would have finished that sentence. Her earlier hopes seemed to have crumbled at her feet.

"Is that what you truly want?" Alex asked softly and she realized he was repeating her earlier question, but she was so confused, she didn't know how to answer.

Eleanor felt tears burning behind her eyes and she clenched her jaw and fisted her hands to keep the tears from flooding her eyes. She forced herself to speak calmly as she said, "There is nothing for me here in London. Aside from my family and Juliette, there is no one I care to be around." She turned and stared out into the dark gardens. She was startled when she felt his hand on her arm.

"Truly? There is no one?"

She glanced at him and frowned. "I'm hardly marriage material any longer. Your father's announcement aside, I know what men of your position wish in a wife." She tried and failed to keep the bitterness out of her voice. It was silly because she'd been perfect "marriage material" before she'd left society and she had no desire to return to that life, but curse it all, she wished he wanted her anyway.

"Men of my position? I've been Lord Reading for exactly four hours! Do you really think I've changed so greatly in that short of time?" His voice was tense, his gaze fierce.

She opened her mouth to speak but he continued.

"When I've wanted nothing but to marry you from the first moment I saw you?"

"Oh," Eleanor gasped.

"Yes, 'Oh,'" he said, grasping her upper arms and gently pulling her toward him. "I was an ass not to ask you directly two years ago. I know we tiptoed around the subject but I was afraid you didn't really care for me as I—" he caught his breath.

"Damnit, as I loved you. As I love you still.

"I will do anything to win your forgiveness, to win your heart. Will you marry me, Eleanor?"

"I—" she froze, not knowing which emotion to feel: delight, trepidation, excitement, or fear. "There are so many things to work out. We are not the same people we were two years ago."

"No, we're not. But I think we are wiser, more compassionate, more tolerant. We are better suited to matrimony and each other."

"But—"

"What is it? What's holding you back? Do you—do you not care for me?"

"It's not that," she prevaricated.

"Then what?"

"I wish to continue working with my cousin."

"Of course you do," he said matter-of-factly, seeming surprised that she would mention it.

That startled Eleanor out of her reticence. "And you would support that?"

"Well of course I would. You clearly thrive managing hordes of people and patching them back together. Why would I seek to deny you that?"

Eleanor inspected him from the corner of her eyes. "Most men would wish their wives to stay home."

"Perhaps I am not most men," he said archly.

Well that was certainly true, Eleanor decided. "There are so many details to work out," she repeated.

His hands slid down her arms to catch up her hands, which he brought to his mouth for a kiss. "No more than when I was a worthless bastard."

Eleanor inhaled sharply. "Don't say that! You were never worthless."

He grinned and drew her hands up to rest on his shoulders. "Is that all?"

Eleanor felt her heart beat faster and flutters low in her

belly spread delicious tendrils throughout her body. "It never mattered to *me* that your father didn't recognize you."

"And why was that?" His voice was a low rumble that seemed to strum her very nerve endings. Her eyelids drooped and all she saw was his mouth.

"Because," she paused. There was scarcely a breath's space between their lips. She lifted her gaze to his. "Because I loved you. I love you still," she said, mirroring his own words.

She saw the flare of passion light his eyes in the split second before their lips met. It was a slow kiss, lacking in the fevered rush of their first embraces, but all the richer for its celebration of what they'd experienced apart and what they would now experience together.

Their kiss deepened and Alex pulled her tighter to him with a low groan. Eleanor felt as though she could not get enough of him—she ran her hands through his hair, cursing the gloves that prevented her from enjoying the silky strands. Her thin gown allowed her to feel every inch of his body and without thought she pressed herself closer to his evident arousal.

"Now let's not undo all my hard work making you two respectable." Southampton's sardonic voice startled them apart. Eleanor felt her cheeks flame with embarrassment, but Alex's hand was reassuring in the small of her back and his voice expressed amusement as he said, "If we're betrothed, surely we're allowed a bit of leeway."

"Is that what leeway looks like?" Southampton said with a grin as he approached them. His expression sobered as he looked at Eleanor. "I apologize for not discussing my plan with you in advance. I hope I did not do you a disservice."

"It was high-handed of you in the extreme," Eleanor said severely. "But in the end, I find I am quite pleased with the outcome."

Southampton smiled at that and dabbed at the moisture in his eyes.

"Then allow me to escort you back inside where we will

arrange with Lady Augustus to send your funding sooner rather than later. You," he said over his shoulder. "May enter through another door. I'll not tolerate any criticism of the future Countess of Southampton."

Alex seemed ready to argue, but capitulated with a bow and an ironic smile.

As Southampton led her back inside, Eleanor asked, "What *did* you say to Lady Augustus to change her mind?"

He shook his head and patted her hand in a fatherly manner. "It is too salacious to repeat to one so refined an innocent as yourself, my dear. May I call you that? I very much find myself wishing to have a family after—well, I'm sure my son will fill you in on all that has transpired.

"I shall make sure he does. I shall press him most for the salacious details," she said tartly.

"Oh I do like you, my dear. Alexander is a lucky man."

Eleanor felt her gaze pulled across the room Alex had just entered, his hair still mussed from her fingers, his eyes still glazed with the same passion she felt warming her cheeks. He stared at her with all the love in the world.

"That may be," she murmured. "But I am a lucky woman."

Epilogue

Eleanor stood and massaged her lower back, relieving the stiffness caused by bending over a laboring mother all night. The aches were well worth it as both mother and child had come through the long and painful process and were resting comfortably. She stretched a bit more before turning to gather up the soiled linens and her basket of simples. With a final farewell to the family, she made her way through the dawn-lit streets back to the kitchen where she and Sarah fed hundreds of people each day. Women were already at work preparing large batches of porridge as she entered the steamy kitchen and made her way to the back where she deposited the linens in the pile of never-ending laundry and fetched herself a cup of tea.

"You look done in, missus," said one of the women. "We can manage here today, you go on and get some rest."

Eleanor smiled wearily and decided she was right. There was no way she'd be able to attend her afternoon meetings with donors if she didn't get at least a few hours of sleep.

She returned home to the small townhouse she and Alex had moved into after their wedding to find the man himself returned from a fortnight's trip to Bristol.

"There you are!" Alex exclaimed, sweeping her off her feet and twirling her around. "I've missed you! I was about to send the cavalry out for you."

"Mrs. Robinson's baby decided to arrive early. I was there all night delivering it."

"Oh, you must be exhausted then," Alex said and though

he was sympathetic, she could tell he was also disappointed.

"I am but you look like you have news. What is it?"

"It's only that I wanted to show you something—a gift, as it were. Something I've been working on for months and now it's ready. It can wait though."

She could see that he was practically hopping from foot to foot with excitement and she smiled. Every day with Alex was an adventure and she'd missed him desperately while he was gone. "Where is this gift?" she asked, suddenly filled with anticipation.

"We'll have to go for a drive. You can sleep on the way."

She raised her eyebrows. "It's that far away?"

"Well, not terribly far, just...well, come along then."

She might have dozed in the well-sprung carriage except that she *was* a newlywed and her husband *had* been gone for a fortnight. Though they forbore from being quite *that* intimate, Eleanor was sure when she emerged from the carriage thirty minutes later that her hat was askew and her lips kiss-swollen.

"Oh!" she exclaimed. They were at the docks in front of Alex's warehouse. "Did my present arrive on your latest shipment?" she asked.

"No," he said with a grin.

"Oh," she said again, this time with a small frown.

They walked through the bustling warehouse where men were moving large crates and burlap-wrapped bundles. The air was filled with a dusty mix of spices, coffee, wooden boxes, and brine.

"M'lady!" someone called. Eleanor turned to see Lenny hopping down from a stack of crates and rushing over to her. He tugged his forelock respectfully and bowed.

"Lenny! It's so good to see you here. Are you enjoying your work?"

"Aye, m'lady. I thank ye and yer husband there," he said with a nod to Alex, whom Eleanor could see was growing more anxious. She laughed at the thought that her husband resembled a small boy at Christmas.

"Yes, well, we must be along, Lenny. It was so nice to see you."

Lenny winked and returned to his task and Alex practically dragged Eleanor through the maze of cargo. Eleanor laughed and said, "Good heavens, Alex. Is my prize going to run away?" She stopped abruptly, tugging on her husband's arm. "You didn't send for something ridiculous like a camel or an elephant, did you?"

Alex looked crestfallen. "Do you mean to say you wouldn't like something like that?"

Eleanor found herself rapidly calculating where on earth they would house an elephant as she pasted a smile on her face and said, "Well, ah, of course I would. It's just—"

Alex laughed and pulled her along after him. "I'm only teasing No exotic animals today." Eleanor swatted his shoulder but it was an ineffectual strike at best, seeing as how she was practically having to run to keep up with his long strides as they exited the back of the warehouse and headed down the dock.

"Alex!" Eleanor exclaimed. "Do slow down!"

He came to an abrupt stop and she nearly collided with his back. Only her years spent on a ballroom floor enabled her to sidestep him and still maintain her balance. She shot her husband an aggrieved glance but he was staring rapturously at something ahead. She followed his line of sight but could see nothing other than tall masted ships.

"What do you think?" he asked, gesturing proudly.

"Er, about what?" she asked.

"The ship!" he said, pointing to the one just to their right.

It looked very much like every other ship at the docks but Eleanor knew that to a sailor such as her husband, each vessel was as unique as a person so she smiled again and nodded encouragingly. "It's very nice."

He looked at her and laughed, then turned her so she could see the stern of the ship in question. "LADY ELEANOR" was painted in gold letters over a large bank of mullioned windows.

"Oh!" Eleanor gasped. "You named her after me!"

"Come see why," he said, urging her toward the wide gang-plank. Once on deck he pointed out various accoutrements that he assured here were the latest in shipboard equipment. She nodded and responded with appropriately placed "Oohs," and "Aahs," even as her eyes drooped and she could think of nothing so much as how she wished for her bed.

He guided her below deck and along a narrow passage, then threw open the door at the end dramatically. "Here is your present!"

She stepped inside the brightly lit room and realized they were on the other side of the mullioned windows she'd seen from the dock. She glanced around and saw a luxuriously appointed berth, complete with plush chairs, a large table, and a bed that looked positively heavenly. Her gaze stayed on the plump pillows longingly as she asked. "I'm not sure I understand."

"You said you wished to see more of the world. This way you can do so in comfort. We can finally take our honeymoon."

Eleanor's fatigue fell away and she felt her drooping eyelids spring wide. "Oh Alex, do you mean it?" She began exploring the built in drawers and cabinets, and peered out the large bank of windows.

"Do you like it, then?" he asked hesitantly.

"I love it!" she said, throwing her arms around him. "And I love you," she said, smiling up at him. "Where shall we go first?"

Alex crossed to a flat drawer built into the wall and pulled out a handful of maps. He spread them on the glossy surface of the table and began throwing out ideas. "France and Italy, of course, but beyond that I think you would enjoy Morocco."

Eleanor smiled and said "Mmhmm," while she climbed up onto the down mattress and stretched out. "Lovely," she said, though she wasn't sure if it was the idea of the French Riviera or the embrace of the bed. She closed her eyes, imagining the colorful markets of Morocco Alex had described to her.

Never had she expected her life to turn out as it had, and yet she wouldn't change a thing about it. Aside from her work, which had become a part of her, she and Alex had a love based on understanding, passion, respect, and support—things she'd never realized were important when she'd been caught up in the marriage mart. Plus he was so delightfully handsome, she thought, lifting one eyelid enough to admire his trim form and dark hair. She sighed happily and nestled deeper into the pillows. Yes, she thought, as she drifted off to sleep, life was good.

"How soon do you think you could get away? You don't think Sarah is going to wish to take a honeymoon at the same time, do you?" When he received no answer, Alex glanced over his shoulder to find his wife sound asleep. He smiled as he crossed the cabin and pulled a blanket up over her sprawled form. He tenderly smoothed her hair back off her face and pressed a kiss to her brow. He carefully sat on the edge of the bed and stared at her sleeping face. His heart swelled with love and he felt a suspicious sheen of moisture in his eyes as he realized that while he'd met every business goal he'd set for himself, his true treasure was right before him. Eleanor was the love of his life. She brightened his mornings and heated his nights. He missed her when she was absent—which was often considering their busy schedules—and relished each moment spent with her. She filled his life with love and he would give her anything she desired. He chuckled as he realized that the "new" Eleanor desired nothing so much as him. Fancy gowns and beautiful homes, which he could now afford, meant nothing to her since her experiences in Southwark. The only thing she wanted was him, and he was more than happy to accommodate her.

He stretched out next to her and gathered her close. His body hardened at the feel of her soft form pressed against his but he willed it into submission. There was time aplenty for that when his wife had had a restorative nap. He closed his eyes as he inhaled her sweet scent. Yes, life was good.

I hope you enjoyed Eleanor and Alexander's love story. If you did, it would mean so much if you would leave a review—they really help independent authors! Thank you so much and please come visit me at www.michellemorrisonwrites.com

Read on for a sample of Book Three of the Unconventionals...

Chapter One

If ever there was a fish out of water, Sarah Draper reflected, it was she. Dressed in borrowed finery, her hair properly styled for the first time in years and surrounded by a society she'd long since given up, Sarah clung to the wall and watched as her cousin's engagement was announced.

She couldn't be happier for Eleanor. Her cousin was the sweetest, most caring person Sarah had ever met in spite of, or perhaps because of the heartbreak she had suffered. Though Eleanor had been born into nobility, she treated everyone with compassion and genuine interest. And while Sarah rejoiced for her cousin, she recognized that her own life would soon be growing lonelier. Surely once Eleanor was wed, her new husband wouldn't approve of her working with Sarah in their charitable aid organization in one of London's most notorious slums. In fact, she realized with a frown, Eleanor's time was sure to be taken up immediately with wedding plans, for it wasn't every day that an earl's daughter married a bastard-turned-legitimate-heir-to-another-earldom.

With a sigh, Sarah resigned herself to the solitary life she'd lived before her stunning cousin had hurtled into her life two years ago. She'd managed to run her aid kitchen by herself before Eleanor had joined her; surely she could do so again. The only problem was that now she knew what it was like to have someone to share the load, someone with whom to share frustrations and victories alike. She had not realized how lonely she'd been before Eleanor had joined her, but she certainly would recognize it now.

Sarah's morose thoughts were distracted by the boisterous laugh of a man standing a few feet away. She blinked several times, her ruminations dispersing. Glancing over, she saw a tall, broad-shouldered man still grinning with mirth. His hair was a riotous mass of gold and honey and champagne, worn loose and uncontained by pomade as was the fashion. His face was stunning, with eyes so intensely blue Sarah could discern their color from several feet away. The strong lines of his face and sun-kissed complexion distinguished him from the fashionably pale faces of the other men standing next to him and when he spoke—more loudly than was seemly, the nasal tone of his accent gave him away as an American, bold as brass and confident as they came. He was exactly the sort of man who would glance at her dark hair and eyes and drab gown and see right through her to the dazzling debutante behind her.

Sara glanced down and fingered the rich dark blue satin of her borrowed gown. Well, perhaps not everything was so drab about her this evening. Eleanor's friend Juliette had loaned her this gown and it had taken very little alteration to make it fit like a glove. The regal swish of the heavy fabric made her walk more slowly and the nearly off-the-shoulder cut of the neckline caused her to stand up straight lest the gown slip. While she wasn't completely comfortable out of the familiar coarse broadcloth of the gowns she normally wore, it felt rather nice to know she could still appear presentable when the occasion called. Tonight, she felt like a different person than the woman who arose before dawn every day to feed and tend to hundreds of people.

MICHELLE MORRISON

She allowed herself one more glance at the golden Adonis when he laughed aloud again. He was too handsome by half. Or perhaps handsome wasn't exactly the right word when one compared him to the well-groomed men of the ton surrounding him, but there was something undeniably attractive about him nonetheless. He was exactly the sort of man she scorned if for no other reason than he was clearly the type given to frivolity and excess. One who lived only for pleasure. She had no idea why she was so certain about the American's character, but she knew it as absolutely as she could see that he was as at ease in his skin as she was uncomfortable.

As if feeling her gaze upon him, the Adonis looked over at her and she quickly turned her head, affecting interest in the crowd of people who were still congratulating her cousin and her new fiancée.

Eleanor appeared a bit dazed, and glancing at Eleanor's future husband, Lord Reading, Sarah realized he had the same bemused expression. Sarah wondered if either had known of the Earl of Southampton's plan to announce their betrothal less than twenty minutes before.

"I'm glad to see I'm not the only one you scowl at," a deep voice to her left said.

Startled, she turned to find the Adonis smiling at her. Crinkle lines around his eyes suggested he smiled a great deal. Or squinted from near-sightedness, she thought uncharitably.

"I'm not scowling," she replied sourly, but as she felt the muscles of her forehead relax, she realized she had indeed been frowning. "You're American," she said, trying to change the subject.

He held up both hands and said, "Guilty as charged. But what did she do to you?" he nodded in Eleanor's direction.

"She seems as English as they come. Did she steal your fellow?"

"What?" Sarah asked, suddenly flustered. "No! She's my cousin. If she's happy, I'm happy."

"Uh huh," he said, clearly unconvinced, and Sarah realized her eyebrows had drawn together again. She reached up to smooth them with a gloved finger.

"It's just—I shall miss her, is all. We have grown very close in the last few years and I suspect I will not see her as much once she is wed." Or at all, Sarah thought, but she forced herself not to frown at the idea. She wondered why she felt the need to explain herself to this man. She certainly was unaccustomed to sharing any such personal feeling with people.

She was surprised when he simply nodded in understanding, a shuttered look in his eyes. "A feeling I can well relate to," he murmured. Then, in a quicksilver change of mood, he said, "What is it about you English and food?"

"I beg your pardon?" she asked, trying to figure out how that related to their conversation.

He lifted up his glass in demonstration. "You do spirits very well, I'll grant you, but would it kill you to put out some finger sandwiches?"

"There will be a large dinner later," Sarah explained.

"Yes, at midnight. Who wants to eat at midnight?"

Though she said nothing, Sarah agreed with him. She knew the answer was, "people who don't arise early to work," and wondered if this American worked. If so, she wondered that he found himself at a duke's party. Perhaps he was as much a fish out of water as she was. Except he didn't seem the least bit bothered by the notion, she thought sourly. He exuded the confidence of one who felt at home anywhere.

"And who are you to be here at the Duke of Andover's

ball?" she asked sharply, turning her discontent against him.

He executed a slightly mocking bow. "Forgive me. I forgot I'm not supposed to be speaking to a lady without a proper introduction."

She almost told him she was no lady, but realized in time just how that would sound and bit her tongue and said instead, "That is only at public events, not at private ones such as this."

He nodded. "In that case, I am Samuel James. American, as you so astutely pointed out."

She narrowed her eyes at this, but he didn't appear to be mocking her.

"Though I suppose if I looked hard enough I could find a distant relative here in England. My great grandfather was from Surrey. Say, you don't suppose I might be related to royalty, do you? That would be awfully useful now, wouldn't it?"

"Er, I'm sure if your great-grandfather was related to the royal family, he would not have emigrated to America."

"Hmmm. Good point," he conceded. "Still, if there was even an off chance of my having a drop of royal blood, it would mean my sister's future mother-in-law would have to welcome, me, wouldn't it?"

Sarah frowned, trying to follow his rapid-fire dialogue. It had been so long since a man had simply conversed with her, she felt a bit out of her element. Then there was the way he was looking at her, as if she was, well, beautiful—something she had not felt in many years. Finally unraveling his last statement, she said, "Your sister is to be married, then?"

"Oh yes, that's the reason I am here in jolly old England and why I was invited to this foodless soiree. She's to be married to Lord Treason."

"Lord Treason?" Sarah was not familiar with the London social scene, but the name struck her as distinctly odd.

"That's just what I call him. Trowbridge is his name, but I rib him that he's a traitor to his country for marrying a Colonial."

"Oh," Sarah said, a bit overwhelmed at his overall volume and strength of personality, even as his invigorating dialogue awoke a part of her brain that had been long dormant.

"Of course, marrying a dollar princess to fill the family coffers may be considered a noble sacrifice to his kin, but who am I to judge."

"I beg your pardon. A what?"

"Dollar princess. No blue blood to speak of, what with all of our American-ness, but plenty of money in the bank to ensure we're tolerable. I'm given to understand dowries are the easiest way to save failing estates these days."

Though his tone was still humorous, Sarah saw a hardness in the bright blue eyes when she hazarded a glance at them.

"But who are you to judge?" she asked slyly.

He stared at her for a moment before bursting into that boisterous laugh that had first drawn her attention. She noticed people glancing in their direction and felt herself physically shrinking, trying not to draw attention to herself. Realizing what she was doing, she deliberately straightened her shoulders and refused to meet the wondering glances. She looked back at Mr. James and found him looking at her in a manner that made her feel positively fascinating.

"Disdain fairly drips from your tongue," he said, making it sound like the highest compliment. "You're a sharp one, my lady."

"I'm not—" she'd started to say again she wasn't a lady. "You do not address me as 'my lady.'"

"Why not?"

"I am not the daughter or wife of a nobleman."

"I thought everyone at these parties was a lord or lady. Except for we wealthy Americans, of course," he added.

She overlooked that acerbic comment and continued, "My parents are members of the gentility and so I am only addressed as 'Miss.'"

"Not 'Mrs.,' then?"

He seemed surprised and Sarah felt her chin raise defensively. She was old enough that were she active in the London scene, she would be considered a spinster, the most piteous position in society.

"As I am unwed, no." she said tersely. She pretended to study the crowd and noticed that her cousin and Lord Reading were nowhere to be seen.

"So what is under gentility?"

"I beg your pardon?" she asked, turning back to him.

"If you have nobility and then gentility, what comes next?"

"Royalty," she replied.

He grinned. "Royalty is beneath gentility?"

"No!" she exclaimed, unaccountably flustered. "You forgot royalty. Royalty, nobility, gentility."

"And then what?"

"Well, I suppose you would simply say 'everyone else.'"

"We commoners, eh?" he said with a grin. "Unless, of course, I turn out to be related to the Prince."

In spite of herself she felt her lips quirk at his irreverent humor and strove to suppress the smile, forcing herself to think of the struggles of the people she tried to help every day through her aid society. She supposed they were common enough problems—trying to find food, shelter, security.

At his expectant look, she realized she hadn't responded. She also realized that for one evening she didn't want to think of her work. She wanted to enjoy herself, enjoy a spirited conversation with an outrageous and handsome man.

"Oh I can assure you, you do not have a drop of noble blood."

His tawny brows rose in surprise even as a smile tugged at his mouth. "Do tell. Is there some secret test? Shouldn't you need a sample of my blood to verify your assertion?"

"Not at all. It is simply evident in your carriage, your mannerisms, and the way you hold your liquor."

He looked a little taken aback and she wondered if she had overplayed her jest.

"I thought the Prince Regent was considered to be an abysmal drunk."

"Indeed," she said primly.

A sly smile curved his lush lips. *Lush?* She asked herself. Why on earth should she notice such a—

"And as I can stand erect without the aid of a corset, don't spend myself into the poorhouse and do not engage in public drunkenness, I clearly have not a drop of royal blood?"

She gave him a brief single nod, tilting her head a bit to the side so she could watch him beneath her lashes.

"And here I thought you English considered it perfidious to criticize your royal house."

"Perfidious?" she asked with a smile.

"Treasonable," he clarified.

She shook her head sadly. "Yet further proof you are not English and therefore cannot be related to the prince."

He grinned and his gaze roamed over her face with a look that made her feel as if she'd drunk an entire bottle of champagne. "Please explain."

"We consider it a point of honor to malign the Prince Regent. After all, we've received little other recompense for the hundreds of thousands of pounds we've provided to redeem his profligate debts."

"So you verbally abuse him amongst yourselves in return?"

She bit the inside of her cheek to keep from laughing. She could not remember the last time she'd had this much fun.

He cocked one eyebrow and stroked his chin thoughtfully. He looked nothing less than piratical. A golden, bronzed Adonis-like pirate.

She took a breath to deliver a further witty set down on the chances of him being related to royalty when a petite blonde strolled by in the company of an elegant redhead and Mr. James' appreciative gaze followed them.

Instantly Sarah felt her skin go cold and she drew back, wrapping her arms protectively around her waist. Ire replaced any charitable thoughts she had been developing for Mr. James. Ire and no small amount of hurt. Very well, a large amount of hurt. They'd been having such a lively conversation, and the way he'd looked at her made her feel interesting, almost… desirable. She should have known he was fickle, should have known she was poor company for one such as him. Ignoring her hurt feelings, she focused on anger as it was a far less debilitating emotion. This American was no different than any privileged nobleman. She pressed her lips into a disgusted line.

He was a typical man, she thought scornfully, and reminded herself this was only one of many reasons why she didn't attend society functions. She turned to leave but felt a hand on her arm.

"You didn't tell me your name. Miss…?"

"I didn't, did I?" she replied before turning again and weaving her way through the crowd.

"Lady Disdain!" she heard him call out. "That's what I'll call you."

Her shoulders hunched as people turned at his loudness and she barreled out of the room as quickly as possible, only stopping when she found a quiet hallway.

I hope you enjoyed Eleanor and Alexander's love story. If you did, it would mean so much if you would leave a review—they really help independent authors! Thank you so much and please come visit me at www.michellemorrisonwrites.com

Books By This Author

Lord Worthing's Wallflower

What do you call a woman with a penchant for scandalous novels, a complete lack of small talk skills, and a quirky sense of humor?

In Juliette Aston's case: a wallflower.

Juliette would like nothing better than to find a husband and start a family (especially when the alternative is serving as her father's housekeeper for the rest of her life). As the best friend of society's reigning debutante, however, Juliette is invisible to the men of London. Compounding her problem is the fact that the only man she wants is courting her best friend!

Jacob Wilding considers himself a good son; at his father's deathbed insistence, he reluctantly agrees to court London's most popular debutante, only to discover he is more interested in an opinionated, headstrong wallflower.

Passion simmers beneath their verbal sparring matches as an all-consuming love blooms between them.

Lady Disdain

Sarah Draper has run a charity kitchen in the dregs of London's Southwark for five years. What began as penance for her disastrous fall from grace has become her vocation and passion, and a lonely one at that. She has built a protective cocoon around her heart and has become a master of self-sufficiency even as she secretly craves more from her life.

Samuel James is a brash American printer, gregarious, handsome, and bossy. His attraction to the fairer sex extends only so far as amusing companionship....until he meets a coolly aloof woman who seems immune to his most charming smile and attempts at flirtation. Sarah Draper is everything he never realized he was looking for.

The combination of a fiercely independent woman and a well-intentioned but high-handed man is disastrous until their need for one another proves overwhelming.

The Lady Ordinary

Amanda Hayworth's life is the epitome of ordinary. With a dash of average thrown in for good measure. Which makes it all the more inconvenient that she feels a burning desire for more out of life than an indifferent husband and a busy social schedule. But when the rough and dashing Viscount Howard pays her court, Amanda dares to dream big.

The death of Oliver Howard's cousin and heir left him with more than a broken nose. He feels responsible for the death of the man who was closer than a brother and is scarred by the pain the man's wife and children suffered at his loss. He vows to have a marriage based on compatibility but never love. That way, should either of them die, the other will be spared unbearable grief. But the heart is not so logical.

Their passions more than make up for the hesitancy of their hearts as they struggle to let go of past heartbreaks and give into an extraordinary love.

The Daring Mrs. Kent

Josephine Kent risked everything to escape an abusive husband: a perilous sea voyage, a new life in the Caribbean, and the constant worry that Mr. Kent would find her. She settles into a safe new life in her brother's house, content to avoid society and serve as her brother's housekeeper...until her identity is discovered by one of her husband's henchmen.

Hungerford Spooner walks a careful line among the residents of St Kitts' capital. As the son of a wealthy English landowner, he has holdings and a successful shipping business. But he is also the son of a former slave, a combination that puts him on the fringes of Basseterre's high society. When he rescues a young woman fleeing a pursuer, he finds himself drawn to her beauty and spirit. And he recognizes in her a fellow soul carrying a heavy burden.

To save her, he hides her aboard his ship. In such close quarters, their feelings intensify. But just when happiness seems in their grasp, their journey is cut short by a rogue slave ship and now Josephine must overcome her past fears to save the man she loves.

The Stolen Crown

A Kingdom at Peace...
Harold Godwineson, Earl of East Anglia and member of King Edward the Confessor's advisory council ignores both tradition and his father to marry a common-born woman to join him in his quest to maintain England's fragile peace.

Adith Svanneshal has survived a Viking attack and the death of her promised husband, neither of which prepare her to become the Countess of East Anglia. But she is determined to prove herself, and discovers a knack for gathering information her husband would never hear..

Together, Harold and Adith survive exile, betrayal, and a visit to Duke William's Normandy. When Harold finds the crown of England on his head, they begin their most treacherous journey yet.

The King's Rebel

Amidst the turmoil of the battle for the Scottish throne, bonny red-haired Meghan Innes and darkly handsome Black William meet at a Mayday celebration. They delight in the blush of newfound love until Meghan learns that Black William is actually William Bruce, cousin to the self-proclaimed king of Scotland, and enemy to her own clan. But when Meghan's father is captured by the English, she must swallow her pride and appeal to King Robert and his cousin William for help in freeing her father.

Forced into each other's company, can they conquer their differences and rekindle their love?

War disrupts their tenuous bond as they find themselves pawns in the deadly battle between Scotland and England.

A Dishonorable Knight

A forced betrothal to a brutal nobleman is the worst thing that has ever happened to Elena de Vignon, pampered lady in King Richard III's court. That is, until she finds herself stranded in the English wilderness with Sir Gareth ap Morgan, a disenchanted Welsh knight who has decided to leave Richard's army and join the challenger to the throne, Henry Tudor. She finds him rough, ill mannered, and far beneath her. He sees her as spoiled, petulant, and a hindrance to his plans. But their mutual animosity masks an intense attraction.

Forced to take her with him to his meeting with Henry Tudor's rebels, Gareth begins to see past Elena's haughtiness to the woman beneath the mask. She in turn finds herself wondering about a marriage of love rather than prestige. Before either can explore their budding feelings, they are forced back into the treacherous atmosphere of Richard III's court and Bosworth Field, the staging ground for the final battle in the Wars of the Roses where they will battle for a new king and their love.

Made in United States
Orlando, FL
28 March 2023

31499072R00189